THE BERSERKERS BRAND

BOOK 1 FROM THE AGE OF SCARS

DAVID J. HODGES

MILTON & HUGO L.L.C.

1001 3rd Avenue West,
Suite 430 Bradenton,
FL 34205, USA

Website: *www. miltonandhugo.com*
Hotline: *1- 888-778-0033*
Email: *info@miltonandhugo.com*

Ordering Information:
Quantity sales. Special discounts are granted to corporations, associations, and other organizations. For more information on these discounts, please reach out to the publisher using the contact information provided above.

ISBN-13:	979-8-89285-747-5	[Paperback Edition]
	979-8-89285-748-2	[Hardback Edition]
	979-8-89285-746-8	[Digital Edition]

Rev. date: 12/04/2025

CONTENTS

This book is dedicated to my beautiful wife
Stacia and my daughter Liliauna.

PROLOGUE

The hum of honeybees in the lavender was the sole sound, a contented drone against the profound silence of the Monastery of the Sun-Warmed Stone. Sunlight, a heavy gold, bled through arched windows, warming flagstones centuries of shuffling sandals had worn smooth. Faded silk prayer flags, strung between columns, whispered in a draft too slight to feel, their hushed benedictions mingling with the bees. The quiet settled, heavy as a shroud, over everything.

From her bench, Baelfire registered the monastery's slow breath. Brother Thaddeus, his eyes the color of worn granite, had once called this quiet "peace." The word was a stone in her throat. Her jaw tightened. Her gaze traced the intricate patterns of the meticulously kept flowerbeds, the ordered rows of herbs; they were not soothing, they were the tightening bars of a gilded cage. Every pruned bush, every perfectly aligned stone became an accusation.

The hum of the bees drilled into her skull, a high-pitched whine threatening to split the bone. A filigree of violet lightning, thin and venomous, crackled at the edges of her vision, transforming the garden's gentle greens into a bruised, sickly tapestry seen through warped glass. A dissonant thrum vibrated beneath her skin, a low counter-frequency to the bees' drone, making the muscles in her arms and legs twitch with a tension that found no release. She tried to draw a full breath, but it hitched in her throat as something cold uncoiled against the inside of her ribs, evaluating the limits of its cage.

Her head was a drum skin stretched taut, pressure building behind her eyes as if a captive star fought to force its fiery wings against the constraining bone. She drew her knees tight to her chest, spine rigid, muscles coiled to spring from the sidelong glances that burned. She counted the flagstones—twenty-three of them, sun-warmed and pale, an ocean of uncrossable stone separating her from the trellis where two brothers worked.

Thaddeus stood among them, his ancient, gnarled hands steady as oak roots, guiding a delicate rose cane with a tender touch. Brother Michael, his face a round moon that curved easily into a smile, murmured a jest, his voice a soft burr in the sun-drenched air. Then came Thaddeus's laugh—a low, warm rumble of contentment. The sound twisted something sharp in Baelfire's chest. Heat flooded her cheeks, staining them scarlet.

The scent of sun-baked stone, thick and earthy, rode the breeze.

A memory flared, unbidden. The kiln courtyard. Glare. The smell of clay and ash. Children's laughter, a sharp, cruel blade.

Joric sneered, his voice a lazy drawl meant to land like a stone. "Moon calf. Always staring. Like a spook."

Lyra's sing-song taunt followed, brittle as shards of glass. "Half-breed. Bad seed. Bet you'll turn on us, just like your kind."

Baelfire's hand rose, trembling, to the pointed curve of her ear, a physical mark she tried to bury beneath her spill of silver hair. A low hum started behind her ribs, escalating into a high-pitched ringing behind her eyes.

Joric, emboldened, shoved Elara. The small, frail girl stumbled, a sharp intake of fear escaping her lips.

The world inside Baelfire's six-year-old chest went silent, a void where a deafening roar began. A phantom wave of impossible cold washed out from her. She looked at Joric's sneering face, and her vision flooded with amethyst energy. The sun-drenched stones of the courtyard became a landscape of bruised purple.

CRACK.

The sound was a geological event, the shattering of primordial rock. Rime, white as ground bone, exploded from the courtyard well, the sun-hot stone hissing like a quenched blade. The well water became a thirty-foot spear of crystalline ice, glittering under the midday sun. Joric's sneering mouth hung open, arrested mid-taunt. A breath Baelfire hadn't realized she was holding escaped her lips, and for a single, sickening beat, the terror in his eyes was a balm.

Then her gaze found Thaddeus's face. No fear. No anger. Just sorrow carved his features, an ancient grief like a mountain mourning a single, broken stone. Her rage starved the amethyst light in her vision; it guttered and died. Sickness bloomed hot in her stomach. The ice, the power—it all vanished, leaving only a bone-deep chill and the devastating echo of his eyes.

The memory receded, leaving her on the sun-warmed bench, the scent of lavender and baked stone thick in the air. The brothers' easy camaraderie was a deliberate mockery. A fragile, desperate need took root in the hollow space the memory had left behind—a need to create something, anything, to counter the echo of that shattering cold, to silence the memory of Thaddeus's sorrowful eyes.

Her gaze fell upon a single sun petal lily, a casualty of the afternoon heat, its golden petals curled and brown. The garden was empty. The brothers had moved on. She was utterly alone with the silent, pleading lily.

Kneeling on the warm flagstones, she reached out, her trembling hand hovering above the wilted bloom. She closed her eyes, focusing her entire will not on the roaring storm, but on a single, controlled drop of dew.

"Please," she whispered to the captive thing within her. "Create."

A warmth, soft and tentative, flowed from her fingertips. It was not searing; it was gentle. On the lily, a single, golden petal, the most withered of them all, slowly unfurled. Its anemic yellow deepened, strengthening, until it became the vibrant, living gold of a sunrise.

And then the storm answered.

The warmth became a torrent, the spark a conflagration. The lily did not revive; it erupted. The ground convulsed beneath her. Vines, the color of old bruises and thick as a hangman's rope, writhed from the soil. They were not green, but a slick, venomous purple-black. Blossoms swelled, their golden petals thickening into fleshy, bruised amethyst. She scrambled backward, a cry caught in her throat as a chorus of soft, wet tearing filled the quiet.

"By the Sun Mother's grace…"

Brother Michael stood at the cloister's edge, a laundry basket of fresh linens half-dropped from his hands, his round face a mask of slack-jawed wonder. He fixed his eyes on the writhing life that consumed the lily bed.

"A miracle," he breathed, his hand instinctively tracing the sun's ancient symbol over his heart. "Truly, a miracle from Solara herself."

His awe was a new kind of condemnation. She fled. Fled the blossoming horror, fled the twisted mockery of creation, fled the round, wondering face that saw a miracle where she had wrought only a monster. For a month, she buried herself in the archives, breathing the scent of old paper and beeswax. She ignored the uplifting Parables of Solara, their words now hollow. Instead, she lost herself in the dry, factual histories of ages with names but no stories, in the cold truths of things long past and irrevocably finished.

Alone, a single flickering candle her only companion, the night a thick, impenetrable blanket around the stone building, a presence settled in the quiet—a cold weight on her shoulder. She was tracing a faded map of a forgotten kingdom when a thought, crystalline and alien, bloomed in her mind like a drop of ink in clear water.

They do not truly understand you, child.

Her head snapped up, her breath catching. She scanned the towering shadows between the shelves. The archives were empty.

"Who's there?" Her voice was thin; the immense quiet listening swallowed it. A cold, sharp, psychic grip seized her mind. Her own mind scrabbled for an explanation—a trick of exhaustion, a phantom isolation birthed, the lingering effects of some poison she had half-forgotten.

Then, the voice came again, clearer, more resonant, a hum inside her bones.

They fear the innate light you carry, little star, even as they pretend to embrace it. They would see you a candle's flicker when you were born to blaze.

This time, she did not cry out. The words were a silken weight. The tremor in her hands stilled. A breath she had held since the kiln courtyard shuddered out of her. It was the feeling that someone saw her for the first time. She fled the library, her chair scraping a harsh shriek against the stone. Curled in the suffocating darkness of her cell that night, she placed a hand over her own chest. The space inside no longer felt entirely her own.

A week later, at the midday meal, Brother Michael slid the honey pot toward her. "You are too thin, child," he said, his smile kind.

As her hand reached for it, the voice whispered in her mind. *He pities the broken little bird. His kindness is a cage to keep you small.* Her hand froze an inch from the pot. She looked at Michael's open, friendly face and forced a smile that felt like cracking ice. "Thank you, brother." She took the honey but did not eat it.

At night, in the cold of her cell, the darkness pressed in. The voice was a warmth against the chill. *Your power is not a curse. It is a birthright. A glorious fire. They fear it because they are moths, and you are a star.* A warmth, small and treacherous, spread through her chest, a flicker of pride she had not allowed herself in a decade. As she left the refectory, it was different. A deep, physical ache settled in her bones, a yearning for something more than quiet contemplation and hushed prayers. The voice's gentle pull, which had been a silken thread for a month, now tightened into an iron hook in her soul.

Her feet moved toward the statue of the forgotten Hero King, one step and then the next, a grim magnetism pulling her forward. With every footfall on the warm flagstones, a ghost of a memory rose: the phantom sting a taunt left on her cheek, the crushing weight of Thaddeus's sorrowful eyes she remembered. The air near the statue was distinctly cooler, sharp and metallic, the scent of lavender replaced by the coppery tang of old blood.

"Who are you?" she whispered to the unmoving stone.

I am a memory of a better world, the voice replied, a resonant hum that seemed to emanate from the stone itself, wrapping itself around her solitude. *A world of absolute purpose, of perfect order. A world where they do not fear power like yours, child, but celebrate it. A world your supposed parents callously abandoned you to.*

The words were not a blade; they were the cold space a blade leaves behind. Baelfire's breath hitched. A warmth she hadn't known she still carried in her chest was suddenly gone, leaving only a hollow ache. Thaddeus's gentle story of heroes lost in war crumbled to dust. They hadn't died. They had simply left her.

Duty, the voice purred, the word a drop of poison in the new wound. *That is what they chose over their own blood. They cast you aside. But we...*

we would not abandon you. We would make you a queen, a force of glorious, unyielding order.

A faint, sickly violet light pulsed from the statue's ancient stone eyes. The air grew colder, thick with a low, dissonant thrum that was the same vibration she felt constantly beneath her own skin. The chaos of it, for the first time, resolved into a terrible, majestic symphony.

"What do you want from me?" she asked, her voice trembling.

A home, child, the voice declared. *The world, as it stands, is a fever, a chaotic sickness of pointless, messy emotion. We are the surgeons, Baelfire, who have come to bring it a final, perfect peace. Your mother, the Chronomancer, clings desperately to the disease of a dying age. We would have you be the cure.*

A vision unfolded in her mind: a cold, exquisitely elegant truth. A universe of perfect, interlocking gears, a vast machine humming with silent, absolute purpose. A world entirely free from the agonizing pain of a broken heart, the sting of betrayal, the gnawing, endless ache of loneliness.

Her voice, when she finally spoke, was clear and calm.

"I accept."

The violet light flared violently, and the world dissolved into a screaming vortex of raw, untamed feeling. The vortex pulled her through a torrential tide of human moments: a soldier's last, ragged breath on a bloody battlefield; a lover's gentle hand on a summer night, already a ghost in the morning light; a mother's bottomless sorrow over a lost child. This was the sickness. This was the chaotic emotion she would now cure.

Then, silence. Absolute. She stood in a void beyond mortal comprehension. Black stars, devoid of light, pulsed in a sky of screaming nothingness. Before her, a throne of black iron and frozen sorrow. A swirling aura of malevolent yellow light wreathed a towering figure— the psychic echo of the King she had come to serve.

He did not speak, but a wave of cold, crystalline, validating logic washed over her. A shard of solidified silence, smooth and stark as polished bone, detached itself from the gloom of the throne and flowed toward her. She did not flinch. As it molded itself to her features, a perfect, unblemished porcelain mask, the roaring storm within her finally went quiet.

The silence was a gift.

She raised the mask, impossibly smooth and cool in her hands. As it touched her face, a chill did not seep in; it crystallized. The last fragile echoes of doubt, the last lingering tendrils of warmth, shattered into brittle stillness. Her pulse slowed to a steady, measured rhythm, her blood running cold and precise. The inner tempest was gone; the calm of a single, absolute purpose replaced it.

She turned from the black iron throne and stepped back into the vortex of feeling. A barrier of absolute detachment now cloaked her. She was a surgeon observing a fever dream. She passed through the raw sensations of fear, sorrow, and delight, not as a participant, but as a dispassionate judge, assessing the flaws, the weakness, the ultimate sickness of it all.

When she solidified back on the monastery grounds, the garden's riot of color and scent was an assault, a jarring cacophony of life. The vibrant, chaotic world she had once so desperately desired now seemed flawed, loud, and utterly meaningless. Through her new eyes, masked and cold, she understood the elegant promise of a perfect, final silence.

Chapter 1

A Silence of Stone and Silver

Clawing at a slate-grey sky like grasping talons, the skeletal branches of long-dead bog-oaks, with their gnarled forms, offered no hospitable perch for feathered life, nor any comforting murmur of wings. The marsh offered no bird song, no chirping symphony of nature; only the stagnant, fetid breath of forgotten time, a pervasive stench of decay clinging to the air. Its silence was not an absence of sound but a profound, physical weight that pressed upon Gundroff's eardrums, a crushing presence that filled his skull with the echoing thrum of his own pulse. It felt like being plunged into the deepest, lightless chasms beneath the earth, the world above crushed to a hollow hum, a distant, muffled memory of sound disconnected from the Zemleglas—the stone and echoes he understood, the Voice of Earth that was his birthright. No insect hummed its ancient song of survival, no rustle betrayed the furtive passage of hidden life through the sodden, grasping reeds. The wind, stirring the low mists, appeared to sigh, soundless, as if it feared interrupting the profound stillness. This was an unnatural quiet, a void where the Earth's pulse should thrum-roar-vibrate, a silence that grated against his dwarven soul.

His own breathing, the strong, controlled respiration of a mountain-born warrior, broke the cavernous stillness like tearing cloth, even though it was a quiet, steady rhythm. Each inhale was a thief's gasp, raw and grating, a profound betrayal of the pervasive hush that swallowed all other noise. It felt... loud, uncouth, a clumsy disturbance in a world holding its breath, desecrating the natural order of quiet. The mire stretched before him, an endless expanse of murky, black water and decaying vegetation, a vast, ancient lung of putrescence that seemed to hold its own putrid breath, waiting. Tendrils of thick, grey fog clung like spectral shrouds to the surface, obscuring the horizon and twisting the skeletal forms of submerged trees into gnarled, spectral limbs, menacing and silent.

With his calloused hand, thick and scarred like granite, formed by a life spent hammering steel and shaping stone, he further tightened his grip on the worn leather of the axe haft. The familiar cold bite of the weapon's tempered steel, its substantial weight – the reassuring mass of Grief and Vengeance – offered a grounding counterpoint to the suffocating silence, a solid promise of immediate action in a world that felt frozen. A tremor, sharp and sudden a fault line shifting deep within the earth, traced an icy path down his spine, leaving a slick film of cold sweat on his skin. It was not fear, not precisely, but the visceral resonance of the place, a deep-seated hum that awakened the brutal purpose etched into his being, the solemn vow he had sworn to Grolnir. The world around him did not wait for the turn of the tide; it held its breath in a profound, unsettling stillness, poised and ready, like the finely honed edge of a sharpened blade. It waited for the terrible reckoning he carried within him, a burden of vengeance as heavy and unyielding as the mountains from which he had sprung.

His immense weight shifted, the heavy, steel-toed boot pressing deep into the sodden, yielding ground. The churned earth beneath it sucked and squelched, a grotesque, wet sigh that shattered the oppressive quiet like a physical blow, a sound that grated against his dwarven sensibilities. The air around him seemed to thicken, coalescing into a palpable pressure that built and vibrated deep in the marrow of his bones, a premonition. Coarse hairs on his forearms pricked under the weak, watery sun that fought a losing battle against the perpetual gloom, a silent alarm against the unseen chill that seeped into his bones. His jaw clenched, a lock of bone he did not command, a grim sentinel against the rising tide of memory that threatened to engulf him.

A relentless, freezing drizzle tapped its insistent hammer against the anvil of his skull, each drop a tiny, frigid shard that pierced the thin veil of his composure. His breath hitched, a fight against an unseen hand pressing on his chest, squeezing the air from his lungs, a ghostly reminder of the smoke-choked air of his dying home. Knuckles, white as bone, tightened further on the worn leather of his axe haft, slick with the chill rain and old, dried sweat, anchoring him to the desolate present. The constant ache in his knees, a testament to countless weary miles and battles fought, sharpened into a throbbing insistence, a pulse of old pain. Then, a new scent, rich and undeniably familiar, cut through the grave-stink of rot fouling his nostrils, pushing the ache aside with startling force. A phantom warmth, impossible and vivid, seeped from the damp, cold stone beneath him, a warmth he hadn't truly felt, truly lived, in decades.

The grave-stink of rot vanished utterly, replaced by the sharp, metallic tang of coal smoke swirling through the vast spaces, then the clean, powerful bite of hot iron being hammered with the precise rhythm of a master, and the hearty, mouth-watering aroma of roasting boar. He stood in the Great Hall of Hjarta-Fell, fifteen again, his heart swelling in his chest, ready to burst with an uncomplicated, youthful pride. A deep, resonant hum vibrated through his boots, the rhythmic clang-clatter-thrum of a thousand hammers on a thousand anvils – the Kladiv-grom, the Hammer-Thunder, the heartbeat of the mountain echoing for miles into the living rock and vibrating in his marrow, a Zemleglas song of creation he would forever carry. Colossal veins of raw mithril, woven like luminous arteries through the living stone, pulsed with a soft, internal light from the vaulted ceiling, making ancient, intricate runes depicting the deeds of ages dance on massive, mirror-polished pillars of polished obsidian. He squinted up, his young eyes tracing the etched triumphs of his Ragingfire ancestors—tales of forge-lords mastering fire, warriors cleaving dragons, engineers taming mountains—each carving a testament to their strength and ingenuity. A fierce, proud tightening seized his chest as he spoke their names silently, a litany of legacy that bound him to his kin, an unbroken Tuathas—a clan, eternal. Sweet, intoxicating honeyed mead from colossal wooden vats mingled with the cool, damp, earthy scent of lower cisterns, the metallic tang of molten steel, and the rich, savoury aroma of roasting boar turning slowly on gargantuan spits. Each scent declared itself, vibrant and immediate, a perfect, irreplaceable chord in the symphony of his home. All of it lost, yet searingly present, a phantom pain and joy entwined, forever intertwined in the deep stone of his memory.

"Still trying to make a sword that is not a lopsided paperweight, little brother?" The voice, sharp and melodious as a perfectly tuned harp string, yet with a hint of Zemleglas's deeper resonance, cut through the clamor of the great hall, drawing his gaze like a magnet. He turned, and Audhild's image, vibrant and full of life, struck him like a hammer blow to the breastplate. She moved with the unbridled grace of a whirlwind, a blur of incandescent light and furious energy, a stark contrast to his own more grounded, deliberate movements. Her head tossed, sending countless silver beads woven into her fiery, copper-braid torrent chiming like miniature bells, a joyful counterpoint to the deep, percussive thrum of the forge. One corner of her mouth quirked, a familiar, mischievous tilt of her lips, and her smile, sharp and crackling with playful intent, seemed to electrify the air around them, sparking with an undeniable zest for life. He felt the phantom jab of her finger in his ribs, a precursor to the barb he knew was inevitably coming, a playful torment he would come to dearly miss.

"It was a dagger," he grumbled, the heat of embarrassment crawling up his neck like fire up a freshly stoked flue. He stared down at the hunk of metal in his hands, intended to be a sleek, balanced throwing dagger, but instead slumped into a grotesque, lopsided parody of a blade, its edges uneven, its point frustratingly blunt and ineffective. A week of tireless, muscle-aching hammering, patient tempering, and endless grinding had yielded only this stubborn lump of ferrous shame, a monument to his current lack of skill. "And I weighted it for throwing, Audhild. For precision, that it was. Not just raw force, zhdran it all."

"Oh, it would throw splendidly, that it would," she chirped, her voice a lilting, mocking melody, her eyes dancing with mischievous light, reflecting the forge flames. "If you desired to knock out a sleeping goblin. From a distance of two feet. And only if you aimed for its head, which, as we both know, you never truly mastered, little brother." Her laughter, unrestrained and pure, rang through the vaulted expanse of the great hall, a sharp, joyous music that, in this precious moment, defined his entire world. He rolled his shoulders, a futile attempt to project the stoic bearing of a clan lord's son, a facade he found increasingly hard to maintain, but the posture crumpled under the unyielding, discerning scrutiny of her gaze.

"Father says the soul of steel only truly awakens after you have failed a hundred times, sister," he recited, the ancient wisdom resonating within him, a fundamental truth of their craft, a truth as immutable as the stone beneath his feet. "This is just the tenth. Ninety more failures to zhd– endure– before true mastery can ever be forged, that is the way."

Across the expansive hall, at his personal forge, his father, Borin Ragingfire, stood like a granite sentinel, a figure of immutable strength, hammering a shield boss with meticulous, practiced strokes. A literal mountain of a dwarf, Borin's formidable, blood-red beard, now gloriously streaked with silver like veins of purest mithril through living rock, caught the flickering light of the roaring forge, making it gleam like spun moonlight. Each deliberate strike of his Kladiv on the glowing metal rang out, a perfectly measured, resonant note that wove seamlessly into the mountain's ancient, rhythmic song, a symphony of purpose and strength. Sparks, like tiny, ephemeral constellations, cascaded from the impact point, briefly incandescent against the cavernous darkness before winking out on the cold, unforgiving stone floor. Borin, his great shoulders a testament to generations of forge-work, paused. His molten iron eyes, deep and knowing, swept the vast expanse of the hall, taking in the myriad apprentices and journeymen, before settling with unwavering intensity on Gundroff. The rhythmic clang of his hammer ceased abruptly, leaving a sudden, profound silence in its wake, broken only by the sharp, ethereal hiss of quenched steel cooling rapidly in the trough beside him. With a forearm thick and knotted as an ancient oak bough, he wiped a bead of sweat from his furrowed brow. Then, a quiet nod. A small, almost imperceptible gesture, yet it was a fundamental truth, anchoring Gundroff's wavering world. A profound warmth, like molten gold settling into a perfect mold, flooded his chest, chasing away the chill of his self-doubt. His shoulders squared instinctively, no longer a forced posture but a natural bearing, and his grip on the stubborn, imperfect practice dagger tightened, suddenly imbued with renewed purpose and unwavering resolve.

The memory of Audhild's laughter, bright and clear as newly-struck mithril, echoed within his mind, a sweet melody abruptly cut short, shattering mid-note like crystal against unforgiving stone. It was the laughter of a sister, a sound woven into the fabric of Hjarta-Fell's living rock, as integral as the mithril that coursed through its veins. But now, the forge's sudden, profound silence—a stillness so absolute it throbbed like a fresh wound—devoured that cherished sound. It swallowed the vibrant, rhythmic beat of a thousand hammers, a ceaseless symphony of creation that had once been the heartbeat of his home, of his clan, of the Ragingfire legacy. This oppressive quiet, heavy as a fallen mountain, choked out the phantom sounds of dwarven life, leaving only a hollow ache in its wake, an abyss that could never be filled.

The memory's vivid glow extinguished with cruel finality. It snuffed the mithril veins' warm, inner light, which had once pulsed with the promise of prosperity and the deep comfort of ancestral halls, replacing that life-giving brilliance with the cold, pale grey of a dying day. It was the barren light of a tomb, the spectral illumination of a world brought to ruin. This stark, brutal contrast struck Gundroff with the force of a battering ram, a profound void opening in his chest. Where a bustling, living world, vibrant with the clang of steel and the rich scent of coal smoke, had just vividly existed in his memory, now there was only a gaping chasm, a desolate absence, leaving behind a cold, terrible draft that whispered of ash and forgotten warmth. This was the curse of his Oath of Rage, the eternal oscillation between the vibrant ghosts of what was and the desolate reality of what remained, a torment he endured daily.

The grave-stink of rot offered no truth, no solace. A sharp, musky spoor cut through it, the unmistakable scent of the Gloomfang Boar. Acrid, wild, and utterly corrupted. He lay motionless between the gnarled, scarred roots of an ancient oak, the muck half-burying him like a granite slab over a coffin. Three days he had endured in this hollow, his body becoming one with the earth, moss beginning to claim the edges of his shoulders, obscuring the Berserker's Brand from the casual eye. His chest rose and fell, slow and controlled, a testament to his unbreakable will. He was stone, breathing stone, a living monument to Grolnir's command to Endure. He counted his own heartbeats against the slow creep of a shadow across the mud. A twig snapped. An acorn fell. He blinked, his steel-grey eyes unmoving, fixed on the murky world before him. He waited, patient as the mountains themselves, a Dub of unwavering patience.

He shifted his head a fraction, a slow movement taking three heartbeats, sending a rivulet of black water through the grime on his cheek. In a still pool no larger than a dinner plate, a stranger's face stared back, reflected in the oily surface. Gaunt cheekbones, etched with deep lines of suffering and endless vigilance. Eyes the color of old steel, dulled by countless battles, yet burning with an inner, ceaseless fire. He touched his chin, fingers catching on the rough iron rings woven into his beard, each one a vow, a name for the dead, a memory he carried. The metal clinked softly, a faint whisper, and the mud swallowed the sound. His gaze locked on the skin beneath his beard. Intricate spirals of blue-black ink crawled from his scalp to his soles, covering every inch of his visible flesh. These were not mere tattoos. These were the Chronicle of Skin, the Berserker's Brand, each mark a chapter of his clan's glorious past and tragic fall, a book closed forever on his people, a living tombstone. He stood its last, wretched keeper, his body a canvas of grief and fury.

The cold marsh water blurred, replaced by the warm, flickering light of a hearth-fire in a quiet antechamber of Hjarta-Fell. Young Gundroff, barely ten, sat cross-legged, a small slate tablet in his lap. Beside him, his father, Borin, sat hunched, his great finger tracing rough lines on the stone. The air was thick with the scent of pipe-weed and ancient paper, not coal smoke, a rare stillness in their bustling home.

"These, boy," Borin rumbled, his voice low and gravelly, "are the Khovnik. The Earth-Voice made visible. Twenty-four symbols, for twenty-four truths." He poked the slate with his calloused finger, indicating a straight, vertical line. "This is Slovo – Stone. The foundation of all we are. See how it is straight, unyielding? No soft curves, no weak horizontal stroke that would break the grain of the rock." He moved to another. "This, Tvar – Strength, or Treasure. It mirrors the strength of the mountains, the value of what we pull from its heart. And the greatest, the deepest." Borin drew a complex, angular symbol. "This is Zhd. It means to wait, to endure. It is the deep truth, the most ancient power. When carved, it contains its own meaning, holds it fast, like a mountain holds its heart. Each rune is a piece of the mountain's soul, made into word. When we carve our laws, our grudges, our lineage, into the living stone, or into the flesh of an oath-taker, we speak the Earth-Voice. We bind ourselves to permanence, to what cannot be broken." He tapped Gundroff's chest, a surprisingly gentle thud. "This is why the Tuathas, the Clan is more than blood, boy. It is the unbreaking Slovo of generations, etched into the world."

The warmth of the memory faded, the hearth-light receding, replaced by the chill of the marsh. Borin's words, once a comfort, now sharpened the barb of grief. Gundroff's own skin, a tapestry of those runes, burned.

His breath hitched, a sharp, ragged sound. His hand trembled, then curled into a fist so tight his nails bit into his palm, a small, self-inflicted pain grounding him. The phantom taste of ash coated his tongue, acrid and bitter. The world lurched, a violent lurch of memory and pain. He knelt again in the desolate ruins of Hjarta-Fell, forty years ago. The sky, a monstrous bruise of purple and grey, choked with thick, black smoke from his people's funeral pyres. His knees ground into a slurry of rubble, shattered marble, and the grey, insidious dust of incinerated kin, a perverse mixture of the glorious and the grotesque. Before the shattered stump of a statue of Grolnir, the Axe-Lord, his voice grated like stone on stone, a raw, desperate plea tearing from his throat, shaping the ancient guttural sounds of Zemleglas.

"I am Gundroff, son of Borin, of the clan Ragingfire," he began, each word scraping his throat raw with grief and unadulterated fury, a primal Zemleglas chant. "I who failed. I, who survived. The last survivor, left to bear witness." Blood flecked his lips, a testament to the agony of his invocation. He slammed a fist against his chest, a dull thud like a funeral drum beating out a final cadence. "I forsake the shield, for it failed to guard my kin, that it did. I forsake armor, for it failed to protect my home, for it turned to slag and offered no succor. Let my skin be my shield, a testament to my people's glory and their brutal end. I will carry the story of our fall upon my flesh, etched in ash and sorrow. No more hearths. No more holds. No ease. No comfort. Only the enemy. Only the hunt. I am a weapon. Nothing more. This is my Oath of Rage, the vow of the unshielded, the last son."

The final, choked word escaped his lips, a broken sound echoing in the ravaged halls. The world fell silent. The crackle of distant embers, the mournful moaning wind, all ceased, a cosmic hush acknowledging his terrible pact. Pressure built, an immense and ancient weight, as if the mountain itself settled upon his shoulders, crushing him, yet purifying him. The god's reply came. Not a voice, for the grief-stricken Grolnir had no need for words, but a deep, resonant rumble that vibrated through the bedrock beneath his knees, rising from the mountain's molten core. It was a pressure of immense, sorrowful, and terrifying approval, a weight of retribution given form. It branded a single, iron word directly onto his soul, a divine command and promise from his god: Endure. The Rune of Earth, Zhd burned onto his soul, a silent, unyielding decree.

The memory blurred, shifting like smoke in a draft. The grim, dead-eyed face of old Elgrom, the lore master, twisted into view, his hands steady despite the horror of his task. The obsidian needle, impossibly sharp, glinted in the flickering torchlight. The profane ink, a mixture of soot, his own blood, and the literal ash of their dead kin, shimmered ominously. He felt the first scrape of obsidian over his heart, tracing the terrible maw of the dragon. Fire, not pain, erupted, a ghost of the dragon's unmaking breath searing his lungs again, a phantom inferno. He tasted ash anew. He heard screams he couldn't silence. Each line of the needle, each Slovo of the Khovnik script, kept a wound open forever, fresh and bleeding, ensuring his hatred would never cool.

A deep tremor in the earth shattered the vision, a brutal jolt back to the marsh. The present crashed upon him like a breaking wave. The reek of rot, the biting cold, the solid, familiar weight of his axe in his hand. He raised a scarred hand, touching the inked dragon's maw that gapes over his heart, its black eyes staring accusingly. This hunt, this small, brutal encounter, offered another blood offering to his god. It was one more measured step toward the glorious, violent end Grolnir had promised him.

The ground trembled again, closer now, a low thrum through the saturated earth. The Gloomfang Boar. Gundroff rose from the mud, a dripping monolith of muscle and ink, rising like an ancient stone from the earth. In his hand, Grief and Vengeance, the twin-headed axe, settled with a perfect, deadly balance. Forty years of survival, forty years of constant vigilance and unyielding purpose, shrieked through him, a silent roar, a guttural Ryn of unwavering resolve. A stench of corruption, a foulness beyond the marsh's natural decay, filled his nostrils, the mark of true evil. He moved low in the skirmisher's shuffle, a ghost gliding through the skeletal trees, invisible to all but his prey. The boar, a mass of muscle and fury, bore brittle grey patches on its hide, where its hair flaked away like burnt parchment. Its breath rattled, a dry hiss of ash and decay, sickeningly familiar. Yellowed tusks dripped thick, green slime that hissed as it touched the earth, scorching the reeds. Its eyes, two dull rubies, pulsed with the faint, violet light of the void, a sinister glow. For a searing instant, the boar shifted, became a Mor-kin Soul Eater, its skin like obsidian shards, its form twisting into the enemy. Those same eyes, glowing with violet light, flared as it sundered his father's shield, a final, horrifying memory. The vision died, leaving a blaze behind, burning white hot in his mind. The beast before him echoed the true enemy, a minor echo of the great destruction.

The boar squealed, a sound of raw fury and pain, and charged. Gundroff stood. He rooted to the spot, an unmoving mountain, an iron statue, his feet feeling the deep bedrock beneath the bog, a connection his god had granted. Purpose settled him, cold and empty, yet perfectly clear. He waited until the stench of its decay filled his nostrils, until the violet light in its eyes burned into his own. Then, he moved. He set his feet, feeling bedrock through his boots, a firm, unyielding foundation. The pivot turned, a measured arc like a siege engine, slow, powerful, unstoppable. The swing swept, not a wild, desperate blow, but the precise arc of a master smith's Kladiv, perfectly aligned and focused. The axe head named Vengeance sang a single, perfect note as it cleaved the air, a song of righteous retribution.

A wet, percussive crunch echoed through the dead woods, a sound of bone and sinew tearing. The blade bit deep, shearing spine and sinew with terrifying finality. The spray that erupted was not crimson. Fine, black, acrid dust laced it, coating the air. The sterile, foul taste hit the back of his throat, the same taste as the air of Hjarta-Fell after the dragon's unmaking breath had erased stone and dwarf into nothingness, leaving only ash and memory. Dark blood followed, sluggish as tar, reeking of ozone and the foul rot of a disturbed grave.

He knelt beside the twitching carcass, its dying gasps rattling. The scent of its corruption seized his memory, twisting it into a fresh, agonizing wound. The ghost of his sister's laughter died again. The phantom warmth of his father's forge went cold, utterly. The silence where a world once lived roared in his ears, a crushing weight that hollowed a space in his chest he could never refill, no matter how much vengeance he wrought. A choked sound escaped him, a primal Khaz of grief, a single, broken sob he refused to acknowledge, swallowed by the guttural rasp of his breath.

He worked with the boar, his touch finding the flesh unnaturally cold, clammy beneath his scarred fingers. The meat, tough and stringy, bore dark veins that pulsed faintly with the same violet light that had burned in its eyes. As his blade, Grief, sliced through, the muscle flaked away in dry, brittle pieces, crumbling like ancient parchment, devoid of life. The bone felt light and porous, the same texture of unmaking he'd seen in stone after the dragon's fire had scoured Hjarta-Fell. He selected the least affected cuts with a mason's care, discarding the rest into the muddy bog, knowing that even this meat carried a taint.

Shouldering the pack, its weight familiar, Gundroff trudged south, leaving the desolate marsh behind. He paused at the crumbling ruins of a human border fort, its stones scattered like forgotten teeth. He ran a calloused hand over the mortar; it powdered to gritty dust between his fingers. "They poorly mixed sand and lime," he rumbled, his voice like grinding rock, a low growl of disappointment, a deep Zemleglas-edged disapproval. "Such shoddy work would shame an apprentice in Hjarta-Fell, that it would. No Tvar – no enduring strength." He kicked a rotted timber beam. It collapsed in a cloud of dust, a testament to its impermanence. "Wood," he spat, the word a curse, a sign of weakness. "They build with wood. They build to fail, always. They build no Khorv – no true hold."

Inside the collapsing shell of a barracks, his heavy boot struck metal. A human sword, its blade a pitted sliver of rust, lay half-buried. He picked it up. It hung light and insubstantial in his hand, a toy. He flicked the blade with a thumbnail, expecting to hear the clear, high ring of true-forged steel, the resonant song of metal hammered with purpose, the sound of a dwarven Kladiv striking well-tempered Khlad.

Instead, only a dull, lifeless thud. No song. Just dead iron. His world of eternal stone and resonant song vanished, replaced by a grim clarity. This world offered twigs and rust, fragile and fleeting. A burning clench seized his gut, a familiar anger. He tossed the thing aside. Its clatter, a hollow, pathetic sound, swallowed by the ceaseless wind.

Hours later, as twilight bled across the sky in hues of bruised purple and grey, he crested a ridge overlooking Tetra. Lights flickered against the encroaching dark, tiny, vulnerable beacons in the vast wilderness. He ignored them, his attention fixed on a deeper concern. His gaze locked on the medallion from the Mor-kin chieftain: a heavy, cold disc of burnished silver bearing the sigil of the Stonehammer clan. Dwarf-work. Its surface bore no flaw, no imperfection. Its weight spoke of strength, of enduring craft, a testament to ancestral Tuathas. His hand trembled, a barely perceptible tremor that belied the granite resolve of his stance. The forty-year oath, a fortress of granite built upon the foundations of vengeance, flexed under an unbearable strain. This medallion, with its impossible sigil, threatened its foundation. His fingers curled, trying to crush it, to deny its existence. His thumb, however, traced the familiar hammer-and-stars sigil, carved with the precision of Khovnik runes, a symbol of hope and lineage. His breath hitched. Had they survived? Had forty years of suffering been a bitter, pointless joke, a cruel jest by a laughing god?

A colder, more practical thought entered, cutting through the emotional maelstrom like a shard of ice. No one in that flimsy, wood-built town could craft an item of such quality, of such undeniable dwarven lineage. A city, even a human one, held taverns. Taverns carried gossip, whispers of travelers, news from far-flung lands. He focused the mission, reducing it from a monumental leap of faith and identity to a single, calculated step. A new quarry. A means to an end, however uncertain that end might be. The logic settled like solid stone in a swamp, firming his resolve. Yet the tremor of the flaw persisted, a leaden weight in his chest, a deep-seated doubt that defied all logic.

He fell to one knee, the rough stone biting into his flesh, a solid anchor against the swirling uncertainty within him. He pressed the medallion into the dirt, tracing the sigil with a calloused finger: a hammer for strength, seven stars for guidance, a forgotten prayer echoing in Zemleglas, the Earth-Voice. He bowed his head, breath misting in the frigid air, a physical manifestation of his internal turmoil. "Father of the stone, Grolnir," he rumbled, his voice raw and grating, thick with a desperation he rarely allowed himself to show, shaping the words with the deep, uvular trill of his people. "I have lost my path. My oath is my heart, that it is, but this is a new seam to follow, a vein of ore that challenges the bedrock of my purpose. Grant me a true path. Let this road lead to my end, a glorious death in your name. Or let it be a lie I can cast aside, that I can return to my vengeance without question." He waited, breath held tight, for the familiar rumble, for the divine command. No rumbling answer from the earth. Only the cold wind, whistling through the skeletal trees. Grolnir had already spoken his will, long ago, in the ashes of Hjarta-Fell: he would Endure.

He rose slowly, joints cracking a protest against the cold, a symphony of old age and unending battle. His face settled into a mask of granite, hardening against the unwelcome vulnerability. Comfort eluded him, replaced by a harsh, unavoidable clarity that now pierced him to the bone. He closed his fist around the medallion, the cold silver digging into his palm, a reminder of the sharp, unsettling truth. His first step down the ridge toward the temporary, fragile lights of Tetra felt no triumph. It began a new, uncharted hunt, one that held no promise of solace, only more questions. And it marked the heaviest, most uncertain step of his long, brutal life.

Chapter 2

The Blighted.

The rain that fell on Tetra was a temporal sickness, a malevolent whisper from a dying world, an insult to causality. It carried no clean scent of earth, no petrichor, only the sterile dust of a tomb unsealed, a slow decay that caught in the throat like a nobleman's poison, burning with a phantom chill. It descended from a sky bruised an unhealthy, sickening purple, drumming upon the gleaming white marble of the Royal Spire with a hollow, arrhythmic beat that seemed to echo from the city's bones, a funereal cadence for a civilization unaware of its demise. Seraphina ran a gloved finger along the balustrade. Its flawless surface, pristine at dawn, was now gritty with a fine, greasy silt that clung like a shroud. As she pulled her hand back, a century of fine, grey cracks spiderwebbed across the ancient stone in a single, gut-wrenching moment, then vanished, leaving a surface *almost* whole, but irrevocably tainted. A wound disguised. The rot left a scar, even when it retreated. The air was not merely damp; it was thin, brittle, tasting of dust and cold, ancient stone, the slow, agonizing exhalation of a forgotten age. The city breathed death. No one noticed, or no one admitted it.

She drew the hood of her deep purple robes tighter, the formal, austere vestments of the Order of Chronomancy from her ancestral home in Aethelgard. The intricate silver wires braided through her blonde hair, usually reflecting the sun with cool precision, now caught only the weak, grey light, lending her an ethereal, almost spectral quality. A single morning had delivered a hundred years of wear and corrosion to the city, yet she remained an anchor in the accelerating chaos. Someone had to see what they refused to. A cold precision sharpened within her, a slow, crystalline accretion, unyielding as a theorem. This was not grief; it was an equation demanding correction, an incandescent precision against a logical flaw refusing rectification. Her mind, an instrument honed for reading reality's subtle geometries, screamed at the city's shared, elaborate lie, a collective delusion that allowed the decay to fester. How could they be so blind? This shared delusion would be their undoing. Below, the capital staged a grand, tragic performance of denial, its rain-slicked streets reflecting the hurried faces of its people, each step a tacit agreement to ignore the unraveling. Each hurried step, a concession. Each averted glance, a lie.

She watched a young mother, her features etched with weary tenderness, comfort a crying child. For a searing, split second, a deep wrinkle. the kind etched by decades of sorrow. appeared on the child's smooth cheek before vanishing like a phantom echo.

A causality violation, small but absolute. A lifetime of grief, condensed into a single, impossible moment.

The child's future sorrow, momentarily impressed upon its face.

Nearby, a portly merchant, his waistcoat taut over a comfortable belly, paused by a street stall. As his fingers, accustomed to the soft delusion of a stable world, reached for a loaf of bread, its crusty surface devolved instantly into a puff of grey, stale dust.

The syntax of reality is fraying.

The matter sifted through his wide-eyed grasp to vanish into the street's slick grime. The young baker's practiced smile, a brittle facade of normalcy, faltered. His eyes widened, the controlled expression giving way to something wild before he managed to rein it in.

There. He saw it. For a flicker, the truth stared out from behind his eyes.

"A bad loaf," he said, his voice strained and unnaturally high, a forced lightness that rang false. "A one-off mistake."

The merchant, his face slack, quickly accepted a fresh loaf that, for the moment, held its shape, and hurried away. They played their parts in the brittle, dying theatre, both participants in the comforting, catastrophic lie. This denial was a second rot, an infection of the will, more insidious than the one consuming their world.

Her predetermined path led her to a secluded, high-walled garden nestled within the Spire's labyrinthine confines, a place she had quietly claimed as her impromptu laboratory. The air here, once thick with the vibrant scent of loam and the cheerful hum of life, now clung, heavy and still, the silence a suffocating weight. Even here, where life should thrive, the rot did not discriminate. She moved through the ruin, her gaze fixed on a single, withered Sun Petal, its intricate, once-golden life stolen in a single, inexplicable night. With the dispassionate, clinical care of a coroner examining a corpse, she plucked a brittle petal. Another patient on the slab. Another victim. The dry, papery snap it made was the only sound in the oppressive, profound quiet, a stark punctuation mark in the city's silent elegy.

Back within the cold, echoing silence of her scriptorium, a chamber lined with forgotten texts and the scent of aged parchment, she placed the desiccated specimen upon a slab of polished obsidian that felt unnaturally, morbidly warm, a small island of oppressive heat in the gloom. A heat not of life, but of consumption. From her satchel, crafted of dark, supple leather, she withdrew the *Tome of Kronos*, its strange, light-devouring cover a patch of absolute, unfathomable blackness in the dim light, as though it absorbed not just photons but joy itself. Its pages were blank, yet it was a manifestation of time itself, a living artifact and a heavy, silent burden of knowledge. The cost of this knowledge... she paid it then, she paid it now. This was her burden. She remembered the arduous, years-long journey to find it, hidden deep within a forbidden vault beneath Aethelgard, where a temporal ward, not a physical lock but a complex, ancient song, sealed the entrance. When she had finally learned its impossibly intricate melody and sung it back with perfect pitch, the way had opened, and the book had been waiting, pulsing with an ancient, profound stillness.

She laid her will upon the book, a silent command reverberating through the fabric of causality, and her mind plunged into the petal's brief, tragic existence. She witnessed its golden thread of causality, from the first stirring of a seed in the dark earth to its vibrant, full bloom, unravel in an instant, rewound and undone. The thread was severed. Not frayed naturally, but cut. Violently. Then came the violation. a hostile geometric theorem, anathema to life, had brutally inserted itself into its timeline, fraying its future into nothingness, like a perfectly woven tapestry torn asunder by an unseen force. Anathema. A contradiction. A deliberate act. This was not simply death. This was... an assassination of existence. This was not decay. This was war.

Duty, cold and uncompromising, demanded she take this terrible discovery to her master. He must know. He had to. He had taught her to see this. As she walked the echoing, increasingly desolate corridors toward his sanctum, a sharp memory, clear as glass, surfaced unbidden. The dusty study dissolved, and she was a girl again, standing in the heart of the Spire's Grand Orrery, a marvel of celestial mechanics that mirrored the cosmos. The Corvin before her then was not the hollowed-out, weary man of today, but a figure vibrant with intellectual fire. That man... where had he gone? What had become of that fire? His eyes burned with scholarly passion, alive with the light of a thousand constellations, and his voice was a low, resonant hum, perfectly in harmony with the Orrery's soft, whirring song of turning gears and shimmering spheres. "A chronomancer is a musician, Seraphina," he had said, his face a mask of fierce, absolute focus, his hand gesturing to the turning heavens. "We listen to the universe's endless song of causality, the symphony of moments. We must learn to hear the discordant chords, the notes out of place, the subtle flat or sharp that signals imbalance. The most dangerous silence is not the absence of sound, but the quiet where a song should be, a void that portends only unraveling." He had taught her to hear the silence. Now the city was a song unwritten.

That vibrant, achingly alive memory sharpened the present, carving a stark contrast between a glorious past and a decaying now. She arrived at his door, its heavy oak seeming to absorb all light and sound, the ghost of the man he had been fading with each step, leaving only the cold, hard reality of what he had become, a shadow of his former self. A sepulcher. He had buried himself here.

Corvin Nightshade sat in his sanctum, a place of perpetual twilight where shadows clung to every corner and the air hung heavy with the scent of old paper, dust, and something else. a faint, metallic tang of unspent magic. His profound weariness seemed a physical presence that drained the light from the room, making the motes of dust dance in slow, tired eddies. He was a masterpiece of arcane illusion, outwardly appearing in his late prime, his dark hair untouched by grey, his posture impeccable, a testament to powerful, ongoing glamour spells. A glamour, a lie. Even he, the master of truth, hid behind illusions. But his obsidian eyes, ancient, held a soul-deep fatigue that went beyond any mortal sleep, hinting at burdens carried across forgotten epochs.

He looked up from a profane, skin-bound grimoire, its pages illuminated by a faint, sickly green glow, the air around him cold and heavy with scholarly detachment, a fortress built of intellect. Seraphina's hands trembled, not from fear, but from a burning drive to make him see the truth unmaking their world. He must see it. He must. This was not theoretical, it was visceral. It was happening now. She placed the brittle Sun Petal on the dark, polished table between them. "Master," she began, her voice dangerously precise, each syllable an intellectual weapon. Her report poured out, a torrent of intellectual urgency. fraying timelines, hostile geometry, a targeted assault on existence itself. She withdrew a pristine, gleaming silver and gold coin, minted just a fortnight ago, its edges sharp, its shine untarnished, a symbol of supposed constancy. A constant. A baseline. Something undeniable. "Observe. A thing of the city, untainted. A constant, a measure of our stability."

He did not look at the coin, nor did his gaze linger on the withered petal. He looked at her, his ancient eyes seeing only her fervent, exhausting urgency, a relic of a time he no longer inhabited. He saw only her, and her inconvenient truth. He raised a hand, thin and veined, as if to ward off a physical blow, a radiating conviction. "A fascinating anomaly," he murmured, his voice the dry rustle of forgotten leaves, utterly bored. An anomaly? No, Master, a symptom. A demonstration. His movements were glacial, each gesture an act of profound effort. He waved a languid hand over the coin, and the silver instantly tarnished, cold, creeping rust blooming across its surface in an instant, devouring its luster. He glanced at it with immense, weary dismissal and, with another dismissive wave, sent the corroded metal vanishing into a large, woven basket already filled to overflowing with other broken, forgotten things. shards of pottery, rusted keys, faded ribbons. a veritable graveyard of temporal failures. And he merely discarded it. So easily. A graveyard. He'd been collecting the evidence, then ignoring it. Why?

"In a decaying age, Seraphina, we should expect temporal fluctuations," he said, his gaze already returning to the demonic script of his book, dismissing her concerns as trivial academic curiosities. "A ripple in a stagnant pond, nothing more. Note it, of course, for the archives, but do not waste your extraordinary gifts chasing ghosts of causality. There are greater burdens to bear." A ripple? The pond was already a swamp. This was not mere fluctuation; it was a systematic dismantling. Ghosts of causality? He had taught her to see them. He had taught her to hunt them down.

A cold precision, sharper than any blade, tightened the line of her jaw. She placed her knuckles on his desk, the bone-white contact a silent challenge. He forced her hand. He forced her to speak the undeniable truths. "With all due respect, Master, a third of the royal granary just turned to dust, enough to starve a district. The hinges on the Old Gate, centuries old and forged by master smiths, rusted through overnight. These are not ripples. The pond is draining, Master, draining while you admire its reflection, while Malakai poisons the well." This was not academic. This was the unraveling of a kingdom. Malakai. He was always there, always profiting from the chaos.

"The world is full of flawed variables, Seraphina. You have merely found one more," he said, his voice flat, final, impenetrable. Flawed variables? Was he so weary he could not discern a deliberate attack? "Note it, file it, and move on. My work is vital; your distractions are not." Distractions? This was the work. What could be more vital than this?

His absolute dismissal left a bitter, metallic taste, cold on her tongue, when a figure stepped from an archway, blocking her path, his presence commanding and inescapable. Prince Alexander. Alexander. Always appearing when she was most exposed. A complication. And a reminder of her own surgical cruelty. His face was a grim mask of duty, hardened by responsibility, a wicked, jagged scar tracing a stark line across his right cheekbone, a silent testament to battles fought. But his kingly green eyes, though shadowed by the present gloom, held a familiar, intense gaze, a lingering ghost of a past she had painstakingly forced herself to unmake. That gaze... a question she had left unanswered, unanswerable.

For a searing instant, the memory flooded her, vivid, as real as the air she breathed. A moonlit balcony, years ago, high in the Royal Spire, the city lights spread beneath them like scattered diamonds. His voice, a low, resonant rumble, confessing a truth that could unravel kingdoms. *"The laws of this kingdom are a cage, Seraphina. I would give it all up for you. My crown, my duty, my name… all of it."* He would have. He would have sacrificed everything. And she, the guardian of time, could not let that happen. He had leaned in to kiss her, a disarming openness in his eyes, not duty or royal decree, but a singular intensity. But she, the master of causality, the surgeon of time, understood better than anyone the true cost of such stolen moments. A single, forbidden kiss, a momentary lapse of judgment, could cost a kingdom its rightful king, plunge it into chaos. She had faced the impossible equation. the fate of an entire kingdom, its future balanced against the life and love of a single, extraordinary man. and, with an achingly precise, intellectual incision, chosen the kingdom. A single variable, removed. For the greater equation. The fate of Tetra outweighed one future, one heart. She had pulled back, whispering an apology that created a hollow ache, and with a single, sharp act of will, wove a spell of precise subtraction, an excision from the tapestry of his memory. She did not erase the moment entirely; such a brute force manipulation was crude. Instead, she excised it from *his* recollection, leaving only a lingering ache, a phantom limb of memory. She had watched the soft light in his eyes give way to a silent, pointed question that still lingered there today, a constant, unspoken accusation. The ache in his eyes. Her punishment, self-inflicted. She chose the cold logic, the greater good. It was the only choice.

"Seraphina," he said now, his voice a low, hard rumble, cutting through the echoes of the past. "You requested an audience with the council. It is a fool's errand, a dangerous waste of your time. They will dismiss you out of hand. Worse, they will twist your words, use them against you, and ultimately blame you for the decay you seek to understand." He was right, of course. He understood the political rot, if not the temporal. But what choice did she have?

"Then let them blame me," she replied, her voice sharp, driven by resolve, a glint of steel in its usual cool precision. She would not be silenced. Not while this city fell. "If I am the only one who sees this truth, this fundamental flaw in reality, then let me be the one to speak it. Let me be the one to face their accusations."

He reached out, his hand taking her arm with a gentle urgency, his touch warm even through her robes. She registered a phantom echo of a warmth that had never truly been theirs, a memory of a future that she herself had denied them. That warmth... a ghost of what might have been. A lie she created. "The council listens only to Malakai now," he said, his voice dropping to a conspiratorial whisper, edged with a heavy weight. "They are too blinded by fear and ambition to see the truth. But my father... he sees it. He knows there is a deeper rot. He is in his private rooms, away from Malakai's gaze. The rot has taken a toll on him that the royal healers cannot put a name to, a sickness that defies their salves and potions. Come with me. He will listen to you." The King. Yes. He had always seen beyond the surface. Perhaps there was still hope for a logical mind.

They found King Theron in his private chambers, a space once vibrant with royal authority now steeped in an oppressive stillness. The ermine-trimmed robes of state, usually symbols of grandeur, seemed to swallow his frail, emaciated form, making him appear even smaller, more vulnerable. He was fading. Even his symbols of power betrayed him. A tarnished silver bell, his personal symbol of authority, sat on a bedside table, its once gleaming surface now swirling with an accelerating rust, a microcosm of the city's decay. His eyes, though clouded with weariness and the grey film of sickness, held a flicker of the old fire, a defiant spark of regal intelligence as he looked at her. But that spark... it remained. "My son tells me you see the rot not as a plague, not as a disease of the body, but as a feeling," he said, his voice a weak whisper, broken by a dry, rattling cough that shook his entire frame. "Describe it to me, Archmagis. Not in the cold, logical language of books, but as a feeling, a raw sensation." A feeling? He asked for the subjective. A challenge to her clinical mind, but a necessary one, if he was to truly comprehend.

Seraphina knelt beside his divan, bowing her head in respect. A tightness settled in her chest for the dying monarch. She took a slow, deliberate breath, steadying her voice, her gaze unwavering as she met his. "It is a cold, psychic stillness, Your Majesty. A hollow space where a vibrant life once was, a void where reality should hum with purpose. It is the silence where a song should be, the absence of causality, the terrifying void of a broken equation." The truth. Unvarnished. Unyielding.

The King closed his eyes, letting out a long, slow breath. a ragged sigh that named his impending death, the unraveling of his kingdom. He opened them again, and they burned with a defiant, kingly purpose, a resurgence of his former strength. He understood. Finally, a mind that grasped the magnitude. A king worthy of his throne. "She is right," he said, his voice firming, imbued with a final, authoritative tone. "I have seen this wrongness for too long. The stones of this Spire weep with it. We will grant the Archmagis the resources she requires, all the power of the throne. Form a royal commission. Investigate this. " A violent, racking cough cut him off, doubling him over with a ragged sound that stole the air from the room, leaving him gasping. Malakai, who had followed Alexander and Seraphina into the chambers with a small retinue of council members, was instantly on his feet, his face a perfect, polished mask, devoid of any genuine expression. Malakai. Always present, always twisting. A predator in plain sight. His concern was a performance. A manipulation. And the council, his unwitting audience. "Your Majesty, you exert yourself unduly. The Royal Physicians have been explicitly clear on this matter." He turned to the council members, his voice smooth and commanding. "Our King's heart is true, but his body is frail. We cannot burden him with these phantoms, these unsubstantiated claims. Phantoms? This was their reality, disintegrating before their eyes. I dismiss the motion, effective immediately. The King requires rest."

Later, under the shroud of impending night, Malakai entered the King's private chambers alone, his footsteps soft on the thick carpets. The air was thick with the scent of dried herbs, stale medicines, and profound weariness, a suffocating aura of finality. King Theron lay on a divan, his face still and blank, his breath shallow and ragged. Malakai knelt beside him, his gaze fixed on the tarnished silver bell, a symbol of the promise he now intended to break, of the throne he would usurp. "My King," he said, his voice a low, raw rumble, imbued with a profound pity that twisted his ambition into something he believed was righteous. "The city is falling. I have done what is necessary, what you were too frail to do. I have ordered the purge. The mages are a cancer, a poison unmaking our world from within, a contagion spreading the temporal rot. I must cut them out. I must erase them. I must unmake them, for the good of Tetra." The King did not respond, his eyes staring blankly at the ceiling, lost in the creeping void. Malakai, a man who had once believed he could control the world through charisma and cunning, was now merely a witness to its unmaking, convinced he was not a usurper, but a tragic hero tasked with a terrible, necessary surgery upon a diseased kingdom.

Back in her observatory, high within a secluded turret, Seraphina stood before the grand astrolabe, its intricate brass rings and polished lenses usually a source of fascination, now an instrument of grim prophecy. The city had become a cage of whispers, the council a nest of self-serving vipers, her master a ghost of his former self. She stood utterly alone, adrift in a sea of decay and denial. Alone. Yes. But not powerless. Her logic remained. Her purpose remained. They denied. They whispered. They faded. But the rot was real. And it had a signature. An assassin. A cold, deliberate hand at the throat of reality. With grim resolve, her mind a whirling vortex of calculations and chronomantic theorems, she began her complex equations, feeding the astrolabe the hostile energy's unique geometric signature. the precise, cold fingerprint of the world's assassin, the entity responsible for Tetra's unraveling.

Her long, elegant fingers traced glowing runes across the central crystal, each symbol shimmering with stored arcane power. The ancient instrument released a low, mournful chime, a sound like glass shattering in a dream, as its needle ceased spinning its erratic, chaotic dance. It snapped into place with violent finality, forming a single, unwavering vector pointing toward the foreboding, untamed wilderness of the north, toward the jagged peaks of the Dragon's Teeth mountains. The north. Dragon's Teeth. A wild land for a precise solution. The air grew sharp with the metallic scent of ozone and burning magic, crackling with barely contained power. A crack, fine as a hair, shot through the central crystal, a jagged scar that bled a faint, pulsating violet light, a wound carved into the heart of her instrument, a testament to the power of the enemy. This power... it resisted. It broke her instrument. But it did not stop it from revealing the truth.

The rot had a heart. A source. And if the King and his council refused to acknowledge it, refused to act, she would. A heart. She would find it. She would excise it. The decision settled in her soul like a shard of black ice, cold and immovable, sharpening her resolve to a diamond point. They would not act. So she must. The equation would be balanced, one way or another. Alone. Always alone. But a scalpel was precise. A single point could sever a tumor. There would be no royal commission, no grand investigations sanctioned by the crown. The kingdom's great, intricate machinery had broken, fear and Malakai's ruthless ambition rusting its gears into immobility. She stood alone, a scholar armed with an undeniable truth, the last line of defense. She studied the unwavering vector on the wounded instrument. a silent, accusing finger pointing toward a war no one else would fight, a battle she would wage alone.

She moved through her scriptorium, no longer an mage calculating probabilities, but a soldier preparing for a long, arduous campaign. The time for contemplation was over. The time for action had begun. She packed a simple, sturdy leather satchel not with arcane scrolls or dusty tomes, but with dried rations, a waterskin, and potent alchemical reagents that might mean the difference between life and an unremembered death in the desolate north. Survival. The most fundamental of all calculations. She drew a deep breath, the cold air filling her lungs, steadying her spirit. "Fine then. Come along, Mike."

Her miniature basilisk, Mike, responded instantly, his single milky white eye swiveling to meet her gaze, his forked tongue tasting the air. Her only constant companion. Her only true witness to this unraveling. Seraphina, the High Elf Chronomancer of Aethelgard, apprentice to Archmagis Nightshade, took her first determined steps beyond the decaying walls of Tetra in nearly two hundred years, searching for a war no one had yet declared, a solution no one else dared to seek. A solution. A final cure. Even if she must apply the scalpel alone.

Chapter 3

Crossroads

The old trapper, Elias, knew the Gravewood with a certainty etched deeper than the gnarled lines on his weathered hands. An intimacy forged over six decades, a covenant steeped in pine sap and damp earth. His worn boots had mapped its labyrinthine veins onto his memory. He deciphered its secrets from snapped twigs and dry rustles, but more profoundly from wind-whispers through high pines—currents alive with unseen energies, carrying tales only the truly attuned discerned, speaking of the Gravewood's ancient memories as tangibly as the resin on his fingertips.

The forest pulsed with intricate rhythms, its temperaments as varied as the day's shifting light. He had breathed the profound stillness of winter, his exhalations pluming white in air so sharp it stung the lungs, frosted branches scraping a brittle tune against a sky the colour of aged iron. He had tasted the vibrant crescendo of spring, a glorious tumult of scent and sound: the yielding ground teeming with the rich, earthy perfume of decay and rebirth, birdsong erupting in a joyous, deafening chorus, nascent green leaves drinking the light from the sky. Yet, through all these deep cycles, the Gravewood had always offered a raw, profound honesty, its fundamental truths laid bare. It was a wild, untamed entity, a sprawling, verdant kingdom where primeval instincts still roared and whispered through the canopy. Even in its fierce beauty, it moved with ancient, predictable laws, a rhythmic pulse Elias trusted with the marrow of his bones—until now.

A profound betrayal, a searing disappointment, coiled like frozen steel in Elias's gut, tightening into a hard, aching knot. The Gravewood, once a bastion of primal truth, had become a liar, its essence warped into a grotesque parody. The first, most chilling sign was the silence—not the crisp hush of a frost-kissed winter, pregnant with unseen life, but an alien, profoundly predatory quiet. It had ravenously consumed every bird call, hawk's cry, and frantic rustle, leaving a suffocating void, a vast, echoing vacuum that hummed with palpable, unseen menace, pressing in from all sides, threatening to steal his breath. The air itself, usually invigorating with pine and damp earth, now felt thin and brittle, like old, sun-cracked glass, threatening to shatter with the slightest disturbance, leaving a metallic taste upon his tongue. Elias moved with the practiced stealth of a predator, a lifetime of tracking etched into his lean frame, through skeletal trees whose gaunt, bare branches clawed at the heavy, leaden sky. His worn leather boots, usually a soft scuff on damp leaves, now tramped through an unnatural quiet, the absence of crunching sounds making his own heartbeat deafeningly loud. This place, once a cathedral of shadow and light, was now a profanity, a desecration against the gods, a silent scream of agony rising from the violated earth.

He found fresh tracks of a magnificent buck, cloven hooves pressed deep into the soft earth—a prize worthy of a week's hunt. But a few paces further, a cold, leaden knot tightened within him, chilling him to the bone. The creature's droppings, usually dark, firm pellets, were instead a small, anomalous pile of fine, uniform grey dust, sterile and lifeless, like ash from a forge long cold. Elias followed the trail deeper into the hungry, devouring silence, his hunter's instincts warring fiercely with a primal, overwhelming urge to turn and flee.

An hour later, he found the buck standing motionless in a small, shadowed clearing. It simply... stood, neither dead nor truly alive. Its great, dark eyes, once keen and alert, now stared into a vacant, unfathomable stillness, devoid of life or light, like ancient stones worn smooth by forgotten rivers. Thick, grey, web-like fungus, pulsing with faint, sickly luminescence, coated its magnificent antlers, casting an eerie glow on the gloom, a grotesque mockery of life. A single, withered leaf, brown and crisp, drifted down from a branch overhead, settling with an almost imperceptible whisper on the buck's broad back. The moment it touched, a patch of thick, brown fur flaked away like ancient, desiccated parchment. The skin beneath was not pink and healthy, but brittle and grey—the colour of old, forgotten stone and an older, fathomless grief, the skin of something long dead, yet still standing.

Then, with a soft, dry rustle, like the turning of a brittle page in a thousand-year-old book, the creature collapsed. It simply... crumbled: a cascade of ancient, brittle bones and fine, grey ash, a monument of dust in the shape of a deer, settling onto the forest floor, stirring a silent cloud that hung briefly in the air. The magnificent antlers, moments before a crown of life, were the last to go, shattering into countless fragments with a sound like breaking glass, each shard adding to the grey dust that now marked where the buck had stood. A high, thin, utterly human scream tore itself from Elias's throat, ragged and desperate, but the oppressive, consuming silence of the woods immediately devoured it, as if the forest itself had actively swallowed his agony. He turned and fled, stumbling blindly from a quiet so profound, so absolute, that it felt as if it were actively unmaking the world around him, unravelling the threads of existence. He ran until his lungs burned, a raw, searing agony in his chest, the horrifying image of the crumbling buck a final, terrible testament to the insatiable rot that had begun to devour the Gravewood.

The coaching inn, optimistically named 'The Traveller's Respite,' was a cruel deception. Respite found no purchase within its sullen, leaning walls, nor in the sour, cloying smell of wet wool, old despair, and the pervasive damp rot that clung to the air, seeping into bones with chilling persistence. An unseasonably fierce storm had broken over the plains hours ago, turning the already treacherous roads into churning rivers of mud, forcing a tense, uneasy truce between the disparate souls now trapped within its flimsy confines. The meagre hearth fire sputtered, battling relentless damp that crept through a dozen cracks, making the air thick, close, and heavy with unspoken anxieties, pressing down like a physical weight.

Gundroff, a mountain of muscle and granite sunk in a stony silence, had endured its confines for a full day. His massive back pressed firmly against the only wall that offered a semblance of permanence, a futile attempt to find true stone in this crumbling edifice. The inn was a profanity against the enduring craft of his people, a masterwork of shoddy human building. Floorboards groaned, sagging perilously beneath his bulk, each creak a testament to weak timber and unseasoned pine. Poorly fitted hearthstones wept acrid smoke, stinging his eyes. The great central beam, unseasoned pine, had an ominous bow, threatening collapse with every gust. An apprentice in Hjarta-Fell, a mere boy in his first year of Fyrn studies, would have faced shame, utter disgrace, for such amateurish work. This flimsy, rotting human world, built on shifting earth and green timber, was a constant, grrrating insult to his memory of stone and permanence—of mountains like Hjarta-Fell that *should* have endured, not crumbled. That it was not. He listened, golden gaze fixed on the struggling fire's shadows, to the hushed conversations of the inn's other patrons—farmers and trappers, their faces etched deep with weariness and palpable anxiety. They spoke in low tones, their collective unease a guttural murmur beneath the wind's relentless howl, a chorus of rising apprehension.

"It ain't natural, I tell ye," Elias insisted, his knuckles white as he gripped his tankard, as if seeking an anchor in a drowning world. His voice, usually steady and seasoned by years of solitude, now frayed, barely contained. "The quiet... it just eats things. A bird sings, and the sound is just... gone, swallowed whole before it can even echo, leaving only the cold emptiness." Gundroff's golden gaze remained fixed on the struggling fire's flickering shadows, seeing nothing and everything, the spectres of his past rising in the smoke. "It's the rot," a farmer's wife added, her voice a barely audible whisper, her eyes wide with terror. "My Ned, he cut a cord of firewood from the edge of the Gravewood. Two weeks later, the whole pile just... crumbled to dust. Turned to grey ash, like it had been there a thousand years, as if time itself had sped up only for those logs." A burly carter scoffed loudly, though a tremor in his hand betrayed him. "It's a blight, is all. Happens to the crops sometimes." The trapper shot back, his voice rising, "I've lived in these woods sixty years! I know a blight when I see one. This is different. The air feels... thin. Brittle. Like it's about to snap." Gundroff's hand, resting heavily on his tankard, slowly tightened until the wood moaned in protest. The words—of things turning to ash, of time speeding up— struck a chilling, discordant chord in his soul, a Zemleglas lament. They stirred dormant memories of his own clan's fall, of a world that had crumbled to dust around him, leaving only him to endure (✗).

Then, a furious blast of wind and rain threw open the inn's heavy, oak door, admitting a presence so utterly alien it immediately altered the room's sullen, stagnant chemistry. She stood a full head taller than most men present, her lithe, ethereal form an affront to the clumsy, earthbound patrons. Rainwater streamed from her oilskin cloak as she swept back her hood, revealing a cascading torrent of pale blonde hair, braided meticulously with silver wires that caught the firelight like moonlight on ice. Her face was a thing of cold, aristocratic beauty, as if carved from a glacier. Two brilliant, cerulean lines of arcane tattoos spiralled from her elegant brow down her sharp jawline. Her eyes, the colour of a frozen, unforgiving sea, swept the room with clinical detachment, dismissing each face as an irrelevant variable. Coiled on her shoulder, a miniature basilisk with sea-green scales and milky, unblinking eyes surveyed the squalor with reptilian disdain.

Gundroff snorted into his ale, the low, rumbling sound of stone grinding on stone vibrating through the floorboards. She looked utterly out of place, a meticulously cut diamond in a pigsty. Seraphina's heightened senses suffered a brutal assault. The stench was a blow: wet dogs, unwashed bodies, stale ale, and beneath it all, the insidious scent of temporal decay. This, then, was the reality beyond her Ivory Tower: crude, loud, and unacceptably filthy. She walked with imperious purpose, taking the only empty table, not far from the hulking dwarf. She set her light-devouring *Tome of Kronos* upon the scarred wood with a surgeon's precise care. The patrons' superstitious drone was an irritating distraction until a single phrase cut through the noise: "...turned to grey ash, like it had been there a thousand years."

Her head snapped up, glacial eyes alight with fierce, intellectual focus. It was the same terrifying phenomenon. To hear it described so far from Tetra's protected borders was a chilling confirmation: the sickness was far more widespread than even her direst prognoses suggested. Her gaze fixed inexorably on the red-haired dwarf. He watched, not with confusion, but with grim, terrible understanding etched into his face, a veteran's insight into devastation. Their eyes met across the dim, smoke-hazed room. He did not ask permission. He simply pulled out the other creaking chair and sat, placing his heavy, twin-headed axe, Grief and Vengeance, on the earthen floor beside him, its scarred metal gleaming dully.

"You are a long way from your ivory towers, elf," Gundroff rumbled, his voice a low, gravelly rasp, like the grating of stone on stone.

"You are a long way from your mountain, dwarf," Seraphina countered, her voice a low chime of polished ice. "Assuming you still have one."

Gundroff's golden eyes, usually molten pools, narrowed to glinting slits. A deep, grrrating rumble started in his chest. "The mountain endures. The worrld has grrown weak, that it is." He leaned forward, massive forearms on the table, his presence commanding, filling the space like a newly-hewn boulder. "You heard them. The ash. You've witnessed what it does."

"It is a phenomenon beyond their comprehension," she stated, her words a clean, dispassionate cut.

"Call it what you will, elf," Gundroff grrrowled, the sound like stone on stone. "It killed a boar in my hands, turned it to dust. It is turrning their forrest to dust, killing all in its path. It is real, that it is. Yourr books, forr all theirr dead weight, will not stop it." He tapped a calloused finger on the scarred tabletop. "I see things as they arre— stone, steel, rrot. You see only the worrds you have forr them, the abstrract equations. There is a rrot, a deep sickness, in the heart of this worrld. Have yourr books taught you how to cut it out, how to end it?"

"My books have taught me that ravings are not empirical evidence, dwarf," Seraphina retorted, her composure an unbroken shield of ice. "What you see is merely a symptom. I seek the disease, the root cause of this temporal anomaly. A disease of such insidious nature cannot be cured with a sharpened piece of iron."

Before Seraphina could form a suitably withering retort, a sound outside ripped through the storm—the stable's heavy wooden door splintering, then a horse's shriek of pure fright, brutally silenced by a wet thud. Then, a ragged chorus of guttural snarls, punctuated by a dry rattling like brittle bones. A heavy, clawed body slammed against the inn's main door, and the old wood groaned, splintering further. The innkeeper scrambled frantically to bar it. Another thunderous thud made the iron hinges scream. Gundroff was already on his feet, moving with the terrifying speed of a landslide, his massive axe clutched in his hands. "That is the rot," he said, his voice a low, grim certainty. The door splintered inward, and a massive, grey-furred wolf, eyes burning with rabid, unnatural light, burst through. Patches of its hide were brittle, flaking away in dust, exposing sickly grey skin. Its breath was a dry, rattling hiss, exhaling fine ash. It lunged for the nearest farmer, a man frozen in utter dread.

In mid-air, its feral lunge faltered, caught in an unseen current. Its living muscle turned sallow, shrinking violently against bone. Its fur turned a sickly grey and fell away in a cloud of sterile dust. It landed not as a predator, but as a shower of ancient, brittle bones that shattered into countless fragments on the floorboards with dry, clattering finality. Through the broken door, a dozen more pairs of glowing, malevolent eyes watched from the driving rain, their forms wavering at existence's threshold.

The moment of paralysis broke. Patrons screamed, a cacophony of raw fright. Gundroff roared, a sound of pure dwarven wrath that shook the inn's foundations. He charged—not to attack, but to defend. He slammed his massive body against the ruined door, his immense strength the only bulwark against the dying, frenzied pack clawing at the threshold. "The bar rrom!" he rumbled, his voice a raw, grrinding stone, cutting through the din. "Now! Get the damn bar rrom in place, zhdran it!" Seraphina was already moving, an oasis of calm control. As the farmers fumbled with the heavy iron bar, she stepped forward, weaving patterns in the air, her arcane tattoos glowing faintly. A cold, razor-sharp focus reduced the chaos to a simple equation. She spoke a single, sharp word of power, a low chime that struck two lead wolves with concussive force, sending them flying backward into the mud. Galvanised, the farmers slammed the iron bar into place just as the rest of the pack crashed against the makeshift barrier.

The inn fell silent once more, save for the mournful howl of the wind and the frantic, ragged breathing of its occupants. The patrons, huddled together, stared at the two strangers—the towering dwarf and the ethereal elf—with a profound, almost superstitious wonder. Gundroff stood guard, his adrenaline draining, leaving the familiar, gnawing ache of grief and the cold weight of his Oath: the responsibility of enduring. He looked at Seraphina. Her hands still glowed faintly, her face pale, but her frozen eyes burned with fierce, analytical light. A grudging, unspoken respect replaced their initial animosity. Her parlour tricks, he now knew, were potent, terrifying weapons.

The innkeeper, his face ashen, slid two tankards of dark ale across their table. His fright gave way to the grim calm of a survivor, his voice a hollow echo. He settled onto a stool, his gaze lost in a memory the night had dislodged. "I've heard the stories," he said, his voice low, conspiratorial. "Old Man Wilford always said the Gravewood was... hungry. Always taking, never giving." He took a long, fortifying pull from his tankard. "He stumbled from the woods a month ago, a hollowed-out ghost, clutching a half-dozen smooth, grey stones. 'The wood took the song,' he whispered, over and over. For days, he sat by the hearth, speaking to those stones, telling them his life's story, as if pouring his soul into them. Then one morning, his cottage was empty. No struggle. Just his clothes, neatly piled, and the six grey stones lying cold on his empty pillow, shimmering faintly. They held his memories now." The innkeeper shuddered. "His song was gone," he finished, his voice a profound, chilling whisper. "The rot... It steals the song from a man's heart, memory by memory, until nothing's left but silence and dust."

Gundroff's hand tightened on his tankard. He saw the Great Forge of Hjarta-Fell, a hollowed-out space where a roaring song of hammer and anvil once was, now replaced by unnatural silence. Seraphina's face was pale and set, her jaw clenched as she processed the innkeeper's raw story with detached precision, searching for causal links. He saw in her not merely an arrogant elf, but a bulwark of unyielding resolve. She looked back, seeing not a brutish dwarf, but a bastion of pragmatic strength who had, without question, become a living shield. Her books had given her the theory; he had given her the raw, physical truth of its horror. It was then that an old man in the brown robes of Solara, the Sun Mother, set down his untouched mug. He produced a small, leather-bound book. "A sad story, that it is," he said, his voice a low, gentle rumble. "And an old one. It reminds me of a tale from the *Parables of Valerius*."

"The Tale of the Gardener," he began, his voice taking on a rhythmic cadence. "There was once a gardener, whose hands were blessed with patience. He was given a single seed that had fallen from the distant stars, a gift of pure light. He tended it with all the love in his simple heart, and it grew into a magnificent star blossom, its petals unfurling in brilliant hues, a beacon in the darkness. But a creeping blight, a rot that lived in the deep, forgotten soil, a jealous shadow born of ancient emptiness, was envious of its light. It poisoned the blossom's roots, twisting its vibrant colours into dull, necrotic greys, turning its fragile beauty into a weapon of thorns. The gardener... he never forgave himself, for he saw the blight's victory as his own failure, the corruption of beauty as his own sin.'"

He closed the book softly. The simple, allegorical tale hung in the heavy air, a mythic counterpoint to the innkeeper's raw tragedy. The two stories began to resonate, their truths intertwining. Gundroff saw a jealous, ancient evil, a primordial shadow that hated the vibrant light of his roaring forges, the enduring song of his people. Seraphina saw a historical precedent, an ancient, recurring sickness in creation's fabric, a causality gone horribly awry. The two truths were no longer in opposition; they were two verses of the same terrible song.

"You travel north. To Tetra," Gundroff stated, his voice flat, a decree carved in stone.

"The source of this decay is in the north," Seraphina replied, her voice steady. "I mean to find it. I mean to eradicate it. My solution is a final cure."

"Then you will need more than books and parlour tricks, that you will," he rumbled. He gave a single, sharp nod. "I will walk with you. My axe for yourr... knowledge. My strength for your mind. My oath is to endure, not for vengeance, but for the sake of others who cannot."

The storm outside had passed, leaving profound stillness and the scent of rain-washed earth, a faint promise of a new, troubled dawn. In the quiet of the battered inn, amidst dust and burgeoning hope, they forged an alliance—a grim, necessary contract bound by encroaching darkness. With terrifying certainty, they understood they were perhaps the only two in the world who truly grasped the nature of the insidious war that had just begun, a war that sought to steal existence's song.

Chapter 4

Long Road to the Heart

The morning after the storm unveiled a world scrubbed clean and aged beyond its years, a haunting tableau painted in shades of grey and bruised violet. The deluge had passed, its roaring fury now a phantom echo in the ringing silence, leaving in its wake a profound stillness that pressed down with a physical weight far greater than the tempest itself. A pale, aqueous sun wrestled through the tattered edges of bruised clouds, casting a sickly, jaundiced light over a landscape of shattered branches and pooling, stagnant water. The air, thin and metallic, tasted of sterile dust and ozone, as if the heavens had scoured the life from the earth, stripping it raw. This unnatural quiet hung thick and oppressive, pregnant with an unspoken tension that made the skin prickle and promised only further unraveling.

Within the damp, musty confines of 'The Traveler's Respite,' the few surviving patrons shuffled with the aimless, broken gait of specters. Ghost-pale, drawn faces revealed the centuries they had weathered in a single night; the timber of the inn itself seemed more weathered, its grain deeper, the floorboards groaning with a newfound antiquity. The previous evening's superstitious awe had curdled into a sour, fearful resentment. Their eyes, once wide with wonder, now tracked Seraphina's cloak with a low, cold scrutiny, gazes tightening into hard knots of suspicion at the sight of Gundroff's great axe resting against his shoulder. Magic and monstrous strength were primal, unpredictable energies, and their fragile world had been torn by them. A grizzled trapper's hound, its milky, cataracted eyes catching Seraphina's alien scent, let out a low, mournful whine deep in its chest. It flattened itself to the floor before retreating beneath its master's table, tail clamped tight between its legs, trembling uncontrollably, the raw scent of fear thick on its fur.

"This debt here, I must settle it," Gundroff rumbled, the words a formal declaration of honour, a deep-seated dwarven need for order asserting itself against the encroaching chaos. Purpose was etched on his brow like an ancient runemark as he approached the innkeeper, his heavy purse held ready.

The innkeeper, his frame bowed under the sudden, crushing weight of his ruined stables and the invisible ruin of his own stolen years, raised a trembling, arthritic finger. It wavered, a fragile twig in a gale, then steadied, pointing with rigid finality directly at the door. His wide eyes, empty of recognition or gratitude, fixed on the empty road beyond. It was not a gesture of dismissal but of desperate expulsion, a hollow, palpable force pushing them toward the exit, away from his broken threshold and the reminder of the nightmare they had brought.

They departed without a word, two solitary figures swallowed by the grey dawn. The mud of the road, thick and clinging, was marked by patches of fine, grey powder and brittle splinters of bone—all that remained of the wolf pack the temporal storm had consumed. Seraphina knelt beside one such ash-patch, a faint cerulean light blossoming in her palm, cool and analytical. Her breath misted in the chill air, held on a razor's edge as her spell dissected the ash, reducing the visceral terror of the previous night to a clean, clinical equation of cause and effect.

"The decay accelerates exponentially in moments of extreme physical or emotional exertion," she stated, her voice as calm and dispassionate as the wan morning light, utterly devoid of the horror the sight inspired. She rose to her feet, meticulously wiping the clinging dust from her hands with a fine silk cloth. "Cellular structure loses its temporal cohesion under acute stress. It doesn't truly die in the conventional sense. It simply... *unspools*. Its entire future timeline collapses into a single, catastrophic instant of being."

Gundroff grunted, the low, guttural sound caught in the thicket of his beard. His formidable gaze was already mapping the northern road, claiming their next mile before they had even taken a step. Her intricate, academic theories, fine and delicate as Elven lace, held little sway for a being of stone and steel. To him, the rot was a spreading poison, a corrupting blight that violated the fundamental dwarven principle of endurance. It was an insult to the natural order of stone, a profound wrongness that needed to be forcibly rectified. His hand sought the worn leather haft of his great axe, its familiar weight a solid, grounding truth in this unraveling world, a tool designed to *solve* problems. "Such knowledge is useless if it does not lead to a cure," he rumbled, his voice a low, gravelly rasp that grated like stones shifting in a riverbed, "or a blade to cut the corruption out. *Aye.*"

Their alliance began as a grim march of purpose, not companionship. The initial days unfolded in a strained, heavy silence, a tangible barrier of culture and perspective erected between them. They walked with a careful, measured distance—he, a creature of stone and earth, his heavy, deliberate tread a percussive rhythm against the muddy road, a relentless metronome of duty; she, a being of air and intellect, her long-limbed stride so light and effortless she seemed to glide over the ground she disdained, barely disturbing the ash of forgotten futures.

The further north they ventured, the more profoundly sick the world became. The lowlands bled into a sallow, anemic palette of sickly yellows and faded ochres, as if the land itself were suffering from a wasting disease, a slow, chronological consumption. The trees sagged under the weight of their own unnatural age, their leaves a brittle, unhealthy yellow that crumbled to dust at the slightest touch, dissolving into grey powder on the wind. This was no sudden blight, but a slow, creeping corruption that leached the vitality from everything. The woods held their breath, the deep, pervasive silence less a sign of peace, more the sound of a void where life had simply... ceased. No birdsong sliced the air; no rustle of unseen creatures in the undergrowth broke the stillness. Only the dry, crackling crunch of their boots on brittle leaves punctuated the quiet. They passed a dead robin on the path, its body not mangled or preyed upon, but simply ancient. Its tiny form was withered, its feathers faded to a ghostly grey, as if it had run out of time mid-flight and tumbled from the sky, a husk of what it had been a moment before. A fine, grey dust, the ash of forgotten futures, covered the forest floor, powdering their boots with every weary step, a constant, chilling reminder of the world's inexorable decay.

As they crossed a rickety wooden bridge spanning a sluggish, brown creek, Gundroff halted abruptly. He ran a calloused, knowing hand over the weathered stonework of its foundation. The granite, which should have stood for centuries more, wept fine, shimmering cracks that spiderwebbed across its surface. Thick, green-grey moss that should have taken decades to form clung to the stone in dense, velvety patches, soft and unnatural against the failing granite. The air around the bridge hung heavy, a viscous quality that hummed with unseen tension, a low thrum of temporal stress. "The mortar is failing," he stated, his voice a low growl of disgust, grinding like stone on stone. "Sand and lime, poorly mixed and hastily applied. A dwarf in the deeps would have his clan shave his beard and break his Kladiv for such pathetic work. It is a disgrace to the stone and to the Khlad who shaped it, *that it is*." A challenge glinted in his molten gold eyes as he faced her, a direct jab at her world of abstracts. "Your books cannot hold up a bridge, elf. Nor your frail magic, that it cannot."

"Nor can your axe rebuild it," she retorted, her gaze as cool and unyielding as his, a surgeon's calm before a complex operation. "I am not observing shoddy craftsmanship, dwarf. I am observing a localized temporal distortion field. Something is artificially accelerating the stress on the stone's causal timeline, forcing it to endure a century of erosion in a matter of weeks. This bridge, your axe, your own physical form— matter composes you all, and all matter submits to the iron law of time. The rot is a parasitic force. It attaches itself to a timeline and feeds upon it, drawing out all potential futures and leaving only a hollow, exhausted present. The trees do not sicken from a disease of the body, but of their chronological essence. Something is *unraveling* their temporal thread. They are living out their entire lifespans in weeks, dying of extreme old age, and this rot is the cancer that feeds on their borrowed time."

He snarled, a guttural sound grinding from deep in his throat like dry stone. "A man dying of a gut wound does not care for the name of the blade that stabbed him," he retorted, his voice low and dangerous, edged with primal frustration. "He cares only for the hand that can stitch him closed. You obsess over the theory of the rot, Seraphina, as if naming it gives you power over it. My concern is the practical reality of it—stopping the bleeding. This is a problem of action, not of observation. A beast to be slain, not a specimen to be dissected. That it is."

"A physician who stitches a wound closed without first removing the poison within is not a healer," she replied, her voice dangerously quiet, each word a scalpel's edge, sharp and precise. "He is a fool committing murder by incompetence. You would stop the bleeding, Gundroff, and leave the infection to fester. My solution is a final cure. A complete eradication of the source."

Their first night's camp was a tense negotiation of their opposing natures. He made camp in a defensible hollow within a rocky outcrop, his movements economical and certain, the ingrained wisdom of a dwarven warrior seeking security. He cleared the brush, built the fire pit, and set snares with an efficient, brutal grace born of a lifetime of survival in harsh lands. She, in turn, paced the perimeter of their small sanctuary, whispering words of power that were ancient when the surrounding hills were young, her fingers tracing faint, glowing runes in the air. A shimmering, invisible barrier of arcane energy, smelling faintly of ozone and starlight, settled over the hollow, an unbreachable wall of pure causality.

They sat on opposite sides of the fire, a small, defiant star in the encroaching, silent dark. The snares had yielded a single, scrawny rabbit, which Gundroff was now roasting over the flames, turning it slowly on a sharpened stick. He tested the shimmering barrier with the tip of his axe, a firm, unyielding resistance meeting the honed steel. The air hummed where metal met magic, a low, resonant thrum of power. "Your magic," he rumbled, the words a grudging concession, forced from his throat like rough stone, "It holds like good mortar, *aye*. Not just parlor tricks, that it is not."

Just then, a voice, soft as moss on stone, drifted from the deep shadows just beyond the firelight. "A fine fire on a dark night. Might an old man trouble you for a bit of its warmth?"

A figure emerged into the flickering light, an old man in the simple, travel-stained brown robes of a lay brother. After a curt, assessing nod from Gundroff, he settled himself near the flames, his knees cracking audibly. His bright blue eyes, clear and unclouded by the decay that plagued the land, reflected the firelight as his gaze shifted from the dwarf's stony, impassive face to the elf's cold, guarded appraisal.

"A fire like this, it reminds me of a tale from the Parables of Valerius," he said, his voice warm and soothing, a welcome balm in the silent, suffocating woods. He produced a small, leather-bound book, its cover worn smooth with countless readings, and opened it to a page marked with a faded ribbon. "The First Forging," he began, his voice soft yet resonant, carrying easily through the silent woods. "In the time before time, the Mountain Heart, Grund, looked upon his works and found them wanting. He had raised the great peaks and forged the bones of the world, but it was a silent, empty place. So he took a piece of the Deep Core, the heart stone of the world, and on an anvil of pure gravity, with a hammer of cosmic force, he forged the first seven dwarves. He gave them three great gifts: the stubbornness of the mountain, the fire of the forge, and a soul of unbreakable loyalty. And he gave them their great charge: to be the keepers of the deep places and to keep a fire lit in the heart of the mountain, so the world would never fall into a final, cold darkness."

He closed the book with a soft snap. Gundroff remained silent, his gaze fixed on the dancing flames, but his knuckles, gripping the roasting spit, had gone bone-white. The words were an echo from his father's hall, a sacred creation myth he had not heard anyone speak aloud since he was a boy, before the fire and the fall of Hjarta-Fell. Seraphina, however, dissected the tale for its underlying structure, an intellectual exercise to extract its core data. "A heart stone," she mused aloud, her voice a low, analytical whisper. "A central, stabilizing element. A Pillar, perhaps. And a charge to keep a fire lit… a source of constant energy, a ward against a great cold… a darkness. A core causality, one might say, from which all other dwarven history proceeds."

Gundroff tore a piece of the roasted rabbit from the spit and, after a moment's hesitation, offered it to her on the flat of his knife. She eyed the greasy meat, then his calloused, grime-stained hand, her lip curling in a faint, almost imperceptible twitch of distaste. Yet his molten gold eyes held the offer, not as a challenge, but as a simple fact of their shared circumstance: a grudging necessity for survival. She took the meat, her long, elegant fingers carefully avoiding his. A quiet, shared weariness, not tension, settled into the silence between them as they ate.

The next day delivered them to the village of Oakhaven, a place steeped in muted despair. The central square lay empty, save for a few listless figures slumped on benches, staring with hollow, vacant eyes into the middle distance. There was no laughter, no children playing, no merchants calling their wares; only the oppressive hush of a forgotten world. The town's great oak, a five-century testament to life and resilience, stood skeletal and leafless, its bark peeling away in papery sheets like sunburnt skin, exposing the ancient, dying wood beneath. The church bell, a villager later told them in a monotone, had fallen that morning, not with a crash, but by crumbling silently to a pile of green dust in its belfry, its voice erased from memory.

They found the village elder on the steps of the silent church. He did not look at them as they approached, but at his own gnarled, trembling hands, which he turned over and over as if they were foreign objects, trying to place them. "The bell... it fell this morning," he rasped, his voice a dry, reedy whisper, thin as ancient paper. "Crumbled. Turned into a pile of green dust. It had a fine voice, our bell. For four hundred years, it called us to prayer, warned us of fires, celebrated our weddings. Now... now I can't quite remember what it sounded like." He looked up, his eyes clouded with a terrifying confusion, his voice cracking. "My wife... her name is Elara. I have known her for sixty years. Loved her for sixty years. This morning, I woke up, and for a full minute, I could not remember her name. It was just... gone. A hole in my head where her name should be. I can see her face... I can see her smile, but I cannot find the word for her."

Seraphina's face, so often a mask of cool, intellectual disinterest, went stark pale. The decay was not merely physical; it attacked memory, identity, the fabric of the self, unraveling the essence of a soul. She placed a delicate hand on the old man's forehead, whispering a single, diagnostic word, a prayer of chronological inquiry. A faint, silver light bloomed from her palm, invisible to all but her. She saw the thread of his personal history, and it was fraying, thin and fragile as an old rope about to snap. Gaping holes of pure nothingness appeared in the thread, moments and memories un-written from existence, erasing his past from the inside out, turning him into a ghost in his own life.

They left the village of silent bells behind them, a new and colder dread clinging to their souls like a shroud. A crumbling world was a tragedy; a world that was forgetting itself was an apocalypse. Their path led them into the fringes of the King's Wood, where the temporal decay became a violent, chaotic madness. Distorted birdsong slowed to a mournful dirge that hung in the air, a broken lament for lost time. The rustle of leaves rasped like brittle bones rubbing together, a dry, percussive sound of dying. The trees themselves writhed, their branches twisting into impossible, agonized shapes, growing and decaying in the same instant, their forms blurring at the edges of reality. They were forced to make camp early, the oppressive wrongness of the place making further travel impossible. The hairs on Gundroff's arms rose and stayed risen, a primal alarm blaring through his dwarven blood. He sat by the fire, his great axe laid across his knees, relentlessly scanning the deep, churning shadows, feeling the weight of unseen eyes.

"There is something out there," he rumbled, his voice a low growl that was felt as much as heard, vibrating through the cold ground. "Something large. And it is not hunting for food. It is hunting for a fight. *Aye.*"

A chill, unrelated to the evening air, traced an icy path down Seraphina's spine. A profound and ancient life force brushed against her arcane senses—but it was corrupted, twisted into a screaming mockery of its true nature, a temporal predator.

The attack came in the grey light just before dawn. A colossal black bear, a true forest monarch, burst from the treeline, its gait staggering and hideously unnatural. It should have been a magnificent creature; instead, it shambled, a walking ruin, a grotesque parody of strength. The left side of its face was a hairless, withered mask, the skin stretched thin and translucent over the bone beneath, aged centuries beyond its time. Its left eye was a clouded, milky white orb, blind and weeping; its corresponding ear was a shriveled, leathery husk. The claws on its left paw were long, yellowed, and brittle, while those on its right were keen and sharp. It was a living paradox of vitality and ruin, half-ancient, half-prime, an abomination against the natural order.

It roared, not in challenge, but in a symphony of confusion and pain, a raw, broken sound from a noble spirit trapped in unraveling time. It charged, not at them specifically, but at the flickering fire, at the wrongness of their ordered presence in its fractured, chaotic world. Gundroff met the charge, planting his feet like the roots of a mountain, his body a bastion of unyielding stone. The impact of the bear's charge against his axe sent a jarring tremor up his arm that numbed his fingers to the elbow, a shockwave that resonated deep in his bones. The creature was mighty, its agony granting it a terrible, supernatural strength, a force fueled by temporal paradox. It swiped, its one good paw a blur of razor-sharp claws, forcing him to shift and absorb the blow along his side with a grunt of pain. The creature's one good eye held a raw, terrified confusion—the horror of a king who had found his own mind a traitor, his own reality in rebellion against itself. He became a bulwark, a wall of granite and will, his only purpose to turn the creature's mad charge away from Seraphina, to shield her with his own unwavering body.

Her offensive spells were too crude, too destructive for this. She needed a surgical strike of healing causality, not a blast of raw force that would merely add to the chaos. Pouring her will into a single, complex spell, her fingers wove intricate, arcane gestures in the air, a dance of pure logic. A delicate web of silver light bloomed from her fingertips, a geometric pattern pulsing with quiet, ordered energy, a temporal matrix forming in the fractured air. She wove no spell of harm, but one of peace, of temporal stabilization, a desperate attempt to mend the bear's fractured timeline, to impose cosmic order on its internal storm. The effort of imposing such order on chaos, of mending a wounded timeline, left a hollow void aching in her chest, a profound exhaustion that resonated deep in her bones.

A gentle wave of pure silver light washed out from her hands, a timeless, silent embrace. The great bear, claws raised for another strike, froze mid-lunge, caught in the spell's precise grip. A profound calm washed over its features, replacing the rage in its one good eye with a quiet, peaceful awareness. Its heaving, ragged chest slowed to a steady rhythm, the frantic temporal anomalies around it settling into a calm, continuous flow. It stood for a long, silent moment, a statue of black fur and ancient sorrow, then it simply lay down upon the forest floor. It closed its eyes and, with a final, shuddering sigh, fell into a deep and dreamless sleep, its suffering finally at an end.

Seraphina collapsed to her knees, pale and trembling, the hollow void of spent power aching deep in her bones, a raw, emotional toll for a purely intellectual act. Gundroff lowered his bruised body beside her, the lingering aches from the bear's blows a dull thrum. He reached out, his grime-stained hand settling heavily on her shoulder. She did not flinch or pull away. Instead, her head leaned into his touch, the solid heat of his body an anchor in the swirling chaos of the wood, a tangible point of reality. Her gaze met his over the bear's slumbering form, and in that shared look, an unspoken understanding passed between them, a silent pact forged in the heart of chaos.

The last days of their journey became a grim, silent march of unity, their separate purposes now aligned. The King's Wood gave way to the rolling hills and farmlands surrounding Tetra. Here, the decay offered no subtle secrets; it was a screaming, open wound across the landscape. The fields wove a tapestry of death, a patchwork of withered life. Squads of the Royal Guard, their faces hidden behind grim steel helms, put entire fields of withered wheat to the torch, sending plumes of sickly, acrid smoke to stain the horizon, a pall of unnatural decay. Farmers with dead eyes led skeletal livestock to the cull pits, the creatures stumbling on atrophied legs, their hides hanging loose, their bones sharp, cruel angles against emaciated forms, their timelines having accelerated to a point of no return.

The official story, from a nervous young soldier at a checkpoint, was of a fast-acting blight of unknown origin. But the frantic fear in his eyes told a different story, one of orchestrated terror. "The priests say it's a punishment from the gods," he whispered, darting quick, terrified glances around as if the trees were listening, as if the rot itself had ears. "But the new Lord Regent's men… they are calling it a 'mage blight.' They say some rogue sorcerer has laid a curse upon the land."

The soldier's darting eyes confirmed the cynical, calculated lie. Malakai's men were not fighting a blight; they were hunting magic itself, using the rot as a bloody excuse for a purge. He described a scene from the week before: a hedge witch in a small hamlet, a woman who had delivered half the village's children, her small magics a comfort, not a threat. The Regent's men had come, inciting the crowd, whispering of "mage blight," expertly stirring up ancient, dormant fears that had simmered beneath the surface of the realm. "They pointed at her garden," the soldier recounted, his voice trembling with a mixture of horror and shame, "said the blight started there because her herbs hadn't withered. The townspeople, driven mad by fear and hunger, dragged her from her cottage and built a pyre in the town square."

The words struck Seraphina like a cold, physical slap, a realization that chilled her to the core. Lord Malakai's political poison was seeping into the soil, taking root in the fear and ignorance of the common folk, twisting their minds. She and Gundroff were not walking toward a sanctuary; they were walking into a carefully prepared trap.

As they crested a high hill, the city of Tetra gleamed in the setting sun. Its slender, white marble spires pierced the sky like elegant needles, and its impossibly smooth walls shimmered with the faint, ancient arcane wards woven at its founding, promises of protection that now felt like a cruel joke. It was a perfect jewel nestled in the green cradle of the valley, a beacon of hope, but the memory of Oakhaven's silent bells and the whispers of a coming purge rendered the city fragile, distant, and doomed. This was no sanctuary. It was a beautiful cage, its bars forged not from iron, but from a calculated, weaponized fear, its purpose not to protect, but to imprison. They had walked through a dying world only to arrive at the heart of the cancerous disease.

Chapter 5

The Serpent's Court

The Grand Hall of the Royal Spire was built for awe, but now it was a stage for decay. Its vaulted ceilings soared hundreds of feet into a perpetual gloom the midday sun could not banish, its ribs of white marble laced with shimmering veins of gold that now seemed tarnished and skeletal beneath a film of grime. Colossal statues of Alexander's ancestors, the kings and queens of his line, stood sentinel in arched alcoves along the walls. Their stone eyes, once inspiring, now gazed down upon a history forged with steel and sorrow, their expressions seeming to curdle into silent accusation. A fine, sterile black dust coated the mosaic floor, dissolving the gilt from the sills and window casings. It lay thick on the broad shoulders of the marble sentinels, clinging to their carved faces like grave mould, giving them the appearance of forgotten corpses. The air, heavy with the cloying sweetness of wilting funeral flowers and a sharp, metallic ozone, tasted of rot.

Prince Alexander stood rigid beside the Sunstone Throne, a pillar of gilded black wool in the vast, echoing space. His hand, white-knuckled, clamped the silver pommel of his longsword—a grip that flexed and released in a frantic, involuntary rhythm, like a failing pump. The lineage, the crown, the city—all of it pressed inward on his ribs, a crushing physical weight that made each breath shallow and sharp. He was a prince in name, a king in waiting, yet his only absolute authority at this moment was to hold his chin high and command his own limbs not to tremble.

He closed his eyes, shutting out the suffocating present, and the metallic tang in the air was momentarily replaced by the ghost of beeswax polish and clean, sun-warmed stone. A memory, so sharp and unbidden it felt like a physical blow, pierced the gloom. He was a boy again, small enough to hide behind the throne's great carved legs, watching his father dispense justice from that seat. The hall had been different then; it had thrummed with a warm, living hum—the shuffle of petitioners' feet, the rustle of scribes' quills, the low murmur of a hundred conversations. A farmer, his knuckles thick with the soil of his birthright, had knelt before the throne, his fields stolen by a greedy, neighbouring lord. King Theron, his back straight as a spear shaft and his voice a resonant baritone, had not needed to raise it. He had held the farmer's gaze and asked two simple questions: "What is the truth of this matter? And what is the just path?" The answers, spoken in a voice that was both a king's command and a father's patient lesson, had been enough. The lord was humbled, the farmer made whole, and the hall had settled into a quiet, powerful rightness. The memory dissolved, leaving a hollowness in his chest, a physical ache for a time when justice was a solid, tangible thing, and his father was the unshakeable stone at the centre of the world.

He opened his eyes and looked at his father, King Theron. The magnificent ermine robes, heavy with gold thread, pooled beneath the Sunstone Throne, swallowing his frail form until he seemed little more than a ghost lost in finery. The Crown of the Sunstone, a circlet of sun-forged gold, sat heavy on his brow, tilting slightly. His skin was the pale, waxy colour of old tallow. At his temples, a disturbing web of black veins pulsed like thin, agitated snakes just beneath the skin, a venom the Royal Physicians had no name for and no cure. He listened to the supplicants before him, his eyes half-closed, his breathing a shallow, laboured rasp that was almost lost in the vast, dead air of the hall.

"Your Majesty," a stout man named Jorun, head of the city's Granary Guild, cut through the oppressive silence, his voice trembling with a mixture of fear and outrage. He held up a handful of wheat, and even from the dais, Alexander could see its profound corruption. The grains were shrunken, blackened husks, coated in the same fine dust that veiled the great clock tower, visible through a high, arched window.

That tower, a masterpiece of dwarven ingenuity and a symbol of Tetra's precision, was now a silent monument to a morning that had refused to end, its bronze hands frozen at a quarter past nine, its face grimed with the foul dust the people had begun to call the "Liar's Rain."

"This is from the royal silos, sire," Jorun continued, his voice cracking into a pleading whisper. "The harvest was blessed, the silos sealed by the priests themselves. And yet... It rots. Not a natural rot, but a... a withering. An emptiness. A third of the city's winter stores have turned to this dust in a fortnight." His hands shook, and the blackened grains sifted through his fingers like sand from a broken hourglass, a tiny, soundless cascade of ruin onto the marble floor.

Beside Jorun stood Captain Lyra of the Mariner's Guild, her face a mask of hard lines carved by a life at sea and now deepened by a new, terrestrial dread. "Our anchors, Your Majesty. Good iron, forged in the dwarven style, meant to last a thousand years. Now they crumble like old bread when they strike the seabed. The nails in our hulls weep with a hungry, unnatural rust. We dare not make port for long, for fear our ships will fall apart in the harbour." Her voice was raw with an exhaustion that went deeper than any long voyage, the sound of a woman who had lost faith in the materials that had defined her world.

A third man, his hands calloused and grey with stone dust, shuffled forward, his body stooped as if under the invisible weight of the city itself. He held a mason's hammer as if it were a holy relic he no longer knew how to use. "The west wall of the Citadel, Your Grace. The foundation stone, laid by the First King himself. It weeps—the mortar powders at a touch. My guild... we patch it by day, and by morning, the cracks have returned, deeper than before. The city's bones are turning to sand." His voice was a dirge, a funeral song for a dying city.

The air around the stonemason shivered faintly, smelling of pulverized stone and ozone. As the man turned his head, a single, tiny flake of dust drifted from the silver trim of Alexander's own sleeve, dissolving before it hit the floor. Alexander's grip tightened on the pommel, the metal feeling strangely light and porous, like dry bone, beneath his palm.

It was the same litany of decay they had heard for weeks, a chorus of despair from every corner of the kingdom. The sickness. The rot. The phenomena Seraphina had tried to warn them about. The thought of her name was a sudden, sharp pressure behind his ribs. He saw her fierce, brilliant eyes, felt the cool intensity in her voice as she had presented him with a withered Sun Petal, its golden life leeched away to a brittle grey. Her words had been a cascade of alien terms—'temporal distortion fields' and 'hostile geometry'—that the Council had dismissed as hysterical fantasy. He had believed her, but his belief had been a useless, silent thing. He had failed to champion her cause, failed to make them listen. He had failed her then, and he was failing his people now.

Before the King could offer another weary platitude, a voice, smooth and resonant as a cello, cut through the charged silence. "The good people of Tetra are frightened, Your Majesty. And they are right to be so."

Lord Malakai stepped forward from the assembled Council, a slash of serpent green silk and elegant, controlled menace. He moved with the fluid, predatory grace of a panther, his handsome face carefully composed into a mask of profound pity. He glided toward the supplicants and placed a palm—not comforting, but possessive—on Jorun's trembling shoulder, a calculated gesture that aligned him with the common man while the King sat distant, silent, and enthroned.

He did not wait for a response, his gaze moving past the King's drooping form to address the crowd directly. "For generations, we have lived in the light of Anor's blessing," he continued, his voice filling the vast hall, each word polished and weighted for maximum effect. "But a shadow has fallen upon our land. This is no natural blight. It is a poison. A poison of the spirit, a curse that targets the heart of our prosperity, our strength." He let the words hang in the air, a palpable threat. He gestured to the stonemason. "The bones of our city crumble. To the good captain, the iron of our commerce turns to rust. To Master Jorun, the bread of our people turns to ash. This is not the work of nature. This is the work of an enemy."

He paused, letting the silence build, his piercing gaze sweeping over the assembled crowd. A nervous cough rippled through the front row. A woman in a worn wool cloak wrung her hands, her knuckles white. Alexander watched him survey them, not as people seeking aid, but as instruments waiting to be played. "And where do such curses find their root, I ask you?" he said, his voice dropping to a conspiratorial whisper that nonetheless carried to every corner of the hall. "They are born in the shadows, in the dusty studies of those who meddle with forces beyond mortal ken. They are brewed in the cauldrons of the arcane, by those who have turned their backs on the honest light of the sun to whisper secrets to the dark."

A deep, angry murmur went through the assembled supplicants. They had come with a problem; he was giving them a solution, simple and satisfying. A cold knot formed in Alexander's stomach. Malakai was not just speaking; he was conducting an orchestra of fear. "My heart aches to see you so distressed," Malakai said, his voice dropping to a warm, intimate tone, as if he were sharing a private grief with each of them. "I have not slept for weeks, consumed by the same questions that plague you. I have consulted with priests, with scholars, with men of reason and men of faith. And all paths, my friends, lead to a single, inescapable truth." He took a dramatic breath, then spoke the words they were all now waiting to hear. "The nature of this rot—its deliberate, malicious corruption of our vital industries—is the hallmark of arcane malevolence. It is the work of a sorcerer, or a cabal of sorcerers, who resent the light of our prosperity."

A ripple of recognition passed through the crowd. Their postures shifted, shoulders straightening, expressions hardening from victimhood to something colder, more resolute. They had a name for their tormentor. The stonemason, who had stood hunched in defeat, now stood tall, his eyes narrowed with newfound purpose. Jorun's knuckles, which had been white with fear, now clenched into a tight fist of anger. "We cannot fight a ghost," Malakai continued, his voice taking on a new, firmer cadence, the voice of a commander addressing his troops. "We cannot reason with a shadow. We must find the source. We must bring the poison out of the dark and into the light. The people of Tetra need to know that their King, their government, is doing everything in its power to protect them, to hunt this sickness to its root and burn it out once and for all."

The crowd stirred, their whispers no longer hushed but sharp, edged with fury. The Guild master, Jorun, found his voice, a low rumble that became a shout. "He speaks the truth! Give us the power to purge them!" Another voice, then another, joined the chorus. The Captain, Lyra, whose face had been a mask of weary defeat, now looked at Malakai with a dangerous flicker of hope in her eyes.

"Lord Malakai speaks out of turn," Alexander said. His own voice sounded thin and reedy in the vast space, swallowed by the rising tide of anger. The collective weight of the crowd's hostile gazes turned on him, a physical blow that made him flinch. "This is a matter for the Royal Scholars and the High Priests to investigate, not for baseless speculation."

Malakai turned, and the look in his eyes was not anger, but a condescending pity that was far more insulting. He took a slow, deliberate step toward Alexander. "Ah, my dear Prince." Malakai's hand remained on the stonemason's shoulder, a gesture of solidarity against the throne. "Your heart is noble. A credit to your lineage." He looked out at the faces, now hard and expectant. "But a soft heart is a luxury we can no longer afford." He took another step forward, his voice dropping, becoming a shared secret between him and the crowd. "They don't need another investigation. They need a shield. They need a surgeon's hand to cut out this rot. And they need it now."

He turned back to them, his voice rising to a passionate crescendo. "We must be vigilant! We must be strong! We must give our King the strength to purge this arcane sickness from our city, once and for all!" A ragged cheer went up from the supplicants, a wave of angry consensus that crashed against the dais. He had taken their formless anxiety and forged it into a weapon. Alexander looked to his father, desperate for a sign, but the King merely gave a slow, weary nod, his head sinking further into the ermine collar of his robes.

—※—

The private session of the Royal Council, held an hour later in the Chamber of the Sunstone, was a colder, more intimate affair. The chamber was a perfect circle, its walls made of a warm, golden-hued marble that was said to glow faintly at dawn. Today, under the perpetually grey sky, the stone was dull and lifeless, and the room felt like a cage. The air was thick with the residue of Malakai's performance, a tangible layer of unspoken tension. The councilors, a collection of wizened old men and sharp-eyed lords, sat around the great, circular table, their faces grim and unreadable.

Malakai stood at the head of the table. He was no longer the impassioned orator; he was the pragmatic statesman, all smooth reason. "The proposal is a simple matter of public safety," he began, his voice a low, reasonable hum that belied the cruelty of his words. "The 'Mage Purity Act' is not a persecution. It is a registration. A simple census to ensure that all practitioners of the arcane arts within the city walls are known to the Crown, and that their studies are... aligned with the interests of the kingdom. It would require a mandatory cataloging of all arcane artifacts and a royal seal of approval for any high-level thaumaturgical workings. A small price to pay for security."

"It is a witch hunt, and you know it," a voice, sharp and clear as a winter morning, retorted. Lady Elara Vess, her iron-grey hair pulled back in a severe bun, fixed Malakai with a glare that could have chipped stone. She sat ramrod straight, her hands folded on the polished wood before her. "You are proposing we treat our scholars and healers as criminals, that we give your 'Serpent's Hounds' leave to break down doors and confiscate priceless artifacts based on the whispers of frightened peasants. This is the language of tyranny, my lord, not of governance. We are a kingdom built on law, on reason. An Act such as this is a betrayal of that law, a stain upon our history, and a self-inflicted wound upon a city that is already bleeding. You are not offering a solution; you are offering a scapegoat. You are offering a public spectacle to distract from the true nature of the disease that consumes us."

"It is the language of survival, Lady Vess," Malakai countered, his voice losing none of its silken composure. "A language you seem to have forgotten in your long, comfortable years behind these high walls. The world outside is not a library. It is a dark and dangerous forest. And there are wolves in it."

An elderly lord, Baron Uther, a man whose family had sat on the council for three hundred years, cleared his throat. His liver-spotted hand trembled slightly as he gestured. "The times are... uncertain, Lady Vess. The people are afraid. Perhaps a measure of... caution... is not unwarranted. If this registration reassures the populace..."

"It will legitimize their fear!" Alexander snapped, his control finally breaking. The words tore from his throat, louder than he intended. "The only wolf I see is the one who uses that fear as a leash! Seraphina Noelle, the Archmage's own apprentice, presented evidence that this decay is not the work of some hedge wizard brewing curses in a cellar. It is an ancient and powerful force, a threat to us all!"

Malakai's gaze, which had been fixed on Lady Vess, now shifted to Alexander. The genial mask slipped, revealing a flash of reptilian cunning. He smiled, a slow, knowing thing that did not reach his cold eyes. "Ah, yes. The lovely Miss Noelle," he purred, his voice dripping with an oily sincerity. He leaned forward, resting his elbows on the table and lacing his fingers together, a predator settling in. "A brilliant, if... excitable, young woman. One for whom you have always shown a particular... scholarly interest. I had heard she had been dispatched to some remote parish to study a crop blight. A task more suited to her... passions, I should think. Did she not once argue that the structure of the Grand Orrery was 'causally inefficient'? A radical, one might say. A mind untethered from tradition." He paused, his gaze boring into Alexander, and his smile widened just enough to reveal the malice beneath it. "One might even say... untrustworthy. You see, Your Highness, a mind that can so easily dismiss centuries of established arcane principle... who is to say what other foundations it might seek to unmake? And what, my Prince, of those who champion such a mind? Who is to say what radical sympathies have tainted his judgment?"

Heat flooded Alexander's face—a public shame he hadn't earned. The silver pommel of his sword felt suddenly slick, wet with the sweat that had sprung instantly to his palm. He held the blade's weight, but the guard's familiar, solid shape seemed to twist, its metal mocking his failure to protect the woman Malakai had just slandered. The cold flush of exposure ran down his spine. Malakai knew. He knew of the stolen moments in the library, of the forbidden affection that had bloomed between them before duty and station had forced it into a sterile memory.

"Enough," the King's voice, a mere thread of its former strength, cut through the tension. He lifted his head slowly, and the air in the chamber seemed to stiffen. Though his eyes were clouded with weariness, they held a flinty resolve that made the councilors flinch. "This council is divided. The fear in the city is a tangible threat, but Lady Vess is correct. We will not become tyrants in our own home." He looked at Malakai, his gaze hard as granite. "The Act is tabled. We will not vote on it today. This session is concluded."

It was a small victory, a temporary stay of execution. But as Alexander left the chamber, the weight on his shoulders had not lessened. He had tabled the Act, but the war for the city's heart was being lost. Malakai's influence grew with every withered crop, with every fearful whisper. He was not just a politician; he was a priest, and the god he served was fear itself.

—⚭—

Later that afternoon, Alexander walked the Sovereign's Walk, the long gallery that led to the royal apartments. His footsteps echoed in the unnatural silence, a ghost haunting the halls of his own future. He stopped before the statue of his grandfather, Theron the Great, a giant of a man who had single-handedly broken a barbarian horde at the Battle of the Blackwater Pass. The stone hero held a great, two-handed sword, his jaw set in unbreakable resolve. A familiar, bitter clenching settled in Alexander's gut.

He stood there for a long time, the cool air of the gallery doing nothing to cool the fire in his veins. He remembered Seraphina's last plea, weeks ago, just before the council had sent her away. "They will not listen to me, Alexander," she had said, her voice tight with an intensity that had stripped away all pretense. "They see a woman. An elf. They see theory, not truth. But you… You are the Prince. Your voice carries the weight of a thousand years. Make them listen." He had tried, and his words had turned to dust. He had let her be sent away, dismissed as a girl, and now the sickness she had warned of was lapping at the foundations of his home, a cold, silent tongue licking at the mortar between the stones. He could feel his own inaction pressing down on him, a physical weight. He could not wait for the council. He could not wait for Malakai's next move. The kingdom needed a symbol. The people needed to see their King, not as a frail, dying man, but as the rock upon which their nation was built.

He strode past the rest of the silent, judging kings, his stride lengthening, his back straightening, a purpose hardening in him with every step. He found his father in his private chambers, not resting, but staring out the window at the frozen clock tower, his reflection a pale, ghostly image in the glass. The King's face was a mask of utter exhaustion, the web of black veins at his temples pulsing visibly. His hands, resting on the arms of his chair, trembled with a constant, fine tremor.

"Father," Alexander said, his voice quiet but firm.

The King turned, a faint, sad smile touching his lips. He gestured to the window, to the silent city. "My heart... it beats with a weary drum, my son. The kingdom's pulse is growing weak, and I no longer feel its beat as I once did."

"No," Alexander said, stepping forward, his own voice now imbued with a strength he had not known he possessed. "A king is a fire. And even the lowest embers can be fanned into a flame. The people listen to Malakai's poison because it is the only voice they hear. They need to hear yours. They need to see their King. They need to know there is still a King on the throne willing to fight for them. They do not need a prince. They need the lion."

King Theron looked at his son, and in his weary eyes, a flicker of the old fire ignited. He saw the man who had loved his people, had bled for them, and had wept for them. The flickering flame of his prime, long dormant, sparked back to life. "You are right," the King's voice snapped back from the edge of the grave, gaining the weight of tempered steel. He shoved himself up from the chair, his back straightening with a defiant, painful slowness, a tremor running down his spine. He challenged the black veins that consumed him, forcing his feet to root on the cold marble. When his eyes settled on Alexander, they held the flinty focus of a man who had burned away all fear, leaving only duty. His breathing hissed between his teeth—a necessary, agonizing cost for the command he was about to deliver.

"Summon the council. Summon the mercenary captains, the guild masters, the nobles. I will address them all in the Grand Hall tomorrow.

I will remind them what it means to be a kingdom of the sun. I will remind them what it means to be a people of stone and fire. I will not let fear be the last king of this city."

A warmth pushed back the cold that had been Alexander's constant companion. For the first time in weeks, hope felt like a real and tangible thing. He saw his father not as a dying man, but as a king, ready for one last battle. He bowed, a deep and reverent gesture of a son to his father, of a prince to his king. "It will be done, Your Majesty," he said.

He left the chambers with a new, lighter step. He did not see the way his father slumped back into his chair the moment the door closed, a single, wracking cough shaking his frail frame. He did not see the flicker of a shadow in the corner of the room, a shadow that was not cast by any object, that listened, and watched, and then silently, hungrily, dissolved back into the gloom. He knew only that the fire was not yet extinguished. A new dawn was coming.

Chapter 6

The Black Arrow

They arrived at the gates of Tetra as the sun bled out across the western sky, painting the clouds in the bruised and wounded colours of a dying monarch. The city's great white walls, veined with gold, seemed to glow with a final, defiant beauty against the encroaching twilight. From a distance, it was a vision of serenity and strength, a perfect jewel of civilization. Up close, it was a corpse in cosmetics.

The temporal decay, a subtle, creeping unease in the remote countryside, was a palpable, physical presence here. It was a low, sub-audible hum that vibrated up from the flagstones, a dissonant note in the city's symphony that settled in the teeth and made the bones ache. The grand, iron-banded gates, emblazoned with the golden Gryphon of the royal house, were tarnished with a strange, swirling patina of rust that seemed to defy the frantic polishing of the guards. This was not the kind of rust that came from rain and time; it was a hungry, living thing, a cancerous bloom that ate through the metal from the inside out, leaving behind a fine, sterile dust.

The guards themselves were a study in barely contained panic. They stood their posts with a rigid discipline, but their eyes beneath the rims of their polished helms darted everywhere, scanning the faces of travellers, lingering on anyone who looked out of place. A merchant's cart, its axle groaning under the weight of barrels of salted fish, was stopped for a meticulous, paranoid inspection. A soldier ran a gloved hand along the cart's wooden frame, his brow furrowed, as if he expected the wood to crumble at his touch. He checked the iron bands on the barrels, his fingers trembling. They were not defending the city from an external threat; they were protecting it from itself, from the sickness that was already within the walls. They were a symptom of the city's self-consuming fear, a living embodiment of the Lord Regent's paranoia.

Gundroff felt the city's sickness in his soul. This was a place of soft wood and brittle stone, of men who put their faith in high walls that were already turning to dust. He pulled the hood of his cloak lower, the sight of the shoddy masonry a personal insult. The foundation of the city gate, meant to be a bulwark of granite, was filled with a soft, crumbling mortar that would have shamed a dwarf apprentice. He felt a deep, profound disgust. His hand rested on his axe, its weight a familiar comfort in this alien world of fragile beauty. He was a creature of the deep, enduring stone, and this city felt like a house of glass in a hailstorm. He grunted, a deep sound of a warrior's contempt, as a guard prodded a barrel of fish with his spear tip, the clang of the metal a harsh and unwelcome sound in the gathering gloom.

Seraphina, for her part, felt the hum as a direct assault on her senses. To her, it was not just a sound; it was a schism in the architecture of causality, a constant, grating static that made her mind recoil. She could see the subtle ripples in the fabric of time, a shimmering, almost invisible distortion that made the city's lines waver at the edges of her vision. She felt the gaze of the Serpent's Hounds, Malakai's private guard, who stood apart from the Royal Guard. Their green-trimmed leather was a jarring note against the royal gold. They were not inspecting carts; they were watching people, their eyes cold and assessing, predators who had already claimed this territory as their own. She pulled her own hood forward, her face a mask of cold, controlled urgency. They were not entering a sanctuary. They were walking into the heart of the disease.

Their entry into the city was a descent into a theatre of denial. Merchants hawked their wares with a brittle, forced cheer, their smiles as fragile as spun glass, their voices too loud. The air was thick with the scent of wilting flowers and fear, a cloying perfume of death that had settled over the entire city. Children played in the streets, but their laughter was too loud, too sharp, a defiance against a quiet they did not understand. A woman in the square was selling candied apples, but the fruit was shrunken and dry beneath the glistening, ruby-red sugar. The citizens of Tetra moved around the fantastic clocktower, their gazes carefully averted, as if refusing to acknowledge the monument to their dying world, a silent, damning accusation in the heart of the Grand Plaza. The frozen hands of the clock were no longer a mere inconvenience; they were a public symbol of a moment that had passed, a kingdom that was running out of time.

They found lodging in a quiet, respectable inn in the Artisan's Quarter, a place of clean linens and the distant, reassuring sound of a potter's wheel. But the fear was here, too. The innkeeper, a man with kind eyes and a nervous tremor in his hands, spoke in hushed tones of the new "mage blight" and the Lord Regent's promises to restore order. The political poison had seeped down from the Spire and was now flowing through the gutters of the city. He looked at them with a nervous suspicion, his eyes darting to their hoods. He was a man who had heard the whispers and was already looking for a scapegoat.

"We must get to the library," Seraphina said, her voice a low, urgent whisper as they sat in their plain, candlelit room. The cheap tallow candle on the table between them guttered, its flame weak and anaemic, as if the air in the city was thin on hope. "The King is making a grand address tomorrow. According to the innkeeper, he has summoned every noble, guild master, and mercenary captain in the city. It is our only chance to present what we have learned to someone who might listen."

"And who might that be?" Gundroff rumbled, his voice a low, guttural sound of a warrior's contempt for a world he did not understand. He had not touched the stale bread or watery ale she had procured. His gaze was fixed on the street outside, watching the flicker of torchlight and the passing shadows. "The soft-handed lords who let their walls crumble? The Prince who hides behind his father's robes?"

"Lady Vess," Seraphina answered, her gaze distant as she stared into the candle flame. "She is the head of the council. She is… pragmatic. She deals in facts, not fears. Malakai's theatre will not sway her. And Prince Alexander… he will listen. He must." The way she spoke his name held a weight that Gundroff could not decipher, a note of something older and more complex than simple political manoeuvring. The sound of his name, a familiar ache on her tongue, was a quiet, personal defiance against a world that was trying to unmake her past.

The Grand Hall was a sea of colour and sound, a convergence of every thread of power in the kingdom. The air, which had been thick with the cloying scent of fear and decay in the streets, was here replaced by the perfume of a hundred different flowers, a heavy, insistent scent of denial and wealth. The hall's high, vaulted ceilings echoed with the nervous hum of a thousand different conversations, a low, thrumming murmur that was punctuated by the sharp, brittle sounds of polite laughter. The light, which streamed in from the high, arched windows, was a pale, weak gold, as if it, too, had grown thin and weary.

As Seraphina and Gundroff moved through the throng, they were a study in silent, grim purpose, their simple cloaks and travel-worn boots a jarring contrast to the finery around them. She leaned in, her voice a low whisper that only he could hear. "Look to your left, Gundroff. The men in crimson tabards. That's the Crimson Hounds, a mercenary company. Malakai brought them in to enforce 'order' in the city. They answer to his gold, not the King's law." Gundroff grunted, his gaze fixed on their leader, a brute of a man with a scarred face, loudly complaining about the lateness of his company's pay. He recognized the type: men who lived for coin and blood, and had no loyalty to either.

"To our right," she continued, "the men in the dark blue silks and the silver falcon sigil. That's House Valerius. They are the great scholars and archivists of the kingdom, keepers of the King's library. They have long been allies of the Crown, but their power is in knowledge, not in steel. They look nervous." She was right. The Valerius nobles looked out of place, their faces pale and their eyes darting about the room as if a physical threat were about to materialize.

"The stout men in the green velvets and heavy gold chains are the Guild Masters," she said, her voice dropping to a lower, more conspiratorial tone. "The heart of the city's commerce. Their conversations are a quiet litany of lost profits and rotting goods. Their faith in Malakai is a fragile thing, built on the promise of a scapegoat. They want an end to the bleeding, and they don't care who they have to blame to get it."

The nobles, draped in the silks and sigils of their ancient houses, moved through the crowd with a practiced, predatory grace. There were the proud lions of House D'Avergnac, a family of old money and traditional power, their faces a mask of careful, aristocratic boredom. Their fortunes were not tied to the city's trade, but to vast, isolated estates, and their concern was for their own standing, not for the common folk. Then there were the younger, more aggressive nobles, the upstarts who had aligned themselves with Malakai's rising star. They moved with a swagger and a confidence that the older houses lacked, a quiet, dangerous hunger in their eyes.

They had all been summoned to hear the word of their King, to be reassured, to be led. They were a flock of nervous sheep, gathered in the pen, not yet realizing the wolf was already among them, wearing the shepherd's finest clothes.

Seraphina and Gundroff moved through the throng like ghosts, their simple, travel-stained cloaks making them all but invisible amongst the finery. They found a position in the shadows of a great pillar, a vantage point from which they could observe the dais without drawing attention. From here, Seraphina saw him: Prince Alexander, standing beside the throne, his face a pale, taut mask of duty. Their eyes met for a fraction of a second across the crowded hall. In that single, silent glance, a novel's worth of unspoken history passed between them—of shared studies in the library, of a forbidden affection, of a bitter, necessary parting. She saw in his eyes the same trapped, desperate frustration she felt in her own heart. He gave her a single, almost perceptible nod, an acknowledgment, a promise. He would listen.

Then Lord Malakai made his entrance. He did not walk; he flowed, a river of serpent-green silk and condescending charm. He moved through the crowd not as a peer, but as a master, a comforting hand on a mercenary's shoulder here, a whispered word in a noble's ear there. He was weaving his web, and the entire hall was caught in it. He took his place at the head of the Royal Council, his face a perfect portrait of loyal, sober concern.

As he neared the councillors' designated area, he paused to greet a figure who had been standing quietly in the shadows of an archway, a figure so still he seemed to be a part of the architecture itself. He was so still, in fact, that the people around him seemed to actively avoid him, as if they instinctively recognized a void in his presence.

A murmur went through the nearby nobles as the figure stepped into the light. He was a Dark Elf, a rarity in the human court, and his appearance was arresting. He was tall and impossibly elegant, clad in robes of pure black silk, the fabric so dark it seemed to drink the light of the hall's high windows. The robes were etched with thin, spidery lines of Dark Elf script that seemed to writhe and shift at the edge of one's vision. His skin was the colour of polished obsidian, a stark and stunning contrast to his long, flowing hair, which was the pure, silver-white of fresh-fallen snow. But it was his eyes that held the room. They were the colour of amethyst, glowing with a faint, internal light, and they swept the hall with a serene, intelligent, and utterly dispassionate calm.

A cold, sucking vacuum pulled at Seraphina's arcane sight. It was not the quiet of death, but the perfect, terrifying stasis of non-existence, a temporal void in the shape of a man. Every living person's history pulsed like a chaotic, rhythmic fire; Katho was a stone dropped into the river of time, causing no ripples. It was an insult to causality, and the feeling made the fine hairs on her forearms stand stiff and cold. This creature, this Dark Elf, had no past, no future. He existed. It was the most terrifying thing she had ever encountered, and it made the rot feel like a child's game. Gundroff, beside her, merely grunted, a low, guttural sound of a warrior recognizing a predator. His hand tightened on the hilt of his axe, his senses telling him that this man was a weapon, and a hazardous one.

"Lord Katho," Malakai said, his voice a smooth purr of welcome. "I trust your journey was uneventful? The roads are so fraught with peril these days."

The Dark Elf, Immeral Katho, inclined his head, a gesture of liquid grace. "The road's end always justifies the journey's hardships, Lord Malakai," he replied, his voice a calm, melodic baritone that carried a strange, chilling resonance. "Some paths must be cleared to ensure a peaceful future."

Prince Alexander, his face a mask of royal duty, approached the pair. "Lord Katho. On behalf of my father, I welcome you to Tetra. It is a rare honour to receive a dignitary from Nyx'Tolos."

Katho's amethyst eyes turned to Alexander, and a faint, serene smile touched his lips. It did not reach his eyes. "My condolences for your father's illness, Your Highness. It's a real shame when the old pillars of the world start to crumble. It creates such... opportunity... for new growth."

The words were a perfect, polite sympathy, yet they landed like a veiled threat. Alexander's jaw tightened, but before he could form a reply, Katho had already given a slight bow and glided toward a seat reserved for foreign dignitaries, his movements a silent, serpentine dance. Malakai watched him go, a flicker of cold, triumphant understanding in his eyes, before taking his own place at the head of the Royal Council, his face once again a perfect portrait of loyal, sober concern.

The trumpets sounded, a high, clear note that cut through the murmur of the crowd. The great doors at the back of the hall swung open, and King Theron entered. A collective gasp went through the hall. He was not the stooped, frail figure from the throne room. He was a king. He wore a simple, unadorned suit of polished steel plate, the same armour he had worn at the Battle of the Blackwater Pass. The Crown of the Sunstone sat firmly on his brow, and he walked with a straight, steady stride, his eyes clear and filled with a fire that had long been absent. It was a magnificent performance, a final, desperate act of will from a dying man who had chosen to be a king for one last day.

He reached the Sunstone Throne, but he did not sit. He stood before it, his hand resting on its carved arm, and his voice, when he spoke, was not the reedy whisper of a sick man, but the clear, commanding voice of a monarch. "I see the fear in your eyes," he began, his gaze sweeping the hall. "I have heard the whispers in the streets. You speak of a blight, a curse. You look to the shadows for a source of our ills. You are looking in the wrong direction."

He raised a hand, pointing to the high, arched window. "For a thousand years, this city has been a bastion of the sun. Our strength has not been in our walls, but in our unity. Our wealth has not been in our gold, but in our shared purpose. This sickness that has befallen us... It does not feed on our crops or our stone. It feeds on our fear. It feeds on our division. It is a poison of the soul, and it asks only one thing of us: that we turn on one another."

He looked directly at Lord Malakai, his gaze as hard and unyielding as a winter frost. "There are those among us who would offer you a simple cure for this fear. They would give you a villain to blame, a shadow to hunt. They tell you that the arcane is our enemy, that our scholars and mages, who have guarded the lore of this kingdom for centuries, are now the source of its suffering. This is the oldest and most cowardly lie in the history of mankind: to blame the learned for a fear the ignorant cannot comprehend."

A ripple went through the hall, not of agreement, but of pure, disbelieving shock. This was not the speech they had been expecting. This was a direct, open challenge. The nobles from House D'Avergnac, their faces frozen in a mask of aristocratic boredom, now exchanged hurried, wide-eyed glances. The Guild Masters, their expressions of carefully maintained neutrality, now had their brows furrowed in a deep, unguarded confusion. The mercenary captains, grim and calculating, watched their leader, the Crimson Hound, whose scarred face was a mask of furious, disbelieving rage. Lord Malakai's perfect portrait of loyal concern faltered. For the briefest moment, the mask slipped. A muscle in his jaw clenched so hard that it showed through his smooth, unblemished skin, and a flash of pure, cold fury replaced the cold triumph in his eyes. The king was supposed to be a broken thing, a puppet whose strings were already cut. This defiance was an act of terrible, brilliant art, and it was unmaking his masterpiece.

"I will not lead you on a witch hunt," the King declared, his voice rising, filled with a sudden, brilliant passion. "I will not let this kingdom devour itself from within. We will face this threat as our ancestors did: together. As a people of the sun, united, a fortress of will and purpose! We will find the true source of this rot, and we will cut it out, not with the fire of persecution, but with the unyielding steel of our resolve!" He gestured to his son, his hand holding a firm, unshakeable command. "My son has dedicated his life to the arcane arts, to the science of the sunstone, to the magic that has brought prosperity to this kingdom. He is my heir. And he is a king in his own right. To believe that he, or any of our scholars, would bring this disease upon us is to believe a lie that is unworthy of the people of Tetra! Our strength is not in our gold, but in our knowledge. Our hope is not in our steel, but in our unity!"

For a moment, there was a stunned silence. The sheer audacity of the King's speech, its directness, its utter lack of diplomacy, left the hall in a state of suspended animation. Then, a single, proud Gryphon Knight, a man who had served the King for thirty years, his hand on his heart, let out a tremendous roar. "For the King and the light!" The Royal Guard took up the cry, their voices a single, unified bellow. It was not a cheer of triumph, but a roar of defiance, of recognition. It was followed by a handful of the older, more traditional nobles who had stood by the King in the past, their voices a trembling, but resolute chorus. A flicker of hope, bright and defiant, ignited in the tense, fearful atmosphere of the hall. Alexander's face was filled with a fierce, filial pride. He had his father back. The fire was not yet extinguished. It was a flame in a sea of shadows, a final, beautiful, and incandescent decisive moment.

It was in that precise moment of hope, that single, brilliant spark of defiance, that the assassin struck.

A single, sharp *thwip* came from a shadowed archway high above the hall, a sound so small the echoing cheers swallowed it. For a heartbeat, nothing happened. The King stood, his face filled with the fire of his speech, his hand raised in a gesture of command.

A sound—a soft *thwip* from the rafters, lost in the cheers. Father's hand was still raised. A final command. Then he faltered. He looked down. There was a black line in the centre of his breastplate. A crack? No. A splinter. A black splinter of... what? It wasn't possible. The steel was an inch thick. He saw a single drop of red bloom on the white tabard. Father's mouth opened. His eyes held not pain, but a look of blank, clinical surprise. Then he fell. The sound of his armour on the marble was the loudest thing in the world. He opened his mouth, but no sound came out. A single, perfect drop of crimson bloomed on the white tabard beneath the steel. Then, his eyes rolled back in his head, and he collapsed, a puppet whose strings had been cut, crashing to the marble floor with the hollow, final sound of a falling statue.

The hall was filled with a collective, horrified gasp that was swallowed by an instantaneous, profound silence. For a single, shared heartbeat of pure, disbelieving shock, the world stopped. A mercenary captain, his mouth open in a triumphant cheer, froze, his fist raised in the air like a grotesque statue. A noblewoman in a crimson gown fainted, a splash of colour against the white marble, but no one moved to catch her. The royal guard, their swords half-drawn in salute, stood motionless, their faces masks of perfect, agonizing confusion. Even the whispers of the guild masters, the eternal hum of their greed, ceased. All sound was gone. All movement was arrested. The only thing that remained was the sight of the fallen king, a man of fire and steel reduced to a shattered thing on the floor. It was a moment of truth, a silent accusation that settled on every soul in the hall.

And then, the spell broke. A single, cold, commanding voice cut through the stunned silence. "The King is dead," Lord Malakai announced, his voice ringing with a false, terrible authority. He did not rush to the dais or mourn. He took a step forward, his eyes, for a fraction of a second, holding a cold, reptilian gleam of triumph before they hardened into a mask of solemn sorrow. "A vile, cowardly assassination." He turned to his men. "The Prince has conspired with these arcane terrorists to murder his own father. For the safety of the realm, I am assuming the authority of Lord Regent. Arrest him."

The Royal Guard, confused and leaderless, hesitated. They looked to the crumpled form of their King, then to their Captain, a man whose face was a mask of utter bewilderment. They were a force of order, and in this moment, order had ceased to exist. The Serpent's Hounds did not. They moved forward, a wall of green leather and naked steel. Alexander's gaze snapped from his fallen father to Malakai. His face went paper-white, the sound of his blood roaring in his ears. His right hand shot to the silver pommel, drawing the sword in a screaming arc of steel. The blade's tip trembled violently, not from fear, but from the sheer, physical force of the betrayal. "You will not take me!" he bellowed, his voice raw with a grief he could not yet process.

"We have to go!" Seraphina hissed, grabbing Gundroff's arm. "Now!"

In the chaos of the standoff between the Prince and the Hounds, another figure moved. Lady Vess, her face a pale, determined mask, stepped from the crowd of nobles. "The Prince is innocent!" she cried, her voice a sharp crack of defiance. She drew a small, silver-bladed parrying dagger, a courtly weapon that was little more than a toy, and stood beside Alexander. "You will have to go through the Royal Council first, you traitorous snake!"

Her brave, foolish act of defiance was the diversion they needed. As Malakai's attention was fixed on this new political challenge, Seraphina pulled Gundroff towards a small, overlooked postern gate at the far end of the balcony, a service entrance for the castle staff. "This way!" They plunged through the gate and into the winding, narrow service corridors of the Royal Spire, the sounds of shouting and steel ringing behind them. The Spire, the seat of power and the symbol of order, had become a cage. The hunt had begun. They were no longer investigators. They were fugitives.

The noise was a distant, dying thing. The shouts of the guards, the terrified screams of the supplicants, the defiant cry of Lady Vess—it was all a fading echo in the vast, cold space of the Grand Hall. Malakai stood alone at the centre of the dais, the air around him still and quiet as a tomb. He did not feel triumphant. He did not feel joy. He felt a profound, bone-deep satisfaction, a sense of cold, perfect order restored. His gaze, unblinking, was fixed on the fallen king, a crumpled, fragile thing on the polished marble.

The king had been a good man. A sentimental fool. His speech, so full of fire and resolve, had been a final, foolish gesture of a dying age. He had spoken of unity, of strength, of a fortress of will and purpose. He had been a man who believed in a world that no longer existed, a world where truth and courage were enough. The rot had proven him wrong. The rot was not a blight, not a curse. It was a test—a test of the world's strength, and it had found the old ways wanting. The kingdom was a beautiful house, but its foundation was crumbling, its mortar was failing. King Theron, with his grand speeches and noble heart, was not a solution. He was a sentimental delay, a weak and crumbling pillar that had to be brought down before it brought the entire structure with it.

Malakai looked at the scene before him, at the chaos he had so meticulously orchestrated. The confusion of the Gryphon Knights, the swift, unquestioning obedience of his Hounds. He was not a villain; he was a surgeon. He had cut away a rotting limb to save the body. He had performed a necessary, brutal, and merciful act. The people were frightened, lost, and hungry. They did not need a symbol. They needed a shepherd who would lead them to safety, a hand strong enough to clear the wolves from the field. He would be that shepherd. He would be that hand. He was the cure.

He stepped over the King's body, his polished boots making no sound on the marble. He did not sit, but settled onto the Sunstone Throne, and a cold, terrible power solidified over the room. The air grew heavy and utterly still, the gilt on the high ceilings dimming as if his presence drew the light from the space. His voice, when he commanded, "Find them," was a low, cold wire, and the sound did not echo in the vast hall—it was swallowed completely.

Chapter 7

Fellowship of Ghosts

The world dissolved from the high, wind-swept grandeur of the Royal Spire, shattering into a million shimmering motes of light and sound as if reality itself had fractured. One moment, they were poised precariously on the edge of a precipice, the thin, frigid air biting at their exposed skin, the distant, frantic echoes of battle from the balcony still clinging to their ears. The next, they plunged headlong into a tight, suffocating darkness that assaulted their senses with the stale, heavy scent of damp, ancient stone, the pervasive musk of rat droppings, and the countless, forgotten secrets of centuries. The cacophony of shouting men and clashing steel from the battlements above faded abruptly behind them, swallowed by the profound, oppressive silence of the Spire's unseen, stony guts. They had landed, with a jarring thud, in the castle's secret circulatory system—a hidden network of narrow, winding service corridors that lay a world away from the gleaming marble, sunlit halls, and political machinations of the upper floors.

Here, no vibrant tapestries adorned the walls; only the raw, weeping stone of the mountain's deep foundation greeted them. The air was thick, heavy, and utterly still, disturbed solely by the frantic rasp of their own ragged breathing and the soft, rhythmic, maddening drip of water from some unseen, tenacious crack high in the ceiling. Seraphina's magelight, a small, trembling sphere of cerulean energy that felt as fragile as spun glass, cast long, dancing shadows that seemed to writhe and claw at them from the oppressive darkness ahead, transforming familiar shapes into monstrous specters.

68

They moved as a study in controlled desperation, a tableau of weary determination against overwhelming odds. Seraphina, her face a pale, grim mask of concentration in the magical glow, led their desperate retreat. The monumental effort of holding the King's life in a fragile bubble of frozen time had left her utterly drained, her body trembling uncontrollably with a magical exhaustion so profound it was a deep, physical ache that permeated her bones. Her will, usually a precise, unyielding instrument of causality, now felt like a frayed, unraveling theorem, its elegant logic teetering on the brink of collapse. The cerulean light of her spell flickered erratically, a dying star struggling against the encroaching gloom, its unsteady glow a stark reflection of her waning resolve. Every deepening shadow seemed to hold the glint of a Serpent's Hound's polished helmet, every distant drip of water sounded like the ominous cadence of an approaching footstep. The once logical, ordered fortress of her mind was now a city under siege, its meticulously constructed walls beginning to crumble under the relentless assault of fear and fatigue. Her thoughts, which usually flowed with the pristine clarity of a perfect equation, had been reduced to a chaotic scramble of variables, coalescing into a single, primal, desperate imperative: escape.

As she stumbled, her foot catching on an uneven stone, a disjointed image flickered at the edge of her consciousness: a warm, inviting tavern, flickering firelight dancing on polished wood. A sudden flash of a kind, knowing smile, almost familiar. A pair of startlingly blue eyes that seemed to hold ancient secrets. The fleeting image was gone as quickly as it came, a ghost of a memory she was far too exhausted to grasp or categorize. She shook her head violently, attempting to clear the encroaching fog, but the memory, tenacious and unbidden, stubbornly persisted. *Who was that man?* The question echoed in the cavern of her fatigue, unanswered and unsettling.

Gundroff, a veritable stumbling mountain of pure, unadulterated rage and unyielding dwarven will, followed closely behind her. The poisoned wound in his shoulder burned like a searing forge fire, a malevolent brand upon his flesh, and the deeper, more insidious wound of the assassin's shattered dirk in his arm pulsed with a throbbing, hateful drumbeat that perfectly matched the furious rhythm of his own unyielding heart. But the greatest wound, the one that festered deep within his iron spirit, was the crushing weight of betrayal. The world of men, with its deceptive, pretty words and its fragile, easily broken honor, had proven to be just as rotten, just as treacherous, as he had always instinctively suspected. A kingdom supposedly built on noble ideals had crumbled into lies, cemented with a coward's blade thrust into a good king's back. He had journeyed to this sprawling city seeking a lead, a flicker of hope, a tangible thread of vengeance, and he had found only deceit and treachery. He gripped the scarred leather haft of his great twin-headed axe, Grief and Vengeance, its familiar, weighty balance the only solid, unyielding truth in a world that had dissolved into shifting shadows and treacherous plots. His Oath of Rage, branded onto his soul, screamed at him to turn back, to charge headlong into the heart of the chaos above, to meet this new, insidious enemy with the honest, brutal language of steel and dwarven fury. Vengeance was his sacred purpose, not this cowardly flight. But the sight of Seraphina's trembling form, of the rapidly fading light she so desperately maintained, held him in check, a bitter pill to swallow. He was bound by a life debt, a chain forged in a tavern brawl that now felt as heavy and as unbreakable as any oath-gold he had ever sworn in the solemn halls of his ancestors.

And then, his own memory, a flash, unbidden and unsettling, surfaced from the depths of his granite mind: the familiar, unsettlingly calm face of a man from the road, a man who had walked into their camp with unnerving nonchalance and offered them a warm, spiced apple. The same man who had been sitting in the quiet corner of that bustling tavern, watching them with those same unsettlingly bright blue eyes. The dwarf's brow furrowed, a deep canyon etched into his granite face. *Impossible*, he rumbled to himself, the thought clashing against his dwarven practicality. *It cannot be.* He forcefully pushed the thought away, focusing instead on the searing, insistent pain in his shoulder, a more tangible reality.

Their desperate, stumbling flight through the labyrinthine corridors became a harrowing descent into the forgotten, dust-choked history of the Spire itself. They passed through dark, web-choked storage rooms, filled with the discarded, decaying furniture of forgotten kings and the remnants of long-abandoned courtly finery. Gundroff, ever the master craftsman, couldn't help but note the shoddy, hastily executed joinery of moth-eaten thrones, the cheap gilding already flaking away from brittle wood. *Human kings build thrones of wood and silk, destined only to rot,* he thought, a bitter taste in his mouth. *Dwarves build thrones from the living stone, meant to endure for ages.* They navigated a bewildering maze of narrow, winding staircases that spiraled relentlessly down into the roots of the mountain, the air growing colder, damper, and heavier with every strained step. The Spire's guts were a silent, vast, stone cemetery, a stark, unyielding testament to the fleeting nature of human power and the implacable, eternal permanence of the earth beneath it. They were little more than ghosts, haunting a tomb.

It was in a small, circular junction, where three identical, dark passages converged like the spokes of a forgotten wheel, that their desperate flight was finally forced to a halt. Seraphina leaned heavily against the cold, unyielding stone wall, her breath coming in ragged, painful gasps, the magelight dimming to a faint, ghostly glimmer that threatened to wink out entirely. "I cannot maintain the light much longer," she whispered, her voice a thin, fragile thing, stretched taut by exhaustion. "And I do not know which way to go. These passages are not on any of the Spire's official schematics, nor do they align with any known ley lines. The causality is muddled."

The oppressive silence of the subterranean chamber swallowed Gundroff's low growl of frustration. They were lost, wounded, and bleeding in the suffocating dark, a perfect, bitter metaphor for their entire, doomed enterprise. He tasted the metallic ash of defeat in his mouth, acrid and unwelcome, like the dross of a failed smelting, the slag left behind when a good ingot refused to form.

"Well now," a surprisingly cheerful voice suddenly chirped from the profound darkness of the central passage, a sound so utterly unexpected and so completely out of place in their grim predicament that it was like a sudden, dazzling shard of sunlight piercing the impenetrable gloom of a crypt. "That does seem to be a bit of a pickle, doesn't it? A real conundrum, as my old tutor used to say, often with a twinkle in his eye, I might add. The left passage leads to the old wine cellars, which I'm told are quite drafty, not to mention entirely overrun with rather aggressive giant cave spiders, which do love a good vintage, apparently. The right leads directly to the under-barracks, which I imagine are currently teeming with some rather unfriendly gentlemen in green, probably quite eager to make your acquaintance. I suppose that only leaves the middle path, doesn't it?"

They spun around in a single, fluid motion, a desperate, shared instinct driving them, weapons instinctively raised and ready. Gundroff's great axe, Grief and Vengeance, was a silent, menacing shadow, poised to strike; Seraphina's hands crackled with the last, desperate vestiges of her arcane power, ready to unleash a final, calculated strike.

A figure emerged slowly from the encroaching gloom, stepping calmly into the faint, flickering glow of the magelight. It was an old man, clad in the simple, unassuming brown robes of a lay brother of Solara, the Sun Mother. He was of middling height, with a sparse fringe of wispy white hair circling a bald, spotted pate, and a truly magnificent, snow-white beard that reached almost to his chest. His face was a cheerful roadmap of countless wrinkles, each crease a testament to a life of quiet amusement, and his eyes, a bright and startling blue, held a look of such profound, untroubled calm that it was, paradoxically, more unsettling than any overt threat. He was holding a half-eaten, ruddy apple in one hand and a small, leather-bound book in the other.

"Brother Thaddeus," he said, taking another cheerful, loud bite of his apple and offering them a small, pleasantly unassuming bow. "At your service, such as it is. I was merely visiting poor Brother Michael in the lower scriptorium – a terrible case of the bone aches, you know, especially when the damp settles in – when all that dreadful shouting started up above. The doors were sealed, rather inconveniently, and I'm afraid I've been wandering about down here ever since, trying to find my way back to supper. A bit of a to-do, isn't it, all this unpleasantness?"

Seraphina stared at him, her highly analytical mind struggling desperately to categorize this new, impossible variable, this utterly illogical element in their equation of survival. He showed no discernible fear, no surprise, only a mild, almost academic, pleasant curiosity. "Who *are* you?" she demanded, her voice sharp with suspicion, cutting through the damp air.

"I told you, my dear. I am Brother Thaddeus," he said with a serene smile, as if stating the most obvious of facts. "And you, unless I am much mistaken by the patterns of causality and the whispers of the air, are Lady Seraphina Noelle, the Archmage's finest apprentice, though perhaps a touch more disheveled than usual. And this fine fellow," he continued, his bright gaze falling on Gundroff's immense axe with an appreciative, almost connoisseur's twinkle in his startling blue eyes, "must be the Hill Dwarf who caused such a magnificent stir on the high balcony. A rather impressive bit of work, that, the way you handled those Serpent's Hounds. Malakai's men are still trying to scrub the mess from the cobblestones, I heard from a rather chatty gargoyle. A true master of the axe, you are."

He seemed to know everything, to possess an unnerving omniscience, and yet to be utterly unconcerned by any of it. Gundroff took a half-step forward, his massive, imposing form a looming shadow of menace, an unyielding granite bulwark. "How do you know these things, old man?" he growled, his voice a low, gravelly rasp, like stone grinding on stone.

"Oh, the Spire is a talkative old place, if you know how to listen to the whispers in its walls and the echoes in its ancient foundations," Thaddeus said, waving his half-eaten apple in a vague, dismissive gesture. "And I have been listening to its secrets, and to the secrets of the world, since I was a mere boy. Now, if you are quite finished with the introductions, which, while charming, do delay our progress, I believe several rather determined young men are, at this moment, making their way down the right-hand passage, probably looking for a promotion. I would humbly suggest we take the middle one. I recall there's a rather charming, if somewhat damp, forgotten cistern that way. A perfect place for a quiet chat about destiny and fate, don't you think?"

He turned and, with the calm, unhurried air of a man embarking upon a pleasant afternoon stroll through a sun-dappled meadow, began to walk down the central tunnel, humming a jaunty, off-key tune that seemed utterly out of place in the dark, foreboding depths. Seraphina and Gundroff exchanged a profound, baffled look of mistrust and disbelief. But from the right-hand tunnel, they could now distinctly hear the faint, distant, but rapidly approaching sound of armored footsteps, echoing ominously, followed by muffled, angry voices. They had no choice. With a shared, grim nod, a silent acknowledgment of their desperate straits, Seraphina extinguished the magelight, plunging them into absolute, suffocating darkness, and they blindly plunged after the cheerful, impossible old man.

The middle tunnel soon opened into a vast, cavernous space, the sudden expansion of the air a welcome, if chilling, change. It was a forgotten cistern, a monumental, ancient basin where the Spire's inner waters once collected and purified themselves, now abandoned to the ages and utterly dry. The air was noticeably colder here, filled with the unnerving echo of their footsteps and the persistent, rhythmic *plink* of a single, tenacious drip of water, like a solitary, slow-ticking clock. Thaddeus settled himself comfortably on a low, moss-covered stone ledge with a soft sigh of contentment, as if he had just arrived at his favorite armchair.

"Please, have a seat, my dears," he gestured genially to the dusty floor, his voice echoing slightly in the cavernous space. "It's not precisely what the King's architect would have chosen for a royal council chamber, I'll grant you, but it's remarkably private. And it's quite old, you see. So old, in fact, that it was built long before the founding of the shining city of Tetra itself. It hums with the memory of pure water, and older things still."

Gundroff did not sit. He stalked forward, planting the colossal head of his great axe into the stone floor with a hollow, resonant clang that reverberated through the cistern, a deliberate gesture of aggression and a silent, unyielding challenge. "You haven't answered my question, old man. How do you know these things? The secrets of my Oath are not for the ears of men."

"And you have not answered mine, my dear Lady Seraphina," Seraphina countered swiftly, her voice sharp with a cold, terrifying certainty that cut through her exhaustion. "The tavern on the winding road to Tetra. The camp in the King's Wood, under the pale moonlight. That was you, wasn't it? And… that was you. In the garden." Her voice, which had been so brittle with exhaustion only moments before, now held a note of pure, terrifying clarity, a sudden, stark realization. She looked intently at his face, at the familiar roadmap of cheerful wrinkles, and suddenly, impossibly, she saw a face she had last seen a decade ago, one that had been etched into the deepest, most guarded corners of her heart. "Brother Thaddeus… you are my foster father. Juniper Ray Noelle remembers."

The old man smiled, a kind, knowing smile that was now more unnerving than any outright threat, for it held the weight of impossible knowledge. He took another deliberate bite of his apple, the sharp, percussive crack of it echoing unnaturally in the quiet of the cistern. "The world is an impossibly small place, my dears, a tapestry woven with threads that often cross and recross. I've been watching you for a long time, Seraphina, since before you were even named. I was there when you took your first steps in the monastery garden, Baelfire, when you first heard the whispers stirring in your own soul, the chaotic song of unmaking. I was there when you wrestled with your own dangerous power, even then."

He turned his bright, startlingly blue eyes, filled with an ancient, profound wisdom, to Gundroff. "And I was there when you swore your terrible Oath of Rage, the Vow of the Unshielded, over the cold, bitter ashes of your hold, calling upon Grolnir as the God of Endings and Retribution. I was there when you chose to honor a life debt in a tavern brawl, a decision that diverted the course of your roaring vengeance. And I was there when you chose to stand beside a scholar, a fragile wielder of the mind, instead of charging headlong into a senseless war. Your great destiny, my dear Gundroff Ragingfire, is not vengeance. It is a purpose of another, far more profound, kind."

Gundroff's massive hand tightened around the haft of his axe, the leather groaning under his immense grip. Every fiber of his being screamed at him to rage, to demand answers, to challenge this impossible old man. But the old man's words, delivered with such casual certainty, such impossible truth, held him utterly in check. This was not a liar, not a charlatan. This was a force of nature, an entity that had seen his deepest past, his greatest triumphs, and his most profound, secret failures.

"You're not a brother of the Sun God," Seraphina stated, her voice a hushed whisper of awe, a tone usually reserved for profound arcane discovery. "You are… something else entirely. You are Valerius, aren't you?"

Thaddeus laughed then, a soft, low rumble that was the sound of a happy, ancient secret, a quiet, joyful melody. "Labels are for grocers and for scholars attempting to categorize the infinite, my dear. I am a simple monk, watching the currents of the world. I hear the song of the world, you see, a great, beautiful, and utterly chaotic symphony of cause and effect, of fate and free will, as laid before me in my holy scripture. And your song, Seraphina, is a bright, beautiful, and utterly chaotic note in that grand symphony, a melody that should be heard, not silenced. And you, Gundroff... you are the deep, resonant bass note, the unyielding heart of the mountain, the foundational rhythm. The two of you... You are rare and beautiful beings, a confluence of opposing forces: the precise mind of causality, and the unyielding heart of the mountain. A truly fascinating duet."

He stood, dusting off his simple robes, his gaze filled with a quiet, profound conviction that transcended mere observation. He was not a savior. He was not a guardian in the traditional sense. He was an observer, an ancient chronicler of fates, and he had come to watch the unfolding show of their destiny, up close. "And that is why I'm here. I have a great desire to observe the great destiny unfolding within you two, up close and personal. I wouldn't want to miss a single, pivotal moment of it." He pulled the small, worn, leather-bound book from the fold of his robes. The cover was worn smooth by countless years of handling, and the pages within were stained with the rich, earthy colors of age. He opened it to a specific page with surprising ease, his finger tracing a line of ancient text before he cleared his throat gently.

"The Parables of Valerius," he said, holding it up slightly, as if presenting a priceless artifact. "A little-known text, I'll admit, often overlooked by those who seek only power. Valerius was the first writer of the world's song, you see, a visionary, they say. He didn't build for power, or for kings, or for dominion, but for the light of the Sun God to shine upon the people, to foster community and growth." He began to read, his voice taking on a low, sonorous quality that filled the vast, quiet space of the cistern, transforming it into a sacred hall.

"In the beginning, before the High Spire's gleaming tip pierced the clouds, a beacon against the vast, indifferent sky, there was only the immense, ancient mountain and the scattered people who lived in its long, uncertain shadow.

And these people were fragmented, and they spoke in a thousand dissonant tongues, and they knew only suspicion, fear, and tribal animosity. And the first King, whose true name is now whispered only by the enduring stone itself, came to the mountain. And he carried not a scepter of dominion, but a single, unadorned stone, smooth and unassuming, plucked from the cold riverbed below. And he said to the fragmented people, with a voice that echoed with conviction, 'I have come not to rule, but to build a lasting legacy. Let us together construct a home, a sanctuary for Solara, the Sun Mother, a place where her light may truly nourish us, and let us build it with the honest, unyielding truths of the earth itself.' And the people, moved by his vision, came, laying aside their quarrels, and they worked together, hands stained with soil and purpose. And each stone was laid with a solemn promise: a promise of truth, a promise of guiding light, a promise that the people would be as united and enduring as the mortar that bound the stones together. And thus they built the Spire, stone by arduous stone, and it rose, a magnificent beacon of hope, a towering monument to their shared purpose and their collective spirit. And the King, when the monumental work was finally done, did not craft a throne of gold and jewels for himself. Instead, he laid his single, unadorned stone at the base of the Spire, a humble, yet powerful act, and he called it the 'Cornerstone of Trust.' And he declared, with a voice that carried across the ages, 'As long as this humble stone remains, steadfast and unbroken, so shall the honor and the integrity of this city endure.'"

Thaddeus closed the book gently, the soft, reverent thud of the worn leather cover a final, solemn period on the tale. Seraphina and Gundroff exchanged a look, a shared moment of profound, unsettling realization. The parable, told in the forgotten, decaying guts of a castle where a treacherous act of regicide had just been committed, felt less like a hopeful lesson and more like a cruel, bitter joke. The city above them, once a testament to shared purpose and honest truths, a shining beacon of human endeavor, had just betrayed its foundation, its core principles shattered. They were, impossibly, in the one place where its true history could still be found—the ancient, forgotten secrets buried deep in the earth—while its false, glittering facade crumbled above them, consumed by treachery and ambition.

Gundroff shifted his weight, his rage momentarily replaced by a cold, hard sadness that felt heavy in his chest. "A strong foundation, aye," he growled, his voice a low rumble, "for a rotten structure. There is no honor left in this city of men, only deceit and decay."

"Perhaps not in the glittering halls above, where the shadows play their cruel games," Thaddeus said, a strange, knowing smile returning to his face. "But the city's true heart is still here, beating deep within the earth. It just… got a bit buried under layers of ambition and neglect." He stood, dusting off his robes with a characteristic lack of haste. "Now then, if we want to get to the sea, where the ships await, we must go through the sewers. They're a bit unpleasant, I'll grant you, but they'll get us out of here, and they are generally free of political intrigue, if not other unpleasant things."

He walked toward a low, dark archway, the inky blackness within it palpable, almost inviting.

The stench hit them first, an immediate, suffocating wall of foulness that made their eyes water instinctively and their stomachs churn with revulsion. It was the collective miasma of an entire, sprawling city, a cloying, putrid mix of human waste, decay, and stagnant, sluggish water that seemed to cling to their clothes. Seraphina gagged, her hand flying to her mouth, but Gundroff, a veteran of countless dark, reeking places beneath the earth, gritted his teeth, his jaw hardening. The stench of orc-holds, he mused grimly, was often fouler, a primal, guttural reek, but this was the unique, insidious filth of men, a city rotting slowly from the inside out, its corruption made manifest. The passage was narrow, the ancient stone walls slimy to the touch, and their boots slipped precariously on the slick, refuse-strewn floor.

"Watch your step, my dears," Thaddeus chirped cheerfully from the front, his voice echoing with unsettling lightness in the gloom. "The Sump rats here are quite large, some as big as a small dog, and they've got a rather nasty bite, I'm told. They have a particular fondness for stray fingers, it seems."

As if on cue, a sudden, frantic rustling sound came from the darkness ahead, followed by a pair of beady red eyes that glinted malevolently in the gloom. An unseen thing scurried away with a high-pitched squeal, but the sound seemed to multiply, a thousand tiny clicks and whispers that followed them as they walked, a restless, unseen chorus. They were no longer alone, no longer just ghosts haunting a tomb. They were trespassers in a world of unseen, scuttling things, and the oppressive claustrophobia of the slimy, echoing tunnels pressed in on all sides, a tangible weight.

The passage eventually opened onto a wide, subterranean canal, its murky, sluggish water a slow, fetid river of filth. A narrow walkway of slick, treacherous wooden planks ran precariously along the side, the only discernible path forward through the Stygian gloom. As they began to cross, a sound, faint but unmistakable, reached their ears: the metallic clang of a helmet against stone. A low, gruff voice, then another, answering in the gloom. They were close. The Serpent's Hounds were patrolling the deeper sewer network.

Thaddeus gestured wildly, urgently, for them to flatten themselves against the wall, his cheerful demeanor momentarily replaced by a tense, focused intensity. Seraphina and Gundroff pressed themselves into the narrow, dank space between the rickety walkway and the cold, slimy stone, their bodies tense, their breaths held tightly, every muscle screaming for release. They could hear the voices now, drawing inexorably closer, the words becoming clearer.

"Any word from the Captain, then?" a voice grumbled, thick with weariness.

"No, not a whisper. He says the King is dead, proper done for. Malakai is King now, he declared himself on the balcony, bold as brass. He's ordered a full sweep of the Spire and all the surrounding tunnels, a real bloody purge. He wants them found. The Archmage's apprentice, the one with the silvery hair, and the dwarf, the big brute who wields that monstrous axe."

Gundroff's great hand clenched around the axe handle, his knuckles turning white, a silent, murderous oath forming on his lips. Seraphina's heart hammered frantically against her ribs, a frantic drumbeat of terror and adrenaline, threatening to burst from her chest. They could now clearly see the faint, flickering glow of the Hounds' lanterns, their uncertain light casting long, grotesque shadows that danced and twisted like malevolent spirits on the slimy, ancient walls. The heavy thud of their boots on the wooden planks was getting closer, closer, their voices growing louder, more distinct.

"What a mess this whole bloody business is. He's promising a reward, though. Gold. So much gold, they say, enough to buy a small manor."

"I'd rather have a warm bed and a pint of ale than all the gold in Tetra. This place stinks to high heaven, enough to rot a man's teeth."

The Hounds passed directly above them, their heavy boots thudding ominously on the planks, their voices gradually fading into the echoing distance. It was an agonizingly close call, a life-or-death suspense that left Seraphina trembling uncontrollably and Gundroff's muscles aching with the strain of suppressed violence. When the sounds of their passage had completely died away, swallowed by the sewer's depths, Thaddeus motioned for them to move, his previous cheerfulness restored.

"Right," he said, his voice a calm, reassuring counterpoint to their hammering hearts. "Just through that last grate, you see. It leads out into the old irrigation fields. Follow me."

He led them to a metal grate set deeply into the stone wall at the end of the tunnel. It was ancient, thick with layers of rust, and held firmly in place by a heavy-duty padlock, its chain as thick as a man's thumb, oxidized almost to immobility.

"I imagine it's here to keep out... unwanted guests of the four-legged variety," Thaddeus said with a characteristic shrug, peering at the rusty lock. "But it seems it's doing a rather fine job of keeping us in."

Seraphina's magic was a spent force, a flickering ember of what it once was, and Gundroff's poisoned arm was useless, a leaden weight at his side. Their combined strength, fueled by a desperate, shared need for escape, was all they had left. They took hold of the rusty grate, their knuckles turning white with the immense effort, and pulled. The ancient metal groaned and protested, emitting a high, tortured screech that echoed painfully through the enclosed tunnel. Gundroff, his face a mask of straining effort, pulled with a strength born not merely of muscle, but of his sacred oath to *Endure*, the muscles in his good arm screaming in agonizing protest, threatening to tear. Seraphina pushed from the other side, her body trembling violently with the last, desperate reserves of her physical strength, her teeth gritted against the pain. It was a hopeless, collaborative effort, a brutal test of their collective resolve, and for a terrifying moment, it seemed that the grate would hold, that they were truly doomed to rot in the filth.

Then, with a final, shattering clang that reverberated through the tunnel, the padlock gave way, shearing apart under the impossible strain, and the grate swung open with a final, protesting screech of tortured metal. They stumbled out into the cool, clean night air, their lungs greedily drinking in the fresh scent of damp earth and distant, dew-laden fields. The Royal Spire, a black, monstrous silhouette against the pale, indifferent moon, loomed silently behind them, its scattered lights like cold, unblinking, judgmental eyes. They were free, their desperate journey through the foul guts of the mountain finally over. It was a rebirth, a new beginning in a world that had betrayed them, with a quiet, impossible old man they didn't fully understand, but who had, for some strange, inscrutable reason, decided to save them.

Chapter 8

The Hunt

The stench of the sewer was a familiar thing, the layered history of a city's waste baked into the stone. For Captain Philip, it was not a foulness but a language, a complex text that told him everything he needed to know about the secrets Tetra tried to flush away. He stood at the edge of the open sewer grate, a cold, elegant monster in the pre-dawn gloom, his gauntleted hand resting on the polished pommel of his longsword. A dozen of his men, the Serpent's Hounds, stood a respectful distance behind him, their faces grim and disciplined masks of unwavering loyalty. They were not brutes or thugs; they were professionals, instruments of a will greater than their own, and their purpose was a holy one. In the Grand Hall, the nobles and priests had been swayed by lies, by the cloying poison of sentiment. But here, in the city's forgotten guts, the truth was as plain and undeniable as the filth at their feet. The town was sick. It had a disease festering in its heart. And a shepherd's duty was not to coddle the ill lamb, but to cull it before the entire flock was irrevocably poisoned.

He knelt, his movements an economy of motion that spoke of a lifetime of training, a perfect, fluid articulation of steel and leather. He ran a gloved finger over the grime-smeared handle of the old padlock that now lay broken on the flagstones. The iron was grooved, not picked or forced, but sheared through with the marks of immense, unnatural force. He saw the faint, tell-tale splinters of brittle, ancient bone caught in the threads of the thick chain. They were the shards of the wolf's teeth, a calling card he had been trained to recognise. He had listened

82

to the overwrought tales of the dwarf's monstrous power in the Grand Hall, dismissing them as the hyperbole of frightened men. Now he saw the proof of it, cold and solid in his hand. This was not a man who had lifted a lock; this was a force of nature that had broken it, a being whose strength defied the engineering of a city built to endure for millennia. The subtle, cold fury he felt was a professional's respect for a formidable opponent, a hunter's quiet acknowledgment of a worthy quarry.

He looked from the shattered lock to the grate itself, the heavy, circular slab of rust-eaten iron, and a slow, professional smile touched his lips. They had not lifted it. They had broken the hinges from their stone moorings. He examined the trail—a single set of deep, heavy dwarven boot prints, the light, long-limbed stride of the elf, and a third, fainter set of prints that spoke of an old man with a light, surprisingly specific step. The tracks led north, away from the city walls and into the deep, dark tangle of the King'swood.

He stood, dusting the grime from his gauntlets with two precise claps, his mind already three steps ahead of the chase, the entire board laid out in his thoughts. "They are not running to the southern roads," he stated, his voice a low, cold hum of pure, unquestionable certainty that cut through the morning mist. "They are running into the mountains." His second-in-command, a grim-faced man named Kael whose loyalty was as sharp as the axe on his back, furrowed his brow in confusion. "Sir, they will die in the mountains. The passes will be treacherous. We can catch them easily in the lowlands."

"A fool's errand," Philip said, his voice laced with the cold, complex logic of a man who had left sentiment behind a long time ago. "They would expect us to chase them directly. They are not running from us; they are running from the rot they have helped to spread. They will expect us to follow their trail, to blunder after them like common thugs. But that is not what we do. We are not hunting; we are herding. They are a virus, a contagion that has infected the heart of the kingdom. Now they flee, attempting to carry their poison to the rest of the land." He looked out over the sprawling, sleeping city, its great white walls a final, defiant gesture against the creeping, invisible sickness that gnawed at its foundations. He was not just a mercenary captain; he was the Shepherd of the City, and he was charged with protecting his flock from the wolves. "Send a dozen men to the north. Have them spread out, a wide net, but do not engage. Do not let them escape to the lowlands. Let them believe they are escaping us. Push them, gently, into the foothills. Send word to the Watcher. Tell him they are on their way."

His men did not question him. They simply nodded, their grim faces alight with the cold, hard purpose of true believers. They were not hunting men. They were purging a sickness. Philip watched them go, a thin, satisfied smile on his face. The hunt had begun. It was not a race, but a carefully orchestrated ballet of death, and he was the master choreographer. He had a tremendous and terrible purpose to fulfill.

—൝—

The first breath of freedom was a lie. The cool, clean air of the King'swood, so miraculous after the suffocating filth of the sewers, had become a chill premonition in the pale, grey light of dawn. The gentle rustle of the wind in the ancient oaks was no longer a song of sanctuary; it was the whisper of approaching death. They huddled in a shallow, moss-lined hollow, three ghosts haunted by the city they had just escaped, their brief, ragged relief already curdling into the cold, hard certainty of the hunted.

Gundroff materialized from the pre-dawn gloom, moving with a predator's silence that belied his heavy, iron-shod boots. His face, etched with the grim lines of a lifetime of vigilance, was a mask of unyielding stone. The crude sling for his wounded arm was already soaked through with fresh, dark blood, the pain a low thrumming he had long since learned to ignore. He did not speak of his pain. He spoke only of the enemy.

"They arre already herrre," he growled, his voice a low, grinding sound, like rocks shifting in the deep earth. "A dozen of them. Serpent's Hounds. Moving fast, sprreading out in a hunter's sweep. They arre not just patrrolling the walls. They arre hunting us, that they arre."

Seraphina looked up from the crude map spread across her knees, its fine, elegant lines smeared with the filth of their escape. The cold, challenging mathematics of their situation presented a singular, brutal conclusion: they were going to die here, in the shadow of the city that had cast them out, trapped between the walls of their prison and the blades of their executioners.

Thaddeus, who had been quietly watching the first rays of the sun pierce the high canopy, turned to them. The raw fear on his companions' faces seemed to find no purchase on his own quiet calm. His tone was serious now, stripped of all folksy charm, the voice of a scholar, not a storyteller.

"The southern roads are the arteries of the kingdom, and they will be choked with Malakai's poison. Every patrol, every garrison, every bounty hunter with an ounce of greed will be watching them. But the old pilgrim's path to the Ashen Peaks... that is a vein long forgotten. It is not on any modern map. It is a hard road, but it is a road they will not think to look for."

Seraphina's logical mind raced through the probabilities, calculating variables and outcomes. The southern roads were a death sentence, a predictable trap set for fools. The northern path was a desperate, irrational gambit against the terrain itself, a variable too chaotic to properly assess. It was their only hope. She met Gundroff's gaze, seeing her own desperate calculus reflected in his grim eyes. He gave a single, sharp nod. The mountains were a language he understood far better than the politics of men. The decision was made. They turned their backs on the sleeping, hostile city and took the first, painful step on the long, hard road north.

The soft forest floor quickly gave way to a steep, treacherous ascent, the rich earth replaced by loose scree and sharp-edged stone that turned underfoot. The air grew thin and cold, and the sparse, skeletal forms of stunted mountain pines replaced the dense canopy of the lowlands. The scent of damp earth and pine needles was a welcome respite, but the physical reality of the climb was a harsh and unforgiving teacher.

For Gundroff, the physical agony was a familiar companion, but the terrain was a personal insult. He was a creature of the deep, living stone, of planned archways and perfectly balanced keystones. This chaotic, crumbling landscape of the surface world felt like a blasphemy, a place of shoddy, unfinished work by a careless creator. Yet, it was a language he understood. He moved with a slow, deliberate certainty, his warrior's mind subsumed by the hunter's, reading the subtle signs of the world around them. He saw the flaws in the rock, the cracks and fissures that spoke of an old and forgotten kind of weakness. He saw a path that was not forged by dwarven hands, but, in its own silent way, endured. His body, a mountain of granite and unyielding will, was a silent protest against the chaos of the surface world, and he moved with a grim, purposeful grace, his heavy, iron-shod boots finding sure purchase on the loose scree.

Seraphina, however, struggled. Her body, honed by a life of scholarly discipline and arcane study, protested at every agonising step. She was a master of causality, a weaver of the threads of time, and a steep, muddy hill was defeating her. The humiliation of it was a sharp, bitter stone in her throat. She had spent her life navigating the complex geometry of arcane theory, yet her body could not navigate the simple, brutal geometry of a crumbling mountain path. The sharp, burning ache in her lungs, the tremble in her thighs, the stinging pain in her twisted ankle—it was a brutal and humbling reality check. She stumbled, her foot slipping on a patch of loose scree, and would have fallen if not for Thaddeus's surprisingly steadying hand. He was barely breathing heavily, his steps as light and certain as a mountain goat's. "The first step is always the hardest, my lady," he murmured, his voice gentle and devoid of judgment.

They pressed on, driven by the cold adrenaline of the hunted. After hours of grueling climbing, they crested a ridge and saw it nestled in a shallow dale below: a hamlet, a small cluster of stone and timber houses that should have been bustling with midday activity. Instead, it was silent. A profound, unnatural stillness hung over the place, a silence so deep it felt like a held breath. A faint, grey haze, too thin for smoke, seemed to cling to the rooftops like a shroud.

"Water," Seraphina rasped, her throat raw and caked with dust. "We have no choice."

Caution warred with desperate need. They descended into the village of Oakhaven, their movements slow and deliberate, weapons in hand. The place was not abandoned, but its people were ghosts. A blacksmith stood motionless by his cold forge, his hammer held loose in his limp hand, his eyes staring at nothing. A woman sat on her doorstep, methodically polishing a single spoon over and over, her movements slow and listless. They stared through the travelers as if they were made of glass, their faces pale, withdrawn, and utterly vacant.

Then Gundroff saw her. A small girl, no more than six years old, stood alone in the center of the muddy lane, staring intently at a cottage window. She was not crying. Her expression was one of quiet, unnerving vacancy. As they approached, she slowly raised a thin arm, her finger pointing at the glass.

Gundroff looked. Seraphina followed his gaze. On the windowpane, despite the warm sun beating down on the dale, a delicate and intricate pattern of frost had formed. It was not the chaotic, fractal spread of natural ice, but a perfect, swirling spiral, like a frozen galaxy or a complex, arcane sigil of impossible beauty. It seemed to shimmer at the edge of his vision, a pattern of such hostile complexity that it felt profoundly and fundamentally wrong.

Seraphina's exhaustion vanished, replaced by a sudden, razor-sharp focus. "Do not touch it," she commanded, her voice a low and urgent whisper. She took a step closer, her glacial eyes tracing the impossible geometry of the frost. It was the same hostile mathematics she had seen in the heart of the Sun Petal, the signature of the world's assassin. She understood with chilling clarity. The temporal decay was not just a blight on nature; it was a plague on the mind. It was feeding on the memories, the futures, of these people, leaving them as empty husks.

A sudden, sharp bark echoed from the edge of the village, a sound of trained, vicious intent.

"Hounds," Gundroff snarled, his hand already on the haft of his axe.

Panic, cold and sharp, seized them. They were trapped. The village was a bowl, with the Serpent's Hounds descending from the ridge they had just crossed. There was nowhere to run.

"The cellar!" Thaddeus hissed, his cheerful calm finally breaking. He pointed to a heavy, slanted wooden door at the side of the cottage with the frosted window.

They scrambled for it, Gundroff heaving the heavy door open with a grunt of pain from his wounded arm. They tumbled down a short flight of stone steps into a cool, root-scented darkness, pulling the door shut just as the first of the Serpent's Hounds, a man in dark green livery with the face of a hardened killer, entered the village square.

The cellar was a small, cramped space smelling of damp earth and aging apples. Through a narrow, dirt-caked window at ground level, they had a perfect, terrifying view of the lane. They watched as Captain Philip, the same hard-faced man from the Grand Hall, strode into the village, his hand resting on the pommel of his sword as if it were an extension of his own will.

"Search the houses!" he commanded, his voice a sharp crack in the unnatural silence. "They came this way. I know it. Find them!"

His men moved with brutal efficiency, kicking in doors, their shouts echoing in the quiet dale. Philip approached the small, vacant-eyed girl who still stood staring at the window above them. He knelt, his voice taking on a tone of false gentleness that did not reach his cold, calculating eyes.

"Have you seen a big dwarf, little one? And a pretty lady with hair like moonlight?"

The girl did not seem to hear him. She continued to point at the frosted window. Philip looked up, his brow furrowed in a flicker of confusion. He reached out a gauntleted hand to touch the impossible ice.

"No!" Seraphina whispered, a sound of pure, intellectual horror.

The moment his glove touched the glass, the frost pattern flared with a brilliant, violet light. The captain screamed, a high, thin sound of pure agony, and stumbled back, clutching his head as if his skull were about to split open. He collapsed to his knees, his body convulsing, a thin line of blood trickling from his nose. His men rushed to his side, their search forgotten in the face of their commander's sudden, terrifying affliction.

He was not looking at frost. He was looking at a wound in the world. As his gauntlet touched the glass, his mind was flooded with a terrifying vision, a kaleidoscopic nightmare of impossible geometry and a cold, silent void. He saw a world that had been unwritten, a tapestry of history that had been brutally unraveled. He saw a moment that had ceased to exist, a king who had never been born, a city that had never been built. He saw the face of the Rot, not as a disease, but as a consciousness, a cold, hungry intelligence that fed on causality itself. The pain in his head was a slight, physical echo of the cosmic horror his mind was grappling with. He had sought to understand the disease, and for a moment, the disease had understood him, and had shown him a truth so profound and so terrible that it had broken his mind.

"What was that?" Gundroff whispered, his own hand instinctively going to his axe.

"A psychic trap," Seraphina breathed, her eyes wide with a horrified understanding. "A defensive ward. Whoever created this blight is protecting their work. He touched the signature, and it... it showed him something. Something terrible. A glimpse of the void that is unmaking this place."

They watched as the Hounds, their mission shattered by their captain's sudden, inexplicable collapse, dragged his shaking form from the village. They had been saved, not by their own skill, but by the evil they were hunting.

They waited in the suffocating darkness of the cellar until the sun began to set, the silence of the village above returning to its hollow, unnerving rhythm. They emerged into the twilight, the close call having left them shaken and raw. The argument that had been simmering all day finally boiled over.

"Hiding in cellars!" Gundroff roared, the frustration and helplessness of the day erupting from him. He slammed his good fist against the stone wall of the cottage, the impact a dull, angry thud, like a hammer on soft ground. "Saved by a monster's leftovers! This is not how we win, that it is not! This is how we die, piece by piece, in the dark, like rats in a trap!"

"And charging them would have been a victory?" Seraphina retorted, her own voice sharp with fear and exhaustion. She rounded on him, her usual composure stripped away, leaving only a raw, frayed nerve. "Your axe is not the answer to every problem, dwarf! Sometimes, survival is the only victory that matters! A truth your people, in their stone halls, seem to have forgotten!"

Thaddeus stepped between them, his face a mask of profound sorrow. He took a clean strip of linen from his pack, dipped it in their dwindling waterskin, and began to gently clean the grime and tear streaks from Seraphina's face. He then moved to Gundroff and, with a quiet, practiced efficiency, started to unwrap and re-dress the dwarf's festering wound. His simple, silent acts of care were a more powerful rebuke than any words. The anger drained out of them, replaced by a deep, weary shame.

He took a slight, silver sunburst from his pocket, a symbol of his god. He held it over Gundroff's arm, whispering a short, simple prayer for resilience and fortitude. The light from the sunburst was a warm, gentle thing, and it seemed to chase away the cold, quiet poison that was eating at the flesh around the wound. The pain in Gundroff's arm, a searing fire just moments before, became a distant, quiet ache. The blessing was not a spell. It was a promise. A promise that some things, in the face of all the world's fury, will endure.

As they prepared to leave the haunted, dying village under the cover of darkness, Gundroff scouted the northern trail. He returned minutes later, his face grimmer than ever. He was holding a small, crudely carved wooden bird.

"I found this on the trail, a half mile north," he said, his voice low and heavy. "And tracks. A single man. Moving fast. He travels light and knows these mountains like the back of his hand." He turned the bird over in his large, calloused hands. Carved into its base was the single, perfect, and chillingly familiar spiral of the cult.

Seraphina stared at it, the final, terrible piece of the puzzle clicking into place. "They weren't hunting us," she whispered, the words a dawning, cold horror that iced her veins. "They were herding us."

The Serpent's Hounds were merely the dogs, flushing them from the cover of the lowlands and pushing them up into the mountains. But another hunter, a far more dangerous and patient predator, was not behind them.

He was waiting for them on the high paths ahead.

Chapter 9

The Ashen Tower

The hounds were gone, but the hunt was not over. The world had become a cage without walls, and the cold, patient gaze of the unseen hunter was a constant weight on the back of Gundroff's neck. For three days, they had pushed north, into the rugged, wind scoured foothills of the Ashen Peaks, and for three days, the silence had been a more terrifying companion than any pursuer. It was a silence that listened.

Gundroff moved through the broken, rock strewn landscape, his senses stretched to a razor's edge. He was a creature of the deeps, of the reassuring hum of living stone, and this vast, empty sky was an agony. The wind was a constant, probing touch, carrying scents he could not place, whispering of threats he could not see. He tasted the air and found only the clean, cold bite of iron rich stone and the faint, resinous perfume of stunted mountain pines. But beneath it, a sterile, acrid tang lingered in his memory. the ghost of a cultist's poison that haunted his every breath.

It was on the fifth day of their grueling journey that they saw it. They crested a high, windswept ridge, and there, in a bowl shaped valley a league distant, stood a single, jagged tooth of black stone rising from the rolling, grey green hills: a lone, ancient watchtower. It was a stark, menacing silhouette against the bruised purple of the twilight sky, a shard of a forgotten war.

Seraphina stopped, unrolling her map with hands that trembled slightly from the cold. She traced a line with a slender finger, her brow furrowed in concentration. "There," she said, her voice sharp with a sudden, focused intensity. "The Ashen Tower. According to the royal surveyors' charts from a century ago, it guards the only viable pass through these peaks for the next fifty leagues." She looked up, her glacial eyes meeting theirs, a flicker of cold, tactical light in their depths. "The charts mark it as a ruin, held by a disorganized band of hobgoblin raiders. A forward base for Dark Elf slavers."

A grim, terrible logic settled over them. A bandit lair. A nest of filth and chaos. A perfect, anonymous sanctuary for a solitary, patient hunter to use as his base of operations. The pieces fit with the cold, hard certainty of perfectly joined stone.

"He is there," Gundroff stated, the words a flat, final pronouncement. "He has driven us to his den."

"We cannot bypass it," Seraphina continued, her mind already a whirlwind of calculation. "To go around would add weeks to our journey, and we do not have the supplies. To go through the pass under the tower's shadow would be suicide. He would pick us off from the crenellations at his leisure."

A stern, desperate resolve settled over them. They were no longer the prey. They would be the hunters.

"We will burn his nest," Gundroff said, his voice a low rumble of conviction. "We go in hard and fast, and give him a death of stone and steel."

"A frontal assault is a fool's errand," Seraphina countered, her voice sharp. "We do not know their numbers, their defenses. We must be smarter."

The debate that followed was a clash of philosophies, two masters of their respective arts finding themselves at an impasse. Gundroff paced the narrow confines of their sheltered position like a caged mountain lion, his massive hands working the leather grip of his axe.

"Your pretty magic is a scalpel, elf," he growled, his golden eyes burning with frustration. "But sometimes what you need is a hammer. These are bandits. rabble who scatter at the first sign of real resistance. I've seen their kind a thousand times. They're used to preying on merchants and pilgrims, not warriors. Show them the fury of a dwarf's axe, and they'll flee like rats from a burning granary."

"And if you're wrong?" Seraphina retorted, her voice dangerously quiet. "If they have crossbows on those walls? If they've set traps in the approach? Your 'hammer' becomes a corpse in their courtyard, and we lose our strongest fighter before the real battle even begins." She gestured to the tower, its black stone seeming to absorb the dying light. "That structure has stood for centuries. It was built to withstand sieges, not theatrical charges. We need to think, not just feel."

"Think?" Gundroff's voice rose to a growl that echoed off the stone around them. "I've been thinking for forty years, woman. Thinking about duty, about patience, about the proper way to honor the dead. And where has it gotten me? My people are still ash, my home is still a tomb, and my enemy still draws breath." He slammed his fist against the rock, the impact sending small stones skittering down the slope. "Sometimes thinking is just another word for cowardice."

Seraphina's eyes flashed, a dangerous light kindling in their icy depths. "Cowardice? You speak to me of cowardice? I spent years watching my master dismiss the rot eating our kingdom from within while I gathered evidence he refused to see. I've spent my life thinking three moves ahead, dwarf, because the world is full of warriors who charge first and ask questions of the corpses." She stepped closer, her tall frame casting a shadow over him despite his breadth. "Your people had the luxury of dying with their axes in their hands. Mine will die slowly, forgotten, in a kingdom that's eating itself alive while fools like you dream of glorious last stands."

The silence that followed was sharp enough to cut stone. Thaddeus, who had been quietly observing from the edge of their hiding place, cleared his throat gently.

"If I might," he said, his voice carrying that strange quality of calm authority that seemed to come from nowhere and everywhere at once. "This reminds me of a tale from the old chronicles. about two master craftsmen who were commissioned to build a bridge across an impossible chasm. The first was a stonemason, who believed the only way to span such a gap was with the strongest possible foundation, built to last a thousand years. The second was a rope weaver, who argued that flexibility and speed were more important than permanence. that a bridge that could bend with the wind would outlast one that tried to defy it."

He pulled an apple from his pack and took a thoughtful bite. "They argued for days while the chasm remained uncrossed. Finally, a child from the village asked them a simple question: 'What if you're both right?' The stonemason built the pillars, immovable and eternal. The rope weaver built the span, flexible and quick to construct. And the bridge they built together was stronger than either of their individual visions."

Gundroff and Seraphina looked at each other, the heat of their argument slowly cooling into something more practical. The truth of it settled between them like a bridge of its own.

"A synthesis," Seraphina said slowly, her analytical mind already working. "My magic creates the diversion, your strength provides the breakthrough. Not a frontal assault, but not a purely subtle approach either."

"Aye," Gundroff rumbled, his warrior's mind shifting from anger to tactics. "Your illusions draw them to the wrong place, my axe hits them where they're weakest. But it has to be precise. No room for error."

They spent the last hour of daylight planning their approach, their combined expertise creating something neither could have achieved alone. Seraphina would weave a complex auditory illusion. not a grand display that would drain her reserves, but a carefully crafted sound loop projected to the eastern approach. The phantom noise of a large company of men and horses, complete with the clink of mail, the creak of leather, and the low murmur of soldiers preparing for battle.

Thaddeus, despite his apparent frailty, would create a secondary diversion to the south, not through magic, but through the practical knowledge of a man who seemed to understand the secret weakness in every structure. He would trigger a controlled rockslide on the southern slope. nothing dramatic, but enough noise and dust to suggest a second group trying to approach under cover.

And Gundroff would be the hammer, striking at the moment when the garrison's attention was divided. But not a mindless charge. a calculated assault on the tower's weak point, a sally port that Seraphina's trained eye had spotted in the failing light. A servant's entrance, likely poorly defended, as the main threat seemed to come from the east.

As they prepared to move into position, each carrying their part of the burden, Gundroff found himself grudgingly impressed. The plan had the elegance of good stonework. each piece supporting the others, no single point of failure.

"Your magic," he said to Seraphina as they prepared to separate. "It's not just parlor tricks, is it?"

"Your strength," she replied, checking the focus gems on her staff. "It's not just mindless fury."

It was the beginning of understanding.

The plan unfolded with the precision of a master smith's work. As the shimmering wall of mist rose on the eastern plains, erupting with the ghostly neighing of spectral steeds and the distant shouts of phantom soldiers, a chorus of guttural, alarmed voices echoed from the tower. Moments later, a cascade of rocks and dust thundered down the southern slope, Thaddeus's "accident" perfectly timed to suggest a coordinated pincer movement.

Gundroff did not wait. He let out a roar that was pure, primal fury, and charged. His great axe, fed by the righteous anger of a man whose home had been defiled, burst into the divine, white hot fire of Grolnir's judgment. The sally port, a narrow wooden door reinforced with iron bands, stood no chance against the fury of a dwarf blessed by his war god.

The door exploded inward, splinters of oak and twisted metal flying like shrapnel. Gundroff stormed through the breach, his eyes blazing with divine fire, ready to slaughter every last bandit and tear their master limb from limb.

He cut down the first two hobgoblin guards before they could properly raise their shields, their crude iron armor melting like wax under the axe's holy fire. He burst into the central courtyard, his battle cry echoing off the stone walls, ready to face a disorganized rabble of panicked raiders running in all directions.

He stopped so abruptly that dust swirled around his boots.

Before him stood a wall of disciplined, interlocking iron, a phalanx of two dozen hobgoblin veterans, their movements economical and precise, who had slammed their heavy, kite shaped shields together, forming a perfect, unbreakable line, their plate armor was not the mismatched, scavenged junk of bandits. it was well maintained, oiled, and bore a single, unified sigil: a snarling, iron tusked wolf's head. Their spears, held steady over the top of the shield wall, formed a hedge of glittering, razor sharp death.

But it was their discipline that struck him like a physical blow. No shouting. No panic. No wild, desperate scrambling. They moved with the fluid precision of a machine, each warrior knowing their place, their purpose, their duty. This was not a rabble. This was a military unit.

Behind them, his face a mask of cold, professional authority, stood their commander. A massive hobgoblin with a scarred face, a single, milky white eye, and an air of absolute, unquestionable command. He wore the same wolf sigil armor as his men, but his bore the additional markings of rank. a red horsehair plume, and a cloak of deep blue that marked him as an officer of significant standing.

"Hold the line!" the warlord bellowed, his voice a gravelly roar of command, not of panic. "Let none pass the stone gate! For the Legion! For the Treaty! For the Honor of the Compact!"

Gundroff froze, his flaming axe hissing in the sudden, terrible silence. *Treaty?* *Honor?* These were not the words of bandits. These were the words of soldiers. soldiers with a cause, a purpose, a code they were willing to die for.

He looked from their grim, determined faces to his own flaming axe and saw his own blind rage reflected in the commander's single, good eye. He saw a warrior who had come here expecting to fight monsters, and had found only other warriors. warriors he had just attacked without provocation, without understanding, without honor.

His gaze fell upon the two fallen hobgoblin guards, the ones his axe had unmade in his righteous fury. One still clutched a battle axe, its haft wrapped in leather worn smooth by years of faithful service. a weapon maintained by a craftsman, not a raider. The other bore a small, wooden token hanging from his belt: the crude carving of what looked like a child's face.

These were not bandits. They were soldiers. They were fathers, brothers, men who served something greater than themselves. And he had killed them in his arrogance.

The shame of it was a cold, heavy stone in his gut.

The standoff stretched for a heartbeat that felt like eternity. The divine fire of Gundroff's axe cast long, dancing shadows on the grim, determined faces of the hobgoblin soldiers. The moment hung balanced on the edge of a blade. one wrong move, one misunderstood gesture, and the courtyard would become a slaughter.

The arrival of Seraphina broke it. She appeared in the shattered gateway, her hands raised in the clear, universal symbol of parley, her face a pale mask of dawning, horrified understanding. Behind her came Thaddeus, his cheerful demeanor replaced by something graver, more focused.

"We were told bandits held this tower," Seraphina said, her voice cutting through the tense silence, her elven accent sharp and clear. "Your discipline suggests otherwise."

The hobgoblin commander's single eye flicked from Gundroff's still burning axe to the elf's raised hands, then to the old man whose posture suggested neither threat nor submission, but something else. respect. He was a soldier, and he could recognize the signs of a genuine parley when he saw them.

"I am Warlord Grath of the Ironfang Legion," he said, his voice carrying the weight of absolute authority. His scarred face was a map of old battles, and his remaining eye held the deep, weary intelligence of a career soldier. "And we do not raid. We guard."

He spat on the ground, a gesture of profound contempt. not for them, but for whoever had fed them their false intelligence. "The lowlanders are fools. They know nothing of the true war that is fought in these mountains. Every slaver that tries to use this pass, every Dark Elf raid that comes down from the north. we kill them before they can reach your precious farms and villages. The 'bandits' your people fear are the corpses we leave to rot in the high passes."

His gaze fell on the two dead guards, and something terrible and grief stricken flickered across his features. "Those were my soldiers you just killed, dwarf. Good men. Men who have held this post for twenty years, men who have bled to keep your roads safe while your king counts his gold and your nobles play their games."

The weight of the misunderstanding was a physical blow, heavier than any shield. Gundroff lowered his axe, the divine fire sputtering and dying, leaving only cold, hard steel and the bitter taste of his own mistake.

Grath studied them for a long moment, his weathered face unreadable. The shield wall remained steady, but the spears had lowered slightly. ready to strike, but no longer actively threatening. It was the stance of soldiers awaiting orders, not bloodthirsty killers eager for a fight.

"You are not soldiers of Tetra," he said finally, the words not a question but a conclusion drawn from careful observation. "You move like fugitives. You carry yourselves like people who have seen too much and lost too much. And you came here believing lies about what we are." His scarred mouth twisted into something that might have been a bitter smile. "So tell me. what enemy do you run from that drives you to attack strangers in their own halls?"

Seraphina glanced at Gundroff, whose shame was written plain on his face, then stepped forward. "We seek passage through these mountains, Warlord. We are pursued by forces that serve... darker purposes than any king's justice. We were told this tower was a haven for slavers and raiders. We were told wrong."

"Aye, you were told wrong," Grath agreed. His voice carried a weight of old pain, old betrayals. "And I can guess by whom. The same voices that whisper in the lowland courts, the same advisors who have spent three generations rewriting history to suit their convenience." He gestured to his men, and with disciplined precision, they raised their spears and stepped back, creating space but remaining ready.

"Lower your weapons," he commanded. "These are not enemies. They are victims of the same lies that have branded us as monsters."

But he did not dismiss his men. Instead, he planted his own weapon. a massive, two handed blade that bore the same wolf sigil as his armor. point first in the stone of the courtyard.

"You want passage," he said, his single eye boring into each of them in turn. "Very well. But first, you will hear the truth. You will understand what you nearly destroyed in your ignorance. You will know the price of the lies your people have told themselves."

His voice carried the weight of command, but also something deeper. a profound need to be heard, to have the truth of his people's sacrifice acknowledged by someone, anyone, before it was lost forever.

"Sit," he commanded, gesturing to the stone benches that lined the courtyard. "And I will tell you the tale of the Ironfang Legion. I will tell you of the treaty your kings have forgotten, and the honor they have abandoned."

They sat, the strange weight of ceremony settling over them. Even Gundroff, still burning with shame, found himself compelled by the authority in the warlord's voice. Thaddeus settled onto a bench with the air of a man who had been waiting his whole life to hear this story.

Grath began to speak, and his voice carried them back across the centuries.

"In the days when your kingdom was young, when the first King Aethel sought to unite the scattered human clans under a single banner, this land was chaos. Bandits controlled the passes, the high peaks crawled with creatures that had never bent the knee to any authority. Dark Elves from Nyx'Tolos raided at will, taking slaves back to their matriarchal city to serve in their great houses or die in their fighting pits."

His scarred face was distant, lost in the weight of inherited memory. "But there was another force in these mountains. The hobgoblin clans are descendants of warriors who had served the war god Mavorn himself in the Age of War. We were not the rabble your history books describe. we were soldiers, disciplined and organized, but fractured into a dozen feuding tribes."

Grath walked to the center of the courtyard, his movements those of a man accustomed to holding the attention of an audience. "King Aethel was no fool. He saw that he could spend a generation and lose thousands of men trying to take these passes by force, or he could find another way. So he came here, to this tower, carrying not a sword but a treaty."

The warlord's voice grew stronger, filled with the pride of his ancestors. "He spoke with my ancestor, Grath the Unbroken, war chief of the largest hobgoblin clan. And he made an offer that was both simple and profound: unite your people under one banner, hold these passes against all who would use them for evil, and you will be counted as allies of the Kingdom of Tetra. Not subjects. allies. Equal partners in the defense of civilization."

Seraphina leaned forward, her scholarly mind immediately grasping the implications. "A mutual defense pact. Your people would control the high passes, prevent raiders and slavers from using the mountain routes, and in return..."

"In return, we would be recognized as a sovereign power," Grath confirmed. "The Ironfang Legion was born from that treaty. Not a single tribe, but a confederation of all the hobgoblin clans, united under the wolf banner. We swore to guard the Under Gate. the great passage that leads deep into the mountain's heart. and to keep the filth of the north from spilling down into the lowlands."

His voice grew heavy with old sorrow. "For three generations, the compact held. The supply caravans came every season, bringing us what we needed to maintain our vigil. Your nobles visited our halls, treated with us as equals. Our warriors trained alongside your knights. We were not just allies. we were friends."

The pain in his voice was a living thing. "The last caravan arrived ninety seven years ago. A handful of half empty wagons were escorted by bored guards who made it clear they considered the duty a punishment. The official who led them had never heard of the original treaty. He called us 'useful mercenaries' and spoke of 'managing the local goblin problem.'"

Gundroff winced. He could imagine the insult, the slow poison of being forgotten by those you had sworn to serve.

"The kingdoms grew fat and comfortable," Grath continued, his single eye burning with quiet fury. "They forgot that safety requires vigilance, that peace requires guardians. New kings arose who knew nothing of their ancestors' promises. New nobles who saw the old treaties as inconvenient precedents, obstacles to their ambitions."

He gestured to the walls around them, to the worn but well maintained fortifications. "So we have continued our vigil alone for ninety seven years, forgotten and abandoned, but unbroken. Every Dark Elf slaver who tries to use our passes dies screaming. Every demon cult that seeks to establish a foothold in these mountains finds only steel and fire. Every horror that crawls up from the deep places breaks itself against our shields."

The courtyard fell silent except for the whisper of wind through stone. The weight of nearly a century of thankless sacrifice hung in the air like a judgment.

"Your children's stories paint us as monsters," Grath said quietly. "Savage raiders who threaten travelers and demand tribute. They have forgotten that we are the reason their roads are safe, their villages unburned, their children not chained in the slave markets of Nyx'Tolos."

Thaddeus spoke for the first time, his voice soft but carrying surprising authority. "I have read the old chronicles, Warlord Grath. In the archives of the Sun God's temple, there are records of the Great Compact, written in King Aethel's own hand. The treaty stands, according to divine law, until formally renounced by both parties."

Grath's eye snapped to the old monk, something like hope flickering in its depths. "You know the old laws?"

"I know many old things," Thaddeus replied, and there was something in his tone that made even the battle hardened warlord listen with respect. "And I know that honor, once given, does not fade simply because it is forgotten. Your vigil is recorded in the sight of the gods themselves."

For a moment, Grath's face showed the raw emotion he kept buried beneath his warrior's discipline. gratitude, validation, the profound relief of a man who had begun to believe his sacrifice was meaningless.

Then the mask of command settled back into place. "But you have not come here seeking history lessons," he said, his attention returning to his unexpected guests. "You spoke of darker purposes, of enemies that serve powers worse than any king's injustice. Tell me. what brings fugitives to my door?"

Grath led them not to a dungeon, but to the tower's war room, a chamber that spoke of function over comfort. The stone walls were hung with detailed maps of the surrounding peaks, annotated in precise military script. Weapon racks held well maintained arms that gleamed with oil and care. A massive table, scarred by decades of use, dominated the center of the room.

The warlord poured a thick, pungent liquid into horn mugs and pushed them across the table. "Drink," he commanded. "It will put iron back in your blood."

Gundroff took a long pull and grimaced. The ale was harsh, bitter, but warming. It tasted like loyalty. uncompromising and hard to swallow, but good for the soul.

Seraphina, with careful precision, laid out their story. She spoke of the temporal decay eating at the kingdom's heart, of the assassination that had toppled a dynasty, of the cult that moved in shadows to unmake the world itself. She was careful to frame their quest in terms a soldier could understand. not grand cosmic stakes, but a clear and present threat to everything they had sworn to protect.

Grath listened with a warrior's stillness, his scarred face revealing nothing. When she finished, he was quiet for a long moment, his gaze turning to the great map that dominated one wall.

"The hunter you speak of," he said finally, his voice heavy with recognition. "We have seen his work. Three of my patrols have vanished in the past month. good men, experienced scouts who knew every rock and ravine in these mountains. We found what was left of them."

His single eye fixed on Gundroff with something approaching respect. "The kills were... artistic. Staged and left as messages for those who would understand their meaning. This is not some beast that kills for food or territory. This is a predator that delights in the craft of terror."

"What did you call it?" Seraphina asked, her scholar's instincts catching something in his tone.

"The Gray Death," Grath replied. "Our shamans have a different name for the wrongness you describe. the thing that makes stone crumble and time grow sick. They call it the 'Wound That Will Not Heal.' It seeps up from the deep places, from cracks in the world that should not exist."

Seraphina leaned forward, her eyes bright with sudden understanding. This was the confirmation she had been seeking. independent verification of the temporal decay from observers who had no agenda, no political axe to grind.

"You've seen it directly?" she pressed. "The acceleration of decay, the unnatural aging?"

"Aye," Grath confirmed grimly. "Two months passed, one of our watchtowers simply... collapsed, not from siege or storm, but as if it had been standing for a thousand years instead of a hundred. The stones turned to powder, and the iron rusted through in hours. My engineer examined the remains. he said it was as if time itself had gone mad."

He rose and walked to a weapon rack, taking down a massive battle axe whose edge gleamed with careful maintenance. "But we have learned to fight it. Iron blessed by our shamans seems to resist the worst effects. Discipline keeps the mind from fracturing when the wrongness presses close. And faith..." He looked directly at Thaddeus. "Faith in old promises and older powers seems to hold back the darkness."

Grath turned back to them, decision crystallizing in his weathered features. "Your war is not my war," he said slowly. "Your politics mean nothing to these stones. But the shadow that rises from the deep places, the force that would unmake the world itself. that is an ancient enemy. An enemy of all who live in the light."

He planted his axe on the table, its weight making the ancient wood groan. "The Ironfang Legion has held the passes for nearly a century against every foe that has dared challenge us. We have faced Dark Elf raiders, demon cultists, and things that crawl up from caves that have no names. But this... this Gray Death is different. It does not fight. it simply erases. And that makes it a threat to everything we have sworn to protect."

"Then you will help us?" Gundroff asked, hardly daring to hope.

"Help you?" Grath's scarred mouth twisted in what might have been a grin. "Dwarf, if what you say is true, then the only question is whether we fight this enemy in the passes or wait for it to come to our gates. The Legion does not wait for death. we go to meet it."

He moved to the great map, his finger tracing routes through the mountain peaks. "But if you seek to reach the source of this corruption, you cannot take the lowland roads. They will be watched, patrolled, filled with enemies who serve powers you cannot fight directly."

His finger stopped at a point deep in the mountain's heart, marked with symbols that predated the current maps. "There is another way. A path your hunter will not be watching, because it is a path he would not dare to take."

Seraphina studied the map, her trained eye catching the significance of the markings. "The Under Gate," she breathed. "It's real."

Grath led them deeper into the tower than should have been possible, through corridors that seemed to burrow into the mountain's living heart. The air grew cooler with each step, carrying scents of deep stone and ages beyond counting. Torches flickered in brackets carved directly from the rock, their light revealing walls covered in inscriptions that were older than the kingdom above.

"Few living men have seen what I am about to show you," Grath said as they descended a staircase that seemed to spiral down into the world's foundation. "The Under Gate is not merely a passage. it is a relic of the first wars, when the boundaries between realms were not yet fixed."

They emerged into a vast, echoing chamber that stole the breath from their lungs. The space was impossibly large, its ceiling lost in shadows that seemed to move and writhe with their own life. At the chamber's heart stood a massive gate of black iron and silver, its surface covered in runes that seemed to shift and change when viewed directly. The gate was easily fifty feet high and thirty broad, bound with chains that appeared to be forged from starlight itself.

But it was what lay beyond the gate that truly struck them with awe and terror.

Through the iron bars, they could see not another chamber, but an impossible vista. a vast underground sea that stretched beyond the limits of sight. The water was not the blue black of surface oceans, but something more profound, more fundamental. It was the color of midnight given liquid form, its surface perfectly still yet somehow alive with currents that defied understanding.

"The Silent Sea," Grath said, his voice dropping to a reverent whisper. "It is not water as you know it, but something far older. The shamans say it is the first shadow. the space between thoughts when the gods were dreaming the world into existence."

Strange lights moved in the depths of that impossible ocean, not like fish or any living thing, but more like thoughts made visible, ideas given form and set free to swim in the darkness between realities.

"This passage leads under the mountains, under the roots of the world," Grath continued. "It will carry you far to the north, to places where the normal paths between kingdoms mean nothing. But the price..." He turned to face them, his single eye grave with warning. "The Silent Sea keeps its secrets. Men have crossed it and returned, but they are never quite the same. It shows you things. truths that were never meant for mortal minds."

Seraphina approached the gate, her chronomancer's senses reeling from the temporal distortions that radiated from the impossible sea. "This is not just a passage," she said, her voice tight with scholarly excitement and profound unease. "This is a crack in reality itself. A place where the normal rules of space and time break down."

"Aye," Grath confirmed. "The old treaties spoke of it in whispers. King Aethel himself walked this path once, in the darkest days of his reign, when enemies pressed close on all sides. He emerged from the northern caves three days later with hair gone white and eyes that had seen too much. But he had outflanked his foes, appeared where they least expected, and won a victory that saved his kingdom."

Thaddeus stepped forward, his weathered hand touching one of the ancient runes carved into the gate's surface. For a moment, his cheerful demeanor fell away completely, replaced by something far more complex. a weight of knowledge that seemed to press down on his shoulders like a physical burden.

"The Under Gate was sealed for good reason," he said quietly, his voice carrying an authority that seemed to come from deep within. "But there are times when desperate measures become necessary. When the alternative to risk is certain destruction."

Grath produced an iron key from a chain around his neck. not ornate or decorative, but heavy with purpose and age. "The choice is yours," he said. "Face your hunter on the high passes, where he has every advantage and expects you to come. Or take the path that leads through mystery and shadow, where even the darkness itself might not dare to follow."

The key turned in the ancient lock with a sound like breaking glass. The chains fell away with chimes that echoed strangely in the vast chamber, as if the sound was being reflected by surfaces that existed in dimensions the mind could not quite grasp.

The gate swung open on hinges that moved without sound, revealing a narrow stone dock that extended into the Silent Sea. A single boat waited there. if boat was the right word for the craft that seemed to be carved from a single piece of black stone, its hull inscribed with protective wards that glowed faintly in the impossible twilight.

"The journey takes three days," Grath said, his voice heavy with the weight of old warnings. "Keep your minds focused on your purpose. Do not look too long into the depths, and do not listen too closely to the voices that will call to you from the water. Above all, remember. whatever you see, whatever truths the Sea reveals, you are still yourselves. Do not let the vastness convince you that your small, mortal purposes are meaningless."

As they prepared to board the impossible craft, Grath called out one final warning. "The Sea will test you. It will show you the roots of things, the connections between all events. Some who have made this journey emerged believing they understood everything, or that they understood nothing. Both are forms of madness."

The boat moved away from the dock without oars or sail, guided by currents that responded to will rather than wind. As the light from the chamber faded behind them, they were left alone on an ocean that existed between the spaces of the world, carrying them toward a destination that might save everything. or destroy them all.

In the growing darkness of the impossible voyage ahead, each carried their own thoughts. Gundroff felt the weight of his shame transform into something new. not the burning rage that had driven him for forty years, but a colder, more purposeful resolve. He had found allies where he expected enemies, honor where he had been told to see only corruption. Perhaps other truths were waiting to be discovered in the darkness ahead.

Seraphina clutched her notes and maps, her scholar's mind reeling with the implications of what they had witnessed. The Under Gate represented a fundamental challenge to everything she thought she understood about the nature of reality. If such places existed. cracks in the world where normal laws held no sway. then perhaps the temporal decay was not an anomaly but a symptom of something far more profound.

And Thaddeus sat quietly at the boat's prow, his weathered hands folded in his lap, his bright blue eyes reflecting the strange lights that moved in the depths below. Of all of them, he seemed least troubled by the impossible nature of their passage, as if he had always known such wonders existed just beyond the edge of ordinary sight.

Behind them, Warlord Grath stood alone on the dock, watching until the boat disappeared entirely into the luminous darkness. He had given them the most precious gift in his power. not just passage, but hope. The hope that somewhere in the world, there were still those who would fight for more than gold or glory, who would stand against the darkness not because they were ordered to, but because it was right.

He turned and walked back through the ancient corridors, back to his duty, back to his vigil. The Ironfang Legion would continue to hold the passes, as they had for nearly a century. But now they would wait and watch for word from the impossible sea, hoping that three unlikely allies might succeed where armies had failed.

The Silent Sea stretched before the fellowship, vast and full of mysteries that mortal minds were never meant to comprehend. But they sailed into that darkness together, bound by purpose and the strange trust that had grown between them in the shadow of the Ashen Tower.

The real journey was beginning.

Chapter 10

The City of Chains

The air that bled from the Under Gate was more than just a presence; it was a profound, ancient exhalation from the mountain's deepest lungs, a breath of a world that had been sealed off from the light for epochs. It carried a sterile scent of damp stone and forgotten time, a smell as old as the mountains themselves. The chaotic din of the Ashen Tower, the gruff farewells of Warlord Grath's soldiers, the memory of the sun's warmth and the wind's honest song. all of it was stripped away the moment they stepped across the threshold.

In its place was a silence so absolute it felt like a physical weight against the eardrums, a suffocating blanket that muted their thoughts.

The cavern beyond the gate was a cathedral of impossibility, a black cathedral of a lost world. Its ceiling was lost in a darkness that swallowed light, a boundless void where faint, silvery mineral veins in the walls pulsed with a cold, sickly luminescence. Before them lay the shores of the Silent Sea, a vast, perfectly still body of black water that did not reflect their forms but seemed to absorb their presence.

It was a liquid void.

The water was not the water as they knew it. It was a sheet of polished obsidian made liquid, a substance that seemed to exist in defiance of every natural law. When Gundroff dipped an experimental oar into its surface, it yielded with a slow, oily reluctance, parting like thick honey, yet leaving no wake, no ripple, no disturbance to mark their passage. The silence was not just the absence of sound. it was the presence of something else, something that devoured noise itself.

"Well," Thaddeus said, his cheerful voice a sacrilege in the hallowed quiet. He spoke with the forced bravado of a man trying to whistle past a graveyard. "This is a bit more dramatic than the old ferry at Miller's Pond, isn't it?"

But his words died the moment they left his lips. There was no echo, no resonance, no acknowledgment from the vast cathedral around them. The sound vanished, consumed by the hungry darkness as if it had never been. His usual stream of cheerful observations fell silent, the oppressive atmosphere finally breaking through his seemingly inexhaustible good humor.

Gundroff sat in the stern of the small boat Grath had provided, his powerful arms pulling a pair of crude oars through the unnatural water. Stripped of his heavy armor to allow for the possibility of a desperate swim, he was reduced to his most basic elements. muscle, bone, and an iron will that felt increasingly fragile in this place that seemed to exist outside the natural world.

He was a creature of the earth, of the living stone and the deep, reassuring hum of a mountain's heart. This silent, subterranean sea felt like a grave, an endless, drowning darkness that promised only oblivion. It was the antithesis of everything he was. The water did not part with a familiar splash or gurgle. It yielded with a slow, viscous reluctance, leaving no wake, only the faintest whisper of the boat's passage. Every stroke of the oars was a violation, a forced intrusion into a medium that rejected their existence.

The silence pressed in like a living thing, a sentient hunger that seemed to feed on their discomfort. It was getting colder with every stroke, a chill that seemed to seep not just into their bones, but into their souls. The familiar sounds of life. the creak of leather, the rustle of cloth, even the sound of their own breathing. were muffled and distorted, as if filtered through layers of spiritual cotton.

Gundroff found himself counting his heartbeats, using the rhythm as an anchor against the psychological assault of this place. *Thump thump, Thump thump.* It was the only honest sound in this realm of lies, the only proof that he still existed as something more than a fading memory in the darkness.

For Seraphina, seated in the prow, the journey was a slow, intellectual agony. Her entire life, her magic, was predicated on the understanding of causality, of the predictable, elegant flow of time. This place was a violation of that fundamental law. The Silent Sea was not just a body of water; it was a temporal wound, a place where the river of time had pooled and stagnated into a black, motionless mire.

She could feel it as a low, constant pressure behind her eyes, a psychic static that made the precise, logical fortress of her mind feel as though it were built on shifting sand. Her connection to the chronomantic ley lines, a constant, low level thrum in her soul, was now a dead, silent wire. The magic that had defined her since childhood felt as distant and unreachable as the stars.

She felt untethered, a ship without an anchor in a starless sea, and the sensation filled her with a profound and unfamiliar sense of dread. Every instinct screamed at her to reach out with her magic, to impose some order on this chaos, but her power simply... wasn't there. It was as if the concept of causality had been suspended in this place, leaving her as helpless as a child.

The journey stretched on, each stroke of the oars a small eternity. Time itself seemed to have no meaning here. They might have been traveling for minutes or hours. there was no way to tell in this place where the sun had never shone and clocks had no power.

Thaddeus sat in the center of the boat, no longer humming his jaunty, off key tunes. The oppressive silence had finally broken through even his inexhaustible cheerfulness. His usual stream of stories and observations had dried up, leaving him as quiet and contemplative as his companions. The weight of this place seemed to press down on even his irrepressible spirit, crushing it into a small, flickering ember of stubborn hope.

When he did attempt to hum, the sound was wrong. It had no echo, no resonance, no life. It was a small, dead thing that only served to make the silence around it feel deeper, more absolute. It was as if the air was consuming sound itself, feeding on their attempts to impose normalcy on this realm of impossibility.

The walls of the cavern seemed to pulse with that cold, silvery light, creating the illusion of movement in their peripheral vision. But when they turned to look directly, there was nothing. only the endless, watching darkness. It was a place that existed in the spaces between thoughts, in the pause between heartbeats, in the silence between words.

Hours passed, or perhaps days. time had no meaning in this place where causality itself seemed suspended. Their water ran low, their throats grew parched, but still the Silent Sea stretched endlessly before them. The boat moved not through water, but through liquid nothingness, a void that had been given form and substance.

It was only when they saw the distant glow of phosphorescent fungi that they knew they were approaching their destination. But even that light seemed wrong here. muted and sickly, as if the concept of illumination had been infected by this place's profound negation of natural law.

The Silent Sea had tested them, measured them, found them somehow worthy of passage. But it had left its mark on each of them. a cold, hollow space where certainty once lived, a reminder that there were places in the world where even the most fundamental truths could be suspended, leaving only the raw, terrifying reality of existence without meaning.

As they finally approached the distant shore, each of them carried a piece of that silence within them, a small, cold void that would never quite be filled again.

The air that rose from the approaching docks of Nyx'Tolos was thick with alien scents. exotic spices, alchemical reagents, and beneath it all, the cold, metallic tang of a civilization built on cruelty. The ethereal glow of the Silent Sea gave way to something far more sinister: the sickly green and pale violet illumination of captured soul light, thousands of imprisoned spirits providing illumination for a city that had forgotten the sun.

Seraphina's mind, still reeling from the temporal wound of their passage, snapped back into sharp, analytical focus as the reality of their situation crystallized. She turned in the prow of the boat, her glacial eyes fixing on Gundroff with the cold precision of a surgeon preparing for a necessary amputation.

"Before we dock," she said, her voice cutting through the oppressive atmosphere like a blade of ice, "the rules of our engagement must be made clear."

She paused, letting the weight of her words settle in the dead air between them. She had spent the last hour of their journey in a cold, brutal calculus of survival, running every possible variable through the unforgiving logic of her mind. The conclusion was singular, inescapable, and monstrous.

"Nyx'Tolos is an absolute matriarchy," she began, her voice as precise and unfeeling as a coroner's scalpel. "Power flows through the female bloodline, and it is total. Males are, at best, consorts. decorative accessories whose status reflects the power of their mistress. At worst, they are chattel. Property to be bought, sold, and discarded at whim."

Gundroff's paddle slowed in the strange, viscous water. His golden eyes, which had been focused on their destination, now turned to fix on her with growing suspicion.

"I will enter the city under the guise of a visiting sorceress from a minor northern house," she continued, her clinical detachment a shield against the horror of what she was about to propose. "My station, my gender, and my arcane power will grant me a degree of temporary respect and autonomy."

She leaned forward, her pale hands gripping the sides of the boat until her knuckles were white. "You present a problem."

The words hung in the air like a curse. Gundroff's massive frame went utterly still, the only sound the gentle lap of the impossible water against their hull.

"A heavily armed, male Hill Dwarf traveling with an elven mage is not just an anomaly in their society. it is a provocation," Seraphina pressed on, her voice growing colder with each word. "You would be seen as either a threat to be eliminated or a prize to be claimed. You would not survive the first hour in that city as an equal."

"What are you saying?" The words came out as a low growl, a sound that promised violence if she continued down this path.

Seraphina met his glare without flinching. She had anticipated this rage, had factored it into her equations. The mathematics were brutal but inescapable.

"I am saying that for us to survive, for this mission to succeed, you cannot be a warrior. You cannot be an equal." She took a breath, the words tasting like poison in her mouth. "You will be my slave."

The word hit him like a physical blow. The oars went slack in his hands, clattering against the sides of the boat. The rage that had been simmering beneath the surface of his consciousness for days now erupted with volcanic force.

"WHAT?" The roar echoed strangely in the cavern, the sound seeming to be both amplified and muffled by the alien acoustics. "What did you say?"

But Seraphina did not retreat. She could not afford to show weakness now, not when everything depended on his acceptance of this necessary horror.

She watched the male slaves drift past. beautiful, empty things. Property. Gundroff, with his blazing eyes and warrior's pride... they would tear him apart. a cold, sick knot formed in her stomach. There was no other way. "Gundroff," she began, the words tasting like ash. "In this city... You can't be a warrior." He turned, his eyes narrowing. "You have to be... mine. my property. You walk behind me. You don't speak. Ever. It's a mask, Gundroff. Wear it, or we die here. Both of us."

She watched the color drain from his face, watched forty years of dwarven pride and honor crumble in real time. But she pressed on, relentless.

"It is the only way you will survive long enough to be useful."

For a moment, the only sound was the gentle whisper of the impossible water against their hull. Gundroff's breath came in short, sharp gasps, his massive chest heaving as if he'd been running. His hands, which had wielded his axe with such skill and precision, trembled with barely contained fury.

She saw him remember. Saw the phantom pain of old wounds flicker across his scarred features. The massacre of his people. The long, lonely years of exile. The weight of the Berserker's Brand covered every inch of his skin in a tapestry of grief and memory. And now this. the final humiliation, the last shred of his dignity stripped away by the cold logic of necessity.

"You would make me a slave," he said, his voice barely above a whisper. Each word was edged with such pain that it was almost physical. "Me. After everything I have endured, everything I have sacrificed. You would put me in chains."

"I would keep you alive," she shot back, her own composure beginning to crack under the weight of what she was demanding. "Your dwarven pride is a luxury we cannot afford in that city. I have seen what happens to males who forget their place in Nyx'Tolos. They disappear into the fighting pits or the pleasure houses, and they are never seen again."

"And what of your elven arrogance?" Gundroff snarled, his golden eyes blazing with fury. "What of your cold, calculating heart? You speak of necessity, but I hear only cruelty. You would break me to save your precious mission."

"I would preserve you to serve a greater purpose!" The words came out sharper than she'd intended, revealing the raw nerve beneath her clinical exterior. "The world is ending, Gundroff! Forces beyond our comprehension are unraveling the fabric of reality! Your precious honor means nothing if there is no world left to honor!"

The silence that followed was more profound than anything they had experienced on the Silent Sea. It was the silence of two people staring across an unbridgeable chasm, each seeing in the other something they could neither forgive nor forget.

Thaddeus, who had been sitting quietly in the center of the boat throughout their exchange, finally spoke. His voice was soft, thoughtful, carrying none of his usual cheerful levity.

"I knew a man once," he said, his gaze fixed on the approaching lights of Nyx'Tolos. "A proud warrior who was captured in battle and made to serve his enemies. They dressed him in chains and paraded him through their streets. Made him kneel before their altars. For three years, he bore this humiliation, waiting for his moment."

He turned to look at Gundroff, his bright blue eyes holding depths of understanding that seemed far older than his cheerful exterior would suggest.

"When that moment came, when he finally broke free and reclaimed his sword, he did not kill his captors out of rage. He killed them with the cold precision of a man who had never forgotten who he truly was beneath the costume they had forced him to wear."

The old man's words hung in the air between them, neither judgment nor absolution, but something else. a recognition of the terrible burden of survival in an imperfect world.

Gundroff stared at him for a long moment, then back at Seraphina. The fury was still there, burning in his golden eyes like forge fire, but beneath it was something else now. a cold, pragmatic calculation that matched her own.

"A mask," he said finally, his voice rough with suppressed emotion. "Nothing more than a mask."

"A mask you will wear until it becomes your skin," Seraphina replied, her own voice hollow with the weight of what they were doing to each other. "The moment you let that mask slip, the moment you allow your pride to show through, we are all dead."

He nodded once, a sharp, violent motion that spoke of internal warfare and bitter acceptance. "For the mission," he said, the words torn from his throat like pieces of his soul. "For the children who are being unmade while we argue in this accursed place."

"For the mission," she agreed, though the words tasted like ash in her mouth.

As their boat approached the docks of Nyx'Tolos, each of them carried a new wound. not inflicted by any enemy, but by the terrible necessities of survival in a world that demanded they become something less than what they were to serve something greater than themselves.

The transformation had begun, and they all knew that some masks, once worn, could never be entirely removed.

The docks of Nyx'Tolos rose before them like a fever dream carved from living shadow. What had appeared from the distance as merely an unusual city now revealed itself as something far more alien and terrifying. a monument to a philosophy so fundamentally different from anything in the surface world that it seemed to exist in open defiance of natural law.

They ascended through a series of carved stone steps that wound upward along the cavern wall, each step bringing them deeper into a realm that operated by rules that made mockery of everything they had believed about civilization. The city itself was carved from the heart of a single, colossal geode. a natural cathedral of black obsidian that had been hollowed out and shaped over centuries into impossible, soaring architecture.

The spires stretched upward into the cavern's darkness like the grasping fingers of buried giants, impossibly slender towers that should have collapsed under their own weight but somehow maintained their elegant, death defying grace. The obsidian had been polished to mirror brightness, creating a disorienting maze of reflections and shadows that seemed to shift and change with every step.

But it was the lights that truly announced the alien nature of this place.

Thousands upon thousands of crystal lanterns lined the walkways, bridges, and spiraling staircases that connected the various levels of the city. Each lantern contained not flame or oil, but a small, swirling mote of captured soul light. the actual essence of some living being, trapped and compressed into a point of sickly illumination. The lights pulsed with an almost organic rhythm, as if they were still alive, still aware, still screaming their silent anguish into the eternal darkness.

The combined effect was a city illuminated by suffering. a sprawling metropolis lit by the torment of thousands of imprisoned spirits, their eternal screams providing the light by which their captors lived their daily lives.

Seraphina felt the change as soon as they entered the city proper. Her posture straightened, her chin lifted, and her natural elven grace sharpened into something harder, more predatory. The mask of the visiting sorceress settled over her features like a second skin, transforming her from the weary scholar they had traveled with into something else entirely. a creature of power and privilege who looked upon the world around her as nothing more than a collection of resources to be exploited.

Gundroff walked exactly two paces behind her, his massive frame deliberately hunched, his proud dwarven posture crushed into the servile slump of the defeated. His golden eyes, which had always met the world with defiant courage, were now fixed firmly on the polished obsidian beneath his feet. The great axe that had been his constant companion was wrapped in leather and slung across his back like a tool rather than a weapon. Every line of his body spoke of submission, of a spirit broken by years of servitude.

Only Thaddeus seemed unchanged by their surroundings, walking with his usual cheerful, unhurried pace, his bright blue eyes taking in the alien sights around them with the curiosity of a scholar rather than the fear of a visitor to hell.

The citizens of Nyx'Tolos moved through their city with a fluid, predatory grace that spoke of absolute confidence in their dominance. The females. the priestesses, merchants, and nobles. wore robes of black spider silk that seemed to absorb light rather than reflect it. Their movements were economical and precise, each gesture calculated for maximum impact. They were flanked by honor guards of female warriors whose armor was crafted from the chitinous shells of some deep dwelling insect, polished to mirror brightness and articulated with mechanical precision.

And trailing behind them, like shadows given form, were their male slaves.

These were not the crude chattel that Seraphina had described, but something far more disturbing. beautiful, broken ornaments that served as living testaments to their mistresses' wealth and power. They were dressed in fine silks and adorned with jewelry that would have ransomed kingdoms, their bodies pampered and perfected to serve as decorative accessories. But their eyes... their eyes were empty windows into souls that had been systematically hollowed out and refilled with nothing but obedience and despair.

They moved with the mechanical precision of clockwork toys, their every gesture choreographed to provide maximum aesthetic pleasure to their owners. When they spoke, which was rarely, their voices were soft and musical, trained to never rise above a whisper that might disturb their mistresses' thoughts.

As they passed deeper into the city, Seraphina began to play her role with terrifying authenticity. Her voice, when she spoke to inquire about lodging, carried the casual arrogance of someone who had never doubted her command right. Her gestures were imperious, dismissive, and calculated to establish dominance in every interaction.

"You there," she called to a goblin merchant who was arranging a display of phosphorescent fungi. Her tone was not cruel, but it was utterly indifferent. the voice of someone addressing a piece of furniture rather than a living being. "I require directions to the Foreign Quarter."

The goblin, recognizing the authority in her voice, immediately prostrated himself on the polished stone. "Of course, Mistress! Most honored to serve! The Foreign Quarter lies beyond the Spiral Bridge, past the Markets of the Lesser Trades. Follow the purple soul lights. they mark the path for... visitors... such as yourself."

She tossed him a silver coin without looking, already turning away before it hit the ground. The goblin scrambled for it with pathetic gratitude, his eyes never rising to meet hers.

Behind her, Gundroff's jaw clenched with barely controlled fury, but he said nothing. His role demanded silence, and he played it with the bitter precision of a man who understood that his life depended on the performance.

They moved through market squares where the goods for sale defied comprehension. bottled dreams that swirled with opalescent light, weapons forged from crystallized shadow, books bound in what appeared to be living flesh that writhed and pulsed with each turn of the page. The merchants hawked their wares in the musical, hypnotic cadences of the Dark Elf tongue, their voices weaving spells of compulsion and desire that made even the most mundane objects seem precious beyond measure.

But it was in the Artisan's Quarter that the true nature of the city's culture revealed itself most starkly. Here, the greatest creators of the Dark Elf civilization displayed their works. masters of their crafts who had achieved levels of skill that bordered on the miraculous. Their creations were objects of impossible beauty and terrible purpose, artworks that could drive viewers to madness with their perfection or weapons that could kill with a touch.

Yet even these masters, these artisans whose skills rivaled those of the gods themselves, were slaves. Their genius belonged not to them but to their mistresses, and their most significant works were created not for love of the craft but in service to owners who saw their talents as just another form of property to be exploited.

It was here that Seraphina's performance reached its most chilling perfection. She moved through the quarter with the assured confidence of someone who owned not just objects but the souls of those who created them. Her comments on the displayed works were casual and cutting, delivered with the careless cruelty of someone who could destroy a lifetime's work with a few words.

"Adequate," she said of a sculpture that had clearly taken years to complete, her tone suggesting that she found it barely worthy of her notice. "Though the proportions are slightly off. Perhaps with better instruction, the artist might achieve something approaching true skill."

The sculptor, an elderly male whose hands shook with age and exhaustion, bowed deeply at her words, accepting her dismissive critique as if it were a precious gift rather than a casual cruelty.

Gundroff watched this performance with growing horror, seeing in Seraphina's effortless cruelty a reflection of everything he had spent his life fighting against. The woman he had traveled with, argued with, and slowly came to respect was disappearing before his eyes, replaced by something cold and calculating that seemed to take actual pleasure in the suffering of others.

But he said nothing. His role demanded silence, and the weight of their mission hung over him like a sword. Every instinct screamed at him to act, to defend these broken souls, to smash this entire monument to cruelty into rubble. But he was trapped within the costume they had chosen for him, forced to watch and do nothing while the world revealed new depths of horror with every passing moment.

As they made their way toward the Foreign Quarter, each of them carried the weight of what they had become in this place. Seraphina bore the burden of discovering just how easily she could become the thing she had always despised. Gundroff carried the crushing weight of enforced helplessness, of watching suffering he was powerless to prevent. And Thaddeus... Thaddeus walked among the horrors of Nyx'Tolos with the same cheerful curiosity he brought to everything else, as if the systematic brutalization of an entire civilization was just another interesting cultural practice to be observed and catalogued.

The city of soul light had welcomed them into its embrace, and in doing so, had shown them truths about themselves that they would have preferred never to learn.

The Artisan's Concourse was the beating heart of Nyx'Tolos creative soul. a vast, circular plaza of polished obsidian where the city's most skilled artisans displayed their masterworks for the pleasure and approval of their betters. Here, beneath the sickly glow of ten thousand captured spirits, the true genius of Dark Elf civilization was on full display in all its terrible, beautiful glory.

Seraphina moved through the plaza with the fluid grace of a predator surveying her territory, her pale eyes cataloguing the various stalls and workshops with the calculating assessment of someone who saw everything around her as potential property. Behind her, Gundroff followed at the prescribed distance, his massive frame deliberately hunched into the posture of servitude that they had agreed upon.

But even in his degraded state, the dwarf's smith trained eye could not help but appreciate the incredible skill on display around them. These were not mere artisans. they were artists whose abilities bordered on the miraculous, creators who could work miracles in metal, stone, and crystal that would have been the envy of the greatest masters of his own lost civilization.

It was at a small, elegantly appointed stall near the center of the plaza that their carefully maintained masquerade encountered its first actual test.

The jeweler was an elderly male whose hands, despite their tremor of age, moved with the precise, economical motions of someone who had spent a lifetime perfecting his craft. His workspace was a study in organized precision. every tool placed precisely where it needed to be, every surface clean and prepared for the delicate work that was his specialty.

Before him, laid out on a cushion of black velvet, was his latest creation. a necklace of such breathtaking beauty that it seemed to capture and refine the concept of elegance itself. It was constructed from links of silver so fine they appeared to have been spun from moonlight, each one shaped like a delicate leaf and connected to its neighbors with joints so seamless they were invisible to the naked eye. The centerpiece was a pendant carved from a single piece of star sapphire, its surface catching and reflecting the soul light of the lanterns in patterns that seemed to shift and dance with each movement.

Gundroff's breath caught in his throat as he recognized the true scope of the work. This was not merely jewelry. it was a masterpiece that represented months or perhaps years of dedicated effort, each link individually crafted and fitted with a precision that spoke of obsessive attention to detail. It was the kind of work that his own father might have produced at the height of his powers, the sort of creation that proved the divine nature of truly inspired craftsmanship.

Standing before the jeweler's stall was a figure that radiated authority with every fiber of her being. She was tall even by Dark Elf standards, her midnight black skin providing a stark contrast to her silver white hair, which was bound up in an elaborate style that must have taken hours to arrange. Her robes were of the finest spider silk, so dark they seemed to absorb light rather than reflect it, and her jewelry consisted of pieces that would have bankrupted kingdoms in the surface world.

But it was her face that truly marked her as one of the city's elite. It was a study in cruel perfection. beautiful in the way that a blade is gorgeous, with sharp, elegant lines that spoke of centuries of selective breeding designed to produce the perfect predator. Her eyes were the pale violet of poisoned amethyst, and they regarded the world around her with the dispassionate cruelty of someone who had never known what it meant to want for anything.

This was High Priestess Vel'Tar, one of the most powerful figures in the city's hierarchy, and she was currently examining the jeweler's masterpiece with the calculating assessment of someone evaluating livestock.

"Adequate work," she said, her voice carrying the musical cadences of the Dark Elf tongue but lacking any warmth or appreciation. She held the necklace up to the light, turning it this way and that with the casual disregard of someone handling a familiar trinket rather than a priceless work of art.

The jeweler knelt before his workspace, his aged face a mask of hopeful anxiety. "I have labored for three months on this piece, Mistress," he said, his voice barely above a whisper. "Each link was individually forged and fitted. The pendant is carved from a single star sapphire, blessed by the."

"I did not ask for a recitation of your process," the priestess interrupted, her tone dropping several degrees in temperature. "I am capable of assessing quality without instruction from the artisan."

The old jeweler's face went pale, but he merely bowed deeper and fell silent.

For several long minutes, the priestess continued her examination, her violet eyes scanning every inch of the necklace with microscopic attention to detail. The jeweler remained kneeling, his hands clasped before him in an attitude of supplication, while sweat beaded on his weathered forehead despite the cool air of the cavern.

Finally, just as it seemed she might approve the piece, the priestess's expression shifted. A slight frown creased her perfect features, and she held the necklace closer to one of the soul light lanterns.

"There," she said, pointing to a single, microscopic link near the clasp. "A flaw."

The jeweler's eyes went wide with horror. "Mistress, I assure you, the piece is perfect. I have examined every."

"You dare to contradict me?" The priestess's voice had gone deadly quiet, carrying a menace that was far more terrifying than any shout. "You presume to tell me what I can and cannot see?"

"No, Mistress, I would never."

"There is a flaw in the seventh link from the clasp," she continued, her tone taking on the patient cadence of a teacher instructing a particularly slow student. "The curve is infinitesimally off center. The work is imperfect, and imperfection is an insult to my person."

She held the necklace out to him, her pale eyes glittering with something that might have been amusement. "Destroy it."

The word fell into the plaza like a stone into still water, creating ripples of stunned silence that spread outward in all directions. Several other customers and artisans had gathered to watch the exchange, drawn by the drama of a High Priestess conducting business in public.

The jeweler stared at her in complete incomprehension. "Mistress... surely there has been some mistake. The piece is perfect. I have spent three months of my life."

"I am not accustomed to repeating myself," the priestess said, her voice now carrying an edge of genuine menace. "The work is flawed. Destroy it, or I will have my guards destroy your hands, and you will never practice your craft again."

The ultimatum hung in the air like an executioner's axe. The jeweler looked from the priestess to his masterwork, then back again, his face cycling through expressions of disbelief, desperation, and dawning horror.

It was in that moment that Gundroff felt something inside his chest crack like an overstressed beam. He had witnessed many horrors since entering this cursed city, forcing himself to remain silent in the face of countless cruelties and injustices. But this was different. This was not merely the abuse of power. it was the deliberate, calculated destruction of something beautiful for no reason other than the sick pleasure of causing pain.

This was a master craftsman being forced to destroy his own masterpiece, to take the work of months and reduce it to scrap metal with his own hands. It was a violation so profound that it struck at the core of everything Gundroff held sacred.

His carefully maintained posture straightened. His downcast eyes lifted. And for the first time since entering Nyx'Tolos, he met the priestess's gaze directly. not with the servile deference of a broken slave, but with the blazing fury of a master smith who had just witnessed the ultimate blasphemy against his craft.

In his golden eyes was a promise of retribution so pure and terrible that it made the priestess take an involuntary step backward, her mask of cruel amusement faltering for the first time in decades.

The moment stretched between them like a taut wire, pregnant with the possibility of explosive violence. Around the plaza, conversations stopped as dozens of eyes turned to witness this unprecedented breach of social order. a male slave daring to meet the gaze of a High Priestess, daring to show defiance instead of submission.

It was a moment that would shatter everything they had worked to build, a moment that would end their mission before it had truly begun. But in that instant, Gundroff didn't care about missions or greater purposes or the fate of the world. He saw only a master being forced to destroy his masterwork, and every instinct in his being screamed for justice.

The moment hung suspended like a blade over their heads, sharp and terrible and pregnant with violence. The entire Artisan's Concourse had fallen silent, dozens of Dark Elf citizens frozen in place as they witnessed something that did not happen in their ordered world. a male slave meeting the gaze of a High Priestess with naked defiance blazing in his eyes.

High Priestess Vel'Tar's violet eyes widened in shock, then narrowed to poisonous slits. Her hand moved instinctively to the silver whip coiled at her belt, her guards stepping forward with the fluid grace of practiced killers. The air itself seemed to crackle with impending violence as the natural order of their world faced an unprecedented challenge.

It was Seraphina who shattered the deadly tableau.

Her mind, that fortress of cold logic, calculated the rapidly collapsing variables of their situation with desperate speed. She saw the guards' hands moving to their weapons, saw the gathering crowd of Dark Elf citizens whose bloodthirsty anticipation was already turning this into a public spectacle, saw their entire mission disintegrating in the face of Gundroff's momentary lapse into honor.

She had perhaps three seconds before the situation became irretrievably violent. Three seconds to save their lives and their quest, even if it meant damning her soul in the process.

"Beast!" The word exploded from her throat like a whip crack, her voice carrying across the plaza with the authority of absolute command. She spun to face Gundroff, her pale features twisted into a mask of cold, imperious fury that was so perfect it seemed to have been carved from ice.

Her hand shot out, fingers weaving a complex pattern in the air as she spoke a single, sharp word of power in the ancient tongue of chronomancy. It was not a spell of fire or force, but something far more insidious. a minor temporal curse that would achieve exactly what she needed without causing permanent damage.

Gundroff felt the spell strike him like an invisible hammer blow. The air around him seemed to thicken and congeal, turning to something with the consistency of cold honey. His powerful legs, which had carried him across continents and up the sides of mountains, suddenly felt as if they were carved from lead. His sense of balance, that primal confidence that came from a lifetime of sure footing, betrayed him completely.

He tried to maintain his defiant stance, tried to keep his eyes locked on the priestess's face, but his own body rebelled against him. His knees buckled, his massive frame swaying like a tree in a hurricane. He staggered forward, his heavy boots skidding on the polished obsidian, and crashed down onto his knees before Seraphina's feet with a sound like falling stone.

The impact sent shockwaves through his pride that were far more painful than any physical injury. Here, before dozens of witnesses, in the heart of this city of slaves, he knelt like a beaten dog at the feet of his supposed mistress.

"Learn your place," Seraphina hissed, her voice dripping with a contempt so perfect it seemed to have been distilled from pure cruelty. She stepped closer to his kneeling form, her presence looming over him like a pillar of ice. "You forget yourself, animal. Clearly, the lessons of your previous mistress were... inadequate."

She turned to face the High Priestess, her expression shifting seamlessly from fury to apologetic deference. "Forgive my property, Your Grace. It is a new acquisition. barely off the auction block. It has not yet been properly broken to civilized behavior."

The words were delivered with such casual dismissal, such effortless cruelty, that even the Dark Elves in the crowd murmured their appreciation. This was their kind of theater. the public humiliation of the defiant, the reassertion of proper order through the application of superior will.

High Priestess Vel'Tar looked down at the kneeling dwarf, then back at Seraphina, her violet eyes glittering with something that might have been amusement. The moment of danger had passed, transformed from a potential riot into an entertaining display of proper slave management.

"Indeed," she said, her musical voice carrying just a hint of approval. "Though I must say, you show admirable skill in its training. That was a most... educational demonstration."

She gestured dismissively at the still kneeling jeweler, who had watched the entire exchange with the wide eyed terror of someone who had nearly been caught in the crossfire of forces beyond his comprehension.

"Dispose of that flawed trinket," she commanded, already turning away. "And perhaps in future you will remember to check your work more carefully before presenting it to your betters."

With that, she swept away, her guards falling into formation around her, leaving behind only the lingering scent of exotic perfumes and the bitter taste of casual cruelty.

The crowd began to disperse, their entertainment concluded, conversations resuming as if nothing of consequence had occurred. The jeweler, his hands shaking with reaction, began the heartbreaking task of destroying his masterwork, each careful blow of his small hammer a nail in the coffin of his artistic pride.

Seraphina stood motionless for a long moment, her face still locked in that mask of cold authority, watching as the plaza returned to its normal rhythms. Only when she was sure they were no longer the center of attention did she lean down and whisper a single word that released her temporal curse.

Gundroff felt the unnatural weight lift from his limbs, his strength and balance returning in a rush. But the deeper injury, the wound to his pride and dignity, remained as fresh and raw as an open cut. He climbed slowly to his feet, his golden eyes refusing to meet hers, his massive frame radiating a fury so cold it seemed to lower the temperature of the air around him.

"Walk," she commanded, her voice still carrying that note of imperious authority. "Two paces behind. And remember what you are."

As they moved away from the scene of his humiliation, Gundroff followed at the prescribed distance, his jaw clenched so tightly the muscles stood out like cords. Behind them, the sound of the jeweler's hammer continued its mournful rhythm, each blow a reminder of the price of defiance in this city of chains.

Seraphina walked with her spine straight and her chin high, every line of her body radiating the confidence of someone who had just successfully navigated a potentially deadly social crisis. But beneath her composed exterior, her hands trembled slightly with reaction, and her stomach churned with a sickness that had nothing to do with the alien atmosphere of Nyx'Tolos.

She had saved their mission. She had preserved their cover. She had kept them all alive.

And in doing so, she had discovered just how easily she could become the monster she had always claimed to despise.

The sound of that hammer would haunt her dreams for years to come. not because of what it represented, but because of how little it had cost her to make it happen.

Chapter 11

Feast of the Mind

The Foreign Quarter of Nyx'Tolos was a place of quiet, simmering resentment, its discordance a living counterpoint to the pristine, silent spires of the city proper. Here, carved into the lower sections of the incredible geode, was a chaotic jumble of mismatched architecture and sullen inhabitants. The air was thick with the smells of strange, alien spices, acrid alchemical reagents, and the profound, all pervading desperation of those who lived on the sufferance of a cruel and unforgiving society.

Seraphina moved through the narrow, crowded laneway with a slow, deliberate grace, her chin held high, her expression a mask of bored, aristocratic contempt. The role of the mistress had settled upon her like a second skin, a necessary and hateful armor. She passed a knot of goblin merchants, their eyes following her with a blend of avarice and sullen envy. One, a spindly creature with a prominent wart on its nose, spat a series of high pitched, mocking words. Gundroff's shoulders tensed.

"Just an animal, Master," the goblin snarled, its gaze raking over Gundroff's robust frame. "Knows his place, in any case. Good for the pit, I wager."

Gundroff's hand, so close to the haft of his war axe, clenched and unclenched. The desire to reach out, to silence the creature with a single, furious swing, was a physical ache in his arm. But he didn't. He kept his eyes on the ground, the muscles in his neck taut with the strain of submission. The goblin's laughter, a dry, chittering sound, followed them down the lane. Seraphina never glanced back. Gundroff knew she was testing him, and he hated her for it. The mask of the slave was a brand of shame, hotter and more painful than any tattoo.

They passed a pair of Orc mercenaries, their heavy, rust stained plate armor clanking as they shouldered their way through the crowd. One shot a wary glance at Gundroff, but his gaze fell, and he grunted a wordless acknowledgment. He knew the signs of an unbroken soul, even in chains. It was the profound, soul deep misery in the eyes of the few enslaved men who toiled here that felt like a physical blow. Their apathetic stares seemed to say, "Welcome to the gilded cage."

Their destination was a lodging house called 'The Shadow's Respite,' a squat, black stone building that seemed to absorb the already faint light from the soul lanterns. Its proprietor was a Dark Elf woman, ancient and unnervingly still. She sat on a high backed chair carved from pale, petrified wood, her posture ramrod straight. Her face was a web of fine wrinkles, but her eyes, the color of pale amethysts, were sharp and intelligent, missing nothing. She wore robes of black spider silk that seemed to drink the light, and a single, ornate silver pin, shaped like a venomous spider, held the robes together at her throat.

"A room," Seraphina stated, her voice the cold, clear chime of a silver bell in the dusty, quiet standard room. "The finest you have. And a private stable for my... beast." She gestured vaguely in Gundroff's direction without deigning to look at him.

The old Dark Elf's amethyst eyes swiveled from her to Gundroff, a slow, predatory smile touching her thin, bloodless lips. "The Mistress is generous with her titles," she hissed, her voice the dry rustle of old parchment. "He is a fine specimen. Exotic. The priestesses pay well for such... beasts. Especially ones with so much fire in their eyes. The breaking is half the sport."

A low, guttural growl rumbled in Gundroff's chest, a sound he immediately choked back, the effort a physical, painful thing. Seraphina's gaze did not waver. "He is not for sale," she said, her voice dropping a degree, becoming as cold and as hard as the obsidian spires above. "And I will not be questioned by a tavern keeper. The room. Now."

While the words were a shield of pure aristocratic contempt, she felt the phantom sting of her own humiliation. A single, perfect memory surfaced: her father, the Arch Magi, dismissing her most brilliant arcane theory as a "clever parlor trick." She saw his face, not cruel, but indifferent. He had seen her not as a person, but as a potential asset to be managed, a problem to be solved. And in this moment, looking at Gundroff's raw, wounded pride, she realized with a fresh wave of self loathing that she was doing the same. His pain was an inconvenience, a tactical problem to be minimized. She caught her reflection in a polished obsidian wall. the imperious tilt of her chin, the cold set of her eyes. The mask was so convincing that she barely recognized herself. A wave of nausea churned in her stomach. This role was not armor; it was a poison she was forcing herself to drink.

"Of course, Mistress," the Dark Elf purred, the smile never leaving her face. "The Obsidian Suite. The finest in the quarter. It overlooks the alley. But it is private. The price is ten silver."

"Ten silver?" Seraphina's laugh was a short, sharp, and utterly contemptuous sound. "For a damp stone box in a district that smells of goblin spit and despair? You are as amusing as your decor is drab. I will give you three."

The haggling that followed was a masterclass in psychological warfare. Gundroff stood in silent, burning humiliation, his gaze fixed on a crack in the obsidian floor. He felt the old woman's eyes on him, a physical touch that crawled over his skin, appraising him not as a person, but as a piece of livestock. He heard her comments on the rarity of his tattoos, on the potential profit to be made from his sale to a priestess who enjoyed a challenge. He felt the muscles in his jaw clench until they ached, his hand clenching and unclenching at his side, a silent, furious argument with his own rage. He was forced to listen as Seraphina, in turn, used him as a bargaining chip, dismissing him as a "dim witted but loyal animal," his upkeep a constant and tiresome expense. Every word was a fresh whip lash against his soul, another layer of shame piled upon the raw wound of her earlier betrayal.

They settled on five silver and a single, elven travel biscuit, a delicacy in this lightless world. The Dark Elf's eyes gleamed with a greedy light as she took the coin. "A pleasure doing business with you, Mistress," she hissed. "Do let me know if you change your mind about the beast. The Matron of the Third Spire has a particular fondness for... breaking new pets."

They were led to a small, defensible room of damp stone, lit by a single, flickering soul lantern. The moment the door was barred, the fragile, necessary truce between them shattered. Gundroff's silent fury, which had been simmering for days, finally boiled over.

"You shamed me," he said, his voice a low, dangerous rumble, the words ground out from a place of deep, profound pain. "You put me on my knees before them."

"I saved your life," Seraphina retorted, her back to him as she moved to the small, stone table. Her own voice was trembling, not with fear, but with a barely suppressed, self loathing rage. "Your dwarven pride would have had us all flayed in the public square. I did what was necessary."

"Necessary?" he roared, the sound exploding in the small, cramped room. "To break me? To use your tricks to turn me into a puppet?"

"I used my 'tricks' to keep the single most important mission in the history of this world from ending in a pointless, prideful brawl over a broken necklace!" she shot back, spinning to face him, her glacial eyes blazing with a cold, furious light. "You are a hammer, Gundroff. A magnificent, powerful, and utterly unsubtle hammer. And sometimes, the problem is not a nail."

She turned her back on him again, a gesture of finality. She sat at the table, her face illuminated in the eerie, shifting light of the captured soul, and opened the journal. Her hands trembled as she touched the elegant, spidery script. It was filled with a feverish, ecstatic energy. It was not a ledger of plans. It was a book of worship.

"Listen," she said, her voice grim, cutting through the tense, angry silence. Gundroff did not move. His own anger, his own shame, was a vast, roaring fire. But the chilling, prophetic words she began to read were a bucket of ice water on that fire.

The silence that followed the final, terrible verse of the Litany was a physical weight, a suffocating blanket that smothered the air in their small, stone room. The faint, shifting light from the soul lantern cast long, dancing shadows that seemed to mock them with the memory of movement.

Her words were cut short by a sudden, jarring silence. The ever present, low hum of the city, the psychic background noise of a million captured souls, abruptly vanished. It was the silence of a forge going cold, of a heart that has stopped beating. It was a silence that was not empty, but full of a terrible, waiting purpose.

"They are here," she breathed.

Thaddeus had slipped out minutes before their argument, not to escape, but to stretch his legs and enjoy the strange, mundane reality of the lower city. He hummed a jaunty tune, his eyes bright with a simple curiosity that felt out of place in the gloom. He paused to watch a goblin child struggling to carry a basket of shriveled, purple fungi. The child's robes were thin, its knees scabbed and raw. Thaddeus knelt, his movements slow and non threatening.

"A heavy burden for a small one," he said, his voice a warm balm in the sour air. He pulled a wrapped piece of salted pork from his pocket, a ration he'd been saving. "Here. A small gift from a traveler."

The child's eyes, wide and suspicious, flickered to the meat and then to Thaddeus's face. For a moment, a flash of fear crossed them, as if expecting a trap. But Thaddeus's smile was unwavering, his simple goodness a beacon in the spiritual twilight of Nyx'Tolos. The child snatched the pork and scurried away, its disbelief warring with its hunger.

Thaddeus stood, brushing dust from his robes. He didn't see the shimmering, violet aura that had just materialized in the air around him, like a heat mirage on a scorching road. He didn't feel the sudden, psychic tremor that pulsed through the city, the ripple that marked a hungry, predatory consciousness locking onto the single, pure source of light it had found. He just hummed his tune and continued his stroll, oblivious to the hunter that now stalked him.

The wall didn't crumble; it dissolved into a violet mist. Three shapes drifted through. Not walking. Floating. Shapes made of a shadow that ate the light, shot through with a cold, ghostly glow. Where their faces should have been... a nest of pale, writhing things, like blind sea worms. Seraphina's mind recoiled, unable to categorize the sheer wrongness of them.

They had no eyes, no mouths, only a shimmering, violet aura of pure psychic energy that pulsed around them like a malevolent halo.

The first Cephaloid turned its faceless head toward Gundroff, and the world dissolved.

It was not a blow. It was a memory, perfect and pure. The reek of the lodging house vanished. The air tasted of coal smoke and roasting boar. He felt the solid stone of the Great Hall beneath his boots. *Home*. The sound of a thousand hammers echoed in his bones. Audhild's laughter, bright and clear, cut through the din. "Still trying to make a sword that isn't a lopsided paperweight, little brother?" He turned, his heart aching with a joy so pure it was agony. A sound tore from his own throat, a raw, choked sob, and his knees hit the floor. The grief was not the dull, familiar ache of a forty year old scar; it was the fresh, raw, and screaming agony of a new wound.

Seraphina's disciplined mind, while battered, withstood the psychic assault. She felt the intrusive memory wave wash over her. the phantom scent of the sea, the echo of a lullaby her mother had sung to her as a child. but her training allowed her to see it for what it was: psychic chaff, a disorienting tactic, not a killing blow. She erected a hasty mental shield, the arcane equivalent of slamming a door in her mind. But hers was not a simple door. Her mind was a fortress of causality, and she wove her defense from the substance of logic itself. She saw the intrusive memory not as a feeling, but as a thread of cause and effect with a single, crucial flaw. it had no future, no link to the present. She snipped the thread, and the illusion shattered, leaving her gasping and cold, a thin trickle of blood running from her nose from the sheer strain.

The Cephaloids completely ignored them. With a singular, hungry purpose, they drifted back through the breach and were gone.

Seraphina's analytical mind raced. The attack was a diversion. They weren't the targets. A cold, dawning horror washed over her as she realized the truth. They weren't trying to get in. They were covering their escape. And Thaddeus, who had slipped out minutes before their argument began to "stretch his legs," was not with them.

His seemingly simple mind, a beacon of pure, unwavering faith, must have shone like a psychic sun in the dim, faithless twilight of Nyx'Tolos. They hadn't come for the warriors. They had come for the priest.

"They have Thaddeus!" she screamed, her voice a raw, desperate anchor in the sea of Gundroff's grief.

The words cut through his memory fugue like a blacksmith's quench. The violation of his memory and the abduction of his friend fused into a single point of pure, volcanic rage. The argument, the mission, the Litany. all of it vanished. All that remained was the need to save his friend, the only member of his new, bizarre clan who had shown him any measure of simple, uncomplicated kindness.

He let out a roar, a sound of pure, animal fury, and plunged through the still open psychic breach. The journey was a non Euclidean nightmare, a tunnel of shifting, screaming memories that were not his own. He saw the birth of a star and the death of a king, felt the joy of a lover's first kiss and the cold, final despair of a drowning sailor. He burst out into a vast, natural antechamber, a hellscape littered with the hollowed out, dust filled skulls of the Cephaloids' past victims.

And there, in the center of the charnel house, he saw them. The Cephaloids had surrounded their prize. Thaddeus was on his knees, his face a mask of agony, his body convulsing. The largest of the creatures had latched ethereal, shimmering tendrils onto his head, and Gundroff could see the faint, golden light of the old man's faith, the essence of his soul, being siphoned away, a river of light flowing into the creature's shadowy form.

Seraphina emerged behind him, her face pale. "Their feast is the mind, dwarf," she said, her voice trembling slightly. "My mind, which perceives the threads of causality, would be a delicacy for them. I cannot face their psionic attacks directly. You must be the bastion."

Gundroff did not need to be told. He roared and charged, a sound of pure, protective fury. The divine fire of his oath erupted along his axe, a white hot torrent of righteous anger. His first strike connected with one of the lesser Cephaloids. The ethereal flesh sizzled, a silent, psychic scream of agony echoing in his mind. The wound was grievous. But even as he raised his axe for another blow, the creature's shadowy form began to writhe and knit back together, the damage healing with an unnatural, terrifying speed.

The other two Cephaloids turned their full, psychic attention on him. The illusions they used now were not memories; they were weapons forged from his deepest shames.

He saw the face of his father, Borin, his eyes not filled with pride, but with the cold, silent disappointment of a king looking upon a coward. *You let us die.*

He heard Audhild's beautiful laughter twist into a cruel, mocking cackle that echoed the whispers of his own guilt. *You ran, little brother. You hid while we burned.*

He felt the phantom sting of Seraphina's magic forcing him to his knees, heard the jeers of the Dark Elf priestesses, and saw the broken face of the jeweler. *You are a slave. A beast. A thing in chains.*

But the illusions were not perfect. There was a flicker of wrongness in his father's eyes, a discordant note in his sister's laugh. He recognized them as lies, cruel caricatures of his pain. And that recognition was the spark that ignited the actual inferno. The weaponized illusions were not breaking him; they were fueling him. His grief for the past was being forged into a shield for the present.

He let out a roar that was not a war cry, not a sound of pain, but a single, defiant word of absolute denial that shook the stones of the cavern.

"NO!"

The divine fire that exploded from Gundroff's soul was not the clean, white hot flame of a forge; it was a golden, sun bright inferno, the pure, distilled essence of forty years of grief, shame, and righteous hatred made manifest. The heat was so intense it caused the ancient bone dust on the cavern floor to smolder and curl into wisps of grey smoke. He was no longer a bastion. He was a storm. He took a single, thunderous step forward, his eyes blazing with the light of a dying star, the fire of his soul a weapon that the mind eaters had foolishly and fatally stoked.

His first swing was not an attack; it was a judgment. The golden axe clove through the shadowy form of the nearest Cephaloid, and this time, there was no silent, psychic scream. There was a deafening roar of incinerating shadow, a sound of pure negation as the divine fire met the creature of the void. Its ethereal flesh did not just burn; it unraveled, turning to a cascade of shimmering, golden embers that dissolved into nothing before they even hit the ground. The creature did not heal. It was gone, its existence erased from the pattern of the world.

The remaining Cephaloid shrieked, a sound of pure, undiluted terror that echoed not in the air, but directly in Gundroff's mind. It threw another illusion at him, a desperate, final gambit. He saw the great gates of Hjarta-Fell, not as they were, but as they should have been, whole and perfect, swinging open to welcome him home. He saw his father, Borin, standing on the threshold, his arms open in a gesture of paternal pride, his magnificent red beard a banner of welcome.

But the fire in Gundroff's soul was a forge that burned away all lies. He saw the illusion for what it was. a hollow, desperate mockery of his deepest longing, a puppet show of ghosts.

"My home is GONE!" he roared, the words a cleansing fire of their own, a terrible and liberating truth. He swept the golden axe in a vast, horizontal arc, a scythe of pure, holy rage. The illusion shattered like brittle glass, and the axe bit deep into the second Cephaloid's form, annihilating it in another silent, brilliant flash of golden light.

He was a whirlwind of divine destruction, a force of nature that the cold, psychic logic of the Cephaloids could not comprehend. He was not fighting with steel or muscle; he was fighting with a story, the long, terrible, and beautiful story of his people, and it was a story that would not be silenced.

Seraphina watched, her analytical mind struggling to process the raw, terrifying beauty of what she was witnessing. This was not magic as she knew it. It was not a manipulation of time or a bending of physical laws. It was something older, more primal. It was faith made manifest as a weapon. And it was glorious.

But it was not enough. She saw the main Cephaloid, the feeder, its concentration absolute as it continued to drain Thaddeus's psychic fortress. The golden light around the old man was flickering now, a dying candle in a gale. And she saw Gundroff, the divine fire that wreathed him, beginning to dim, his movements a fraction of a second slower. He was burning himself out, a star going supernova. He could not win a war of attrition. They needed to sever the head.

"Gundroff!" she cried out, her voice a sharp crack of insight in the chaos. "The feeder! Break the link!"

He heard her, his head snapping up, his blazing eyes finding hers across the charnel house. He understood instantly. He let out a final, great war cry to Grolnir, a prayer and a curse in one, and charged, not at the feeder, but at the space between, his golden axe a wall of fire that forced the last, terrified Cephaloid to recoil, creating a precious, fleeting opening.

Seraphina did not hesitate. She poured the last of her own desperate, dwindling will into a single, complex spell. It was not a blast of force, but a delicate, surgical strike of pure causality. She thrust her hand out, a single, spidery rune of silver light forming in the air before her. "Anachronos!" she screamed.

A thin, almost invisible beam of silver light shot across the cavern and struck the ethereal, shimmering tendrils connecting the main Cephaloid to Thaddeus. The tendrils did not break. They flickered, momentarily desynced from the present, becoming ghosts of themselves. The connection, for a single, crucial heartbeat, was broken.

At that exact moment, Thaddeus, his psychic shield almost shattered, had a moment of lucidity. The feasting link was severed. He saw the reeling, now vulnerable creature before him. He saw Gundroff, a roaring inferno of divine fire. He saw Seraphina, a pale, trembling figure, blood trickling from her nose from the sheer strain of her spell. He knew he was too weak to survive, his mind ravaged, but he saw his chance, an opening created by the courage of these two strangers.

He gathered the last, flickering embers of his faith. "Fear not the shadow," he gasped, a final, defiant prayer. "For where the shadow is greatest, the light is brightest!"

A brilliant, searing pillar of pure, golden sunlight erupted from his body, a piece of the dawn made manifest in the deepest dark. The stunned, now corporeal Cephaloids, their concentration shattered, their forms destabilized, were caught in the holy radiance. They were incinerated, their shadowy bodies turning to ash and smoke in the brilliant, cleansing light.

The light faded, plunging the cavern back into a sudden, profound silence. The body of Brother Thaddeus, his face serene, fell to the ground, lifeless.

The victory was theirs, bought with Seraphina's intellect, Gundroff's soul, and Thaddeus's sacrifice. They stood in the sudden, echoing quiet, the afterimage of the golden light burned into their vision, over the body of a heroic old man. He was their first faithful ally in a war they were only beginning to comprehend.

The silence that followed was a profound and holy thing, a stark contrast to the psychic screaming that had preceded it. The charnel house was no longer a place of horror; it was a tomb, consecrated by a final, selfless act of faith. Seraphina knelt beside the still form of the cleric, her movements slow and deliberate. Her rational mind, the part of her that was a master of causality and arcane law, was a fortress in chaos, struggling to process a victory that felt so utterly like a defeat. She placed her trembling fingers on his neck, searching for the tell tale thrum of life, a sign of breath at his lips. There was nothing. only the cold, still finality of death.

"He is gone," she confirmed, her voice a quiet, clinical statement that did little to mask the newfound respect in her eyes. The last spark of light, of simple, uncomplicated goodness they had found in this suffocating darkness, had been extinguished. They were alone again, and the shadows felt deeper, more absolute, than before.

Gundroff stood over the body, a deep, familiar ache in his soul. He was no stranger to loss, but the cleric's death felt different. It was not the chaotic, screaming end of a battlefield, but a choice. A weaponized act of faith. He looked at the old man's peaceful face, and for the first time, he saw not a cheerful, infuriating fool, but a warrior who had fought his own kind of war, with his own type of weapon. He had held the line. And he had fallen.

"We cannot leave him here," Gundroff rumbled, his voice thick with a grief that surprised him with its weight. "Not in this place. He deserves the rites."

"We are deep in enemy territory, grievously wounded, and carrying a document that details a plan to unmake the world," Seraphina countered, her pragmatism a cold, necessary shield against the overwhelming sorrow. "We cannot carry a body. It is a tactical impossibility."

She was right. He knew she was right. But the knowledge was a bitter pill. His gaze swept the charnel house, at the hundreds of hollowed skulls, the silent testament to forgotten lives. He would not allow Thaddeus to become another nameless piece of dust in this accursed place.

"Then his deeds will not be forgotten," he declared, the words an oath. He moved to the center of the cavern, his heavy boots crunching on the brittle bone dust. He scanned the rubble, his smith's eye searching for a stone with the right character, the right soul. He chose a single, smooth river stone, a simple, unassuming piece of granite. It was a piece of the earth, a piece of home, and it would serve.

He returned to the body, the stone cool and heavy in his hand. He knelt, the sound of his iron greaves knee on the stone floor a single, sharp crack in the silence. He took out a small, sharp carving knife and closed his eyes. He began to recite the ancient Zemleglas prayer for the honored dead, the Hydra's Lament, his voice a low, resonant chant that seemed to fill the room with the weight of mountains. It was a song of memory, a promise to the stone that it would hold the story of the fallen, that their deeds would become a part of its enduring heart, a memory that would outlast the sun.

He saw in his mind the runes he would carve: the rune of the traveler, for the long road he had walked; the rune of the sun, for the god he had served; and the rune of the shield, for the final, selfless act that had saved them all. His hands were steady, his purpose clear. He was no longer just Gundroff, the last of the Ragingfire. He was a keeper of the dead, a singer of the stone, performing the last, sacred duty of his people.

The cavern was utterly still. Seraphina watched, her own grief a cold, hard knot in her chest. She saw not just a dwarf and a body, but the last flickering ember of a dying world, a final, futile act of honor in the face of an encroaching, nihilistic void. The hope that their victory had rekindled had turned to ash in her mouth. They were alone. They were trapped. And they were going to die here, in this forgotten, lightless tomb. This was the end of their story. This was the edge of despair.

He was about to make the first cut, to commit the cleric's soul to the eternal memory of the stone.

"Oh, don't trouble yourself on my account."

The voice was cheerful, conversational, and directly behind him.

Gundroff's eyes snapped open. The prayer died on his lips. He and Seraphina spun around in a single, fluid motion, weapons instinctively in hand.

There, standing in the archway, looking remarkably and impossibly unharmed, was Thaddeus. He was brushing some bone dust from his simple, brown robes, a pleasant, unfazed expression on his face as if he had just returned from a brief stroll. He looked at their stunned, speechless, and heavily armed faces. He looked at the solemn story stone in Gundroff's hand.

A low chuckle rumbled in Gundroff's chest, a sound of pure, hysterical shock that bordered on a sob. Seraphina stood utterly frozen, her brilliant, logical mind completely short circuited by the sheer, paradoxical absurdity of the situation. Her lips parted, and a single, uncharacteristically faint word escaped. "Impossible..."

Thaddeus's cheerful mask faltered as he took in their expressions. He looked down at his own hands, turning them over as if seeing them for the first time. A flicker of profound confusion clouded his bright, blue eyes.

"You... you were dead," Seraphina finally managed, her voice a raw, strained whisper. "I checked. There was no life. No pulse. No breath. You were gone."

Thaddeus's brow furrowed. He brought a hand to his chest, a look of genuine bewilderment on his face. "Was I? It's... fuzzy. I remember the pain. And then... a light. A great, warm, golden light. It felt like... coming home." His gaze became distant, unfocused, as he struggled to grasp a memory that was like smoke. "But then... There was a pull. A tugging. Like a fishhook in my soul, dragging me back down, back into the cold." He shook his head, a visible shudder running through him. "And then I was... here. My head aches something dreadful. Did I miss supper?"

Gundroff stared for another long second. He looked at the solemn story stone in his hand, then back at the confused, bacon seeking cleric. The tension of the past days. the humiliation, the anger, the battle, the tragic sacrifice, the crushing despair. all of it shattered. A deep, booming laugh that was half madness and half relief shook the stones of the charnel house. It was the first genuine laugh he had uttered in forty years.

He tossed the story stone aside, its clatter a final, absurd note in the impossible scene. He rose to his feet and clapped the bewildered old man on the shoulder, the impact solid and real. "Aye, old man!" he bellowed, his voice filled with a sudden, brilliant mirth. "Bacon sounds magnificent! Let me find you a pan!"

Seraphina did not laugh. She stared at Thaddeus, her analytical mind racing, trying to find a law, a theory, a precedent for what she had just witnessed. There was none. He was not a ghost. He was not an illusion. He was a walking, breathing paradox. a man who had died and returned, with no memory of the journey. The mystery of the world had just deepened, and the most profound enigma of all was the cheerful, befuddled, and impossibly alive old man standing before her.

Chapter 12

Shadow of the Miracle

The victory in the charnel house was a hollow, ringing thing, leaving a silence that was heavier and more profound than the psychic screaming that had preceded it. The aftermath was a somber tableau: a shattered dwarf, a broken mage, and a sorrowful shepherd, standing over the body of a man who was, impossibly, standing beside them. The paradox of Thaddeus's return was a crack in the foundation of their reality, a mystery too vast to contemplate in the immediate, desperate need for escape.

Seraphina's mind, a fortress of causality, sought refuge in the one thing it could control: the mission. The emotional variables were too chaotic. She let her voice, a sharp, precise instrument, cut through Gundroff's relieved bustle. "We are leaving. Now." Her gaze was analytical and cold as she looked at Thaddeus, as if he were a dangerous, unstable artifact she had just acquired.

"Get up," Seraphina hissed, her voice a raw whisper. "The place is compromised. They felt his light... others will have felt it too. We have the Litany. We're leaving. Now. Another minute here and we're dead. For good this time."

The final words were laced with a sharp, unintentional venom born of her own intellectual terror. Gundroff's brief moment of levity vanished, the roaring laughter dying in his throat, replaced by the cold comfort of a familiar purpose. a welcome shield against the chaos of the miracle. He gave a sharp nod. Thaddeus, his own confusion still clouding his features, agreed.

They gathered their meager supplies from the rented room, Seraphina's eyes scanning the cultist's journal one last time. Tucked into a hidden flap in the leather binding, she found it: a small, crudely drawn but meticulously detailed map, not of Nyx'Tolos, but of the tunnel systems beneath it. The map was drawn on a thin, vellum like material that felt unnervingly like flayed skin, and the ink, a deep, rusty brown, seemed to shimmer faintly in the soul light, as if mixed with a trace of blood. A single, winding path was marked with the cult's spiral, a route that led from the Foreign Quarter's waste sluices into a series of ancient, collapsed Mor kin tunnels. It was an escape route.

The journey back through the twisting spires of Nyx'Tolos was a different kind of ordeal. Before, the threat had been the city's cruel, physical laws. Now, it was a silent, psychic pressure.

As they passed a grand archway, a soul lantern burning with a dim violet light suddenly flared, its glow turning a sickly, accusatory green. The captured light seemed to track their movement, following them until they rounded a corner. Seraphina glanced back. It had returned to its dim violet. She felt a cold certainty: the city was watching.

Gundroff walked with his hand resting on the pommel of his axe, a silent, brooding guardian. But his gaze kept flicking to Thaddeus, a mixture of awe, confusion, and a strange, almost superstitious reverence in his eyes. He had witnessed a miracle, a divine intervention that his faith had taught him was possible, but which he had never truly believed he would see. He was walking beside a holy relic, a man who had touched the face of the gods and returned, and he did not know what to make of it. The cold comfort of his forty year certainty was gone, replaced by a terrifying, beautiful question.

Thaddeus himself was a ghost at his own funeral. The cheerful, vacant calm was gone, replaced by a deep, troubled introspection. He would occasionally stop, his brow furrowed, as if trying to grasp a word that was just out of reach, or touch his chest, a look of profound, uncomprehending loss in his eyes. The light he had seen, the pull he had felt. they were not memories, but echoes, phantom limbs of a spiritual experience he could no longer recall. He had been given back his life, but a piece of his soul, a piece of his certainty, had been left behind in the golden light. He was a puzzle to himself, and the cheerful mask he had worn for so long no longer fit.

As they moved through a darkened passage connecting the Scholars' Quarter to the chaos of the Foreign Quarter, Thaddeus stumbled, not from clumsiness, but from a sudden wave of dizziness that seemed to rise from the stone beneath his feet. He swayed, a hand flying to the wall to steady himself. Gundroff, who had been watching him with a hawk's intensity, was at his side in an instant, his massive arm a steadying bulwark.

"Easy, old man," Gundroff rumbled, his voice rough with an uncharacteristic concern.

Thaddeus leaned against the cool obsidian wall, a fine sheen of sweat on his brow. "It is... nothing," he gasped, though his pale face betrayed the lie. "Just a touch of... disorientation."

Seraphina stopped, her analytical gaze sweeping over him. "It is a residual psychic echo," she stated, her voice cold and clinical. "This place is saturated with the city's malevolence. You, after your... experience... are like a freshly rung bell. You are resonating with it." She looked from Thaddeus's shaken form to Gundroff's protective stance, and a new, unsettling variable entered her calculations. The dwarf's reverence for the cleric's "miracle" was a vulnerability, an emotional blind spot that could be exploited. And Thaddeus himself was no longer just a simple cleric; he was a psychic beacon, a walking, talking lure for whatever other horrors lurked in the city's shadows. Their greatest asset had just become their most significant liability.

As they slipped back into the chaotic squalor of the Foreign Quarter, their luck ran out. The low din of the laneway. the high pitched chittering of goblin merchants, the guttural curses of Orc mercenaries, the soft, hopeless whispers of enslaved people. died in an instant. A sudden, profound silence fell over the crowded passage, a silence born not of peace, but of a shared, primal fear. Every head turned down the alleyway.

Blocking their path was a contingent of six Dark Elf warriors, their black chitin armor gleaming like polished insect carapaces in the eerie soul light, their wicked, curved swords drawn and held with a fluid, predatory readiness. At their head was the high priestess from the

Artisan's Concourse, the one who had forced the jeweler to destroy his own masterpiece. Her face was a mask of cold, predatory amusement, her pale amethyst eyes alight with the thrill of a successful hunt.

"My, my," she purred, her voice a silken, venomous thing that coiled around them in the narrow laneway. Her gaze was fixed on Gundroff, a look of proprietary satisfaction in her eyes. "It seems the mistress has lost her pet. A pity. I was so looking forward to our next lesson in obedience." Her gaze flickered to Seraphina, a flicker of contemptuous dismissal in her eyes. "The Matron of the Third Spire was… intrigued… by the psychic disturbance from this quarter. She is always interested in acquiring new and powerful things. She has authorized me to take you all into her custody. You will come with us. Now."

There was no room for negotiation. No possibility of a parley. This was not an arrest; it was a harvest. Seraphina's mind raced, calculating the odds. Six trained warriors, a priestess of considerable power, in a city that was a hostile, living weapon. Their own strength was spent, their magic a guttering candle. The equation had only one brutal solution: annihilation.

The priestess's triumphant sneer was a mask, a fragile and easily shattered thing. She felt a profound, psychic discordance, a dissonant chord that vibrated through the city's labyrinthine conduits of captured souls. It was a silent, insistent alarm, a low hum of a predatory intelligence on the verge of a feast. She felt the sudden, palpable sense of a grand design, a plot to ensnare something of immense and terrible power. The Matron had not authorized a capture; she had authorized a "harvest." And the target was not the pathetic, fire haired dwarf, but the small, silent man with a soul like a sun.

The priestess, a creature of cold calculation, felt a flicker of contemptuous rage. She was a hunter, and they were her prey. This was her city, her rules. But the hunters had been watching. And in the silent, soul filled air of the town, she felt an unseen presence, a predator that was neither of this world nor the next, but of a world in between. The hunt was no longer a sport; it was a war she was not equipped to fight. The hunt was not for them; it was for him. A small, silent, and terribly powerful man who was, in this moment, a beacon in the night. The

Cephaloids had been unleashed. The actual hunt had begun. She was not a part of it. She was in the way of it.

Gundroff did not wait for her calculation. He saw the cold, hard certainty in the priestess's eyes, the hungry way her guards held their blades. He knew this language. It was the language of the blade, the only honest language in the world. He let out a roar, a sound not of defiance, but of pure, pragmatic violence, and charged. But his charge was not a suicidal assault on the priestess. It was a calculated act of chaos. He ignored the warriors and slammed his full, mountain like weight into a nearby stall laden with baskets of grotesque, oversized fungi. He swept his axe in a vast, horizontal arc, a scythe of pure destruction. The stall disintegrated in a shower of splintered wood and crushed, pulpy vegetation. The baskets burst, spewing their contents. a cascade of slimy, phosphorescent, and foul smelling fungi. across the obsidian paving stones. It was a chaotic, vision obscuring, and treacherously slick barricade.

"Run!" he bellowed, the word a command forged in the heart of a hundred desperate battles.

The chase was a desperate, heart pounding flight through the city's labyrinthine underbelly. They plunged into a maze of narrow, twisting alleyways, the priestess's enraged shouts echoing behind them like the cries of a raptor. An arrow, fletched in black spider silk, hissed past Seraphina's ear and shattered against an obsidian wall, leaving a small, spiderweb crack in the polished stone.

They were faster, their movements fueled by a desperate, primal terror. But the guards knew the city. Their booted footsteps were a constant, rhythmic drumbeat behind them, a sound that seemed to come from all directions at once. They were being herded, their path systematically cut off, driven towards the central plaza. It was Thaddeus, in a moment of what seemed to be pure, panicked instinct, who saved them. As they ran past a massive, ornate fountain, its waters a slow, viscous black liquid that seemed to absorb the light, he suddenly stumbled, his foot catching on a loose paving stone. He fell with a loud, theatrical splash into the fountain's basin.

The guards, rounding the corner, saw the commotion and, assuming their quarry was trapped, charged towards the fountain, their discipline momentarily forgotten in their eagerness for the kill. It was the opening they needed. Seraphina and Gundroff, without a backward glance, ducked into a small, unmarked doorway on the far side of the plaza.

They found themselves in the city's waste tunnels, a network of slick, slime coated passages. The stench was overwhelming, a mixture of refuse and alchemical runoff that burned the back of the throat. This was the city's hidden, rotten underbelly, a world away from the cold, pristine beauty of the spires above. The walls, carved from the same black obsidian, were coated in a thick, pulsating layer of phosphorescent slime, casting a faint, sickly green glow on the sluggish, black water that flowed through the central channel. They waited in the suffocating darkness, listening to the enraged shouts from the plaza above fade into the distance. Minutes later, a dripping, mud stained, but miraculously unharmed Thaddeus joined them, a look of profound surprise on his face. "Slippery stones," he muttered, wringing out his beard. "Dreadful hazard."

Seraphina stared at him, her logical mind a fortress under siege. Twice now, a statistically impossible "accident" had saved them from certain death. It was a variable that did not fit her equation of reality, a nagging, insistent paradox that felt more dangerous than any Dark Elf warrior.

They plunged through, the foul water a final, violating baptism, leaving the city of chains and its cruel, beautiful light behind them. The world dissolved from the elegant, seamless architecture of the Dark Elves into something ancient, crude, and filled with a palpable, geological hate. The tunnel was a claustrophobic nightmare, a passage not carved with a craftsman's love for the stone, but hacked with a nihilist's contempt. The walls were sharp edged and dissonant, the angles all subtly wrong, designed to catch the shoulder and trip the foot. This was the work of the Mor kin, the Gray Dwarves, and to Gundroff, it felt like walking through the guts of a beast he had been hunting his entire life.

The air was stale and dead, the silence broken only by the drip of unseen water and the scuttling of things that had long ago forgotten the sun. The faint, borrowed light of Thaddeus's holy symbol, a slight, silver sunburst he held in his palm, cast long, dancing shadows that seemed to writhe and recoil from the hateful, spidery runes carved into the walls. Each symbol was a curse upon the stone, a prayer to a god of dust and endings, and their presence made the air feel thin and cold.

Gundroff ran a hand along the rough hewn wall, the stone cold and dead beneath his touch. Every line was a testament to a philosophy he despised. a belief that the stone was a thing to be broken, not shaped. He felt the phantom echo of his father's hammer, the memory of a song of creation, and the contrast with this place of pure, hateful utility was a fresh wound.

Seraphina, her senses still raw from the psychic energies of Nyx'Tolos, found the tunnels to be a different kind of agony. The runes pulsed with a low, malevolent energy, a background static that was sandpaper on her soul. She walked with her head bowed, her gaze fixed on the uneven floor, trying to shield her mind from the constant, low grade psychic assault.

Thaddeus was a quiet, somber presence. He looked at the hateful runes not with fear, but with a deep, ancient sorrow, as a man might look upon the ruins of a once beautiful garden that weeds had choked. He did not need to read the symbols to understand their meaning. He could feel their intent: the unmaking. the void.

After what felt like an eternity, the oppressive narrowness of the tunnel gave way to a larger chamber, and their path was blocked. A section of the ceiling had collapsed centuries ago, filling the passage with a mountain of rubble and shattered stone. Excellent, wagon sized boulders were piled in a chaotic jumble, their surfaces slick with a fine, damp layer of grime.

"We are trapped," Seraphina breathed, the last of her hope beginning to fray. She slumped against the tunnel wall, the magical and physical exhaustion of the past days finally crashing down upon her.

Gundroff's jaw was a hard, defiant line. He looked at the rockfall not as an ending, but as an insult. "The stone is broken," he growled, his voice a low rumble of defiance. "But it is still stone. I will move it."

He set his shoulder against a massive, house sized boulder, his boots digging into the loose scree for purchase. With a roar of pure, primal effort, he pushed. The muscles in his back and shoulders corded, the intricate tattoos of his Berserker's Brand writhing with the strain. His teeth gritted, a low growl of pure, stubborn will tearing from his throat. The rock did not budge. It was a dead weight, a monument to the futility of his strength. He pushed again, his roar echoing in the dead tunnels, and still, it was like trying to move a mountain.

Seraphina watched him, her mind, even in its exhaustion, racing. She saw the problem not as one of brute force, but of physics, of causality. Her gaze swept the chaotic jumble of rock, her chronomancer's senses tracing the lines of stress, the memory of the collapse. "The keystone," she said, her voice sharp, cutting through Gundroff's grunts of effort. "There. That triangular stone, holding the rest in place. If we can shift it, the rest will follow."

She knelt, placing her trembling hands on the cold, damp stone. She did not have the strength for a grand spell of telekinesis. She had only enough for a whisper. She closed her eyes, her mind reaching out, not to move the stone, but to find the memory of its own weight, the moment of its own falling. She poured the last of her dwindling power into a single, precise act of causality, a gentle nudge against the timeline of the rock itself. A fine, silver light shimmered around her hands, and the air grew cold. She cried out, a sharp gasp of pain, as the effort sent a lance of icy fire up her arms. A trickle of blood, dark in the faint holy light, ran from her nose. The keystone shifted, a single, infinitesimal inch.

It was enough. With a resounding, groaning screech of tortured stone, the rubble began to shift. Gundroff threw his weight against it again, and this time, the great boulder moved, rolling with a thunderous crash that echoed through the dead tunnels, sending up a choking cloud of century old dust. The path was clear. He did not cheer. He stood, his massive frame heaving, his body a testament to the unyielding, stubborn power of the stone itself.

Seraphina collapsed against the tunnel wall, the last of her strength utterly spent. The silver light faded from her hands, and the world plunged into an even deeper darkness, broken only by the faint, holy glow of Thaddeus's symbol. The cost of her magic was a fire in her veins and a coppery taste of blood in her mouth. She had bent the laws of the world, and the world had exacted its price.

The tension in the air was a physical weight, heavier than the Mor kin tunnels themselves. Gundroff, his great frame still heaving from the effort of moving the rockfall, felt a new kind of weariness settle in his bones. It wasn't the honest fatigue of a day's labor, but the soul deep exhaustion of a man who had been pushed beyond his limits. He had faced the ghosts of his past in these tunnels, the silent testament to a philosophy he despised. a belief that the stone was a thing to be broken, not shaped. He ran a hand along the rough hewn wall, the cold and dead stone beneath his touch a fresh wound in his soul, a constant, grating insult to the memory of his father's hammer and the song of creation he carried in his heart.

Seraphina, her face pale with magical exhaustion, slumped against the wall opposite him. A trickle of blood, dark in the faint holy light, ran from her nose, a stark reminder of the price of her desperate act of causality. She watched him, her mind, even in its profound weariness, racing through a new set of variables. The problem was no longer one of brute force or delicate magic; it was one of survival, and their victory felt more like a temporary stay of execution than a genuine escape.

It was Thaddeus, quiet and somber, who broke the silence. He knelt beside Seraphina, taking a clean strip of linen from his pack and, with a gentle, practiced hand, began to wipe the blood from her lip and nose. His touch was a small, quiet act of kindness that felt as out of place in this cold, hateful place as a wildflower blooming in a graveyard. Seraphina flinched at the first touch, her analytical mind recoiling from the emotional variable of a man who would show such unthinking compassion in the face of their impending doom. But the gesture was so simple, so genuine, that she found herself submitting to it, the rigid, defensive walls of her intellect momentarily crumbling.

"I have... questions," she said, her voice a thin, fragile thing. She looked from Thaddeus's peaceful, untroubled face to Gundroff, a silent, brooding monolith standing guard. "The collapse. It was a centuries old event. But my chronomantic senses... they showed me that the moment of its falling had been preserved, like a memory in a stone. A memory that was... being erased. What did you see?"

Gundroff turned, his molten gold eyes now filled with a deep, troubled introspection. "Nothing," he rumbled. "I saw nothing. Only stone. Dead stone, a mountain of it blocking our path. I saw only the insult of it." He looked at her, a challenge in his gaze. "Your magic. Your words. They bent the laws of a world I once knew."

Seraphina shook her head, a cold, dry laugh escaping her lips. "I did not break a law. I merely... reminded the stone of its own history. I gave it a moment of stasis, a heartbeat of memory, long enough for your magnificent, unsubtle hammer to do what it was born to do." She looked at Thaddeus, a flicker of cold, hard light in her eyes. "You, however... You are different. The Cephaloids. Their psychic feast is the mind, not the soul. But they are a part of the Unmaking. They have a new master. A new hunger. What did you see?"

Thaddeus, his hands now resting on his knees, looked up at her, his blue eyes clear and full of a profound, ancient sorrow. "I saw a garden," he said, his voice a quiet, somber thing. "A beautiful garden, full of light and laughter. And then... I saw a hand, a great, cold hand made of shadow, reaching down and plucking a single, beautiful flower. A flower that was... me. It did not crush it. It merely took it. And the laughter in the garden faded, as if it had never been." He looked down at his hands, as if seeing them for the first time, and a look of profound loss crossed his face. "I was a story, my lady. And they took my story." He shook his head, a single, bitter tear running down his cheek and vanishing into the white of his beard. "They left behind a ghost. An echo of a song that can no longer be sung. But they were looking for more. They were looking for the garden's heart. It's true, master. And they came here because they knew it would be found."

Gundroff's jaw clenched. "A garden?" he growled, the word a bitter, contemptuous sneer. "Your soul is a garden? My home was a mountain. A mountain of stone and steel. A mountain that was devoured by fire and hate, and a lie that your people still tell. We are not poets. We are not stories. We are warriors."

"And what good is a warrior without a reason to fight?" Seraphina shot back, her voice now sharp with a cold, desperate passion. She looked at the tattoos on his massive shoulders, a language of ruin and memory that she was only beginning to understand. "Your mountain... it was a story. a saga of creation, of songs and of heroes. And a poet... a poet is a warrior who fights a different kind of war. One that saves the soul, not the body."

Gundroff stared at her, his hands balled into fists, his great chest heaving with a silent, internal war. He saw the cold, hard truth in her words, the truth of his own forty year vigil. a vigil not of vengeance, but of memory. He was a story. A living, breathing, ink stained monument to a world that was dead and gone. And in that moment, he realized with a cold, terrifying clarity, that Thaddeus, the cheerful old man who had died and returned, was an echo of what his people could have been. A different kind of story. And a different sort of ending.

He looked at Seraphina, her face now a mask of exhaustion and despair, and for the first time, he saw her not as an aloof academic but as a warrior in her own right. He saw her mind as a fortress, her words as a hammer, and her magic as a shield that held back not an army, but a terrifying, formless void. He saw a kindred spirit, a fellow survivor. A partner. He saw a cold, beautiful, and startling truth: the war was not just physical. It was spiritual. It was a battle for the nature of existence. And for the first time in forty years, he was not alone in it.

He nodded once, a slow, deliberate gesture of acceptance. "A shield and a hammer," he rumbled, the words a rough, unadorned peace offering. "A poet and a warrior. We are a fellowship of lies. But they are truths we are willing to die for." He turned to Thaddeus, his eyes filled with a new, sober purpose. "What is our next move, poet? Where does this Litany of yours lead us?"

Thaddeus smiled, a faint, sad, but honest smile. "It leads us to the end, my friend," he said softly, his voice full of a sudden, heartbreaking clarity. "The Litany is not a map of salvation. It is a map of a fall. A beautiful, terrible song of a world that is unmaking itself. And it is a song that we, all three of us, have now a part to play in. The sun, my friends. We must find the sun. For where the shadow is greatest, the light is brightest."

They staggered through the newly opened passage, leaving the claustrophobic nightmare of the Mor kin tunnels behind them. They emerged, not into the sunlight they so desperately craved, but into another world entirely. They stood on the threshold of a cavern so vast it felt like a new sky. The ceiling was a distant firmament, lost in a darkness that was pricked by a thousand points of pale, blue green light. vast patches of phosphorescent fungi that clung to the high, vaulted ceiling and walls like constellations in a midnight sky. The air was cool, clean, and smelled of moss and wet stone, a scent so pure after the filth of the sewers and the stale dust of the tunnels that it was like a long, deep drink of water. They stood on a sandy shore, the fine, pale grains of sand cool beneath their worn boots, and before them lay another, smaller arm of the Silent Sea, its black waters still and unmoving. This was the Underworld, not as a passage, but as a place. A world with its own light, its own air, its own deep, unsettling peace. They were free. They were alive. They had the Litany.

The adrenaline of the chase, the tension of their confinement, the sheer, grinding effort of their escape. all of it finally gave way to a profound, bone deep exhaustion. They collapsed on the sandy shore, three broken figures in a beautiful, alien world. Gundroff, moving with the slow, deliberate motions of a man running on fumes, gathered pieces of petrified, phosphorescent wood and built a small, smokeless fire. The cheerful, crackling flames, a defiant star of familiar warmth in the immense, fungal lit gloom, seemed to hold the vast darkness at bay.

For a long time, no one spoke. The silence was not one of anger or mistrust, but of a shared, weary convalescence. Gundroff sat staring into the flames, the firelight casting deep shadows on his scarred, exhausted face. The rage that had sustained him, the humiliation that had burned in him, had been scoured away, leaving only a quiet, grim resolve. He had faced the ghosts of his past in the Mor kin tunnels, and he had survived. He had faced the ultimate shame in Nyx'Tolos, and he had endured. He was no longer just a weapon of vengeance. He was a shield, a protector of this strange, fragile, and impossible fellowship.

Seraphina pulled out the cultist's journal, her hands trembling not from fear, but from the aftershocks of her own spent power. She looked at the first verse of the Litany, then at the crude map of the Underworld. She traced a path from the Mor kin tunnels, a long, winding route through the deep caverns that led, eventually, upwards, towards a remote, forgotten exit into the surface world. She looked up, her gaze meeting Gundroff's across their small, flickering fire. The rift between them, forged in the humiliation of the city, was still there, a raw and unspoken wound. But beneath it, a new, deeper understanding was beginning to form. the quiet, grim respect of two survivors who had walked through hell together. Their victory was not a moment of triumph, but a peaceful, shared moment of survival against impossible odds, a direct result of their combined, desperate actions. She, the master of causality, had been saved by his chaos. He, the master of the direct assault, had been saved by her subtlety. The paradox of their partnership was the only logical truth she had left to cling to.

Thaddeus sat a little apart from them, his back to a large, smooth stone. He was not looking at the fire, but up at the false stars on the cavern ceiling. The shadow of his own death still clung to him, a new and unfamiliar weight behind his eyes. He felt a profound sense of dislocation, a man out of time and place. The cheerful stories, the simple parables. they felt like the memories of another man's life. The golden light he had seen, the fishhook in his soul. it had changed him in ways he did not yet understand.

"Where the sun bleeds on shattered glass, and the old bones sleep," Seraphina whispered, the words a promise and a curse, a new heading on a map that led to the end of the world. "The First Pillar waits."

She pointed to the map, to the long, dark road ahead.

Chapter 13

Decree of the Snake

The Royal Council Chamber of Tetra was a tomb. The air, once vibrant with the scent of beeswax and the lively debate of a kingdom in its prime, was now stale and still, heavy with the dust of a dying dynasty and the metallic tang of fear. The grand tapestries, depicting the glorious founding of the city, seemed to have faded overnight, their once brilliant golds and crimsons now muted, weary shades of brown and rust. They did not celebrate history; they mourned it. The high backed chairs around the great oaken table were filled with the lords of the realm, but they were not councilors; they were statues, carved from a crumbling stone of terror and self preservation.

At the head of the table, in the seat of the Hand of the King, sat Lord Malakai. He did not preside over the assembly; he held it captive. His voice was a soothing balm on the raw nerves of the room, a low, reasonable murmur that was more terrifying than any shout. He was not dressed in armor, but in the fine, dark silks of a scholar, his hands resting gently on the polished oak, his handsome face a mask of somber, reluctant duty. He was not a conqueror. He was the city's last, best hope. And every man in that room knew it was a lie.

The chair to the King's right, the grand, iron shod seat of the Head of the Council, sat conspicuously empty. Lady Vess had not been seen in three days. There had been no official inquiry. No one dared to ask. Her absence was a silent, screaming testament to the new order.

"The kingdom bleeds," Malakai said, his voice resonating with a perfectly pitched note of sorrow. "Our King, our lion, hangs by a thread, the victim of a cowardly and insidious arcane poison. The people in the streets are frightened. They see the rot on the stones, the blight on the grain, and they look to this hall for a steady hand. They look for a shield. And what do they find? A fractured council. A vacant throne. An imprisoned prince whose misguided ambitions have left us rudderless in a hurricane."

He let the words hang in the air, a perfect, poisoned tapestry of fear and reason. He looked around the table, his gaze lingering on each lord in a silent, personal communion. He saw Lord Harlen, the Master of Coin, a portly man whose face was slick with a nervous sweat, his fingers constantly, rhythmically, drumming on the table. He saw Lord Titus, the Master of Law, a man whose spine seemed to have dissolved, his gaze fixed on a knot in the wood grain as if it held the answer to a prayer he was too afraid to utter.

"And so," Malakai continued, his voice taking on a tone of heavy, theatrical reluctance, "for the stability of the realm, I propose the Regent's Mandate. An emergency act to grant a single, steady hand the temporary, but absolute, authority to guide our great city through this storm. Not for power. Not for glory. But for the simple, necessary preservation of the light."

A murmur of assent, a sound of dry leaves skittering over stone, rippled through the room. Lord Harlen nodded vigorously, his jowls trembling. Lord Titus seemed to shrink even further into his chair. The vote was a foregone conclusion. The city was falling, and Malakai was the only one offering a hand to catch it.

"I object."

The words were quiet, but they cut through the suffocating atmosphere like a shard of glass. Every head turned. In a shadowed corner of the room, a figure rose. It was Lord Theron Greywood, a man as old and as unyielding as the grey granite of his northern fiefdom. His hair was a mane of stark white, his face a roadmap of wrinkles, but his eyes, a pale, piercing blue, held a fire that had not yet been quenched. He was the last of the old guard, the final, stubborn friend of a dying king and a vanished Lady Vess.

"You speak of stability, Lord Malakai," Greywood said, his voice a low, gravelly rumble that was accustomed to commanding men on windswept battlements, not whispering in council chambers. "But the law of this land is clear. In the absence of the King, authority passes to his heir. Prince Alexander, whatever his alleged crimes, is that heir. To grant you this... Mandate... is to break a thousand years of established law. It is to spit on the graves of every king who has sat upon the throne."

Malakai's charming, sorrowful mask did not slip. He turned his full attention to the old lord, his expression one of profound paternal pity. "Ah, Lord Greywood," he sighed. "Your loyalty is a thing of legend. a beautiful, honorable, and tragically outdated relic of a simpler age. You speak of laws written for a world that no longer exists. We are not facing a simple succession crisis. We are facing an arcane plague, an enemy that does not respect our traditions or our laws."

He took a half step towards the old man, his voice dropping to a conspiratorial, almost friendly tone. Malakai leaned forward, his voice a friendly whisper. "Your son is still on the northern border, isn't he? A dangerous posting. So many wildling raids this season. It would be a shame if his next request for supplies got... lost in the paperwork. These things happen during times of political change."

The threat was a stiletto, slipped between the ribs with a surgeon's precision. Lord Greywood's face went white, the fire in his eyes flickering for a moment. But he did not waver. "My son knows his duty," he said, his voice hoarse. "As do I."

Malakai's sad smile widened. "As you wish." He turned back to the council, a single, rolled parchment appearing in his hand as if from nowhere. "I had hoped not to have to reveal this. I had hoped to spare this council and the good name of Lord Greywood this final shame. But his stubbornness forces my hand."

He unrolled the parchment. The silence in the room was now absolute. "This," he said, his voice a somber pronouncement, "is the full and signed confession of the mage apprehended in the Grand Hall, a wretch by the name of Elara. It was procured... before her timely demise." He began to read, his voice a clear, cold bell of judgment.

"I acted not alone, but as part of a wider conspiracy to destabilize the throne. Our patrons, who believe the King's rule has grown weak and his bloodline decadent, promised us a new age of arcane prominence.

Their names are known to me. They are Lady Elara Vess… and her most trusted confidant, Lord Theron Greywood."

A collective gasp went through the room. Lord Greywood stumbled back as if struck, his hand flying to his chest, his face a mask of horrified disbelief. "Lies," he choked. "This is… a monstrous lie."

"Is it?" Malakai asked softly, rolling up the parchment. "The seal of the Royal Inquisitor is upon it. The confession is law." He looked at the other lords, his eyes filled with a shared, terrible sorrow. "You see the depth of the rot? It is not just at our gates. It is in this room."

He did not need to call for a vote. Lord Harlen was already on his feet, his face a blotchy purple. "The Mandate!" he cried. "We must approve the Mandate! For the safety of the realm!"

One by one, the other lords rose, their voices a chorus of panicked, desperate assent. Lord Titus, the Master of Law, was the last to stand, his movements slow and pained, as if he were lifting the weight of his own broken soul. The vote was unanimous. The coup was complete.

Malakai did not smile. He inclined his head in a gesture of profound, sorrowful acceptance. He walked to the center of the room, his movements slow and deliberate, the weight of his new, terrible burden visible in the slump of his shoulders.

"My lords," he began, his voice thick with a perfectly feigned emotion. "I did not seek this office. I did not wish for this power. But I will not shirk the duty you have placed upon me." He raised his head, and his eyes, which had been filled with sorrow, now burned with a new, righteous fire.

"The age of weakness is over! The age of whispers and shadows is at an end! For too long, we have allowed the cancer of unregulated magic to fester in the heart of our kingdom. This… Mage Plague… this temporal rot that eats at our stones… it is a sickness born of arcane hubris. And I will be the surgeon that cuts it out!"

He paused, letting the power of his words settle. "From this day forward, a new order begins. The City Watch will be reformed, expanded, and given the authority to act without the shackles of bureaucratic delay. They will be my Serpent's Hounds, and they will hunt the shadows in every corner of this city. Furthermore, I hereby enact the Mage Purity Act. All practitioners of the arcane arts will be required to register with the Crown, to submit their grimoires for review, and to swear an oath of absolute loyalty to the throne. Those who refuse," he said, his voice dropping to a chilling whisper, "will be considered enemies of the state. There will be order. There will be security. There will be peace."

He stood before them, a perfect, beautiful lie, the reluctant savior, the strong hand in the storm. And as the lords of the realm, their faces a mixture of fear and adulation, began to applaud, a single, cold, and triumphant thought formed in the silent, calculating core of his soul: *The board is cleared. The game is mine.*

The applause from the council chamber had faded, but its ghost still echoed in Lord Malakai's mind, a sweet and satisfying music. He stood alone in his private study, the heavy oak door barred against a world he now commanded. The room was his sanctuary, a testament to his ambition, a place of dark, polished wood, priceless artifacts liberated from forgotten tombs, and the faint, lingering scent of expensive Arbor Red. The political victory was a fine vintage, and he intended to savor it.

He moved to the grand, carta stone fireplace, its flames casting long, dancing shadows that writhed and coiled like the serpents on his signet ring. He poured himself a goblet of wine, the deep crimson liquid a perfect mirror to the blood that had been, and would be, spilled to secure his new order. The city of Tetra was a complex and beautiful machine, and he, at last, held all the levers. The Serpent's Hounds were already purging the town of arcane dissidents, the Mage Purity Act was law, and the Prince was a caged lion, his roars unheard beyond the stone walls of his tower. It was a perfect, elegant victory.

And yet, a single, irritating variable remained: the dwarf, the elf, and the strange, old man. Fugitives who carried a knowledge that was… inconvenient. He swirled the wine in his goblet, watching the firelight play across its surface. What he felt was a cold, pure, and intellectual fury, the frustration of a master craftsman who discovers a flaw not in his work, but in the material he has been forced to use. The world was proving to be an imprecise and unruly medium for his ambition.

He set the goblet down and turned to face a specific, unadorned section of his library's shelves. He ran a hand over the spines of the leather bound books, his touch light and practiced. "The nightshade wilts," he said, his voice a low, calm command spoken to the empty air.

It was the password, the key to a hidden mechanism. He expected to hear the soft, grinding sound of a concealed passage opening.

He heard nothing but the crackle of the fire.

A flicker of irritation crossed his face. "Did you hear me?" he asked, his voice sharper. "The nightshade wilts."

"Very wilted, milord," a reedy voice squeaked from the shadows behind his chair. "All brown and crispy at the edges. Not good for eating, I shouldn't think."

Malakai did not startle. To do so would be to admit a flaw in his own security. But a cold, sharp spike of adrenaline pierced the warm haze of the wine in his veins. He turned slowly, his face a mask of bored, aristocratic calm. She was already there. She had been there the entire time, a silent, unseen witness to his private victory celebration.

A goblin emerged from the shadows with a strange, disjointed gait, a series of short, scuttling steps followed by a long, lurching one, as if she were constantly unsure of the ground beneath her feet. She was small, even for a goblin, her form lost in a heavy, black cloak that seemed to absorb the firelight. Her face, a pale, greenish grey, was dominated by two enormous, unnervingly expressive ears that were so long they nearly brushed her shoulders. They twitched and swiveled independently of each other, one cocked towards the door, the other towards the crackling fire, as if listening to two different conversations in two different worlds. A shock of messy, jet black hair fell across her brow, partially obscuring two large, luminous, and deeply unsettling purple eyes. Those eyes were the central paradox of her being. They were the eyes of a skittish, terrified creature, wide and constantly darting, but within their depths was a sharp, focused, and terrifying intelligence. She clutched a small, wickedly sharp dagger in one hand, which she was polishing with a scrap of oilcloth with a relentless, obsessive focus, her movements jerky and bird like. A second dagger was strapped to her thigh, and a small, elegantly crafted crossbow was slung across her back. She did not look at him, but at a point on the floor just to the left of his boots, her head tilted at an odd, inquisitive angle.

"You enjoy giving me heart seizures, Ankle Shanker," Malakai said, his voice a silken purr that did little to mask the cold edge of his displeasure.

"Seizing hearts is not in my contract, milord," she chirped, her voice a high, reedy thing that was at odds with the darkness of her attire. "That's extra. messy. Lots of paperwork." She finished polishing a small section of her dagger and held it up to the firelight, admiring her work with a quiet, self satisfied hiss.

"Your report," Malakai said, his patience already wearing thin.

"Right. The report," she said, her purple eyes finally flicking up to meet his for a fraction of a second before darting away again. "Nyx'Tolos. dark. pointy. Lots of spiders. Not the fun, bitey kind. The big, quiet, judgy kind. The moss in the tunnels tastes terrible, milord. bitter. Not like the good moss near the goblin warrens. That has a nice, nutty flavor. Good with a bit of salt."

Malakai took a slow, deliberate sip of his wine. He was long accustomed to her ways. She was a chaotic, infuriating, and utterly brilliant instrument. One did not command Ankle Shanker; one aimed her and waited for the results. "The fugitives, Ankle Shanker," he said, his voice a low, patient thrum.

"Oh, them. Yes. loud. Not good at sneaking at all," she said, resuming her frantic polishing. "The big one, the dwarf, he smells of old iron and sad memories. He had to pretend to be a slave. He was not good at it. His pride is a boisterous thing, milord. Clangs like a dropped pot. The pointy eared one, the lady mage, is clever. All thoughts and angles. She bought a book. A nasty looking thing. Bound in some skin. Not goblin skin. Too smooth."

She paused, her long ears twitching. "Then the mind squids came."

Malakai's grip on his wine goblet tightened almost imperceptibly. "The Cephaloids," he corrected.

"Squids," Ankle Shanker insisted, her voice taking on a stubborn, childish tone. "They came for the old man. The one who smells of fresh bread and sunlight. strange smell in that place. They sucked his brain thoughts right out. rude. Didn't even ask first."

"And the fugitives?" Malakai pressed, his voice sharp.

"Fought them. The big one got shiny and shouted a lot. The lady mage wiggled her fingers. flashy. The mind squids did not like the shouting. It gave them a tummy ache in their brain parts." She stopped polishing, her purple eyes going wide with a look of genuine, theatrical surprise. "And then the old man exploded. A big, bright, shiny boom. All gold and warm. Burned the squids to little black crunchy bits."

Malakai stared at her. "Exploded?"

"Pop," she said, making a small, sharp gesture with her free hand. "He was dead. dead. The mind squids ate his brain thoughts, and then he went pop. All gone." She tilted her head, a look of profound, academic curiosity on her face. "Then he got up."

The silence in the room was suddenly as heavy and as cold as a tombstone. Malakai's calm, aristocratic mask did not slip, but a small, almost invisible muscle in his jaw began to twitch. "He... got up," he repeated, his voice a low, flat thing.

"Mmm hmm," Ankle Shanker confirmed, now picking at a loose thread on her cloak. "Brushed the dust off. Said his head ached. Most unusual. Messy. Breaks all the rules. Being dead is supposed to be a permanent sort of thing. That's the point, isn't it?"

This was the variable. The impossible, terrifying variable that his cold, perfect logic could not account for. The Litany was a problem, but it was a known quantity. A man who could die and get back up... that was a wild card that could unravel his entire, meticulously crafted plan.

"They escaped into the old Mor kin tunnels," she continued, oblivious to the storm that was gathering behind his eyes. "Have a map. a nasty, skin map. Heading for the surface, I should think. The big one is strong, the lady mage is clever, and the old man is... a conundrum. The rules don't stick to him right."

Malakai walked to his desk and opened a small, ornate box. He took out a single soul gem, a perfect, swirling vortex of captured, violet energy the size of a pigeon's egg. He tossed it to her.

Ankle Shanker's hand shot out with a speed that was a blur, snatching the gem from the air an inch from her face. She held it up to the firelight, her purple eyes gleaming with a greedy, possessive light. She giggled, a high, chittering sound, and then fumbled it, juggling it clumsily between her hands before finally securing it in a hidden pocket of her cloak.

"The next time you see them, Ankle Shanker," Malakai said, his voice a quiet, terrifying threat, "do not lose them. I would hate to have to find a replacement."

Ankle Shanker gave a clumsy, awkward bow, her long ears flopping. "Of course, milord. Sticking to them will be as easy as a dagger in the dark."

He turned his back on her, a gesture of dismissal. When he looked up at the reflection in the dark, polished wood of his desk a moment later, she was gone. There had been no sound, no whisper of movement. She had vanished back into the shadows from which she had been born, leaving him alone with nothing but his thoughts.

The silence that Ankle Shanker left in her wake was a profound and unsettling thing. Malakai stood alone, the firelight casting long, dancing shadows that now seemed less like serpents and more like grasping, skeletal fingers. He picked up his wine goblet, but the rich Arbor Red now tasted of ash. His perfect, elegant victory now felt fragile, tainted by the grit of an unforeseen and unacceptable variable.

He began to pace, his soft, leather boots making no sound on the thick carpet. His mind, a cold and beautiful engine of logic, began to dismantle the problem. The Serpent's Hounds were a magnificent instrument of terror, but they were hounds, fit for running down deer. They were not wolves, fit for hunting in an authentic and savage wilderness. Against a warrior dwarf of Gundroff's caliber, a chronomancer as gifted as Seraphina, and this... this paradox who could simply refuse to stay dead... his hounds were a fool's gambit. They were a political tool, and this was no longer a political problem.

His pacing stopped. His gaze fell upon a heavy, iron bound chest that sat in the darkest corner of the room, a squat, ugly thing that was a stark contrast to the elegant taste of the rest of his decor. It was a relic from a past he had tried to bury, a tool he had hoped he would never have to use again. To do so was an admission of a different kind of failure, a concession that the clean, elegant game of politics was insufficient. It was a blow to his pride. He was Lord Regent of Tetra, and he was being forced to subcontract his will to a monster.

With a sigh that was a quiet hiss of pure frustration, he crossed the room. The chest was not locked with a key, but with a series of complex, interlocking warding runes that glowed with a faint, sickly light as his hand approached. He spoke a single, guttural word in a language that had not been heard in Tetra for a thousand years, a word that felt foul and clumsy in his aristocratic mouth. The runes flared with a silent, violet light, and then died. With a deep, groaning sound of protesting iron, the heavy lid swung open.

The air in the room grew instantly, unnaturally cold. The cheerful crackle of the fire in the hearth faltered, the flames shrinking and turning a pale, sickly blue.

Inside the chest, resting on a bed of what looked like blackened, brittle silk, was a heart. It was the desiccated, mummified heart of a Mor kin commander, the size of a man's skull, its surface a network of cracked, leathery flesh, covered in faint, hateful runes that seemed to pulse with a slow, malevolent light. It was not just a dead organ; it was a profane communication device, a dark and terrible link to a power that had no place in the world of men.

Malakai produced a small, silver pin from a hidden pocket in his robes. With a steady hand, he pricked the tip of his thumb. A single, perfect drop of his own crimson blood welled up. He held his hand over his heart.

"Blood of the living for the ear of the dead," he whispered, the words of the ancient, hateful ritual a sour taste in his mouth.

The blood level dropped. It sizzled, a tiny, angry star of vibrant red against the dead black of the heart. For a moment, nothing happened. Then, with a dry, rustling sound, the heart began to beat.

Thump thump.

It was a slow, dry, rhythmic thudding, the sound of a clod of dirt being dropped on a coffin lid. With each beat, the runes on its surface glowed with a brighter, more insistent violet light. The wine in his goblet, forgotten on the mantelpiece, began to form a thin, spiderweb tracery of frost.

Malakai leaned closer, his face a mask of cold, focused intent. He did not speak with his voice. He spoke with his will. *The fugitives have proven… resilient,* he thought, projecting the words into the cold, dead silence. *They carry knowledge that is an inconvenience to the Master's plan. A paradox guides them. The hounds are not enough.*

The heart's beating faltered for a moment, as if it were listening. Then it resumed, faster this time, a frantic, hungry rhythm.

The north must be sealed, Malakai commanded, his will a blade of pure, cold steel. *They must not reach the mountain. Send your best. Send the one who laughs.*

The name, even unspoken, was a violation, a summoning of a power that the world had rightly tried to forget. The heart convulsed, a violent, spastic shudder that sent a wave of absolute cold washing through the room. The fire in the hearth was extinguished in a sudden, hissing gasp, plunging the study into a deep, oppressive twilight, lit only by the hateful, violet glow of the runes. And then, he felt it. A psychic connection, a brief, terrifying glimpse into another mind. It was not a thought. It was a feeling of a vast, lightless world of stone and silence. A sense of an ancient, patient malice that had been sleeping for an immeasurably long time. And beneath it all, a single, pure, and utterly terrifying emotion: amusement. He felt the phantom echo of a dry, chittering laugh, a sound not in his ears, but in the deepest, most secret corners of his own soul. The connection lasted for a single, heart stopping second, and then it was gone.

The heart's beating returned to its slow, steady rhythm. The contract was made. The answer was given.

Malakai closed the heavy lid of the chest. The cold in the room slowly receded, and the fire in the hearth, with a soft whoosh, reignited itself. But the room did not feel the same. It was colder, fouler, tainted by the brief, terrible communion. Malakai himself felt drained, a subtle, spiritual exhaustion that the wine could not touch. He had rung a bell that could not be unrung.

He walked to the grand map of the northern territories that was mounted on the far wall. From a small, hidden drawer in his desk, he took a single, black stone marker. It was a piece of polished obsidian, cold and smooth to the touch, carved into the shape of a leering, laughing skull.

With a slow, deliberate movement, he placed the marker on the map. He did not put it on a road or in a city. He placed it in the heart of the wilderness, in the rugged, unforgiving expanse of the Ashen Peaks.

The public bounty was a smokescreen. The Serpent's Hounds were a diversion.

The actual hunt had just begun.

Chapter 14

The Sunken Locket

The darkness had become a companion. For days, it had been their world, a press of ancient stone and the scent of damp, mineral rich earth. The cultist's map, a thing of stolen parchment and maddeningly precise ink, had led them through the labyrinthine guts of the world, down passages that twisted like the entrails of a dead god. Seraphina had lost all sense of time, the rhythm of her life reduced to the scrape of her boots on stone, the rhythmic drip of water from unseen stalactites, and the low, steady breathing of her companions. The Underworld was a place of alien beauty. caverns vast enough to hold cities, forests of phosphorescent fungi that cast an eerie, blue green glow on their faces, and silent, black rivers that flowed into nothingness. But its beauty was that of a tomb, and its silence was a weight upon the soul.

Kael moved ahead of her, his broad shoulders a dark shape against the faint luminescence. Thaddeus followed, his staff tapping a steady, reassuring beat that was as much for their morale as it was for his footing. They were a small, self contained world of three, moving through a land that had never known the sun.

The change began subtly. A shift in the air, a thinning of the dampness that had clung to their clothes and hair for so long. Then, a new sound: a faint, high pitched whisper that was not the wind of the caverns, but something else entirely. The passage began to narrow, forcing them into a single file. The glow of the fungi faded behind them, plunging them into an authentic and total blackness, a void broken only by the pinprick of light from the crystal set in the pommel of Kael's sword.

Then, ahead, another light appeared.

It was not the gentle, spectral glow of the underworld. This was a sliver of pure, unforgiving white, so intense it seemed to cut a wound in the darkness. With every step, the wound grew larger, the whispering sound rising to a mournful hiss. The air grew warm, then hot, a dry, baking heat that felt utterly foreign.

"Gods," Kael muttered, his voice rough. He raised a hand to shield his eyes.

The end of the passage was a ragged mouth of rock. One by one, they stepped through it, and the world dissolved into a conflagration of light.

Seraphina stumbled out, her cry a choked gasp. The light was a physical assault, a firestorm that bleached all color from her vision and stabbed at her pupils with a million white hot needles. Her eyes streamed, squeezed shut against the pain, but the glare still burned through her eyelids in a searing red orange. The heat was worse. It was a solid wall, a furnace blast that stole the air from her lungs and cracked her lips in an instant. She felt the moisture evaporating from her skin, a sudden, shocking dryness that made her feel fragile, like old parchment.

She staggered back a step, colliding with Thaddeus, who steadied her with a firm hand on her shoulder. "Easy, lass. Give your eyes a moment."

Slowly, painfully, she forced her eyelids open, squinting through a watery blur. The world swam back into focus, not as a landscape, but as an impossibility.

They stood on a precipice of jagged black stone overlooking a realm of torment. Below them stretched not sand, but a boundless, glittering plain of shattered obsidian. It was a desert of black glass, a frozen sea of razor edges that caught the merciless sun and fractured it into a billion blinding sparks. The air above it shimmered, a visible curtain of heat that warped the horizon into a wavering, liquid line. It was a world seen through a fever dream.

And the bones.

Colossal, fossilized skeletons rose from the glass dunes like the ruins of a forgotten civilization. The rib cage of some impossible leviathan, each bone the size of an ancient oak, formed a line of bleached, curving arches that disappeared into the hazy distance. Further on, the skull of another beast lay half buried, its empty eye socket a cavernous shadow large enough to swallow their party whole. Vertebrae as large as carriages lay scattered like fallen monoliths. This was not a desert; it was a graveyard, a testament to a war fought between gods and monsters on a scale her mind could barely comprehend.

The silence was absolute, profound. The whispering she'd heard in the tunnel was the wind, a tireless, abrasive thing that scoured the glass desert, carrying with it no scent of life, no hint of moisture. only a dry, ancient dust that tasted of ash and time.

"The Ashen Desert," Thaddeus said, his voice a low rumble beside her. There was no wonder in his tone, only a deep, weary reverence. "The Sun God's anvil."

Kael let out a low whistle, his usual bravado stripped away by the sheer, brutal majesty of the place. He drew the back of his hand across his brow, already slick with sweat. "So the maps were true."

Seraphina could only nod, her throat too dry for words. As a scholar, her mind raced, trying to categorize, to understand. Volcanic cataclysm? An ocean of lava that had cooled into obsidian and been shattered over millennia? But her intellect offered no comfort here. The raw, untamable hostility of the landscape defied analysis. It was not a place to be studied; it was a place to be survived.

She looked from the impossible vista to the cultist's map in her hands. Its lines and symbols had seemed like the ravings of a madman in the relative safety of the Citadel's libraries. Here, under the crushing weight of the sun and surrounded by the bones of dead titans, it felt like a prophecy. A prophecy that had led them to the edge of the world.

She took a breath, and the superheated air burned all the way down to her lungs. This desert was alive. It was not a passive landscape, but an active, malevolent entity. Every shard of glass, every shimmering wave of heat, every grain of ashen dust felt like a part of a being that hated them, that wanted to peel the flesh from their bones and scour them into nothingness.

They traveled for a day, and the world became a graveyard. The initial shock of the desert's blinding light gave way to a grueling, soul crushing monotony. The sun was not a source of life; it was a physical antagonist, an anvil of white hot fury that hung in a vast, empty bowl of searing blue. The heat was a physical weight, a constant, oppressive force that stole the breath and baked the will. There was no shade. There was no respite. There was only the crunch of their boots on the black, razor sharp obsidian glass and the soft, maddening whisper of the wind over the endless, sun bleached sand.

Seraphina's tongue felt thick and dry, a piece of old leather in her mouth. She tried to swallow, but there was nothing to swallow. Every logical part of her mind screamed that this desert was an impossibility, a geological paradox. But logic couldn't conjure water. Her body didn't care about paradoxes; it was simply, brutally, shutting down. She felt the moisture being wicked from her skin, the sun a vampire that drank her life force with every passing hour.

Gundroff, in contrast, seemed to draw a grim strength from the desolation. He moved with a slow, steady, and uncomplaining rhythm, his dwarven resilience a testament to a people forged in the heart of the stone. He did not speak of the heat. He did not talk about the thirst. He endured, a walking mountain of scarred muscle and unyielding will.

It was on the second day that the scale of the graveyard revealed itself. They came upon it without warning, cresting a high, shimmering dune. Before them, half buried in the black and white sand, was a rib cage. It was a cathedral of bone, each rib a gracefully curving arch of bleached white fossil, taller than the Royal Spire in Tetra. They walked through the gaps between the ribs, three small, impossibly fragile figures in the shadow of a creature that had died before their races had learned to write their own names.

"By my father's forge," Gundroff breathed, his voice a low rumble of pure, unadulterated awe. He ran a hand over the surface of one of the ribs. The bone was smooth and cool to the touch, a strange, welcome relief from the searing heat of the sand. "The strength of this... the engineering... to hold a beast of this size..." He was not seeing a skeleton; he was seeing a miracle of structural integrity, a piece of the world's forgotten architecture.

Seraphina's mind reeled. She tried to apply her knowledge to categorize the creature and calculate its age. But the scale was too vast, the implications too profound. This was not a creature from any known bestiary. This was a piece of a forgotten, mythic age, a fossilized testament to a world that had once been grander, more terrible, and more alive than her own.

Thaddeus was not awed in the same way. He stood in the center of the bone cathedral, his head bowed, his expression one of quiet, somber reverence. He reached out and placed a hand on the same rib as Gundroff, but his touch was not one of appraisal. It was a gesture of communion, of mourning.

"You stand in a place of great sorrow," he said softly, his cheerful voice gone, replaced by a deep, resonant tone that seemed to be in harmony with the vast, empty silence of the desert. "This is not a graveyard. It is a wound. A scar left upon the world in the first, terrible days of the dawn."

He turned, his bright, blue eyes filled with a light that was older and sadder than the bones around them. "The old songs, the ones that are no longer sung, they tell of this place. They say that in the Age of Dawn, when the Sun God Anor first walked the world, a shadow rose from the void to meet him. It was a beast of pure, unmaking darkness, the first and greatest of Y'harr's children, a creature whose presence was a poison to the light. They called it 'Morogh,' the Great Devourer."

He gestured to the vast, skeletal landscape around them. "Here, on this spot, they did battle. A war that lasted a thousand years and a day, a conflict that tore the sky and boiled the seas. The sun, in its righteous fury, was a torrent of fire and light. Morogh was a storm of shadow and cold. And when the beast finally fell, its death was a cataclysm that unmade the world."

His voice dropped to a whisper, a story told to the bones themselves. "It's blood, a black, oily ichor of pure void, spilled across the land, and where it touched, the rich earth was burned to this black, razor sharp glass. Its final, dying breath, a gasp of absolute cold, froze the clouds in the sky, and they shattered, falling as a rain of sand that buried it for an age. The sun's own grief and rage at the battle was so great that its fire still lingers here, a memory of a pain that has never truly faded.

You do not feel the heat of a simple sun, my friends. You feel the echo of a god's fury."

The story ended, but it did not leave a silence. It filled the world with a new, terrible, and mythic resonance.

Gundroff stared at the bleached bones, his face a mask of grim, profound understanding. To his dwarven soul, a soul forged in a world of myth and stone, the story was not a fable. It was the truth. The desert was no longer a wasteland; it was a holy site, a battlefield where a god had bled to save the world. He felt a new, more profound connection to this harsh, unforgiving land, a sense of a shared, ancient history that resonated with the stone of his own being.

Seraphina's mind was a fortress in chaos. The story was a myth, a primitive, allegorical explanation for a series of complex and unusual geological phenomena. And yet... it fit. It fit with a terrifying, elegant precision that her own cold, complex logic could not replicate. The unnatural, unrelenting heat was not just physical, but seemed to have a spiritual weight. The strange, razor sharp obsidian was unlike any volcanic glass she had ever studied. the sheer, impossible scale of the bones. The story was a beautiful, poetic, and utterly irrational equation that solved every variable. For the first time in her life, she was confronted with a truth that her intellect could not dissect, a mystery that could not be solved, only accepted. The seed of a doubt, a terrifying and beautiful doubt, was planted in the barren soil of her certainty.

They moved on, their journey transformed. The desert was no longer just a physical obstacle; it was a place of mythic, historical, and sacred significance. The sun beating down on them was no longer weather; it was the lingering fury of a god. The path ahead, the path to the First Pillar, now felt like a pilgrimage, a descent into the heart of the world's first and greatest wound. And with every step, the feeling of an ancient, watchful intelligence, a presence that was neither the sun nor the shadow, but something else entirely, grew stronger, a silent, unseen observer in the graveyard of the giants.

The third day in the Ashen Desert was a descent into a deeper circle of hell. The mythic grandeur of the Leviathan's bones had lost its awe, becoming a monotonous, oppressive landscape of death. The sun was no longer just an antagonist; it was a torturer. Its white hot glare reflected off the endless fields of black obsidian glass, creating a disorienting, funhouse mirror effect that made the air itself seem to warp and shimmer. Every breath was a sip of fire, every step a grinding effort against a world that wanted them dead. They moved from one sliver of bone shade to the next, a desperate, creeping pilgrimage across a god's forgotten battlefield.

Gundroff's mind, a thing forged in the cool, quiet dark of the mountain, had retreated into a state of pure, grim endurance. He had rationed their water with a ruthless efficiency, his every action a quiet testament to a lifetime of survival in hostile lands. He watched his companions, his concern a silent, unfamiliar weight in his chest. Seraphina, the proud, untouchable elf mage, was wilting, her pale skin flushed with a dangerous, feverish heat beneath a layer of grime and sweat. Thaddeus, though he still walked with his unsettling, effortless grace, had fallen silent, his usual stream of stories and parables seemingly baked out of him by the oppressive, holy silence of the desert.

It was Thaddeus who saw it first. He stopped, his head cocked, his gaze fixed on a deep, jagged shadow cast by the colossal, fossilized tusk of some forgotten beast a hundred yards away.

"We are not alone," he said, his voice a dry rasp.

Gundroff was moving before the words had even settled, his axe in his hand, his body a low, coiled spring of lethal intent. He followed Thaddeus's gaze and saw it: a flicker of movement in the deep shade. It was lanky and stooped, its form a hunched, pathetic silhouette against the bone white wall of the tusk. It moved with a strange, loping, animalistic gait, its body seeming to twitch and jerk with a spastic, unnatural energy.

Seraphina raised a trembling hand to her brow, her arcane senses, though dulled by exhaustion, reaching out. "I feel… pain," she whispered, her voice a thin, fragile thing. "And a terrible, gnawing hunger. It is not a natural creature."

They watched, a tense, silent tableau under the hateful, unblinking eye of the sun. The creature, a hyena humanoid with fur the color of mangy, dust caked brown, seemed to be trapped in its sliver of shade. It would pace to the edge of the shadow, its long, clawed fingers twitching, its head darting back and forth as it stared across a vast, sun drenched expanse of black glass towards a much larger patch of darkness offered by the shadow of a colossal vertebra. It was a prisoner, and the sun was its jailer.

Then, with a low, mournful whine that was half whimper and half snarl, it made a decision. It broke from cover, its snarling charge an explosion of vicious, desperate intent. It was not charging them. It was charging the shadow.

The moment the first ray of direct sunlight touched its flesh, its charge became a shriek of pure, undiluted agony.

Wisps of oily black smoke rose from its fur, as if it were made of dry tinder. Its skin blistered and popped, a sickening, sizzling sound that was loud in the dead silence of the desert. The creature did not burst into flames; it was being unmade, its substance dissolving under the sun's holy, unforgiving gaze. It recoiled violently, tumbling back into the safety of the shade, clutching its burned snout with hands that were now a weeping, blistered ruin. It huddled at the back of the shadow, its body wracked with violent, uncontrollable shudders, its whimpering a thin, heartbreaking sound that was a profanity in the vast, empty landscape.

Thaddeus's face, which had been a mask of quiet reverence, was now a landscape of profound, troubled sorrow. "Well now," he muttered, his voice grim. "That's not right at all. The sun is a harsh master, but it was never a poison to them. The children of the sand were born under its gaze. This is… a desecration."

Seraphina's reaction was one of pure, intellectual horror. This was a paradox, a violation of the most fundamental laws of the natural world. Creatures of the desert are adapted to the sun, not dissolved by it. She saw not a monster, but a symptom, a walking, screaming piece of evidence in the case against the world's assassin. Her mind raced, a whirlwind of hypotheses and calculations, the scholar in her momentarily eclipsing the frightened, exhausted woman.

Gundroff's hand, which had been white knuckled on the haft of his axe, slowly relaxed. The rage he had felt, the instinct to meet a monster's charge with a warrior's fury, was gone, replaced by a deep, profound, and unfamiliar pity. He was a warrior, and he knew a warrior's duty to grant a clean, honorable end to a tormented foe. This creature was not a foe. It was a victim.

He began to walk forward, his steps slow and deliberate, his axe held low, not as a threat, but as a promise. The creature, seeing his approach, let out a low, guttural snarl and snapped its jaws, but it was a gesture of fear, not aggression. It tried to press itself further into the shadow, its back scraping against the cool, smooth bone of the tusk.

"Wait," Seraphina said, her voice soft but firm. She followed him into the shade, her own face a mixture of pity and clinical curiosity. She knelt, ignoring the creature's weak snarls, and looked into its eyes. And in their depths, she saw the true horror. Beneath the feral, instinctual hunger of a starving beast, there was a flicker of something else. a confused, lucid pain. The ghost of a person, trapped in a cage of corrupted flesh.

Thaddeus, his face a mask of pure, uncomplicated compassion, took a hesitant step forward. He reached into his satchel and pulled out a strip of dried, salted meat. He held it out, not as a lure, but as a simple offering.

The creature, which had been a whirlwind of feral rage, suddenly grew still. Its snarling subsided into a low, mournful whine. For a single, heartbreaking instant, the feral hunger in its eyes was replaced by that same flicker of confused, lucid pain. It did not see a threat; it saw a kindness it no longer understood. It did not take the meat. It simply stared at the offering, a single, viscous tear tracing a path through the dust and blisters on its cheek.

The moment was shattered as the corruption reasserted itself. With a final, agonized shriek, the creature lunged, not in an actual attack, but in a desperate, final spasm of pain and fear, its claws scrabbling at the empty air. The mystery of what this creature was, of what had been done to it, now hung in the air.

They dragged the creature's body into the deep, cool shade of the leviathan's colossal skull, the bone white arch of its jaw a fitting tombstone for the pitiable monster. The silence of the desert returned, a profound, waiting stillness that was somehow heavier now that the creature's agonized whimpers no longer punctuated it. The sun beat down on the black glass outside their sanctuary, the heat a visible, shimmering curtain, but here, in the shadow of a dead god, the air was cool and still.

Gundroff stood guard at the edge of the shadow, his axe held in a low, ready stance, his gaze sweeping the empty, shimmering horizon. He had seen death in a thousand forms, but this... this was a profanity. The creature's end had not been a clean, warrior's death, but a mercy, an unraveling of a knot of pure, pointless suffering. The injustice of it was a cold, hard knot in his gut.

Thaddeus knelt a short distance away, his back to the body. He had taken a small, smooth stone and was quietly, methodically, building a small cairn, a simple, humble monument to a life that had been stolen and twisted into a weapon. He did not speak. He did not offer a story. His grief was a quiet, practical thing, a silent prayer offered to the unblinking sun.

Seraphina, however, was not grieving. Not yet. She was a scholar, and she had a new, horrifying text to decipher. She knelt beside the Sun Scorched, her face a mask of cold, clinical detachment. Her mind, which had been a fortress in chaos when faced with the mythic truth of the desert, now retreated into the familiar, comforting territory of analysis. This was not a tragedy; it was a specimen. It was a problem to be solved.

"Its flesh is brittle," she noted, her voice a low, academic murmur. She ran a gloved finger along its mangy, dust caked fur, which flaked away under her touch like ancient parchment. "The cellular structure has been... compromised. Accelerated decay." She produced a small, silver scalpel from her satchel and, with a surgeon's precision, made a shallow incision along the creature's forearm. There was no blood. Only a fine, black, acrid dust that puffed from the wound and vanished on the still air.

"Fascinating," she whispered, her scientific curiosity momentarily eclipsing her horror. "The life force has been... cauterized. Annihilated at a fundamental level."

But a physical examination could only reveal the symptoms, not the disease. To understand the true nature of this profanity, she would have to read its history, its soul.

She closed her eyes and placed her hands on either side of the creature's head. The fur was coarse and cold. She began to chant, her voice a low, melodic whisper, the ancient, esoteric language of chronomancy. A fine, silver light, cold and sterile as starlight, began to shimmer around her hands. The air grew chilly, a pocket of impossible winter in the heart of the searing desert.

This was not a spell of fire or force. It was a delicate, draining, and deeply invasive act of arcane scholarship. She was not attacking the creature's memory; she was attempting to unwind the threads of its causality, to read the scars that time had left upon its being. Her mind plunged into the creature's timeline, and she was met not with a clean, linear story, but with a chaotic, screaming vortex of temporal noise.

She saw a field of wheat, golden under a warm, familiar sun. The smell of fresh cut hay, the sound of a child's laughter. A life of simple, beautiful, and unremarkable peace. Then, the violation. A flash of violet light. The cold, sterile sting of a needle. The taste of a black, oily serum that was not just a poison, but a paradox.

Her mind reeled from the psychic backlash. She felt the creature's terror, its confusion, its profound, soul deep violation as its own history was forcibly and brutally rewritten. The spell was a torment, a shared agony that sent a lance of icy fire up her arms. A thin trickle of blood, dark and warm, ran from her nose, a stark, crimson line against her pale, sweat slicked skin.

She pulled back, gasping, her heart hammering against her ribs. But she had what she needed. She had seen the ingredients of the poison.

"It is a serum," she breathed, her voice a raw, trembling thing. She looked up at Gundroff, her glacial eyes wide with a new and more profound horror. "A temporal alchemical compound. There are three parts."

She wiped the blood from her lip with the back of her glove, her movements shaky. "The first is a simple, brutish poison. A tincture of night lotus and the venom of the desert scorpion. Designed to break the body, to make it pliable."

She took a shuddering breath, the memory of the psychic scream still echoing in her mind. "The second is the true horror. It is an arcane agent, a particle of pure, temporal decay. The same hostile geometry I saw in the Sun Petal. It does not just poison the flesh; it frays the timeline of the host. It infects their past and devours their future, leaving them trapped in a constant, agonizing present. That is why the sun burns them. They are creatures of shadow now, for the light of the sun is the light of time, of a future they no longer possess."

She fell silent, the weight of her discovery a crushing thing. Gundroff stared at her, his face a mask of cold, brutal fury. "And the third part?" he growled.

Seraphina looked down at the peaceful, dead face of the creature, at the faint, ghostly echo of the farmer it had once been. Her clinical detachment was gone, shattered by the terrible, final truth. Her voice, when she spoke, was a broken whisper.

"The third ingredient... is the person themselves. The serum does not just create a monster. It uses the host's own life force, their own memories, their own soul, as the fuel to power the transformation." She looked up, her eyes locking with Gundroff's, and he saw in them a reflection of his own forty year old horror. "They are not just killing these people, Gundroff. They are harvesting them. They are turning them into weapons, powered by the essence of the lives they have stolen."

The hunt for the First Pillar was no longer just a quest. It was a rescue mission. And it was an act of vengeance.

Chapter 15

Sleep That Steals

The desert was a forge, and they were the iron, being hammered into a new and more brittle shape. The mythic awe of the leviathan bones had long since faded, scoured away by the relentless, white hot fury of the sun. The world had become a monotonous, shimmering hell of black glass and white sand, the horizon a wavering, indistinct line that promised nothing but more of the same. Their water was nearly gone. The last waterskin, passed between them in a solemn, silent ritual, held only a few mouthfuls of warm, brackish liquid. Hope had become a dangerous luxury, a fire that consumed what little moisture they had left in their souls.

Gundroff's world had narrowed to the simple, brutal calculus of survival. The creak of the leather straps on his pack, the rhythmic crunch of his boots on the glass, the raw, dry fire in the back of his throat. these were the only truths. He watched Seraphina, her proud, elven grace reduced to a slow, determined shamble, her face a pale mask of grime and exhaustion. He watched Thaddeus, his cheerful stories silenced by the vast, oppressive quiet, his steps still unnervingly steady, but his bright, blue eyes clouded with a deep, weary concern. He, Gundroff, was the mountain. He would not crumble. He would endure.

It was on the sixth day of their journey, when the last of the water was a memory and their thirst had become a living, clawing thing in their bellies, that they saw it. A dark line on the horizon. A smudge of green in the endless, bleached out landscape. An oasis.

The word was a prayer, a gasp of disbelief. Adrenaline, cold and sharp, cut through the fog of their exhaustion. They stumbled forward, their pace quickening from a funeral march to a desperate, lurching run. The green smudge resolved into the skeletal, reaching fingers of palm trees, the dark line into the promise of cool, life giving water.

But as they drew closer, the beautiful miracle began to curdle into a new kind of nightmare. The oasis was wrong. The palm trees were blackened skeletons, their fronds brittle, ash like claws that rattled in the hot, dry wind. The life giving pool at its center was not a shimmering blue, but a black, oily slick, its surface choked with a fine, black dust that seemed to absorb the light of the sun. The air was not filled with the scent of water and life, but with a profound, all pervading despair, a quiet so deep it felt like grief.

This was not an oasis. It was a grave.

The town of Lastlight was a collection of a dozen or so buildings, their sun bleached wood sagging with a weary resignation, their windows dark, vacant eyes staring out at the desolation. There was no laughter, no children playing in the single, dusty street. The few people they saw moved with the slow, listless shuffle of the damned, their shoulders slumped, their faces hollowed out masks of apathy.

Desperation, however, was a sharper spur than caution. They needed water, any water, and so they walked into the heart of the dying town. Their destination was the only building that showed any sign of life: a grim, squat establishment with a sun bleached sign that read 'The Dry Well.'

The tavern's interior was a cave of cool, shadowed relief from the sun's oppressive glare. The few patrons inside, a handful of weathered, hollow eyed prospectors and traders, looked up as they entered, their gazes lingering on their weapons with a dull, incurious light before returning to their ale. The tavern keeper, a man whose face was a roadmap of worry, approached their table, his initial, fleeting hope for paying customers quickly giving way to a more profound, more desperate plea.

"You're adventurers," he stated, his voice a dry rasp. "You fight monsters. But we... we have a sickness here. A curse."

Before he could continue, a woman rose from a dark corner of the tavern and approached them. She was young, but her face was etched with a grief so profound it had aged her beyond her years, her eyes red rimmed and vacant. She clutched a small, crudely woven doll, made from scraps of twine and a single, faded blue ribbon, to her chest as if it were the last piece of her soul.

"It is not a sickness," she whispered, her voice a shaky, fragile thing, a sound on the verge of shattering. "It is a thief. It steals them away while they sleep."

Gundroff's hand, resting on the horn mug, tightened until his knuckles were white and bone. The tavern, the heat, the thirst. all of it vanished, replaced by the smell of smoke and the phantom heat of a world burning. He flinched, a violent jerk of his shoulders, as if shying from a flame only he could see. The cold, hard wall he had built around his own grief began to crack under the sudden, brutal assault of memory.

The woman did not seem to see them as people. She saw them as a last, desperate, and probably futile prayer. "My daughter," she continued, her gaze fixed on a point somewhere beyond them, a memory only she could see. "It's a thief," the woman whispered, clutching the doll. "It takes them. My Elara... she was laughing one morning. Laughing. The next... just tired. So tired. It's not a fever, you see? They... fade. I could see the candlelight through her hand at the end, like she was made of glass. And then she was gone. Just gone. She was laughing..."

Gundroff's breath hitched in his throat. He saw not the woman's daughter, but his own son, a small, laughing boy with a shock of red hair, his form dissolving into smoke and ash. He took a slow, deliberate breath, the air a fire in his lungs, and forced the memory down, locking it back in the cold, dark vault of his soul. His purpose, which had been a grand, abstract thing. save the world, find the Pillars. was now a single, hard, and brutally simple point of focus. *This would not stand.*

"The night it started," the woman whispered, a new spark of fearful memory in her eyes. "The night Elara first grew tired. I couldn't sleep. I went to the well for water. And I saw a figure there." Her voice dropped, her eyes going wide with the memory of a half seen nightmare. "It was tall, cloaked in dark, fine robes. And its face... it had no face. Just a mask. A smooth, white, porcelain mask. And it was smiling."

Seraphina and Gundroff exchanged a look across the table, a silent, chilling communion. The figure in Lastlight. The impossible, silver fire. The architect of this quiet, creeping genocide. This was not a random plague. It was a deliberate, calculated act of profound and unimaginable evil.

Elara led them from the oppressive gloom of 'The Dry Well' into the searing, white hot light of the dying day. The town of Lastlight was a study in apathy. Dust, fine as powdered bone, coated everything, muffling sound and stealing the moisture from the air. Gundroff's world, a world of sharp edges and clear, honest sounds, was muted here. The silence was not peaceful; it was the hollow, breathless quiet of a town that had already given up the ghost, a place where even the sorrow was too tired to make a sound.

She took them to a small, lopsided cottage, its sun bleached wood the color of old parchment. The door hung open on a single, groaning leather hinge, a dark, gaping mouth that seemed to exhale a sigh of pure despair. Inside, the air was hot, still, and smelled of dust, dried herbs, and a faint, sweetish odor of decay that made the hairs on Gundroff's arms stand up. It was the smell of a life slowly, inexorably, coming undone.

In the center of the single, sparse room, on a small cot made of rough hewn wood and stretched hide, lay a small boy. He was no more than eight years of age, his hair a shock of sun bleached straw against a pillowcase that was grey with dust. He was not sleeping in any way, Gundroff understood. His chest rose and fell with a shallow, almost imperceptible rhythm, but there was no twitch of a dreaming eye, no soft snore. He was utterly, unnaturally still. And his skin… Gundroff's hunter's eye, which could spot a camouflaged grouse at a hundred paces, struggled to focus on him. The boy's flesh was pale, yes, but it was more than that. It was translucent, as if he were a figure carved from pale, milky glass. Gundroff could faintly see the dark, woolen texture of the blanket beneath his thin arm. It was a violation of the senses, a sight that his pragmatic mind could not categorize. At the edges of his form, where his small fingers rested on the blanket, the lines seemed to blur and fray, as if he were a watercolor painting left out in the rain.

Seraphina moved to the bedside, her usual, elegant grace replaced by a slow, deliberate caution. She was no longer a scholar; she was a physician entering a plague house. She did not touch the boy. She stood over him, her glacial eyes scanning his form, her face a mask of cold, clinical concentration. Gundroff watched her, a silent, brooding guardian by the door, his hand resting on the pommel of his axe. He saw the subtle, almost invisible shift in her posture, the way her shoulders tightened, the slight narrowing of her eyes. She was seeing something he could not, a truth hidden in the fabric of the boy's fading existence.

"Hold the light steady, Thaddeus," she commanded, her voice a low, clinical whisper that did not betray the knot of cold dread tightening in her own stomach.

Thaddeus, who had been standing by the window, his face a mask of profound sorrow, moved to the bedside. He held his hand over the cot, and the small, silver sunburst on his palm began to glow with a soft, warm, golden light, a stark contrast to the room's grey, dusty gloom. The holy light seemed to struggle here, its edges fraying against the oppressive, spiritual vacuum of the room.

Seraphina knelt. She placed her hands on either side of the boy's head, her touch as light and as gentle as a falling leaf. She closed her eyes and began to chant, her voice a low, melodic whisper, the ancient, esoteric language of chronomancy. A fine, silver light, cold and sterile as starlight, began to shimmer around her hands, weaving a complex, intricate web of arcane energy around the boy's form. The air in the room grew cold, a pocket of impossible winter in the heart of the searing desert.

Gundroff watched, his jaw tight. He did not understand the words she spoke, but he understood the cost. He saw the fine tremor in her hands, the way the muscles in her jaw clenched with the strain. He saw a fine sheen of sweat break out on her brow, a single, perfect bead that traced a path through the grime on her temple. He saw a thin trickle of blood, dark and warm, run from her nose, a stark, crimson line against her pale, sweat slicked skin. This was not a simple spell. It was an act of profound and costly will. She was not just observing; she was entering the storm, her mind a delicate instrument pushed into the heart of a temporal hurricane.

Then, he saw it. A crack in the ice. Her concentration, which had been as absolute and as unyielding as a glacier, suddenly shattered. Her eyes snapped open, and for a single, unguarded heartbeat, the cold, clinical mask of the chronomancer was gone. He saw not a scholar, but a woman, her eyes wide with a raw, primal, and profoundly personal horror. She let out a soft, choked gasp, a sound of pure, undiluted terror, and her hand, the one not touching the boy, flew to her own chest, her fingers clenching the fabric of her robes over her heart. It was not the reaction of a physician discovering a disease. It was the reaction of a mother seeing her own child in the face of the dying boy.

In that same, terrible instant, a memory, a vision not her own, had lanced through Seraphina's mind. For a single, horrifying second, the face of the pale, sleeping boy was replaced by another: the phantom image of a small, half elven girl with her father's stormy green eyes and her own stubborn chin, a child she had only held once in a stolen, sun drenched moment on a high balcony. The thought. *What if this sickness found her? What if they took my Juniper?*. was not a thought at all, but a shard of pure, unreasoning terror that she had to violently, brutally suppress.

The moment was a fleeting, impossible thing. As quickly as it had appeared, the mask of cold, analytical composure slammed back into place. But Gundroff had seen it. He had seen the ghost that haunted her, the wound that she kept hidden beneath a thousand layers of ice and logic. And in that moment, she was no longer just the arrogant elf mage who had put him in chains. She was a fellow survivor, a fellow parent, a fellow ghost in a world that had taken everything from them.

She pulled her hands back as if the boy's skin had burned her. The silver light vanished, and the oppressive heat of the desert afternoon rushed back into the room.

"He is not sick," she said, her voice a raw, trembling thing that she quickly mastered, forcing it back into its usual, clinical cadence. She rose to her feet, her gaze fixed on a point on the far wall, as if she could not bear to look at the boy any longer. "There is no disease here. No poison. His timeline is… frayed. He is being unwritten."

Gundroff stared at her, his pragmatic, dwarven mind struggling to grasp the arcane horror of her words. "Unwritten?" he growled.

"His life force," she explained, her voice flat and dead, each word a cold, hard stone dropped into the quiet of the room. "His past, his future, his essence. It is being… siphoned. Harvested. It is being used as the fuel for a great and terrible ritual. He is not dying, Gundroff. He is being erased."

The word hung in the air, a final, terrible pronouncement. *Erased.* It was a concept so profoundly, fundamentally wrong that it made the simple, honest violence of a blade or a hammer feel like a mercy. This was not war. This was not murder. This was a desecration of the idea of a soul.

Gundroff turned, his face a mask of granite, his golden brown eyes burning with a cold, clear fire that had not been there a moment before. He looked not at Seraphina, not at the grieving mother who had collapsed into a silent, weeping heap, but through the open doorway, towards the center of the dying town. Towards the well.

"The source," he growled, the words not a question, but a judgment. "The sickness flows from the water."

"Gundroff, wait," Seraphina began, her voice sharp with caution. "We know nothing of what lies down there. It could be a temporal anomaly, a psychic trap. I need time to analyze…"

"The time for analysis is done," he cut her off, his voice a low, dangerous rumble that was not open to debate. "A child is being unmade. There is a poison in the well. I am going to kill it."

He strode from the cottage, his every step a heavy, percussive drumbeat of purpose against the dusty street. The air outside, which had been a suffocating blanket of heat, now felt cool against his feverish skin, the fire in his soul burning far hotter than any desert sun. The few listless townspeople he passed seemed to shrink away from the sheer, focused intensity of his presence. He was no longer a weary traveler. He was a weapon, aimed at the heart of their despair.

He reached the town well, a simple, circular structure of dry stacked stones, its wooden roof sagging with age. The air around it was colder, and it carried a faint, nauseating thrum that vibrated deep in his teeth. It was the same unnatural energy he had felt from the Gloomfang Boar, the same signature of wrongness, but here it was concentrated, a coiled serpent sleeping in the dark.

Thaddeus and Seraphina caught up to him, their faces masks of grim concern. "You cannot go down there alone," Seraphina insisted. "We don't know what we're facing."

Gundroff looked from the dark, gaping maw of the well to the small, lopsided cottage where the unwritten child lay. He saw not the boy's pale, translucent face, but the ghost of his own son, his laughter dissolving into smoke.

"I will not be alone," he said, his voice a low, fierce prayer. He unslung his great axe, its twin heads, *Grief* and *Vengeance*, seeming to drink the harsh sunlight. But he did not read it for a swing. He handed it, with a surprising gentleness, to Thaddeus.

"A slasher is a poor tool for a tight space," he said, his voice a low, practical rumble. From his back, he unstrapped a heavy, one handed great axe, its head a solid block of blued iron, and a round, iron banded shield. He looked at Seraphina. "I will need a light."

She nodded, her arguments silenced by the sheer, unyielding force of his will. She took a small, smooth river stone from her pouch and whispered a single word of power. A sphere of cool, cerulean light bloomed around the stone, casting its long, distorted shadows against the bleached wood of the surrounding buildings.

The townsfolk, drawn by the silent, grim drama, had begun to gather, their hollow eyes filled with a fragile, flickering ember of a hope they had long ago abandoned. They brought a heavy, coiled rope, its fibers stiff with age and dust.

Gundroff tied the rope around his waist, the familiar, rough texture a small comfort. He took the light stone from Seraphina, his calloused fingers brushing hers for a fraction of a second. He gave her a single, sharp nod, a silent promise. Then, he turned and, without a backward glance, began his descent into the belly of the beast.

The world narrowed to the small, shrinking circle of the sky above and the growing, oppressive darkness below. The air grew cool and damp, the scent of the water rising to meet him. not the clean, earthy smell of a deep well, but the sterile, dusty scent of temporal decay, the smell of a forgotten tomb. The fine, dwarven stonework of the well's shaft, a testament to the town's proud, forgotten founders, was coated in a thin, greasy slime.

He passed the water line, the cold shock of it a violent gasp in the darkness, and continued his descent into the submerged grotto below. He let go of the rope, his heavy boots finding purchase on the slick, stone floor. He was in a small, circular cavern, the water up to his chest. The cerulean light of the stone in his hand cast eerie, wavering reflections on the curved walls.

And there, in the absolute, silent dark of the grotto, he saw it.

It was a grotesque, jellyfish like entity, a foot in diameter, its body a mass of translucent, pulsing tubes that seemed to writhe and coil with a slow, malevolent life of their own. It had no eyes, no mouth, only the sickly, violet glow of the cult's spiral symbol at its core, a cancerous heart pumping darkness into the town's lifeblood. It was a Temporal Leech, a living seed of the cult's power, planted in the veins of the world. Its only sound was a soft, rhythmic clicking, a noise that was both physical and psychological, a relentless, maddening noise that clawed at his mind, a perversion of the peaceful hum of his mountain, a clock counting down a stolen life.

The fight was a brutal, claustrophobic affair. The water, thick and heavy, slowed his movements, a grasping, invisible hand that resisted his every swing. But it could not dampen the divine fire that now burned in his soul.

The Leech sensed his presence. It did not charge. It pulsed, a wave of pure, temporal energy washing over him. It was not a physical blow, but it was far worse. He felt his shield arm wither, the muscles turning to a weak, stringy parody of their former strength, the iron bands of the shield blooming with a century of rust in a single, silent second. His mind was filled with the dizzying, nauseating vertigo of his own future death, a fleeting, terrifying glimpse of his own skull lying shattered on a cold, stone floor.

He roared, a sound of pure, defiant life in the silent, watery tomb, and pushed through the psychic assault. He raised his great axe, its iron head seeming to absorb the faint, cerulean light.

The Leech pulsed again. This time, the assault was on his past. He saw his wife's face, not as he remembered her, full of fire and life, but as a withered, ancient crone, her eyes filled with a cold, accusatory light. *You let me burn,* she seemed to whisper, the words a poison in his soul.

No, his soul roared back, a defiant forge fire against the psychic cold. He forced the memory of Elga's true face to the surface. her wild red hair, the laugh lines around her eyes, the fierce love that had been his only sun. He held onto that image, a shield of pure memory against the creature's lies.

He cried out, a choked gasp of pure agony, and stumbled, his boots slipping on the slimy stone. But the grief, the shame, the weaponized memories. they were not breaking him. They were fueling him. His grief for the past was being forged into a shield for the present.

He roared a prayer to Grolnir, the name of his god, a cleansing fire in the profane darkness. "For the children!" he bellowed, the words a promise, an oath.

The divine fire of his faith, a power he had not called upon in forty years, answered him. A brilliant, white hot light erupted from his body, a miniature sun in the subterranean darkness. The water around him boiled and hissed, the steam a cleansing cloud in the foul air. The Leech, a creature of shadow and decay, recoiled from the pure, holy light, its rhythmic clicking rising to a frantic, terrified pitch.

Gundroff brought his great axe down in a single, devastating blow. The divine fire of his oath flared, and the hammer struck the creature's central, glowing sigil. The impact was not a wet, fleshy sound, but a sharp, crystalline crack, as if an excellent, purple diamond had been shattered.

The Leech convulsed, a final, silent scream of pure negation. It did not explode. It unraveled. Its translucent form dissolved into a cascade of shimmering, violet embers that were instantly extinguished by the holy fire, leaving only the clean, cold water and the echo of a nightmare.

The cheer that went up from the townsfolk was a fragile, ragged thing, a gasp of hope from a dozen throats that had long ago forgotten the sound. They hauled Gundroff from the well, their hands surprisingly strong, their hollow eyes filled with a dawning, disbelieving light. He stood among them, dripping, exhausted, and bleeding, the acrid stench of the vanquished Leech clinging to him like a shroud. But he had won. He had faced the poison in their well and cleansed it. For the first time in a long time, the town of Lastlight had a future.

Seraphina and Thaddeus rushed to his side, their faces masks of grim, profound relief. "You did it," Seraphina breathed, her voice a mixture of awe and exhaustion.

Gundroff grunted, leaning heavily on the haft of his Axe. He looked at the faces of the people around him. at Elara, the grieving mother, whose vacant eyes now held a single, perfect tear of gratitude. He looked at the tavern keeper, who was already proposing a toast with a bottle of dusty, saved for a funeral wine. He looked at the children, who were beginning to emerge from their cottages, their steps hesitant but their faces filled with a dawning, childish curiosity. A quiet, unfamiliar warmth had replaced the cold knot of fury in his gut. This was not the grand, glorious vengeance of his oath. It was something smaller, simpler, and in its own way, more profound. It was a shield.

It was then that the cheering died. It did not fade; it was strangled in their throats, cut short by a new and absolute silence. A collective gasp went through the small crowd, and they scattered, a flock of frightened birds, their brief moment of hope shattered into a thousand pieces of primal terror.

Gundroff spun around, his Axe raised, his body a coiled spring of lethal intent. Seraphina's hands, already weaving the complex patterns of a defensive ward, crackled with a faint, cerulean light. Thaddeus, his face a mask of grim, focused resolve, raised his heavy, cast iron frying pan.

Standing on the rooftop of the tavern across the dusty plaza was a new figure. They were clad in dark, impeccably tailored robes of a material that seemed to drink the harsh sunlight, their form a stark, elegant silhouette against the washed out, blue white sky. Their face was hidden behind a serene, white porcelain mask that seemed to smile down at the scene below with a placid, indifferent, and utterly inhuman calm.

Gundroff's mind, a warrior's mind, braced for an attack. He expected a bolt of fire, a whispered curse, a summoning of some new and terrible beast. The silence stretched, a taut, vibrating string that seemed to hum with an awful, waiting power.

The Mage did not speak. They did not move. They raised a single, gloved hand. The air around them crackled with an immense, silent heat.

With a lazy, almost bored gesture, they unleashed a torrent of brilliant, silver white fire. The evocation was one of terrifying, absolute power and purity. The fire did not roar; it was utterly, profoundly silent. It did not strike the party. It engulfed the tavern's empty stable in a quiet, white hot inferno.

It was as if the concept of 'stable' had been rescinded. The wooden walls didn't burn; they thinned, becoming ghosts of themselves before dissolving into motes of sterile light. The stone foundation didn't crack from the heat; it simply ceased to be, its geologic history erased in a silent, white hot torrent.

The entire structure of wood and hay and stone was gone, turned to a pile of fine, shimmering white ash in less than three seconds. The air now held no smell of smoke, but of a hollow, sterile nothingness, the scent of a space that has been violently and irrevocably emptied. The power was not one of destruction. It was one of unmaking. And the Mage had unleashed it with the casual, effortless grace of a master painter cleaning a brush. It was a power that had no cost.

As Gundroff and Seraphina stood, momentarily stunned by the sheer, cosmic scale of the power they had just witnessed, Thaddeus's expression shifted. It was not one of surprise or fear. It was a look of quiet, weary, and profound familiarity, a slight, sad nod, as if he were watching an old, destructive, and heartbreakingly familiar pattern repeat itself.

Before Gundroff could even take a step to charge, before Seraphina's half formed ward was entirely woven, the Mage took a single step back. A shimmering portal of pure heat, like the air over a forge, opened behind them. They gave a slight, mocking bow, a gesture of pure, untouchable contempt, and vanished into it. The portal snapped shut, leaving only the pile of white hot ashes where a building had once stood, and a stunned, terrified silence.

The townsfolk stared at the pile of ash, their brief, beautiful hope not just extinguished, but annihilated. The well, the source of their life, the thing Gundroff had just fought and bled to cleanse, was now buried under a mountain of sterile, unmaking fire. Their small, hard won victory had been contemptuously erased from the world. A single, choked sob broke the silence. It was Elara. She dropped the small, woven doll, the last piece of her daughter, into the dust and fell to her knees, her face a mask of grief so complete it had no sound.

They were no longer just defeated. They were humiliated. And they were in a dying town that now had no water.

Chapter 16

The General's Game

The silence the Masked Mage left in her wake was a profound and terrifying thing, a vacuum where a building had once stood, a void where hope had briefly, impossibly, bloomed. The townsfolk of Lastlight, their faces caked in dust and streaked with tears, stared at the mound of shimmering, incandescent ash. It did not smoke. It did not cool. It simply pulsed with a sterile, white light, a monument to their utter annihilation. The well, the source of their life, the reason Gundroff had fought and bled to cleanse their home, was now buried under a mountain of unmaking fire. They were no longer just defeated. They were humiliated. They were a people condemned, left to die of thirst in a town that now had no water and no future.

There was no time for grief. No time for the crippling weight of despair. Seraphina's mind, a fortress of causality and reason, rejected the emotional abyss threatening to swallow them all. It latched onto the single, tangible thread in the tapestry of their ruin: the energy trail. It was a faint, shimmering distortion in the air, a psychic residue of the portal the Mage had torn through reality, and it was already beginning to fray like old silk. The desert wind, a tireless, abrasive thing, was scouring it away with every passing second.

"We have to move," she said, her voice a sharp, precise instrument that cut through the stunned silence. It was not a request; it was a command forged in the fires of necessity. "Now. That trail is our only link to her, to the source of this."

Gundroff, his knuckles white around the haft of his axe, tore his gaze from the ashen tomb of the well. His face was a granite mask of fury and shame. He looked at the hollow, vacant eyes of the townsfolk, and in them, he saw the ghosts of his own past, the accusing stares of his lost kin. He gave a single, sharp nod, the muscles in his jaw bunching. Thaddeus, his expression unreadable, adjusted the pack on his shoulders, his gaze fixed on the shimmering horizon where their enemy had fled.

They left the dying town of Lastlight behind them. No one spoke a word of farewell. There was nothing left to say. The accusing silence of its people was a physical weight, a chorus of damnation that followed them out into the searing, white hot hell of the Ashen Desert. Their thirst, once a manageable discomfort, was now a raging fire in their throats. Their hope, once a beacon, was a single, flickering ember cupped in the hands of a desperate scholar. They were no longer just running from a shadow. They were chasing a ghost across the anvil of the sun.

The energy trail led them west, a faint, shimmering path visible only to Seraphina's arcane senses. To her, it was not merely a distortion of light but a symphony of sensations. It hummed with a low, dissonant frequency that vibrated behind her eyes; it tasted of ozone and burnt sugar on the back of her tongue; it felt like a cold draft in the furnace like air. Maintaining the connection required a fierce, unwavering focus. The desert itself seemed to fight her, the blinding glare of the obsidian shards and the warping waves of heat conspiring to break her concentration. Each step was a battle, her mind a taut wire strung between the physical torment of her body and the ethereal, fading signature of their foe.

The journey was a grueling, desperate race against time and their own failing bodies. The trail was a living thing, a dying breath on the wind, and with every passing hour, it grew fainter, the hum becoming a whisper, the taste fading to a memory. They moved at a punishing pace, a relentless, stumbling march. Exhaustion became a distant, secondary concern to the all consuming need to keep the trail in sight. The sun was a malevolent god, beating down upon them without mercy. Seraphina could feel the moisture being wicked from her body, her skin growing tight and brittle. Her lips were cracked and bleeding, and every breath was a sip of fire. Gundroff, stoic and uncomplaining, marched with a grim determination, but she could see the strain in the deep lines etched around his eyes, the slight tremor in the hand that gripped his axe.

The landscape grew more alien, more hostile. The vast, open plains of black, razor sharp obsidian glass gave way to a labyrinthine network of canyons, their walls carved by some forgotten river into strange, twisting shapes that, in the distorting heat, looked like screaming faces and grasping, skeletal hands. The world became a claustrophobic maze of stone and shadow. As the sun began its agonizingly slow descent, casting long, dramatic shadows that clawed their way across the dunes, the oppressive silence of the desert was finally broken.

It started as a low panting, a dry, rhythmic sound that seemed to come from everywhere at once. Then, a guttural chittering, the clicking of claws on stone. The dry, rustling sounds of hundreds of creatures moving in the canyon's deep, unseen crevices echoed around them, a sound like dry leaves skittering across pavement. The air, already thick with heat, grew heavy with the smell of musk and a raw, metallic tang of hunger.

"Faster," Gundroff growled, his voice a low rumble. His hand never left the haft of his axe, his knuckles white. He scanned the canyon rims, his eyes narrowed slits against the glare. "We must reach the other side before the light is gone."

The sun sank with agonizing speed, the band of brilliant orange on the horizon shrinking with every desperate, stumbling step. The shadows in the canyon deepened, turning from gray to purple, from purple to a black as absolute as the heart of the Underworld. The sounds grew louder, closer. They began to hear whispered, ragged words in the guttural, debased tongue of the Sun Scorched, a language of pure, animal need: "Hungry… hungry… hungry…" It was not a single voice, but a vast, terrible chorus, a litany of starvation echoing from the rock walls. They could feel the weight of hundreds of hungry eyes on them, a palpable, pressing force in the ever deepening gloom. It was a desperate, kinetic race for survival, their footsteps a frantic, echoing drumbeat against the hungry whispers that surrounded them.

They burst from the canyon's mouth just as the last sliver of the sun vanished below the horizon, plunging the world into the deep, bruised purple of twilight. They turned back, chests heaving, lungs burning, and saw the canyon's maw teeming with them. Hundreds of Sun Scorched, their emaciated forms little more than silhouettes against the fading light, their eyes glowing like malevolent embers. Their chorus of "Hungry!" rose into a terrible, howling crescendo, a sound of pure, thwarted rage that chased them out into the open desert.

Ahead of them, stark against the star dusted sky, was their destination. The energy trail, now a faint, pulsing beacon, terminated at the base of a massive, weather worn pyramid. The structure was surrounded by the sprawling ruins of a once grand city, its towers and courtyards now half buried in the black, glassy sand. As they moved through the silent, ruined streets, a profound sense of dread was their only companion; they found the truth of the Sun Scorched's origin. This was no monster's lair. This was a crime scene.

Here were the remnants of a one sided struggle, a story told in the debris of shattered lives. Discarded shackles lay half buried in the sand, their iron surfaces pitted and worn. Torn scraps of human and elven clothing, the bright colors of a merchant's silk or a farmer's linen, fluttered from the claws of ruined walls. They passed a child's wooden doll, its painted face staring up at the unfeeling stars, lying next to a set of manacles small enough to fit a child's wrist. The dark stains of old blood were everywhere, stark and black against the sand scoured stones. A city whose people had been abducted, dragged away to a fate worse than death, to become the beasts that now hunted the night.

The pyramid's entrance was a massive, arching gateway carved with ancient symbols of the sun, now defiled. The sacred spiral symbol of the cult had been branded over the ancient glyphs, pulsing with a sickly, violet light that seemed to rot the stone around it actively. This was not a forgotten tomb. It was an occupied enemy fortress. It was a factory.

They entered with weapons drawn. The ancient, sun worshipping architecture of the interior, with its clean lines and soaring arches designed to welcome the light, had been grotesquely repurposed into a horrifying alchemical workshop. The air was thick with the stench of blood, temporal decay, and a strange, sweetish odor that clung to the back of the throat, the smell of souls being rendered like fat. Every surface was coated in a fine, black dust that seemed to absorb the light, a physical manifestation of the profane work being done here.

Great, iron vats, each the size of a small cottage, bubbled with a black, viscous solution. Empty, blood stained cages were stacked against the walls, their iron bars bent and broken from the inside, a testament to the agony of the transformations that had taken place within them. They moved stealthily through the hellish workshop, their path lit by the foul, violet glow of the cult's magic.

They passed a room where a half dozen Sun Scorched, their bodies still horribly twisted and glistening from their recent transformation, were being trained by a cloaked cultist. The creatures were chained to the walls, their feral rage being honed into a weapon through a series of brutal, Pavlovian torments. The cultist would hold up a holy symbol of the Sun God, and the creatures would shriek and recoil, their corrupted flesh sizzling and smoking as if touched by a hot iron. Then, he would hold up the spiral symbol of the cult, and they would grow quiet, their heads bowed in a terrified, conditioned reverence. It was a factory for turning faith into fear.

In another chamber, they saw a row of alchemical tables, each one laid out with a horrifying array of surgical instruments: bone saws, cruel looking needles, and vials of the black, oily serum. On one table, an open journal lay next to a half dissected corpse. Seraphina, drawn by a morbid, scholarly compulsion, glanced at the page. It was filled with precise, clinical notes, detailing the alchemical formula's effect on the temporal structure of living tissue. It spoke of "cellular unmaking," "chronal decay," and "re sequencing the soul's anchor to reality." This was not just a fortress; it was a place of profane science, a testament to a cold, calculating evil that was more terrifying than any simple, brutish malice.

They followed the flow of the foul energy, a psychic current that pulled them deeper into the heart of the pyramid. They passed through a final, massive archway and emerged into the pyramid's central chamber.

The sight that met them stole the breath from their lungs.

They stood on a wide, circular ledge overlooking a vast, spherical chamber. The air here was not hot, but cold, a deep, unnatural chill that had nothing to do with the temperature of the desert outside. The walls of the chamber were not stone, but a swirling, chaotic vortex of pure, temporal energy, a contained hurricane of past, present, and future, colors and images flashing and dying within its depths. And in the center of it all, floating in the void, was the First Pillar.

It was a colossal, crystalline structure, a shard of a forgotten sun, and it was dying. It should have been a source of pure, golden, life giving light. But now, it was a corrupted monolith, shot through with writhing, black, oily tendrils of energy that pulsed with a sickly, violet light. The spiral symbol at its base glowed with a hungry, malevolent light, a cancerous heart pumping darkness into the ancient artifact. It was an engine of darkness, a weapon aimed at the heart of creation, and it was already turned on and running.

And floating in the center of the Pillar's corrupted, fiery core, held in a bubble of seemingly pure, untouched light, a single, beautiful, and impossible object of hope in a sea of despair, was a silver locket.

Before they could even formulate a plan, a voice echoed through the chamber. It was deep and resonant, with a wet, guttural, croaking quality, like a toad speaking from the bottom of a deep, dark well.

"So, the little mice have found their way into the pantry."

A shadow detached itself from the far wall, a shadow that grew, and grew, until it seemed to fill the archway of the chamber. A head, horned and massive, scraped against the stone lintel as it stooped to enter fully. It was a demon, a froglike horror of immense size and corpulent power, its bloated form easily twice the height of a man. Its mottled green black hide was covered in warts and bony spikes, and its vast, lipless maw was filled with countless needle like teeth, fixed in a cruel, intelligent grin. Its eyes were small, red, and glowed with an ancient, malevolent amusement. The sheer, monstrous presence hung in the air, a physical weight that pressed in on them. Then, Thaddeus's voice, quiet and thoughtful, cut through the tense silence. It sounded like he was reciting a half forgotten nursery rhyme, a macabre piece of lore that now felt horrifically real.

"A great, groaning general of rot, With a name that was hard to allot, This giant Manduklesh, Made a world all for naught, And ate every soul that he sought."

This was General Manduklesh.

The General did not attack. He moved with a grotesque, ponderous grace, his bloated form seeming to flow rather than walk. He did not look at them as a warrior looks at a foe, but as a gourmand looks upon an interesting new dish, a complex dish with flavors of grief, rage, and a profound, secret sorrow that he intended to savor. His vast, lipless maw was fixed in a cruel, intelligent grin, and his small, red eyes, glowing with an ancient, malevolent amusement, lingered on each of them in turn.

He focused first on Gundroff, his grin widening to a sickening degree. "I smell the dust of a fallen mountain on you, little dwarf," he croaked, his voice a wet, resonant rumble that seemed to vibrate in the bones of the pyramid. "And the forty year old stench of a failed oath. So much... purpose. A vintage of despair, aged to perfection."

He took a slow, deliberate step forward, his immense, three fingered hand gesturing vaguely towards the swirling temporal vortex of the Pillar. "You see this place? This beautiful, chaotic symphony of unmaking? This is what your people could have become. A force of nature. A people of stone and fire, who could have shaped the history of the world." He paused, his red eyes narrowing, the amusement replaced by a look of theatrical pity. "But you were weak. You clung to your songs, your traditions, your sentimental little hearth fires. And so, you were repurposed."

The words were a surgical strike. Gundroff's breath hitched. His hand, gripping his axe, went cold. But the General was not finished.

"Tell me," he mused, his voice dropping to a conspiratorial, almost friendly tone, his gaze boring into the dwarf. "I smell a failed oath on you, little dwarf," the demon croaked. "The stench of a home left to burn. Tell me, do you still hear the screams? So many screams. A whole mountain of them. I wonder which one was your father's?"

The words were a key turning a lock in the deepest, most secret dungeon of Gundroff's soul. He was no longer in a pyramid in a desert. He was back in the ruin of Hjarta-Fell, a boy of twenty, the air thick with the smell of his burning world. He heard the screams, not as a memory, but as a fresh, raw sound in his ears. He smelled the blood and the roasting flesh. He felt the shame, a cold, oily thing that had been his only faithful companion for forty years, coiling in his gut like a serpent.

Before a roar of pure, wounded fury could rip itself from his throat, Manduklesh's eyes shifted to Seraphina. He raised his massive, warty hand, and the silver locket drifted from the heart of the Pillar and into his grasp. "And you…" He sighed, a sound of theatrical pity that was a perfect echo of the one he had used on Gundroff. "Ah, you reek of paradox. Of starlight and heartbreak. A secret love for a golden prince, hidden away like a stolen gem."

Seraphina's blood ran cold. The fortress of her mind, which had been a bulwark against the desert's heat and the horrors of the cult's alchemy, was suddenly and violently breached. The General's words were not a guess; they were a statement of fact, a violation of a secret she had kept locked away for thirty years.

He brought the locket closer to his face, peering into its pristine, silver surface as if it were a scrying glass. "Does he even know of the little star you hid away? The one with his kingly eyes and that little crescent shaped birthmark behind her left ear? She has such potential. I look forward to seeing it burn."

The final sentence, the specificity of the detail, was a shard of pure ice plunged into Seraphina's soul. The implication. that he knew of her secret daughter, that he might have access to her. shattered her composure completely. A cry of raw, undiluted rage, a sound she hadn't made since she was a child, tore from her lips. She unleashed a raw, unfocused blast of pure temporal energy, a chaotic wave of force that warped the air into a shimmering, violent vortex.

Manduklesh held up the locket. "You have come for this, I presume?" he asked, his voice a low, wet sound of amusement as he easily absorbed her unfocused blast into the Pillar behind him. "A memory. A foolish, sentimental anchor to a world that is already dead."

With a grotesque delicacy, he popped the locket open. From across the room, they could see the perfect, miniature portrait of a breathtakingly beautiful woman with eyes like the summer sky.

"So much hope," Manduklesh mused. "So much love. Such a terrible waste of energy."

He held the open locket out, turning it towards the corrupted Pillar. A single, oily tendril of black energy snaked out and touched the portrait. The image did not burn. It did not fade. It unraveled. The woman's smile curdled into a rictus of terror. Her eyes turned to dust. Her features dissolved into a screaming vortex of nothingness, until all that was left was a blank, blackened space inside the silver frame. He had not just destroyed the image. He had murdered the memory it represented.

With a final, contemptuous flick of his wrist, he tossed the ruined locket back into the Pillar's core, where it was caught once more in the swirling temporal energies, a desecrated, empty mockery of what it once was.

The ruined locket clattered to the stone floor, the sound a final, mocking punctuation to the General's pronouncement. For a single, frozen heartbeat, there was only the low, hungry hum of the corrupted Pillar and the ragged, desperate breathing of the three companions. The psychological assault was complete. The General had taken their deepest wounds. Gundroff's failure and Seraphina's secret. and turned them into weapons, leaving them exposed, bleeding, and raw.

And then, the storm broke.

Gundroff's roar was not a sound of simple fury; it was the sound of a soul breaking its cage, a forty year old dam of grief and shame shattering in a single, volcanic instant. Seraphina's cry was a high, keening shriek of pure, undiluted rage, the cold, logical fortress of her mind consumed by the primal, animal terror of a mother whose child has been threatened. They charged as one.

General Manduklesh, with a look of profound, almost weary boredom, sighed.

"Such passion," he croaked, a low, wet sound of disappointment. "Such... predictable little flames. You are not warriors. You are ingredients. And I have grown tired of this game already." With a final, contemptuous sneer, he took a single step backward, not into shadow, but through a shimmering, unseen tear in reality, vanishing as though he had never been there. He did not need to fight them. He had already summoned their executioners.

He raised his massive, warty hands, not to defend himself, but to conduct. And the elements of the chamber groaned and twisted into monstrous forms.

From a pool of shadow in a far corner, a Fire Elemental coalesced. But it was not a creature of warmth and life. It was a thing of black, soul chilling flames, born from a captured memory of a joyful hearth fire, its warmth twisted and corrupted into a sterile, hollow cold that seemed to leach all color and heat from the air. From the bone dust and shattered stones of the floor, an Earth Elemental erupted, not as a being of solid, unyielding stone, but of shifting, razor sharp obsidian shards, its jagged form a mockery of a lost life, the tormented ghost of a forgotten dwarven warrior. A Storm Elemental of chaotic, violet lightning crackled into existence from the ambient energy of the Pillar, its presence filling the chamber with the sharp, clean scent of ozone and the maddening buzz of a thousand angry wasps. And from a corner where the shadows were deepest, an Ice Elemental formed, a creature of frigid malice that did not just radiate cold, but a palpable aura of temporal decay. The stone at its base instantly frosted over and turned brittle, the world visibly un making itself around the creature's feet.

The chamber became a vortex of elemental chaos. The battle was a desperate, unwinnable dance against the forces of nature, corrupted and turned against them. The floor became a death trap of shifting obsidian spikes and spreading, unnatural ice. The air was a web of arcing, violet lightning. Walls of black flame erupted from the ground, hemming them in, separating them.

It was a tactical nightmare, designed not just to kill them, but to break them. Gundroff, his initial rage now cooled into a grim, desperate focus, became the bulwark. He planted his shield, its dwarven runes glowing with a faint, defiant light, and endured the barrage of obsidian shards from the Earth Elemental, each impact a jarring, bone shaking shock. He roared in defiance, his voice a challenge to the storm, as he parried the lashing tendrils of the Lightning Elemental, the impact sending a shower of sparks skittering across the floor.

Seraphina, her own fury now channeled into a desperate, tactical precision, became the battlefield controller. She was a weaver, pulling at the threads of the chaos. Her magical reserves were a shallow, muddy pool, but her intellect was a honed blade. She did not have the power for grand, destructive spells, so she used her magic like a scalpel. She created a small, shimmering bubble of slowed time around Gundroff, allowing him to sidestep a lightning bolt that would have incinerated him. She saw the Fire Elemental preparing to engulf Thaddeus's miraculously safe corner. She thrust out her hand, not with a blast of water, but by accelerating the moisture in the air into a sudden, dense cloud of fog that momentarily smothered the black flames.

Thaddeus, for his part, seemed to view the cataclysm with the detached interest of a spectator at a particularly loud opera. He had found a miraculously safe corner behind the Pillar's base. After a moment of consideration, he sat down, pulled a small, worn pan from his pack, and with a cheerful hum, began trying to cook the last of his bacon over a small, magically conjured flame, the sizzling of the meat a surreal, maddening counterpoint to the roaring chaos.

They were surviving, but they were losing. For every elemental they managed to disrupt, its energy would flow back into the Pillar and coalesce again, seemingly stronger than before. They were chipping away at a mountain with a teaspoon, and their own strength was beginning to fail. Seraphina's head throbbed with the effort, a thin trickle of blood weeping from her nose.

The pivot came with a horrifying, tangible blow. Gundroff, having just shattered an obsidian shard with his axe, turned to face the Ice Elemental as it drifted through the chaos towards him. The creature's chilling touch radiated a visible aura of decay. Gundroff raised his shield to block a swipe from its icy claws, steeling himself for the impact.

The attack was not a simple blast of cold. Where the chilling touch connected with Gundroff's shield arm, the world seemed to unravel. His thick, dwarven beard on that side of his face instantly grayed and withered, turning brittle as ash. The skin on his knuckles cracked and wrinkled, the hand of a hundred year old man. The iron of his gauntlet tarnished, a century of rust blooming across its surface in a single, silent second. A roar of shock and pain tore from him. He stumbled back, his arm feeling not just cold, but wrong, a hollow echo of a memory that had never been his. The withered skin on his hand, the brittle white of his beard. this was not a wound. It was a theft. He had been visibly, tangibly unmade.

Seraphina witnessed it. In that one, horrifying moment, her tactical mind saw the grim equation of their defeat. This was not a war of attrition that they could win. The elementals did not need to defeat Gundroff with force; they would erase him from time, piece by piece.

Their greatest bastion was a crumbling wall. The clock was literally ticking on his existence.

In the swirling chaos, there was no time for a speech. Their eyes met across the elemental vortex. He saw the desperate, tactical fury that had replaced her fear. She did not speak. She pointed a single, elegant finger. first with a sharp, demanding jab at the ruined Locket still floating in the Pillar's core, and then with a sweep toward the shimmering, unseen portal where Manduklesh had vanished. It was a command born of shared, imminent doom. *The prize. Then the exit.*

He understood instantly. His role was no longer to endure. It was to create one final, desperate opening.

As if confirming her desperate, unspoken plan, a cheerful voice piped up from behind the Pillar. "The brightest fires always cast the deepest shadows, my dears!" Thaddeus called out, his voice impossibly calm over the roaring chaos. "Lovely crisp on this bit here!"

The cryptic words were the final key. Seraphina's eyes widened. She looked at Gundroff, whose axe was already beginning to glow with a furious, divine light. His brightest fire. The deepest shadow. She gave him a single, sharp nod.

Gundroff needed no further prompting. He planted his feet, ignored the agonizing decay in his arm. He focused every ounce of his forty years of grief, rage, and unshakeable faith into his weapon. He let out a final, great war cry to Grolnir, a prayer and a curse in one. He did not aim at a single elemental. He aimed at the center of the chamber. He unleashed the full, divine fire of his soul in a massive, 360 degree shockwave of pure, holy energy.

The blast of golden light was blinding. The four elementals shrieked, a discordant chorus of burning, shattering, freezing, and discharging energy as their corrupted forms were momentarily stunned and thrown back by the raw, holy power.

It was the shadow Seraphina needed.

In that single, crucial instant of distraction, she acted. She poured her own energy, her own desperate hope, into a single, complex spell. It was not a spell of attack, but of theft. She wove a bubble of isolated time, a perfect, shimmering sphere, around the Locket, severing its connection to the Pillar and pulling it through the air into her waiting hand.

At the same instant, the shimmer in the air where the General had vanished began to waver, a sign that its magic was fading.

"Now!" she screamed, her voice raw.

The elementals were already reforming, their mindless fury now focused entirely on the three intruders. The portal was their only hope. Gundroff, his divine fire spent, his body trembling with the effort, charged towards Seraphina. She grabbed Thaddeus, who had calmly packed away his now perfectly crisped bacon, and together, the three of them sprinted for the shimmering, unstable gateway. They leaped through the portal, a maelstrom of elemental fury. of black fire, temporal ice, obsidian shards, and violet lightning. erupting behind them, consuming the chamber in a final, cataclysmic explosion of corrupted power.

Chapter 17

The Sunken Heart

Escaping the General's fortress was an act of severance. One moment, Seraphina's senses were consumed by a roaring vortex of elemental fury. the sterile, soul leaching cold of the black flames, the jagged scream of shattering obsidian, the ozone sharp scent of violet lightning. The next was a violent, wrenching silence and a sickening lurch, as if the universe itself had been pulled out from under her feet.

They did not land. They were vomited out of reality, tumbling through a brief, disorienting void before crashing onto cold, slick stone. The impact drove the air from Seraphina's lungs in a pained gasp. For a long moment, she lay there, the hard, wet surface a shocking contrast to the heat and dust of the desert. The frantic, hammering pulse in her ears was the only sound in a world that had been abruptly muted. The ruined silver locket was still clutched in her hand, its metal unnaturally cold against her skin, a tangible anchor in the swirling chaos of her disorientation.

Slowly, painfully, she pushed herself up onto her elbows. Her body was a constellation of aches and bruises, her magical reserves scraped clean, leaving behind a hollow, throbbing exhaustion that felt like a physical illness. But she was alive. They were alive.

The darkness was absolute, a thick, velvety blackness that felt heavier than the simple absence of light. It was a subterranean darkness, ancient and undisturbed. The air was cool and heavy with the smell of wet stone, of deep earth, and something else... a faint, briny tang, like a sea that had not tasted the sun in a million years. The only sound was the slow, rhythmic *plink... plink... plink...* of water dripping from an unseen height, each drop echoing in the vast, silent space.

"Thaddeus?" Her voice was a raw croak. "Gundroff?"

A groan answered her from nearby. "Present," Thaddeus's voice came, sounding unusually strained. "Though I believe I may have landed on my bacon."

A deeper, more guttural sound of pain rumbled from the darkness a few feet away. "Here." Gundroff's voice was tight, each syllable carved from granite and agony.

Seraphina fumbled at her belt, her fingers finding the small crystal she kept for emergencies. Murmuring a single word of power. a word that felt like scraping the bottom of an empty well. she coaxed a faint, pearlescent glow from it. The light bloomed softly, pushing back the oppressive dark, and what it revealed stole her breath.

They were in a grotto of impossible scale and beauty. The floor was a smooth, dark stone, slick with moisture and carved by eons of flowing water. The walls soared up into an unseen, dripping ceiling, covered in a breathtaking tapestry of bioluminescent life. Great patches of pale blue lichen pulsed with a soft, rhythmic light, like sleeping heartbeats. Veins of glowing green moss traced intricate patterns across the stone, and clusters of phosphorescent fungi, shaped like delicate, alien flowers, cast a gentle, spectral radiance. They had fallen into a secret, living cathedral, a world that made its own light.

Her light found Thaddeus first, already sitting up and inspecting a flattened piece of cooked meat with a mournful expression. He had a long gash on his forehead, but otherwise seemed intact. Then, her gaze fell upon Gundroff, and the air froze in her lungs.

He was on his hands and knees, his head bowed. His left arm, the one that had taken the touch of the Ice Elemental, was a thing of horror. The temporal decay had not stopped when they'd fled the chamber; it had settled, like a disease. From his shoulder to his fingertips, the arm was withered, the skin thin and translucent as old parchment, covered in liver spots and a web of delicate, purple veins. The once mighty muscles had atrophied, leaving the limb looking frail and skeletal. The iron of his gauntlet was no longer merely tarnished; it was pitted with a deep, corrosive rust that seemed to have eaten away centuries of its substance in a matter of minutes. His beard on that side of his face was stark white, the hairs brittle and thin.

He tried to push himself up, and the withered arm buckled, a pained roar ripping from his throat as he collapsed back onto the stone. It was not the pain of a simple wound. It was the deep, grinding agony of ancient joints, of atrophied muscles, of a body that had aged a century in a single, horrifying instant.

Seraphina scrambled to his side, her own exhaustion forgotten. "Don't move," she commanded, her voice sharp with a clinical urgency that belied the knot of horror in her stomach.

She reached out to touch the arm, and the moment her fingers made contact, she recoiled with a gasp. It was not the physical cold that shocked her, but the temporal signature of the wound. To her arcane senses, the wound felt like a tear in the fabric of causality itself. It was a place where the laws of time had been murdered, the natural flow of life and decay perverted into a horrifying, localized paradox. This wasn't merely dark magic; it was a form of profane physics, a blasphemy against the fundamental axioms of reality.

"What is it, lass?" Gundroff gritted out, his good hand clenched into a fist on the wet stone. "What did it do to me?"

"It stole from you," she whispered, her mind racing, trying to categorize this profane science. "It didn't age you. It replaced a piece of your present with a piece of your future. It's... a temporal scar."

Thaddeus had moved closer, his usual whimsy gone, his face grim in the pale, shifting light of the grotto. "Can it be healed?"

Seraphina looked at the withered hand, the brittle white beard, the deep set weariness in her friend's eyes. "I don't know," she admitted, and the words tasted like ash. Healing a cut was a matter of flesh and blood. Rewriting a timeline that had been so brutally corrupted was magic on a scale she could barely comprehend.

They needed to move. They needed shelter. Leaving Gundroff exposed in this strange, unknown place was not an option. With Thaddeus's help, they managed to get the dwarf to his feet. Gundroff was a bastion of pride, but the agony and wrongness of his new limb forced him to lean heavily on the old man, his face pale and beaded with sweat.

They began to explore the grotto, their footsteps echoing in the vast, silent space. The air grew thicker, heavier with the scent of brine. They could hear a new sound now, beneath the dripping of water: a deep, low, resonant thrumming, a sound so profound it seemed to vibrate in their bones. It was the sound of a vast, unseen body of water, the currents of a subterranean ocean.

Following a path worn smooth by some ancient, underground river, they rounded a massive pillar of stone covered in the pulsing blue lichen. They saw it: a fissure in the grotto wall, from which emanated a faint, familiar, and utterly unwelcome violet glow. It was the signature of the cult's magic.

Gundroff stiffened, his good hand reaching for his axe. "More of them?"

"No," Seraphina said, her senses reaching out. "The energy is old. Stale. This place is abandoned."

With a shared look of grim resolve, they approached the fissure. It was a narrow opening, just wide enough for them to pass through one at a time. Inside, the violet light was stronger, emanating from a single, fist sized crystal embedded in the wall of a small, dry cavern. The cavern had been turned into a crude but functional alchemical laboratory.

A stone slab served as a workbench, littered with discarded glass vials, tarnished copper wiring, and a series of complex, arcane diagrams scratched directly into the stone. A pile of rusted, broken shackles lay in one corner, next to a stack of moldering clothes. the simple, homespun garments of farmers and villagers. The stench of temporal decay, the same foul odor from the pyramid's factory, still clung to the air, though it was faint and old. This was a forward operating base, a place where the cult had experimented, researched, and perfected its monstrous creations.

"They were here," Thaddeus murmured, his fingers tracing one of the arcane symbols on the wall. "They studied the Pillar's energy from a distance, it would seem. Perfecting their poison before moving in to corrupt the source."

Seraphina's attention was drawn to a series of notes etched onto several large, flat pieces of slate stacked on the workbench. They were fragmented, written in the same precise, clinical script she had seen in the pyramid. They spoke of "harvesting emotional resonance," of using "soul prints as a temporal catalyst," and, most chillingly, of "the Sunken King's Locket as the ideal emotional key."

It confirmed their worst fears. The cult was not just twisting flesh; they were weaponizing memory, using the most profound emotions. love, grief, faith. as fuel for their profane alchemy. The people they abducted were not just bodies; they were the raw ingredients in a formula designed to unmake the world.

And then, leaning against the far wall, they found it. A crude map, not on parchment that would rot in the damp, but painstakingly etched into a large, cured piece of leviathan hide. It depicted a vast, complex network of underworld tunnels, rivers, and caverns. It showed the location of the pyramid they had just fled, and it showed other places, other points of interest marked with the cult's spiral symbol. But most importantly, it showed a way out. A path that, according to the map's strange, alien geography, would lead them away from the desert and towards the northern mountains.

It was a small, desperate piece of hope in the suffocating darkness. They were wounded, hunted, and trapped in a hostile, alien world miles beneath the sun. But they were not lost. They had a path.

While Thaddeus helped Gundroff to a relatively clean corner of the abandoned lab, settling him against the cold stone wall, Seraphina took a moment to secure their position. She used the last dregs of her energy to weave a simple ward across the fissure's entrance. a fragile, shimmering net of magic designed not to stop an intruder, but to give them a moment's warning. It was a flimsy defense, but it was all she could manage. Her head throbbed with a dull, persistent ache, the price of her over exertion in the pyramid.

Gundroff sat slumped against the wall, his breathing harsh and shallow. He refused any offer of comfort, his pride a shield as solid as any he had ever carried. His good hand rested on the haft of his axe, but his gaze was fixed on his withered left arm, a look of stony disbelief on his face, as if it were a foreign object, a monstrous parasite that had attached itself to him. The temporal scar was not just a wound; it was an artifact of his own grim future, a constant, physical reminder of his own mortality and decay. Every pained breath he took was a testament to the General's surgical cruelty.

Thaddeus, ever practical, produced a small, battered tin from his pack. "The bacon is a tragedy," he announced with a sigh, "but I believe a spot of tea is in order. Excellent for morale." He set about summoning a tiny, clean flame, his quiet, mundane actions a small, defiant protest against the grand, cosmic horror of their situation.

With the camp secured and her companions tending to their own wounds, Seraphina could no longer ignore the object in her hand. She sat on the cold stone floor, the cult's map spread out beside her, and finally allowed herself to look at the locket honestly.

In the faint, violet glow of the cult's crystal, the silver was tarnished and dull. The delicate clasp had been broken, and the surface was marred by a fragile, black tracery of cracks, like a spiderweb of frozen lightning. the result of the General's profane unmaking of the memory within. It felt cold, unnaturally so, a cold that had nothing to do with the cavern's temperature. It was the cold of a void, of an absence. It was a reliquary whose saint had been exorcised.

Her rational, scholarly mind told her to be cautious. The cult had called it a "key." The General had used it as a weapon. This was no mere trinket; it was a nexus of powerful, volatile energies. But the scholar in her was insatiably curious. What was it, precisely? A soul jar? A chronal anchor? A vessel for a captured emotional echo? The fragmented notes on the slate tablets provided a terrifying theory, but she needed to be certain.

Closing her eyes, she gently cradled the locket in both hands. She extended her senses, not with a surge of power, but with a delicate, probing touch, like a surgeon feeling for a pulse. She did not try to force her way in, but merely to listen, to feel the faint, residual resonance of the magic it had once contained.

The moment her arcane senses touched the silver, the world vanished.

She was not prepared for the violence of the connection. She was hurled into a moment in time with the force of a physical blow. The damp, violet lit cavern was gone, replaced by a world of impossible light and color.

She stood on a balcony of white marble under a sky of the deepest, softest blue. A gentle, warm breeze carried the scent of salt and a flower she had never smelled before, a sweet, heady fragrance like honey and starlight. Below her, a city of breathtaking beauty glittered, its towers and bridges built not of stone, but of what looked like solidified sunlight, all of it overlooking a calm, turquoise sea. This was a memory of the world as it had been, in a forgotten, golden age.

And she was not alone.

A man stood at the balcony's edge, his back to her. He was tall and broad shouldered, clad in armor of gleaming, sun gold plate that radiated its own warmth and light. A white cloak, embroidered with a symbol of a radiant sun, billowed softly in the breeze. This was a hero whose presence was a bulwark against the darkness. She could feel the power emanating from him, the pure, unshakeable power of conviction, a righteousness so absolute it was a physical force.

A woman came to stand beside him, and the breath caught in Seraphina's throat. The miniature in the locket had been a pale shadow of her true beauty. Her hair was the color of spun moonlight, and her eyes, the color of the summer sky, were filled with a light of their own. She wore a simple white gown, yet she possessed a grace and majesty that outshone his golden armor.

He turned to her, and Seraphina saw his face for the first time. It was a face carved from nobility, with a strong jaw and eyes the color of molten gold. But the strength in his features was softened by the expression he wore now. As he looked at the woman, all the power, all the kingship, all the divine purpose fell away, replaced by an emotion so pure, so profound, it was a work of art in itself. It was a love that was both a surrender and a conquest, a perfect, harmonious chord of devotion, passion, and a deep, soul shaking tenderness.

"My love," he said, and his voice was not the guttural rasp of a lich, but a deep, resonant baritone, warm and full of light. He took her hand, his armored fingers infinitely gentle. "Is it not the most perfect day?"

"Every day with you is perfect, my king," she replied, her voice like music. She reached up and touched the silver locket that hung around his neck. the same locket Seraphina now held. "But this one... this one feels like a promise. The beginning of a thousand years of peace."

"Our peace," he said, his golden eyes filled with her. "A world we will build together."

He leaned in to kiss her, and in that moment, the universe seemed to hold its breath. The pure, uncorrupted emotional energy of that single instant. the absolute certainty of their love, the boundless hope for their future, the perfect, radiant joy of their union. was a force of nature, a supernova of the soul.

And Seraphina, an unwilling conduit, could not contain it.

Back in the cold, damp cavern, the locket in her hands flared with a silent, invisible light. The psychic shockwave bypassed sound and sight, striking them as a direct, violent, and overwhelming infusion of pure, heroic love.

The effect on her companions was immediate and devastating.

Gundroff, who had been sitting in stoic, stony silence, cried out as if he'd been stabbed. It was a choked, guttural sound of agony. The wave of emotion hit him not as a comfort, but as a poison. For a man whose entire identity was built on a foundation of failure, whose soul was calloused by forty years of shame and a grim, unwavering belief in the harsh, unforgiving nature of the world, this sudden, invasive flood of pure hope and love was anathema. It was a sweet, cloying poison that highlighted the bitterness of his own existence. It was the memory of a warm hearth to a man freezing to death. It was a mockery.

He staggered to his feet, his good hand clenched, his face a mask of revulsion. "What is this?" he roared, not at Seraphina, but at the air around him. "This… weakness! This lie! Get it out of my head!" He saw in the vision's purity not a strength, but a fatal flaw, the sentimental foolishness that had led his own people to ruin. Love was a fairy tale told to children. Duty, stone, and the cold, complex reality of steel. those were the only truths. This feeling was a violation, a defilement of the grim strength he had cultivated in the ashes of his home.

Thaddeus's reaction was quieter, but no less profound. The wave of emotion washed over him, and the old man froze, the tin cup of tea halfway to his lips. His cheerful, enigmatic facade dissolved, replaced by a look of deep, ancient, and utterly unexplainable sorrow. A single tear traced a path through the grime on his cheek. The pure, perfect love of the vision did not inspire him or disgust him; it broke his heart. It was as if the vision's joy had struck some long dormant, secret chord of grief within him, a sadness so profound that he himself seemed unable to comprehend its source. He looked at Seraphina, his eyes filled with a terrible, silent question, not for her, but for a ghost only he could see.

Seraphina herself was thrown back out of the vision, gasping, her heart hammering against her ribs. The locket clattered from her numb fingers onto the stone floor. She was left trembling, not from fear, but from the sheer, overwhelming force of the paradox that had just been seared into her mind.

The monster they hunted, the profane intelligence behind the Sun Scorched, the architect of an evil that sought to unmake reality itself... had once been a man. A good man. A hero who had been capable of a love so pure and potent it had survived for millennia, a love strong enough to be weaponized. The knowledge didn't excuse his evil or lessen the horror of his actions. It twisted it, complicating the entire war. Their enemy was not a simple abyss of darkness, but a fallen star, and the light still echoing from his past only made his present shadow all the more terrifying.

The three of them were left in a heavy, ringing silence, broken only by Gundroff's ragged breathing and the slow, steady drip of water from the cavern ceiling. The psychic storm had passed, but it had left them shipwrecked, each stranded on the shores of their own private, wounded island. The locket lay between them, no longer just a prize or a clue, but a terrible mirror, reflecting the broken pieces of their own hearts.

The silence that followed the psychic storm was heavier and more profound than the subterranean darkness that surrounded them. The single, shared vision had shattered their unity, leaving three isolated individuals trembling in its wake. The air was thick with unspoken thoughts, with the echoes of emotions too powerful to be easily dismissed.

It was Seraphina who broke the spell. She drew in a shuddering breath, forcing the cold, damp air into her lungs to quell the frantic beating of her heart. The scholar within her, the rationalist who built fortresses of logic against the chaos of the world, was reeling. But she was also their leader. She had to be the one to put the pieces back together, even if she wasn't sure what shape they were supposed to make anymore.

She rose to her feet, her legs unsteady, and retrieved the locket from the stone floor. It was inert again, just a piece of ruined silver, but it felt heavier now, weighted with the tragedy it contained. "That was... a soul print," she said, her voice still shaky as she tried to fit the experience into the framework of her arcane knowledge. "A captured emotional echo, imprinted onto the object at a moment of extreme significance. It was more than a memory. We experienced what he felt."

Gundroff finally moved. He pushed himself away from the wall, his face a thunderous mask of contempt. "I know what I felt," he snarled, his voice a low, grinding rumble of disgust. "Poison," Gundroff snarled, spitting on the floor. "You want me to feel *pity* for the thing that's unmaking the world?" "I want you to be smart!" Seraphina shot back, her voice shaking. "That *thing* was a man! He loved someone! That's a weakness, a crack we can break!" "Love is a weakness! My people died for it! They died for songs and hearth fires while the world burned! You want to fight him with a sad story? I'll fight him with an axe!"

"It wasn't weakness, Gundroff," Seraphina countered, her voice gaining strength as her conviction returned. "It was the opposite. The sheer power of that emotion... It's what the cult has been trying to harness. It's the fuel for their alchemy. Don't you see? This changes everything."

"It changes nothing!" he roared, taking a step forward, his good hand balling into a fist. "What does it matter what he was? A dragon was once a hatchling. do you dull your axe on its scales for memory's sake? You strike it down for the monster it has become! This... this pity you feel is a luxury we cannot afford. It is the sentiment that brought my own people to ruin!"

"This isn't about pity, it's about strategy!" Seraphina shot back, her frustration boiling over into anger. "Knowing your enemy is the first law of warfare! Before this, he was just a force of nature, an abstract evil. Now we know he was a man. He had a heart. And anything that can be built can be broken." She held up the locket. "He loved that woman. That love was his greatest strength, and its loss must have been his greatest wound. That is a vulnerability. That is a flaw we can exploit!"

"A flaw?" Gundroff laughed, a harsh, bitter sound with no humor in it. "You speak of his heart as if it were a weakness in his armor. Do you really think you can defeat this god of decay with a sad story? He will use that hope of yours to choke you. He will use that compassion to gut you. He did it to me, not an hour since! Did you not see? He took the memory of my home and used it to sharpen his blade!"

"And he took the memory of my daughter," Seraphina said, her voice dropping to a low, dangerous whisper, her eyes flashing in the violet light. The argument was no longer academic. "He threatened my child, Gundroff. Please do not presume to lecture me on the nature of this enemy or the stakes of this fight. I will use any weapon I can find to destroy him, and the knowledge of what he has lost is a weapon."

They stood facing each other, a chasm of philosophy and experience separating them. Gundroff, the pragmatist forged in tragedy, saw only the monster that must be slain. Seraphina, the scholar thrust into a war, saw a puzzle that must be solved.

It was Thaddeus who finally broke the standoff. He had remained silent throughout their argument, his teacup forgotten, the single tear having dried on his cheek. He looked from one to the other, his gaze filled with that same deep, inexplicable sorrow from the vision.

"A memory," he said softly, his voice barely a whisper in the echoing cavern, "is a heavier burden than any stone. And a broken heart is the most fertile ground for monstrosity." He sighed, a sound of ancient weariness. "You are both right. And you are both wrong. He is the monster Gundroff sees, and he is the broken man you see, Seraphina. The tragedy is that the two are the same."

He slowly rose to his feet and picked up the leviathan hide map. He unrolled it on the stone floor, its crude lines a stark, practical reality in the face of their metaphysical debate. "This," he said, his finger tracing a path through the dark tunnels, "is the only truth that matters right now. This is the path ahead. The nature of our enemy's soul is a question for the gods. The location of the next cult outpost is a question for us."

His simple, profound words cut through their anger, leaving a raw, uncomfortable silence in their wake. He was right.

Seraphina let out a long, slow breath, her shoulders slumping. She looked at Gundroff, whose own fury had subsided into a grim, stubborn resentment. The rift between them had not healed, but Thaddeus had built a fragile bridge across it.

"He's right," she said, her voice quiet. She knelt beside the map, forcing her mind back to the immediate, the tactical. "The trail leads north, through a series of river caverns. We need to rest. Gundroff needs his wound tended to, as best I can. And we all need to conserve our strength."

Gundroff gave a stiff, jerky nod, refusing to meet her eyes. He retrieved his axe and went back to his corner, sinking against the wall, the picture of grim defiance. The argument was over, but it was not resolved. A fracture had appeared in the foundation of their fellowship, a hairline crack of ideology that threatened to widen under the pressures to come.

Seraphina watched him for a moment, then turned her attention to the map. But as she plotted their course through the alien darkness of the Underworld, her thoughts were not on the path ahead. They were on the impossible paradox of their enemy, the fallen hero, the Sunken King. They had won the locket, but in doing so, they had invited a ghost into their fellowship.

The silence stretched, punctuated only by the rhythmic drip of water and Gundroff's pained, shallow breathing. The immediate, tactical need to move warred with the profound, bone deep exhaustion that had settled over them. Seraphina knew they couldn't stay in the cult's abandoned laboratory. Its stale, violet tinged magic felt like a beacon in the dark, and every moment they lingered was a risk.

"Gundroff," she said, her voice softer than before, devoid of the sharp edge of their argument. "Let me see your arm."

He didn't look at her. His gaze remained fixed on the far wall, his face a stony mask. "There's nothing to see. It's done."

"It is not done," she insisted, pushing herself to her feet and walking over to him. She knelt in front of him, forcing him to either meet her eyes or look away pointedly. "The temporal decay has stabilized, but the wound is... an open gateway. It's leaking. I can feel the life draining out of you, a little at a time. I may not be able to fix it, but I have to try to seal it."

He flinched as she reached for his withered hand. "Don't touch it with your magic, witch. It was magic that did this."

The word 'witch' was a slap. It was the term peasants used, a phrase born of fear and ignorance, not one she ever expected to hear from him. A flare of anger ignited in her chest, but she smothered it. He was in agony, lashing out from a place of deep, primal fear.

"It was profane science that did this," she corrected him, her voice a low, firm instrument of reason. "And I am going to use arcane science to contain it. This is not a debate, Gundroff. Either you let me try, or we leave you here to crumble into dust. Now, hold still."

Her tone brooked no further argument. With a low growl of frustrated resignation, he held out the blighted limb.

Seraphina took his hand. It was cold, the skin thin and dry as papyrus over the bird like bones. She closed her eyes, focusing her will, gathering the last vestiges of her power. She did not attempt a healing spell; that would be like trying to fill a sieve with water. Instead, she visualized the flow of time itself, seeing his timeline as a golden thread. The wound was a frayed, tangled knot in that thread, a place where the past, present, and future bled into one another in a chaotic, decaying mess.

She couldn't untangle the knot, but she could cauterize it.

Murmuring a soft, complex chant, she wove a delicate matrix of pure, temporal energy. It was not a grand, powerful magic, but a thing of intricate, precise patterns, like a weaver setting a loom. She carefully wrapped this matrix around the temporal scar, not touching it, but containing it, creating a shimmering, almost invisible shell of stable causality around the wound. The goal was to isolate the corrupted timeline, to stop it from leaking into the rest of him.

The effort was immense. Sweat beaded on her brow. The hollow ache behind her eyes intensified into a sharp, stabbing pain. She felt her own life force being drawn into the spell, the cost of meddling with such fundamental forces. Gundroff let out a sharp hiss of pain as the arcane energies settled, the sensation of having a piece of his own soul caged and quarantined clearly agonizing.

When she was finished, she slumped back, gasping, a wave of dizziness washing over her. The arm looked no different. It was still the withered, ancient limb of a dying man. But to her arcane senses, the leak had been sealed. The bleeding had stopped.

"It will hold," she said, her voice a weary rasp. "For now."

Thaddeus, who had been watching the entire exchange with a sad, knowing look in his eyes, chose that moment to intervene. "The path will not walk itself," he said, his calm, practical voice cutting through the tension. He offered Seraphina a waterskin, and she took it with a grateful nod. "I have secured the map. Our supplies are meager, but they will suffice for a time. We should move while the cover of this... well, this perpetual darkness, is upon us."

His gentle, mundane words were a balm. Gundroff, cradling his sealed arm, pushed himself to his feet with a groan, his pride forcing him into motion. He was unsteady, but he was standing.

They gathered their few belongings in silence, the earlier argument hanging between them like a physical presence. They were a fractured fellowship, moving together out of necessity, not unity.

Seraphina led them out of the cramped laboratory, back into the breathtaking, spectral beauty of the main grotto. The sight of it was no less awe inspiring. The vast, silent chamber, lit by the pulsing, organic light of its strange flora, was a world unto itself. And there, at the grotto's edge, was the source of the deep, thrumming sound: the Under Ocean.

It was not a lake, but a true sea, stretching out into an infinite, silent blackness. Its surface was unnaturally calm, a sheet of black glass that perfectly reflected the glowing moss and fungi on the ceiling, creating the illusion of a star filled sky beneath their feet. Slow, powerful currents moved within its depths, great, dark shapes that hinted at the passage of immense, unseen creatures. The air was cool and tasted of salt and stone.

They stood on the shore of this impossible sea, three small, wounded figures in a world that should not exist. The map showed a narrow, walkable ledge that followed the coastline for miles, a treacherous path into the deeper dark.

Without a word, Seraphina took the first step onto the path. Thaddeus followed a few paces behind, his staff tapping a quiet, steady rhythm on the stone. After a long moment of hesitation, Gundroff fell into line at the rear, his heavy, uneven footsteps echoing in the vast, silent cathedral.

They walked together, but apart, each wrapped in their own thoughts. The ghost of the Sunken King had become their fourth companion. Its presence haunted the chasm of silence between Seraphina and Gundroff. It was the source of the deep, unexplained sorrow in Thaddeus's eyes. And it resided in the tragic, impossible love that had ignited a war at the dawn of the world, a love whose corrupted embers now threatened to burn them all.

The narrow ledge snaked along the edge of the silent, black water, a path of damp stone in a world of spectral light. The only sounds were the soft tap of Thaddeus's staff and the heavy, uneven tread of Gundroff's boots, a grim percussion marking their progress into the deep. Above them, the glowing fungi cast shifting, intricate patterns on the water's glassy surface, creating an illusion of a slow moving galaxy of cold, silent stars beneath their feet. The scale of the cavern was oppressive; they were three insignificant specks of life crawling along the shore of an endless, sleeping sea.

Seraphina felt the immense weight of the silence. It was a physical pressure, made heavier by the unspoken resentments and fears that now defined their fellowship. She risked a glance over her shoulder. Thaddeus walked with his head bowed, his face a mask of quiet contemplation, the mystery of his sorrow making him seem more distant than ever. Farther back, Gundroff trudged onward, a solitary figure of stubborn pride. He kept a deliberate distance, his movements stiff with pain and anger. He favored his good arm, cradling the withered one as if it were a dead thing he was forced to carry.

She turned her gaze forward again, the path ahead a winding ribbon of uncertainty. The locket, now tucked safely inside her tunic, felt like a block of ice against her skin. Its vision had given them a weapon, she had argued. A vulnerability to exploit. But as she walked, the certainty of her strategic mind was eroded by a tide of disquiet. The vision had not been a simple recording of the past. She had felt the warmth in the hero's voice, the profound devotion in his eyes.

How do you fight a memory? How do you wage war against a love that was once pure enough to promise a thousand years of peace?

Gundroff was right about one thing: it was a poison. Not the love itself, but the knowledge of it. It was a poison that bred doubt, that complicated the simple, necessary calculus of war. Before, she had been a scholar, a soldier fighting an abstract, monstrous evil. Now, she felt like an executioner, tasked with destroying not just a monster, but the tragic, corrupted ghost of a good man. It was a distinction that settled in her soul like a shard of glass.

A sharp scrape of metal on stone made her pause. Gundroff had stumbled, his withered arm throwing off his balance. He caught himself against the cavern wall with his good shoulder, a low grunt of pain and frustration escaping his lips. For a fleeting second, his stony facade cracked, revealing a glimpse of the terrified man beneath, trapped in a decaying body, haunted by his own future. He recovered quickly, pushing himself upright before Thaddeus could even offer a hand, his pride a fortress rebuilt in an instant. He shot a glare toward Seraphina, a silent warning against any offer of pity.

She said nothing, merely turned and resumed walking. The moment passed, but the image remained: the proud dwarf, the unbreakable bastion of their fellowship, faltering. They were all faltering. The General's assault in the pyramid had been brutally effective, not because of the elementals he had summoned, but because he had understood their hearts. He had wounded them with their own memories, and now, the ghost of his master's memory was finishing the job.

Chapter 18

The Under Sea

The silence of the grotto was the silence of a forgotten grave. They stood on the shore of the Under Ocean, a trio of broken ghosts at the edge of an abyss. The fire they had built was a small, defiant star of warmth, but its light seemed to be devoured by the vast, oppressive darkness of the cavern, a darkness that was ancient, absolute, and patient.

Gundroff's world had been reduced to a symphony of pain. A dull, throbbing ache radiated from his dislocated shoulder, a souvenir from their violent landing. But it was the other wound, the new one, that was a constant, chilling whisper against his soul. He looked down at his left arm, where the Ice Elemental's touch had left its profane signature. The skin was like old parchment, thin and wrinkled, covered in the liver spots of a centenarian. The thick, dwarven beard on that side of his face was a brittle, shocking white. He clenched the withered hand into a fist. It obeyed, but it felt alien, a dead thing grafted onto his living body. The loss was a scar on time itself, a permanent reminder of the power they had faced. His axe, his beloved *Grief* and *Vengeance*, was gone, lost in the chaos of their escape through the portal. His hands, which had so long known the familiar weight of its haft, felt light, alien, and terribly exposed. He flexed his fingers, a clumsy, useless motion, as if his muscles were searching for something no longer there.

Seraphina, her face a pale mask in the firelight, broke the silence. She held up the crude, skin bound map they had found in the alchemist's lab. "There," she said, her voice a low, strained whisper. She pointed with a trembling finger to a spot on the map, a crudely drawn symbol of a gaping maw at the edge of the black, ink blot sea. "The Sunken Road. It is our only way out."

Gundroff followed her gaze. At the far end of their small, sandy shore, the black, still water of the Under Ocean lapped against the entrance to a tunnel. It was a perfect, circular opening in the rock face, a black, gaping throat that promised to devour them whole. His dwarven soul, a thing forged in the deep, living stone, screamed at the sight of it. Stone was safe. Stone was home. Open water was a tomb.

"We cannot go that way," he rumbled, the words a gut reaction, a primal rejection of the path ahead. "It is a fool's path. A grave."

"It is our only path," Seraphina countered, her voice sharp with a desperate, frayed edge. "The tunnels behind us are a maze. The cult will be searching them. This road is the one they would not expect us to take."

"And how do you propose we walk through a drowned tunnel, elf?" he snarled, the old, familiar contempt for her magic rising in his throat. "Do you plan to ask the water to part for you?"

She met his gaze. He saw a vulnerability there that mirrored his own terror. "No," she said, her voice quiet but firm. "I plan to hold it back myself."

She rose, her movements stiff and pained. She walked to the edge of the water, her form a slender, elegant silhouette against the profound, absolute blackness. "The spell is... complex," she began, her voice the calm, clinical tone of a scholar lecturing on a distasteful but necessary subject. "It is a piece of high chronomancy. A weaving of temporal and spatial magic. It creates a lung, not a shield. I will create a bubble of breathable air around us, a pocket of displaced reality. This is not a static ward. It is a constant, active process of transmuting the water into air, of holding back the crushing pressure of a thousand tons of rock and water with nothing but my will."

She turned to face them. In the faint, flickering firelight, Gundroff saw the actual cost of her words. Her face was pale and drawn. Her eyes held a profound, soul weary exhaustion that went beyond any physical fatigue. A fine tremor ran through her hands, a thing she could not conceal.

"I can maintain the spell for perhaps an hour," she said, her voice now a raw, honest whisper. "After that, my will shall falter. The bubble will collapse. We will drown in the crushing, absolute darkness."

The words hung in the air, a simple, brutal, and unadorned truth. Gundroff looked from her pale, determined face to the black, waiting maw of the tunnel. He felt the phantom pressure of the water, the suffocating weight of the mountain above them, the cold, final embrace of a watery grave. Every instinct he possessed, every lesson his father had taught him, every fiber of his dwarven being, screamed at him to stay on the solid, trustworthy stone. Placing his life in the hands of a fragile, trembling elf and her magic felt like an act of profound, suicidal madness.

He looked at Thaddeus. The old man was not looking at the tunnel. He was looking at Seraphina, his bright, blue eyes filled not with fear, but with a quiet, absolute, and unwavering faith. He gave a single, slight nod, a silent testament to a trust that Gundroff could not comprehend.

Gundroff looked back at Seraphina. He saw a fellow warrior, preparing to fight her own kind of battle, a battle of will against the laws of the world. He was a creature of stone and steel. He was being asked to place his faith in a thing as intangible as a word, as fragile as a breath.

His choice was born from a cold, challenging, and brutal pragmatism. To stay here was to die, slowly and indeed, at the hands of the cult. To go forward was to face a possible, though not certain, death. It was a fool's gamble, and it was the only move they had left.

He rose, his own movements slow and deliberate. He walked to the edge of the water, his heavy, iron shod boots sinking into the soft, wet sand. He stood beside her, a mountain of scarred muscle and unyielding will, a silent, grim acceptance.

Seraphina gave him a single, grateful nod. She closed her eyes and raised her hands. She began to chant, her voice a low, melodic whisper that was at odds with the grim, terrible power she was summoning. A fine, silver light, cold and sterile as starlight, began to shimmer around her hands. It coalesced, weaving itself into a shimmering, translucent sphere of pure, arcane energy that expanded from her palms. It pushed back the darkness and the air of the cavern.

Gundroff watched, his breath catching in his throat, as the shimmering bubble touched the surface of the black water. It did not pop. It did not ripple. It simply... entered. The water yielded to the magic, parting with a silent, oily grace.

Seraphina opened her eyes. They were wide with a fierce, burning concentration. "It is done," she said, her voice strained. "Stay within the light. Do not touch the walls of the bubble. And pray to your stone god that my strength holds."

She took the first step, into the shimmering sphere of her own making, and then into the black, silent water. Thaddeus followed without hesitation.

Gundroff stood for a final, heart stopping moment on the shore. He took a last, deep breath of the stale, cavern air. Then, with a grunt that was half prayer and half curse, he plunged into the abyss.

The world dissolved into a silent, silver bubble of impossible air in the heart of a black, crushing sea. Gundroff's first, primal instinct was to hold his breath, his lungs seizing in protest against a reality that should not exist. But the air within Seraphina's spell was cool, clean, and breathable, a pocket of impossible life in a world of absolute death. The only sound was the faint, ethereal, humming thrum of the magic itself and the ragged, desperate sound of their own breathing.

They drifted downwards, pulled by the weight of their own bodies, into an absolute, featureless black. The silver light of the bubble pushed back the gloom for a few feet in every direction, revealing only the rough, gouged walls of the tunnel, a wound in the stone that seemed to descend into the guts of the world. The pressure was a palpable, living thing, a constant, crushing weight that Gundroff felt deep in the bones of his skull. It was a pressure his kind was never meant to endure, making his dislocated shoulder feel as though it might pop from its socket again. He felt a profound, primal terror, a claustrophobia of the soul that was far worse than any narrow tunnel. He was a stone, and he was sinking.

He looked at Seraphina. She floated in the center of their small, silver world, her eyes closed, her face a mask of serene, absolute concentration. Her hands were held out before her, her fingers weaving a slow, intricate, and constant pattern in the air. The silver light of the bubble seemed to emanate from her will, a fragile, defiant star against the abyss. A fine sheen of sweat beaded on her brow, and the faint tremor in her hands was more pronounced now, a testament to the immense, constant strain of holding back a literal ocean.

Thaddeus, for his part, seemed utterly unconcerned. He floated with a quiet, placid grace, his gaze fixed on the shimmering, translucent wall of the bubble, a look of profound, academic curiosity in his bright, blue eyes.

A soft, wet tick against the side of the bubble broke the silence.

Gundroff spun around, his Axe held ready, his eyes scanning the absolute blackness beyond their small sphere of light. He saw nothing.

Tick. Tock. Tick tick.

The sound came again, from another direction this time. A series of minor, sharp impacts against the magical barrier. It was not the sound of an attack. It was the sound of... hail.

"What in the depths...?" he rumbled, his voice a low, dead thing in the strange, echoless air of the bubble.

Seraphina's eyes snapped open, her concentration momentarily broken. "Do not touch the walls," she commanded, her voice strained, a sharp edge of a new and unfamiliar fear in her tone.

Then they saw it. A flicker of movement in the darkness. A pale, ghostly shape that darted into the edge of their light and then vanished again. Then another. And another. Soon, the darkness outside their small, silver world was alive with them.

They were fish, of a kind Gundroff had never seen. They were long and thin, like eels, their bodies a pale, sickly white, utterly devoid of pigment. They had no eyes, only smooth, blank patches of skin where eyes should have been. And their mouths, which were constantly opening and closing, were filled with rows of fine, needle like teeth that glinted in the silver light. They were a swarm of blind, albino, and utterly relentless horrors.

They were not attacking the bubble. They were drawn to it. They seemed to be feeding on the light, or the magic, or both. They pressed against the translucent wall, their pale, writhing bodies a solid, undulating mass of white, their needle like teeth making a hideous, grating sound against the magical barrier, a sound of a thousand tiny files trying to scratch their way in.

"They are blind," Thaddeus said, his voice a quiet, observational calm in the heart of their rising panic. "Creatures of the absolute dark. They have never seen a light before. They are drawn to it as a moth to a flame."

The constant, grating sound was a torment, a physical vibration that seemed to travel through the bubble and into Gundroff's bones. The sight of the writhing, pale mass, the dead, milky white eyes, the endless rows of needle like teeth, was a vision from a madman's nightmare. He felt a primal, warrior's rage surge through him, a desperate, useless need to strike, to smash, to kill. But his Axe was useless here. He was a warrior trapped in a cage of his own ally's making, surrounded by an enemy he could not fight.

He looked at Seraphina. Her face was now as pale as the creatures outside, her brow furrowed, her lips a thin, white line of concentration. The humming of the spell had risen in pitch, a high, strained, keen that spoke of a will that was being stretched to its absolute breaking point. The bubble, which had been a perfect, shimmering sphere, now seemed to flicker and warp where the swarm was thickest, the wall bending inwards for a fraction of a second before she could force it back out.

"We have to keep moving," she gasped, the words a desperate, ragged breath. "I cannot maintain the integrity of the spell against this... this pressure."

Gundroff needed no further prompting. He turned, his back to the horrifying, writhing mass, and began to swim, his powerful legs kicking, pushing their small, silver world deeper into the black, silent tunnel, away from the world of teeth. The swarm followed, a relentless, ghostly procession of a thousand hungry mouths, a quiet, screaming testament to the deep, dark, and forgotten horrors that slept in the bones of the world.

The swarm of blind, pale fish finally receded, their relentless, grating assault fading back into the oppressive blackness from which they had come. A profound and unnerving silence descended once more, broken only by the faint, high pitched thrum of Seraphina's spell and the ragged sound of their own breathing. Gundroff's heart, which had been hammering against his ribs with a warrior's fury, slowly returned to a dull, fearful rhythm. He felt a cold sweat on his brow, a thing he had not felt in the heat of an actual battle for forty years. This was a different kind of war, a struggle against a world that did not fight with steel, but with the slow, grinding pressure of its own alien wrongness.

He watched Seraphina. The silver light of the bubble seemed to emanate directly from her, and he could see the terrible cost of their survival etched on her face. Her skin, already pale, was now almost translucent, her lips a thin, bloodless line of concentration. The tremor in her hands was no longer a subtle flicker; it was a visible, violent shudder. The humming of the spell, which had been a steady, ethereal note, now wavered, dipping and soaring like the song of a dying bird. She was a guttering candle in an infinite darkness, and he knew, with a cold, hard certainty, that she did not have much longer.

The narrow tunnel, which had been a claustrophobic nightmare of scraping teeth and writhing, pale bodies, finally began to widen. The rough, gouged walls receded, pulling back into the oppressive blackness beyond their small sphere of light. The feeling of being in a tight, stone walled passage was replaced by a new, and in its own way, more terrifying sensation: the feeling of being in a vast, open, and utterly space. It was the difference between a grave and the void.

They drifted out of the tunnel's mouth and into a new cavern. This was not a grotto or a passage. It was a subterranean sky. The darkness was absolute, a perfect, featureless black that their small, silver light could not pierce. They were a single, tiny star, floating in an infinite and empty universe. Gundroff felt a sudden, profound vertigo, his dwarven soul, a thing that craved the reassuring press of close, solid stone, crying out in protest against this vast, terrifying emptiness.

It was Seraphina who saw it first. "By the First Star," she breathed, her voice a whisper of pure, unadulterated awe. Her concentration, which had been an unyielding, iron clad thing, faltered for a fraction of a second. The bubble around them flickered violently, the walls seeming to warp and bend inwards, and a wave of crushing pressure slammed against Gundroff's skull.

He followed her gaze, his own eyes struggling to adjust to the new, impossible sight. In the far distance, a light was growing. It was a soft, gentle, blue green luminescence, unlike the harsh violet of the cult or the clean silver of Seraphina's magic. A light that seemed to pulse with a slow, rhythmic, and impossibly ancient life. It was the light of a false moon, rising in a dead sky.

As they drifted closer, the source of the light resolved into a shape, a form so colossal it shattered all of Gundroff's preconceived notions of what a living thing could be. It was a leviathan, a creature from an age before the gods had learned their own names. Its body was a slow, graceful mountain of ancient, bioluminescent flesh, its hide a tapestry of soft, pulsing lights that shifted and changed in slow, hypnotic patterns. It moved with an ancient, indifferent grace, its vast, whale like tail propelling it through the black water with a slow, powerful rhythm that was the heartbeat of the abyss. It was not so much a monster as it was a world, a living, breathing ecosystem of its own, and they were nothing more than dust motes in its path.

They floated in a state of stunned, terrified silence, their own small, desperate struggles rendered utterly, absurdly insignificant in the face of this ancient, indifferent majesty. The leviathan, which had been a distant, beautiful spectacle, began to turn, its vast, slow, and inexorable movement bringing it onto a new course. A course that would intersect with their own.

And then, it saw them.

A single, colossal eye, an orb of liquid, phosphorescent silver the size of the great shield that had once hung in his father's hall, swiveled in its socket. The pupil, a vast, black slit of absolute void, contracted, focusing on their small, defiant bubble of light with a look of slow, dawning, and utterly alien curiosity.

The feeling of being seen was a physical blow, a wave of pure psychic pressure that was heavier than any water. It was the feeling of a god noticing an ant. Gundroff's thoughts, a fortress of grit and pragmatism, felt a sudden, terrifying emptiness. He felt a profound sense of his own smallness, a realization that his forty year war of vengeance was a child's tantrum in the face of a hurricane.

"The light," Seraphina gasped, her voice a raw, desperate croak. "It sees the light! Put it out!"

Her own spell, the source of their life, was now the beacon that was drawing their death. With a final, desperate act of will, she snuffed it out.

The world vanished.

The darkness that descended was a crushing, total void. a presence that smothered the senses, more than just the absence of light. Gundroff could see nothing, not even the faint outline of his own hand in front of his face. He could hear nothing but the frantic, panicked hammering of his own blood in his ears. He could feel nothing but the cold, wet press of his clothes against his skin and the faint, almost imperceptible thrum of Seraphina's now invisible spell against his back.

He reached out a hand, his fingers scrabbling in the void, and found Thaddeus's shoulder. The old man's hand came up and gripped his, a small, solid point of contact in a universe of nothing. They floated in the absolute, silent blackness, three minor, terrified points of life, their own breathing a deafening roar in the sudden, terrible silence.

Time ceased to have meaning. He did not know if they waited for a minute or an hour. His world was the crushing pressure, the frantic beating of his own heart, and the feel of the old man's steadying grip. He felt the bubble flicker once, twice, the wall of it brushing against his back, a terrifying, wet kiss from the abyss. He heard a soft, choked gasp from Seraphina, the sound of a will that was being stretched to its absolute breaking point.

There was no room for prayer in this watery, lightless void; his god was a god of the stone and the forge, of solid, tangible things. All he could do was endure. All he could do was wait for the end.

And then, a new sound. A deep, resonant, and impossibly vast thrumming, a sound that was felt more than it was heard, a vibration that traveled through the water and into the marrow of his bones. It was the sound of the leviathan's passage, the slow, powerful beat of its colossal heart as it moved through the abyss. The sound grew, and grew, until it was a physical, shaking force, and then, just as slowly, it began to fade, receding into the vast, silent dark.

It was gone.

A few, heart stopping seconds later, a small, silver light bloomed back into existence. It was weaker now, a fragile, sputtering thing, and it cast a pale, ghostly glow on their three terrified faces. The bubble itself was smaller, the walls of it visibly closer, the pressure more intense.

They were alive. But the cost of their survival had been high. And they were still a, long way from the surface.

The silver light bloomed back into existence, a fragile, sputtering thing that cast a pale, ghostly glow on their three terrified faces. The bubble itself was smaller, the walls of it visibly closer, the pressure more intense. Gundroff felt it as a physical weight against his skull, a dull, crushing ache that was the abyssal depths trying to reclaim their stolen space.

Seraphina's eyes were open, but they were not focused on them. They stared into a middle distance only she could see, her entire being a fragile, trembling vessel for the spell that was keeping them alive. A thin, dark line of blood trickled from her nose, a stark, crimson tear against her pale, almost translucent skin. The ethereal, humming thrum of her magic, which had been a steady, reassuring note, was now a high, strained, and wavering keen, the sound of a harp string stretched to its absolute breaking point. "The exit," she gasped, the words a desperate, ragged breath, each one a costly expenditure of will. "Above us."

Gundroff looked up. Far above, a hundred feet or more, he saw it. A faint, almost imperceptible disturbance in the absolute blackness, a place where the water seemed to shimmer differently. It was the surface of a hidden spring, an air pocket, their only sanctuary in this drowned world. A hundred feet. It might as well have been a hundred leagues.

"I... I am failing," she whispered, her voice a fragile, breaking thing. "The light... the waiting... it took too much." He saw the bubble flicker again, the wall of it brushing against his back, a terrifying, wet kiss from the abyss. He did not need a scholar to tell him what that meant. The clock was ticking.

He wasted no time on words. He was a creature of action, and the path was clear. He was the mountain. He would not crumble. He turned to Thaddeus, his golden brown eyes burning with a fierce, protective light. "Grab her," he commanded, his voice a low, hard rumble that was not open to debate. "Hold on. Do not let go."

Thaddeus, his face a mask of grim, focused resolve, nodded once. He moved to Seraphina, who seemed to be a dead weight in the water, a puppet whose strings had been cut, her entire consciousness focused on the single, monumental task of holding back the sea. He wrapped a steady arm around her waist, holding her close.

Gundroff turned his back on them. "On my back," he grunted. "Now."

He felt their weight settle upon him, Thaddeus's wiry frame and Seraphina's limp form a strange, desperate burden. He looked up at the distant, shimmering promise of air. Then, with a roar of pure, defiant will that was swallowed by the silent, crushing water, he began to swim.

His powerful, dwarven legs, built for bracing against the weight of the stone, now became pistons, driving him upwards through the black, indifferent water. He was a rising stone, a defiant boulder refusing to sink. The pressure in his skull intensified, a blinding, white hot agony. The muscles in his legs burned with a fire that was hotter than any forge. But he did not stop.

He felt the bubble flicker again, more violently this time. A wave of crushing pressure slammed into them, and he heard a soft, choked gasp from Seraphina. The high, keening thrum of her spell faltered, dipping into a low, guttural groan before she could force it back up. The silver light around them dimmed, the edges of their small world closing in.

Faster, his mind screamed.

He kicked harder, his vision beginning to blur at the edges, his lungs screaming for a breath he could not take. The shimmering surface was closer now, a tantalizing, beautiful promise. Fifty feet. Forty.

The sound of the spell changed. The high, keening thrum dissolved into a wet, sticky, tearing sound, like wet silk being ripped apart. The bubble was no longer a perfect sphere. It was warping, collapsing, the walls of it becoming thick and viscous, clinging to them like a shroud. A trickle of cold, black water, a single, questing tendril of the abyss, forced its way through a momentary weakness in the spell and splashed against his face. It was a promise. a down payment on the death that was coming for them.

Thirty feet.

Seraphina's gasp was louder now, a wet, choking sound. The light was a pale, ghostly glimmer, barely pushing back the absolute, crushing blackness. The bubble was shrinking, its walls pressing in on them, the pressure a physical, suffocating thing. Gundroff could feel the weight of their bodies, a dead, leaden thing on his back. His own lungs were on fire, black spots dancing in his vision.

Twenty feet.

The bubble collapsed.

It was a sudden, violent implosion. The silver light vanished. The world became a maelstrom of crushing, absolute blackness and the cold, shocking, and total embrace of the Under Ocean. The last of the air was driven from Gundroff's lungs in a violent, desperate rush. The pressure was a physical blow, a forge hammer to his skull. He was blind, deaf, and drowning in the heart of a dead god's tomb.

He felt Thaddeus's frantic grip on his shoulder, the desperate weight of two lives depending on him. For a single, agonizing heartbeat, he held them, clinging to the last threads of their shared existence. He could not swim. He could not breathe. But he could push. He gathered all the remaining power in his massive, dwarven frame, all the grief, all the rage, all the stubborn, unyielding will of his people, and he threw them. He threw them upwards, towards the air he would never breathe, a final, selfless act of pure, protective fury. He felt their bodies leave his grasp, a final, selfless release, and the weight of their survival settled upon him, a burden he carried into the silence.

Pain. That was the first thing. A raw, burning, and beautiful pain in his lungs. He was on his back, on a surface that was hard, cold, and blessedly solid. He coughed, a violent, wracking spasm that brought a torrent of black, foul tasting water from his lungs. The air that filled them was a miracle, a sacrament, a fire that was more beautiful than any song. He tasted the dust of the cave and the metallic tang of his own blood. The weight on his body was gone, replaced by the simple, glorious gravity of solid stone beneath him.

He opened his eyes. He was on a narrow, rocky ledge in a small, dark cavern. A few feet away, a small, smokeless fire crackled, its cheerful, defiant light a star in the gloom. Thaddeus was there, his face pale and grim, but he was breathing. And beside the fire, her head resting on her knees, was Seraphina. She was pale, trembling, and utterly, profoundly exhausted, but she was alive.

Gundroff looked from Thaddeus's grim face to Seraphina's trembling, exhausted form. His gaze lingered on the raw, open fear in the elf's eyes, a fear that mirrored his own. He reached out a hand, not to console, but to touch the simple, honest rock of the cave floor. He was a creature of the deeps, and the stone was his only truth. A tremor ran through the mountain of a dwarf, a single, shuddering release of a tension he hadn't known he'd been holding since they had plunged into the abyss. He coughed, a dry, raspy sound, and saw Thaddeus and Seraphina both flinch in unison. They were a broken triad, but they were no longer alone. The fire crackled softly in the silence. It was enough.

Chapter 19

The Laughing Shadow

The first breath of true air was a shock, a beautiful, violent sacrament. They emerged from the last of the winding tunnels, a narrow, moss slicked fissure in the side of a granite cliff, and into a world reborn. The air, after the stale, dead breath of the Underworld, was a living thing. It was sharp, cold, and clean. It smelled of pine needles, damp earth, and a faint, distant promise of snow. Gundroff took a deep, shuddering breath, the scent of the high mountain forest a ghost of a memory he had thought long dead. It was the smell of home, or at least, what used to be home.

They stood on a high, windswept ridge, the world sprawling out beneath them. The sky, after the oppressive, fungal lit blackness of the caverns, was a vast, aching, and impossible expanse of bruised purple and the first, pale fingers of a grey dawn. Gundroff felt a profound, primal agoraphobia, a dwarven soul's terror of the open sky. He fought the urge to retreat into the comforting, solid embrace of the stone.

He looked at his companions. Seraphina stood with her face turned up to the pre dawn sky, her eyes closed, a single, perfect tear tracing a path through the grime and exhaustion on her cheek. The cool, clean air seemed to be a balm on her soul, a respite from the psychic filth of Nyx'Tolos and the suffocating pressure of the Sunken Road. Thaddeus, for his part, had found a small patch of mountain moss and was examining it with the quiet, intense curiosity of a man seeing the color green for the first time. The shadow of his own death still clung to him, but here, in the clean, honest air of the surface world, it seemed a little less heavy.

Gundroff's gaze swept the landscape. They were in the northern plains, a vast, rolling expanse of grey green tundra and dark, brooding forests that stretched to the jagged, snow capped peaks of the Dragon's Teeth mountains on the far horizon. A smudge of smoke, a single, defiant finger of civilization in a vast and empty wilderness, rose from a shallow, mist shrouded valley a few leagues distant. "Grayfell," Seraphina said, her voice a raw whisper. She had the cultist's map, now a tattered and water stained relic, spread on a flat rock. "A frontier town. Prospectors. Trappers. A hard place for hard people."

"Ale," Gundroff rumbled, the word a simple, profound, and deeply felt need. "Food. A fire that is not made of glowing fungus. And information." The journey down from the high ridge was a grueling, day long affair. They were weak, their bodies battered and bruised from their ordeal, and their supplies were all but gone. With every step, with every lungful of clean, cold air, a measure of their strength returned. The world, for the first time in a long time, felt real again.

They arrived at the outskirts of Grayfell as the sun was beginning its descent, painting the bruised sky with strokes of orange and blood red. The town was a wound in the wilderness, a haphazard collection of a dozen or so sod roofed hovels and smoke belching longhouses, all huddled together behind a crude, sharpened log palisade. Gundroff's Smith's eye took in the shoddy woodwork, the poorly stacked stone chimneys, the general air of a place that had been built not with pride, but with a grim, desperate haste. As they approached the town's single, rough hewn gate, a pair of guards, clad in mismatched leather and boiled hide, stepped out to block their path. Their faces were hard, their eyes narrowed with a deep, abiding suspicion. "State your business," one of them growled, his hand resting on the pommel of a rust pitted but wickedly sharp looking hand axe.

"We are travelers, seeking rest and supplies," Seraphina said, her voice calm and measured. The guard's suspicious gaze swept over them. He saw a pale, exhausted elf mage, a strange, quiet old man in a cleric's robes, and a massive, unarmed dwarf whose face was a roadmap of old scars and new grief. He saw their tattered clothes, their empty packs, the haunted, soul weary look in their eyes. They were in trouble. "We don't like trouble here," the other guard said, his voice a low, flat statement of fact. "We seek only a warm fire and a roof over our heads," Thaddeus said, his voice a quiet, gentle balm. "We have coins to pay our way."

The first guard grunted, a sound of reluctant, grudging acceptance. He stepped aside, and they walked into Grayfell.

The town was a single, muddy street lined with grim, functional buildings. The few people they saw. hard bitten prospectors with beards like tangled nests of iron wire, wary trappers draped in furs, a handful of grim faced dwarven miners who gave Gundroff a broad, almost fearful berth. all stopped to watch them pass. Their stares were hard, suspicious gazes of people who had learned, through long and bitter experience, that strangers were a harbinger of ill fortune. The silence was a wall of mistrust.

Gundroff felt the weight of their gazes, a physical, probing thing. He was a stranger in a strange land. The feeling of nakedness, of vulnerability, was a fresh and unwelcome wound. His hands, which had so long known the familiar, comforting weight of his axe, felt clumsy and useless at his sides. He flexed his fingers, a nervous, angry tic, and met the hard, hostile stares of the townsfolk with a silent, stony glare of his own.

"A tavern," he rumbled, his voice a low, hard thing. "There is always a tavern."

He spotted it at the far end of the street, a long, low building with a crudely painted sign of a crossed pick and shovel hanging over the door. It was called 'The Gilded Nugget.' He strode towards it, his two companions following in his wake, a small, defiant island of strangeness in a sea of hostile, suspicious eyes. The door swung open, spilling a wave of warm, stale air and the low murmur of voices into the cold, twilight street. They stepped inside, and the door swung shut behind them, plunging them into the lion's den.

The air inside the Gilded Nugget was thick with the smell of stale ale, pipe smoke, and unwashed bodies. A dozen grim faced miners and trappers sat scattered around a handful of rough hewn tables, their heads bent in conversation that immediately died as the door swung shut.

Every pair of eyes in the room, hard and suspicious, was now fixed on the newcomers.

Gundroff scanned the room, his gaze settling on a group of dwarves at a large table in the corner. They were prospectors, judging by the grime in the creases of their faces and the worn leather of their tools. Their beards were tangled messes of wire and dust, and their hands were thick with calluses. There was a low, simmering tension in their postures, a quiet, defensive menace that felt uncomfortably familiar. One of them, a grizzled elder with a milky white eye and a beard braided with iron rings, was painstakingly arranging a set of flat, grey stones on the table, moving them with the patient, deliberate care of a jeweler.

"We will sit there," Gundroff rumbled, his voice a low command.

The dwarves at the table shifted uncomfortably as the trio approached. The elder looked up, his one good eye a glint of rugged, polished obsidian. "This here table's full, stranger," he said, his voice a low, gravelly rasp. "You'll be better off at the bar."

Seraphina stepped forward, a faint, polite smile on her lips. She carried a small leather pouch that jingled softly. "A game, then?" she asked, her voice as smooth and cool as silk. "A single game for a seat at your fire, and perhaps a measure of information?"

The dwarves at the table exchanged glances, a spark of avarice lighting in their eyes. The milky eyed elder gave a rough, dry laugh that sounded like stones grinding together. "An elf wants to play a dwarven game? What have ye got to wager?" he challenged.

Seraphina untied her pouch and poured a cascade of small, shimmering objects onto the tabletop. They were not coins, but polished stones of agate, tourmaline, and obsidian, each one a perfect, faceted sphere that seemed to hold a sliver of captive starlight. They gleamed with a faint, internal luminescence against the dark wood of the table. The dwarves' eyes widened. This was not a bet for money, but for beauty and rarity, a language they understood far more than coin.

"This is not a game of chance," Seraphina said, her voice dropping to a low, conspiratorial hum. "It is a game of memory, a way to see if your mind is as sharp as your pickaxe." The elder squinted at her, his brow furrowed with suspicion. He picked up one of the spheres, his calloused thumb rubbing its impossibly smooth surface. "What's the trick?"

"No trick," Seraphina assured him. "You arrange your stones in a pattern on the table. You give me sixty seconds to memorize it. Then you cover them, and I must arrange my stones in the same pattern. For every one I get right, I win one of your stones. For every one I get wrong, I give you one of mine."

A greedy grin spread across the elder's face. An elf's memory was good, to be sure, but a human's could be broken. And what could an elf know about the actual, ancient patterns of the stone? He accepted the challenge. As he arranged his stones, a slow, deliberate pattern of circles and triangles, Gundroff watched him. The elder was a master, placing each stone with a surgeon's precision, his single good eye glowing with cold, quiet confidence.

Seraphina did not blink, her head tilted, her pupils dilating as she took in the pattern. She seemed to be weaving the air around the table, a silent, unseen ritual that was as foreign as it was terrifying. When the minute was up, the elder slammed a leather cloth over his stones with a triumphant grin.

"Your turn, elf."

Seraphina's elegant, nimble fingers moved with a speed and grace that defied belief. She placed her stones on the table in a perfect, flawless mirror of his pattern. When she was finished, she looked up, a faint smile on her lips. "I believe I won all of them."

The old dwarf stared at her arrangement for a long moment, his eyes wide. A look of grudging respect, a look Gundroff hadn't seen in a long time, crossed his face. He gestured to the two empty chairs across from him. "Take a seat, master." He then looked to his companions. "And you," he said, nodding to Gundroff. "You will not find ale here, but our beer is a fine, rock hard vintage that will make you forget that you ever drank water."

With that, they were accepted. As the others settled in, the elder gave a heavy sigh that sounded more like a groan. "The roads north are sealed," he said, his voice low and full of a quiet fear. "There's a sickness in the world, a rotting, temporal thing that's turning good stone to dust and good men to nothing." He then leaned in, his voice dropping to a whisper. "And there's a legend, a grim story that's been making the rounds. A shadow that laughs."

He told them of a boogeyman, a shadow that stalked the high peaks, a hunter of such unnatural skill that his victims' bodies were found not broken, but unmade. And every one of them, the elder said, had a single, dry, chittering laugh that would echo from the mountains, a sound that would follow a man's soul into the afterlife.

"A laughing shadow," Gundroff rumbled, the word a question.

"Aye," the dwarf said. "A man, they say, who can take a man's head and leave his ghost screaming." He took a long, hard pull from his beer. "We don't go out at night anymore. Not since the last one. We've heard… the laughter." He shivered, the simple, physical act of a man who was utterly, completely, and deeply terrified. "A ghost of a laugh, they call it. A sign that the world is broken, and getting worse."

The air inside the Gilded Nugget had grown cold. The dwarves at the table had fallen silent, their faces drawn with the grim, resigned fear of men who had heard this legend before. A legend of a laughing shadow, of a hunter who made a mockery of life and left nothing but silence behind. Gundroff felt the weight of the story settle on him, a heavy, familiar burden. This was no simple monster. It was a purpose, a terrible, singular will that sought to unmake. He rose, the scrape of his chair a harsh protest in the quiet room.

"We go to the well," he rumbled, his voice a low, hard statement. "We see it."

Seraphina did not argue. The time for cunning and whispers was over. This was a direct challenge. She nodded to the elder dwarf, a silent promise to return, and followed Gundroff out into the twilight. Thaddeus walked behind them, his face a mask of profound sorrow. He had seen too much death, too much sadness in the last few weeks. This was not the joyous, honest world he had believed in. This was a world of sharp teeth and laughing shadows.

They moved through the huddled, silent town, the suspicion of the locals now laced with a raw, frantic fear. No one met their eyes. They had seen the same thing, had heard the same rumors, and had been reminded of a truth they had tried so hard to forget: that a man's life was a fragile, temporary thing in a world that had forgotten its own name.

They found the well at the center of the town square, a crude, stone monument to a life giving force. But the life that had been given was not for drinking. It was for display.

The body of a grizzled woodsman hung upside down, his legs bound to the well's wooden frame. His limbs were broken at impossible angles, a puppet whose strings had been cut with a brutal, elegant precision. His chest had been meticulously flayed, the skin stretched and pinned to the well's stone frame. The cuts were not savage. They were surgical, clean, cold, and perfect in the unmaking of the human form. Gundroff's stomach clenched. This was the work of a mind that valued pure, ruthless efficiency over all else, a mind that saw a body not as a living temple, but as a problem to be solved. This was the work of a Mor kin.

On the ground at the base of the well, a small pile of pebbles and twigs had been arranged in a perfect, geometric pattern. It was an alien sort of art, a soulless testament to a being that had forgotten how to feel. But what horrified Gundroff was not the blasphemy, but the message. The stones were a crude map of the mountain passes, pointing to a crossroads a few leagues from the town. A waypoint. A location. The hunt was on, and they were the prey.

The woodsman's head was missing, its neck a clean, wet stump. A small leather satchel was pinned to his chest with a single, black obsidian dagger, its blade utterly without shine or reflection. Inside the satchel, folded neatly, was the woodsman's freshly skinned face, his expression frozen in a silent, final scream. A chill that had nothing to do with the cold air crawled down Gundroff's spine. This was the monster from the stories, the unholy assassin who collected the heads of his victims.

But the true horror came not from what he saw, but from what he smelled. A faint, acrid scent of bitter almonds and something cold, something that didn't have a name, clung to the air. A scent that felt as old as the mountains themselves. He knew that smell. It was the Mor kin neurotoxin, a poison that killed not with a searing flame or a brutal crush, but with a cold, elegant logic that simply... ended life. He had smelled it on the battlefield forty years ago, on the bodies of his slain kin.

Gundroff felt the world tilt on its axis. He stumbled back a step, a profound, physical sickness rising in his gut. The weight of his grief, a burden he had carried for forty years, felt fresh and new. This wasn't just a murder. It was an atrocity. An unholy, artistic act of unmaking. It was a ghost that had followed him from the ruins of his home to this remote, desolate town. The whisper he had carried on his soul, the one he had tried to ignore, was no longer a whisper. It was a name. A terrible, forgotten name that only a few souls in the world still remembered.

The Mor kin were the true architects of his clan's fall, not just a pawn of the dragon. A cold, hard certainty settled in Gundroff's soul, a new, terrible purpose that was not of vengeance but of a profound and unending sorrow. This was no longer a personal quest. This was a war. And it had just come to his doorstep.

The miles to the crossroads passed in a grim, silent blur. Gundroff's legs, tired and bruised from the journey, felt nothing. All of his focus, all of his fury, was now concentrated on the single, terrible name he had carried in his heart for forty years: The Mor kin were one thing. a tragic, soulless people born of the void's cold logic. But a demon? A creature of pure, screaming entropy that moved with the patient, meticulous precision of a hunter? That was an abominable paradox, a corruption of the unmaking itself. It meant that the cult had become a thing far more terrible than he had ever imagined.

The crossroads were not a meeting of roads, but a natural confluence of dry, cracked ravines. The wind, a constant, mournful wail, whipped through the chasms, sounding like a thousand ghosts weeping. A clutch of dark, skeletal trees with needles like sharpened knives stood like sentinels, their bare branches scratching at the bruised, twilight sky. This was a perfect place for an ambush. It was silent, desolate, and offered no easy escape.

"No," Seraphina whispered, her voice tight with a sudden, dawning terror. "We need to go back."

But it was too late.

The chittering sound, like the dry, brittle laughter of a thousand dying insects, was not on the wind. It was everywhere. It echoed from the stones, shivered through the branches, and seemed to crawl into their souls. It was not a sound, but a feeling of profound, unending emptiness. The cold that had clung to Gundroff's bones since he had emerged from the Underworld was a warm, comforting blanket compared to the chill that now settled over the small clearing.

"There," Thaddeus said, his voice a low, hard rasp.

A figure, tall and impossibly thin, peeled itself from the shadow of the great, dead tree at the center of the crossroads. It was not a creature of flesh, but of solidified darkness, a silhouette against the dying light. Its skin was the color of dust, its eyes two perfect, empty pools of black. A pair of grotesque, chitinous blades was clutched in its hands, their serrated edges glinting with a faint, oily sheen. Its face was a mask of stretched, desiccated flesh, its mouth a rictus of pure, joyous malice. It did not speak. It simply stood there, its head tilted, and let out a single, dry, chittering laugh that seemed to strip the warmth from the air. This was Y'thrrass'l, the Laughing Shadow.

Gundroff did not hesitate. This was not a fight. It was a suicide charge. The beast had led them here to die, and a dwarf who knew his duty did not run from it. He did not have his great hammer, but the two handed war axe he had bought in the town was a poor substitute. Still, it was a piece of iron, and iron was all a dwarf needed to face a demon. He charged.

Y'thrrass'l did not meet his charge with a counterattack. It simply... moved. It was not a graceful or an elegant motion, but a horrifying, insectoid scuttle, a blur of motion that defied all laws of physics. It moved from the center of the crossroads to Gundroff's side in a single, impossible instant. One of its blades, a blur of black steel, snaked out and laid a long, impossibly clean cut along his forearm. The pain was not a hot, burning thing, but a cold, chemical sting that felt as if his being was unraveling. He smelled it then, the bitter almond neurotoxin, and a cold certainty settled over him. This was not a monster. It was a tool, a weapon, a thing designed to unmake.

Seraphina's magic was already on the wind. She screamed a word of power, a word that would have thrown a man fifty feet, and hurled a bolt of pure, concussive force at the creature. The spell struck its chest with a sound like shattering glass. But the force did not throw Y'thrrass'l back. It simply... dissipated, swallowed by the demon's dark flesh as if it were a drop of water on a hot stone. The demon did not even flinch. It turned its empty, black eyes on Seraphina, its head tilted to the side, and then its body shimmered, a mirage on the heat of the air, and it was gone.

"Run!" Gundroff roared, the word a frantic, panicked cry. He was a creature of a forge and an anvil, a man who had been taught that the best defense was a stubborn stand. But this was no time for stubbornness. This was a time for survival. He turned and ran.

The pursuit was a terrifying symphony of terror. Thaddeus, his face pale and his breath coming in ragged gasps, stumbled as the ground beneath his feet shifted, a silent, terrible tremor. Seraphina, her face pale, was screaming spells into the night, her hands raised in a desperate, last ditch effort to buy them time. The chittering laugh was a constant, mocking presence behind them, and every few seconds, a streak of black steel would flash in the air, leaving a long, burning trail of poison on the ground.

The group was completely outmatched. The demon was toying with them. It was not a predator that wanted a kill. A sculptor wished to showcase their work. A new cut appeared on Seraphina's cheek, a fine line of red against her pale skin. Another ripped Thaddeus's robes, a silent, elegant tear. Y'thrrass'l was not trying to kill them quickly. It was trying to bleed them. It wanted to watch the life drain from them, slowly, deliberately.

Gundroff, blinded by a red mist of pure, unadulterated fury, did the only thing he knew how to do. He turned to fight. He held his axe up, a defiant, snarling mountain of stone and muscle, and stood his ground. "Come on then, you son of a shadow," he snarled. "Come and take me."

The demon's eyes, two empty pools of black, stared at him. It did not scuttle forward. It simply looked at him, its head tilted, and let out a long, dry, chittering laugh that was a sound of pure, unadulterated joy. A sound that was a promise. Then it blurred, a wisp of smoke on the wind, and it was gone, leaving nothing but a lingering, terrible silence and the faint, cold scent of almonds.

The air was silent. The wind had died. The hunt was over, for now. Gundroff's knuckles were white, his body shaking with a profound and terrible rage. He had not won. He had been allowed to live. And the knowledge of that felt like a fresh, open wound on his soul.

Chapter 20

Hunter's Trap

The night following the ambush was not silent; it was a symphony of terror. Seraphina huddled with her back against the cold, unyielding stone of the cave wall, a useless shield. Her mind, a fortress of finely tuned logic, felt as though it was being meticulously dismantled. The laughter was everywhere. a dry, chittering sound that seemed to come not from the wind, but from the air itself. It did not reach her ears so much as it vibrated in the marrow of her bones, a metaphysical assault that made her teeth ache and her head throb with a dull, rhythmic thrumming. She pressed her palms against her temples, trying to force her thoughts back into a linear pattern, to find the geometric source of the sound, but it was an impossible variable, a flaw in the physics of her own sanity. A wave of ice cold dread washed over her, the cold, animal terror of a mouse trapped in a house that was a laughing, conscious thing.

A new, subtler presence began to make itself known, a chaotic whisper in the back of her mind. It was not the demon's cold, intellectual malice. This was a different sort of terror. a frantic, mischievous, and alien curiosity that seemed to flit in the periphery of her senses. a brief, cold spike of adrenaline. *Someone else was watching. Someone else was here.* She suppressed the urge to speak, to betray their position. She had to focus, to hold on to the last, frayed threads of her sanity, for she was the only one who could hear it all.

Beside her, Gundroff's body was a tight coil of silent, grim fury. His hands, clenched so tightly his knuckles were bloodless knots of bone and sinew, rested on his knees. A torn strip of fabric from his shirt was tied around the long, impossibly clean cut on his forearm. His breath came in shallow, ragged gasps, each a protest against the pain eating at his soul. A fine sheen of sweat coated his brow, a stark contrast to the biting cold of the cave. The wound wasn't bleeding. It was worse. The skin around the cut was no longer a healthy, warm color; it was turning a pale, lifeless gray, a slow moving tide of color that was not a bruise, but a form of unmaking. She had seen this before. It was a subtle, insidious form of the same rot that plagued the kingdom of Tetra. a sickness of the soul. This poison did not kill with a brutal, honest pain, but unmade with a silent, patient logic. It was a testament to the unholy genius of a creature who had seen the cosmic wound that plagued the world and had decided to make it his weapon.

Across from them, Thaddeus sat hunched over, his hands wrapped around a piece of jerky, but he made no move to eat. The corners of his mouth, so long turned up in a cheerful, easy smile, were now a thin, hard line. His eyes, usually so full of a quiet, abiding light, were now hollow pools of profound sadness. He saw it all, Seraphina knew. His shoulders, a canvas of quiet strength, now slumped with a crushing weight she could not name. He was the most vulnerable of them all, the living heart of a god who had been made mortal, a perfect vessel for an ideal, cosmic sorrow.

Seraphina reached for him, her hand a cool, reassuring pressure on his shoulder. "Are you with us, Thaddeus?" she asked, her voice a low, precise thing.

He blinked, a slow, deliberate movement that seemed to come from a long way off. "The wound on his arm," he said, his voice a raw whisper. "It is not of the flesh. It is of the soul. It is a poison of... unmaking. My sun god cannot touch it. Not here. Not yet." He shook his head in a single, decisive movement. "The laughter... it is a song. A terrible, beautiful, and lonely song. It is the language of the void. It is singing the world back to sleep."

Seraphina's heart, a cold, hard knot of fear, hammered in her chest. She was a scholar, a chronomancer. She lived in a world of numbers, of equations, of the cold, hard logic of cause and effect. And the math was clear. They could not outrun this. The demon was toying with them.

It was a predator, and they were its prey. It had led them here, a small, terrified herd, and it was simply waiting, enjoying the terror and waiting for them to break.

Gundroff's body shuddered with a profound rage, a silent scream of fury clawing at his throat. He was a creature of duty and stubbornness, a shield for them all, but he was slowly, inexorably, being worn down by a foe he could not fight. His face, a roadmap of old scars, was now being etched with the new, raw lines of a battle he could not win. He was a mountain of a man, an unyielding wall of stone and iron, but even a mountain can be worn down by a thousand years of wind and rain.

The chittering laughter echoed in the blackness. It was a sound of pure, unadulterated joy. It was the sound of a sculptor who was utterly, completely, and terribly pleased with his work. And then, silence.

The silence was a different kind of weapon now. Not the quiet of despair, but the hard, cold peace of a mind that had found a purpose. Seraphina's hands, which had been trembling just an hour ago, were now a model of perfect, unyielding calm as she unfolded the cultist's map on the cold stone floor. The tattered, water stained relic was a language of terrain, a set of variables to be solved. She traced a path with a slender finger, a path not of running, but of deliberate, focused purpose.

"We do more than fight," she said, her voice low and precise, devoid of the raw fear that had been her constant companion. "We choose our own ground. We choose the terms of the fight. We are not prey. We are engineers. We are artisans. We are scholars. We are warriors. He is a sculptor of terror. We will be the architects of his unmaking."

She paused, her gaze flicking between Gundroff's grim, stony face and Thaddeus's hollow eyes. A flicker of movement at the edge of her vision, a cold spike of adrenaline. not the demon's hunger, but a frantic, alien curiosity. pricked at her senses. She ignored it. There was no time for distractions.

"The demon is a creature of the void. He hunts on the plains because the wide, open spaces are his domain. He is a wisp of smoke, a shadow fast enough to evade steel and fire. My chronomancy is built on the elegant laws of cause and effect, on the flow of time itself. But his power, this 'unmaking,' is a flaw in the fundamental nature of the universe. It is an impossible variable. We cannot fight him with magic or strength alone. We cannot win his game."

She looked directly at Gundroff, her gaze unyielding. "But we can change the game. We can force him into a place where the laws of nature are the weapons, where the earth is our ally." She pointed to a location on the map, a narrow, windswept ridge a few leagues from the cave. "The terrain here is treacherous. The mountains rise like jagged teeth, and the plains are a broken sea of scree and loose rock. He will see this as a perfect place to toy with us, to corner us. He will see it as a cage for his prey."

Gundroff shifted, his joints groaning softly. The muscles in his neck, knotted and tense, bulged under the strain of his silent fury. "And what is our role in this cage?" he rasped, his voice a low, hard rumble.

"We can't win," Seraphina whispered, the words a surrender. "Not his game." The chittering laugh echoed outside. Gundroff slammed his fist against the rock. "Then we make him play ours." Seraphina looked up, a wild, desperate light in her eyes. "The scree slope," she said, her voice suddenly sharp. "It's unstable. Thaddeus... you said the mountain remembers the sun." She looked at Gundroff. "He'll come for the weakest first. For me. You... you will be the anvil. And Thaddeus... you will be the mountain that falls."

Thaddeus's hands, which had been clasped in silent prayer, slowly unclenched. A faint, golden light, a ghost of a prayer, seemed to flicker in his eyes. He looked at Seraphina, his expression no longer one of quiet despair, but of a peaceful, abiding faith in her, in the plan.

She smiled, a cold, hard thing without joy. "And I will be the lure. He will come for me first. He will see me as the weakest, the scholar, the one who can be broken with a single whisper. I will sing a song of false hope, of easy prey. I will draw him to the precise point of our choosing. And when he is committed, when the hammer is falling, I will make him believe a lie. It will be the most elegant piece of chronomancy I have ever cast, a surgeon's cut on the timeline, a single second that will make the difference between life and death. He is a sculptor of terror, but we are the architects. We will not kill him with steel or fire. We will unmake him with the earth, with the silence of the mountains, with the laws he so despises. We will show him what happens when a masterpiece decides to fight back."

A grim silence fell upon them. They had been prey. But now, in the cold, unyielding heart of the north, they were hunters. And the hunt, for the first time in a long time, had a name. It was called a home.

The air in the cave was still and cold, but the chittering laughter was gone, replaced by the grim resolve of their plan. Seraphina, the lure, sat cross legged on the cold stone floor, the cultist's map a ghost in her lap. Her mind, a fortress of iron logic, was now a surgical blade, a tool of precision. She was a chronomancer, a master of a magic that allowed her to listen to the silent hum of the universe, to see the elegant, inexorable flow of cause and effect. Her magic was a way to divine a single, sleek truth in an infinite ocean of noise, a means to find a truth buried in the currents of time.

The problem before them was no longer a demon, a whisper of a forgotten god, or a simple hunt. It was a complex and intricate knot of unmaking, a problem of causality. The demon was not an enemy. It was a flaw. And a flaw, no matter how terrifying, could be corrected.

She closed her eyes, her mind reaching out, a delicate, ethereal spiderweb of pure thought. She was not casting a spell. She was listening. She was listening for the flaw, for the single, impossible variable that was Y'thrrass'l. Her mind, a perfect instrument, found its target, a single, cold, and hateful chord that resonated with the profound, silent malice of the void. And then, as she focused, her mind reached a little further, seeking a historical anchor, a name, a truth that could be used as a weapon.

Instead of a name, she found a whisper. Not the whisper of the demon, but a different, frantic, and chaotic signal, a discordant chord from a different song. A mind. A living mind. A mind that was so full of a feverish, disorganized, and beautiful chaos that it was almost impossible to comprehend. She was not seeing a ghost. She was seeing a thief. She was seeing the world through the terrified, unnervingly expressive purple eyes of a goblin.

The images came in a rapid fire, unfiltered flood of raw thought. She saw a flicker of Lord Malakai's handsome, cold face, his voice a single, low command that was a promise of payment and a threat of death. She saw a memory of a time she could only guess at: the cold, unyielding face of a man who looked like Gundroff, but was not Gundroff, and the unholy, artistic chaos of a ritual that she knew, in her soul, was the creation of the demon. She saw the flash of a blade, a blur of motion, and then the still, lifeless body of an unnamed king.

And then, she saw herself. a pale, ethereal figure with a book in her hand, seen through the eyes of a creature who saw her not as a hero, but as a fascinating, dangerous, and intriguing puzzle to be solved. The goblin was not an enemy. She was a scientist. A scientist is fascinated by a flaw in the physics of a universe that shouldn't be so interesting.

The connection lasted for a single, heart stopping second, and then it was gone. Seraphina's eyes snapped open, a single, perfect gasp of cold, northern air escaping her lips. The world, which had been a beautiful and terrible symphony, was now a cacophony of fear and doubt. The demon was not a flaw. The demon was a tool. And the game they were playing was not against a monster, but against a mastermind who had a rogue element in his own command. a rogue element that was now, somehow, a part of their own story.

The silence of the cave was now a different kind of monster. It was a silence of a hundred other, terrible, and chaotic possibilities. A grim, joyless smile touched Seraphina's lips. She was a scholar, a chronomancer. She had just seen a future that was not supposed to happen, and a past that she knew, in her soul, was a lie. The game had not ended. It had simply… gotten more interesting.

The journey was a slow, grinding testament to their desperation, a pilgrimage of pain into the cold, unyielding heart of the north. They were no longer running; they were marching, and the grim calculus of their purpose gave them a strength that had nothing to do with muscle or bone. Seraphina, the lure, led the way, the tattered cultist's map a ghost in her hand. Her mind, a fortress of iron logic, had replaced fear with a cold, precise focus. She memorized every shadow, every rock, every bend in the cracked, dusty trail. She saw not a path, but a battlefield, a chessboard on which every move counted. Her worn, torn boots moved with a quiet, efficient grace that belied the exhaustion that was now a constant, physical weight on her soul.

Behind her, the mountain of granite and grief was beginning to crumble. Gundroff's movements, once so resolute and unyielding, were now slow and halting. His breath came in shallow, ragged gasps, each one a protest against the cold air biting at his lungs. A fine sheen of sweat coated his brow, a stark contrast to the biting wind. The poison was working. The pale, lifeless gray that had first appeared on his forearm was now a creeping stain, a slow, silent wound spreading up his arm and onto his shoulder. She could see it even in the dim, bruised light of the pre dawn sky: a visible, terrible testament to a poison that did not kill, but unmade.

Thaddeus, the hammer, his cheerful smile a thing of the past, was now a quiet, physical presence. He walked beside Gundroff, his hand a constant, steady pressure on his back, a human anchor against a storm that was not of the body, but of the soul. He did not speak. His comfort was in his presence, in the silent, unyielding support of a man who had seen too much sorrow ever to lose his own.

"We are losing him," Seraphina whispered, her voice low and raw.

Thaddeus shook his head. "We are not. He is still with us. He is still fighting."

But she could see it in Gundroff's eyes. the quiet, haunted look of a man fighting a war on two fronts: the physical battle against the poison, and the internal, profound conflict of a soul slowly, inexorably, being unmade. His hands, which had so long known the weight of his axe, were now balled into tight fists, his nails digging into the calloused skin of his palms. He was a creature of iron and stone, a man of profound, physical strength, but he was slowly being worn down by a foe he could not see. a foe that was a fundamental flaw in the nature of the universe.

The path grew steeper, more treacherous. They were now in a high mountain pass, a narrow, windswept trail that was little more than a winding crack in the great, grey stone. Below them, a vast, desolate plain stretched out to the horizon, a sea of jagged, broken rock, a treacherous, unwelcoming landscape of loose scree and crumbling stone. Seraphina's mind, the perfect instrument, saw the cold, brutal beauty of it. It was an ideal hunting ground for a demon, but also a perfect kill box. The memory of the ghost's warning from the night before, a fleeting glimpse of Lord Malakai's face, and a terrifying ritual added a new layer of urgency. The poison on Gundroff's arm wasn't just a threat; it was a ticking clock.

They reached the top of the pass as the sun was beginning its climb, a pale, anemic light that seemed to do nothing to warm the cold, silent world. Before them was a long, gentle slope that descended into a sea of jagged, broken rock; this was the place on the map. This was the anvil.

Gundroff, breathing in harsh, ragged gasps, stumbled, falling to his knees. The sweat on his face was now a cold, clammy thing. The poison had taken its toll. Thaddeus immediately knelt beside him, his hands a gentle, comforting pressure on his broad shoulders.

"I am a mountain," Gundroff said, his voice a low, hard rasp. He looked at Seraphina, his eyes a glint of hard, cold fury. "And a mountain can take a long time to fall."

Seraphina knelt before him, her hand touching his brow. The skin was hot, feverish. She looked at his arm, the creeping gray stain a silent, terrible indictment of her own magical failures. She was a master of chronomancy, a wielder of impossible magic, but she was powerless here. She had no spell for a poison that was a wound on the soul.

"I know," she whispered, her voice full of raw, quiet, and terrible respect. "But a mountain, my friend, can also be a cage."

She stood up, her gaze fixed on the scree slope, her face a mask of cold, surgical determination. It was time to set the trap. It was time to become the architects of their own unmaking.

The world was a study in cold, patient silence. They were not running now. They were waiting. Seraphina lay prone on a high ledge, her eyes scanning the vast, grey emptiness of the plains below. The biting wind was her ally, its mournful howl a perfect cloak for the frantic beating of her heart. She was the lure, the one who would sing the song that would draw the hunter in, a song of false hope, of easy prey. Her mind, a finely tuned instrument of arcane logic, was a flurry of mental calculations, a silent, terrible ballet of numbers and possibilities. She had chosen this place for a reason. This scree slope, this great, crumbling wound in the side of the mountain, was their battlefield. It was an arena of unmaking, a place where a single misplaced stone could become a weapon, and where gravity was a relentless, silent, and terrible truth.

Beside her, Thaddeus sat cross legged, his eyes closed in a silent prayer. His hands were clasped in the cold dirt, his faith no longer a cheerful light but a grim, unyielding truth. His body, once so full of a gentle, quiet light, was now a vessel for a purpose that was cold, hard, and unforgiving. He was a force of nature. He was the rockslide. He was the hammer that would fall upon the anvil.

And Gundroff. Gundroff was the anvil itself. He stood alone on the highest point of the scree slope, a defiant, snarling silhouette against the bruised purple of the sky. His body, a mountain of granite and grief, was shaking with a profound and terrible rage, a fire in the heart of the deep dark. The creeping gray stain of the demon's poison was now a visible stain on his shoulder, a mark of a slow, silent unmaking. He was unarmed, his hands balled into powerful, stone hard fists. He was not a warrior. He was in a war.

The chittering laugh, like the dry, brittle laughter of a thousand dying insects, was not on the wind. It was everywhere. It echoed from the stones, shivered through the branches, and seemed to crawl into their souls. It was a sound that did not just reach their ears but vibrated in the marrow of their bones. It was a sound of pure, unadulterated joy, the sound of a sculptor who was utterly, completely, and terribly pleased with his work.

"He is here," Seraphina whispered, her voice low and raw.

A figure, tall and impossibly thin, peeled itself from the shadow of a great, jagged rock at the base of the slope. It was not a creature of flesh, but of solidified darkness, a silhouette against the dying light. Its skin was the color of dust, its eyes two perfect, empty pools of black. A pair of grotesque, chitinous blades was clutched in its hands, their serrated edges glinting with a faint, oily sheen. This was Y'thrrass'l, the Laughing Shadow.

Seraphina did not wait for it to move. She screamed a word of power, a word that was not of fire or of blood, but of a perfect, elegant, and terrible lie. A shimmering, ethereal mirage of herself rose from her hiding spot and began to scramble down the slope. The demon did not hesitate. It simply blurred, a wisp of smoke on the wind, and was gone, pursuing the lie.

The trap was sprung.

Thaddeus's eyes snapped open, his face a mask of cold, hard purpose. He did not speak a word of power. He placed his hands on the cold ground, his connection to the sun god a cold, hard, and unforgiving truth. He reached into the fabric of the earth, into the great, silent stone beneath them, and he… unmade it. He wove the threads of reality, not into a spell, but into a terrible and beautiful act of pure, silent will. He did not ask the mountain to move. He commanded it.

With a sound like the shattering of a god's heart, the scree slope began to fall. Not a graceful, rumbling avalanche, but a violent, cataclysmic storm of falling rock. A thousand tons of granite scree, jagged and unforgiving, began to cascade down the slope, a silent, beautiful, and terrible weapon of pure, unadulterated purpose.

The demon, caught in the heart of the storm, turned its head, its empty eyes a look of what might have been surprise. But surprise was a mortal emotion. It was not a thing of the void. It was simply… unmade. The falling rock, a torrent of crushing, grinding stone, began to tear at its dark flesh. The chittering laugh was silenced. It was the sound of a god's hammer on a cold, unyielding anvil.

But the fall was not enough. The demon was not a thing of flesh. It was a thing of shadow. It began to shift, to bleed into the stone, to escape its cage. This was the moment. This was the moment that Gundroff had been waiting for.

He leaped from the high ledge, a defiant, snarling mountain of rage and grief. He did not aim for the head. He did not aim for the heart. He aimed for the wound. He aimed for the place where the falling stone had torn away a piece of the demon's shadow flesh. He hit it with a sound like a great, cracking thunder, a sound that echoed through the silent, cold mountains. He hit it again. And again. The demon did not scream. It simply… dissipated, a wisp of smoke on the wind, and it was gone.

The battle was over. The trap had worked. Gundroff stood in the center of the dust and chaos, his fists bleeding, his body shaking with a profound and terrible rage. He had not won. He had made his point. He had wounded a being of pure unmaking.

"We go," Seraphina said, her voice a low, flat statement.

Gundroff did not move. He stood there, his fists clenched, his body shaking with a profound and terrible rage. He had not won. He had been allowed to live. And the knowledge of that felt like a fresh, open wound on his soul.

Chapter 21

The Stonehammer's Banner

The journey was no longer a march. It was a pilgrimage. They moved in a grim, exhausted silence, their bodies a testament to a victory that felt more like a brutal, slow motion defeat. Gundroff walked at the front, his body a silent, stony protest against the cold, unyielding air. His breath, a white plume of steam in the biting wind, was a testament to the cold that had settled in his soul. The poison from the demon's blade had left a creeping, silent tide of numbness, now a cold, foreign presence in his shoulder. The flesh around the impossibly clean cut had turned a sickly, lifeless gray. a silent testament to a sickness that did not kill, but simply unmade. He ignored it. He had a path to walk, a path he knew with the intimate certainty of a waking dream, for he had walked it a thousand times in his sleep, each time to a new, more profound sense of emptiness. The cold that bit at his lungs and turned his breath to white steam was a twin to the cold that had settled in his soul the day he had left his home and his people behind.

The mountains were not just a landscape; they were a cemetery, a world unmade by the Great Dragon Ash Heart. The air was a testament to its power. thin, biting, and acrid with the faint, lingering scent of brimstone. Gundroff's calloused hand brushed against a sheer cliff face, feeling not the familiar grit of granite, but a surface that was unnaturally smooth, polished to a black sheen like obsidian. It was a scar left by the dragon's breath, a fire so hot it could turn stone to glass and melt the marrow of the earth. He remembered the old tales, the sacred stories of the Mountain Father, Grund, forging the first dwarves from the "Deep

Core." He remembered the sound of the Great Peak, the one the god had breathed his spirit into, a silent, rumbling heart that beat with the sound of a thousand forges and a thousand hammers. Now, it was just a rock. A quiet, dead thing with a crown of snow, its heart stilled by a greater, more destructive fire. The mountains did not speak to him. They did not whisper of a lost home or a glorious past. They were just stones. Cold. Unyielding. Silent.

Gundroff's mind, a fortress of iron will, was a lonely, echoing chamber. He was haunted by the ghosts of a thousand songs, a thousand hammers, a thousand voices he would never hear again. He had spent forty years of his life carrying their memory, and the weight of it was a physical thing, a crushing burden on his shoulders that made every step a testament to his grief. He remembered the great hall of Hjarta Fell, not as it was in the end. a tomb of shattered stone and silent ghosts. but as it was in the beginning, when the mountain itself seemed to be alive with their purpose. The great, vaulted ceiling, carved with the stern, proud faces of their ancestors, appeared to touch the core of the world. In the heart of the hall, the Great Anvil stood, a monolith of the purest deep stone. The echoes of the hammers of his people, ringing out a symphony of creation, had been the soundtrack to his life. He could almost feel the rhythmic tremor in his own bones, the same beat that had accompanied the low murmur of conversation and the rich, earthy scent of coal smoke mingling with the sharp tang of forged steel. It was the music of his people, and it was a music that had been unmade.

He remembered the day he had stood on a high balcony, looking down on the great forges. They were not just pits of fire but a spectacle of art and industry, a thousand fires burning with the unyielding strength of stone. Heat rose in waves that danced in the air, tasting of iron and power. The rhythmic clang of a thousand hammers was not a cacophony, but the thundering heartbeat of their world. Beside him stood Prince Fireforge, his face grim with the weight of a crown he was not yet ready to wear. He was a boy prince then, his brow furrowed with a burden too heavy for his youth.

"The song," the Prince had said, his voice a low, hard rumble that fought against the sound of the forges. "It is everything. We are not just warriors, Gundroff. We are artists. The mountain gives us stone and iron, and we give it purpose. We make it sing. That is our truth. That is our reason for being."

Gundroff had watched a forge master, his hammer a blur of motion, shaping a blade into a work of lethal art. He remembered nodding in agreement. "We are the mountain's voice, my prince. We sing for it, and it gives us strength in return."

"Strength is for warriors," the Prince had replied, his gaze fixed on the endless stream of molten ore. "But a song... a song is for a people. It is for our hearts. It is what we must protect." He had looked at Gundroff, and for a brief moment, the solemn weight of his royal duty had fallen away, replaced by the earnest, desperate plea of a young man who knew his people's survival rested on his shoulders.

And Gundroff had believed him. He had thought in the song, a faith as solid as the mountain itself. He had thought that the forges would never fall silent, that the hammers would never stop their rhythmic beat. This belief wasn't a fragile hope; it was a fundamental truth woven into the fabric of his being. He had believed in a god who had gifted them fire and earth, a god who had breathed his spirit into the same stone of the world. But when the demon came, that belief, once a roaring fire, had not been extinguished with a quiet hiss of steam. It had turned instantly to cold, grey ash, a silence that fell with the rest of Hjarta Fell. The silence had not been a sudden end, but a slow, creeping poison that had begun to eat at the heart of his soul.

His sister, Audhild, had carried a different sort of fire. Her hair, a mane of fiery red, was a testament to the life that burned within her, a life that refused to be put out. He remembered a cold, autumn afternoon, watching her work at her forge. Her hammer was not a tool of brute force, but a thing of grace and fury, moving with a dancer's precision. Her laughter, a sound of pure, unadulterated joy, had been a song in its own right, a beautiful counterpoint to the deep, rhythmic clang of the forges around her. She had been forging a wedding gift, a delicate silver crown, a thing of pure, unyielding artistry. He remembered the look of fierce concentration on her face, and the flash of her eyes when she held the finished piece up to the light. a fleeting moment of perfect happiness. A joy that had been unmade with the rest of their world. He had carried the ghost of her memory for forty years, a terrible, beautiful burden, and the weight of it was a curse. He took the grief of his people, the grim, silent duty of the Oath of Rage, a vow that had turned him into a weapon of single minded purpose.

He was the last. The living monument to a people who had been unmade. His Oath of Rage was not a path to vengeance, but a pilgrimage of grief, a long, slow walk through the cemetery of his own memories. The road was a ghost road, and he was walking it alone. He looked at his hands, his fists clenched so tightly his knuckles were bone white. They were empty. The weight of his great hammer, his only friend for forty years, was gone, and in its place was a feeling of naked vulnerability, a fresh and unwelcome wound. He felt himself reduced, a mountain without a peak, a fire without a flame, an anvil without a hammer. He was the end of a story, a terrible, beautiful, and lonely tale that had no other ending but silence.

"We are close," Seraphina's voice was a low whisper behind him, a voice of cold, quiet comfort. "Another day. Maybe less."

Gundroff did not respond. He walked, his gaze fixed on the horizon, on the jagged, snow capped peaks of the Dragon's Teeth. The road was a pilgrimage, and a pilgrimage, by its nature, must have an end. But the end of his pilgrimage was not a home. It was not a reunion. It was not a glorious, final battle. It was just a graveyard. He was a ghost walking a ghost road, and the only end he could see was the cold, unyielding silence of a mountain that had been dead for a, long time.

But then, a whisper.

It was not a sound, but a feeling. A taste of the cold air, a ghost of a scent that was as impossible as it was real. It was the scent of a forge, a smell he had not tasted in forty years: the rich, metallic tang of hot iron and coal smoke, the warm, earthy breath of fire. It was a smell he had thought was lost forever, a part of a memory that was supposed to have been unmade.

He stopped dead in his tracks, his body a sudden, stony statue on the wind whipped pass. He stood there for a long moment, his lungs drawing in the cold, thin air, and for the first time in forty years, his senses were at odds with his reality. The metallic tang of iron, the sharp, pungent scent of coal smoke. they were impossible. They were a cruel trick of the mind. He closed his eyes, pressing the palms of his hands against his temples, trying to force the thoughts back into a linear pattern, to find the flaw in the logic of his own sanity. It was a ghost. a cruel joke.

"What is it?" Seraphina's voice was a low whisper behind him. "I don't smell anything."

Gundroff did not respond. He stood there, his nostrils flaring, his senses a frantic, disorganized torrent of sensation. It was real. It was a lie. It was a ghost of a memory brought to life by the relentless unmaking of his soul. His hands, clumsy and useless without their axe, clenched into fists, the nails digging into his palms, a protest against a world that was suddenly, violently, at odds with his own reality. The silence of the mountain pass was a familiar thing, a companion to his grief. But this ghost... this ghost had a scent.

And then, he heard it. The sound. It was a soft, rhythmic clang, a distant, muffled thump thump that was not just a sound in the air, but a beat in his bones. It was the sound of a hammer against an anvil, the sacred, holy rhythm of his people. It was the sound of a heart he had thought was dead. It was the sound of a promise kept. He turned his head from side to side, trying to find the source of the sound, his face a mask of profound, horrified disbelief. He looked at Seraphina, his eyes pleading with her for an explanation, for a logical answer to a paradox that was threatening to unravel the foundation of his soul. But her face was a mask of cold, quiet concern. She did not hear it. She did not smell it. He was alone in his revelation, the last living mourner at a funeral that had suddenly, inexplicably, come to life.

"The road," he rasped, the words a raw, physical protest against the silence. "The road of ghosts. It has a song."

He turned and began to walk again, but this time his walk was no longer a pilgrimage of grief. It was a frantic, desperate march toward a truth that was so powerful and so terrifying that it might just break him. He was a man who had made his peace with the end of a story, and he was being forced to witness a new, impossible, and terrifying beginning. The impossible scent of a forge fire, the rhythmic thumping of a hammer he had thought was silenced forever. these were ghosts he had to face. Gundroff pushed himself up the final, treacherous stretch of the mountain pass, his lungs burning, his poisoned arm a dead, heavy weight. Thaddeus and Seraphina followed in his wake, their silence a respectful tribute to the war he was fighting in his own soul.

Then, they crested the ridge.

The view that greeted them was a cruel and beautiful paradox. Below them, nestled in a high, secluded valley hidden from the rest of the world by the jagged teeth of the mountains, was a city. It was not the Hjarta Fell of his memory, a grand city of spires and bustling markets. This was a city of war. It was a chaotic, organic sprawl of longhouses and smithies, all huddled together in a grim, functional defiance against the cold. It looked like a wound in the mountainside, a scar of dwarven tenacity and stubborn will. The air was alive with the rhythmic clang of hammers against anvils, the low, rumbling roar of a thousand forges, and the shouts of dwarven guards. The air was thick with the scent of hot iron, of coal smoke, and of a life that was still, impossibly, being lived.

Gundroff's heart, which he had thought was a dead, silent thing, stuttered and then began to pound with a slow, heavy, and profound beat. He looked at the great banner that snapped in the cold wind the banner of the Stonehammer Clan, the royal line of Hjarta Fell. His eyes, which had been a glint of brutal, cold fury just a moment before, were now wide with a profound, unadulterated horror. The banner of the Stonehammer Clan snapped in the wind. Hammers pounded in the valley below. A living sound. A sound that could not be. *I am the last.* The thought was a prayer he had held for forty years. He looked at the smoke rising from a hundred forges. A lie. His hands, which had been fists of purpose, went numb. Forty years of vengeance for a people who were not dead. What was he? A ghost. A joke. The world tilted, the mountain itself seeming to crumble beneath his feet.

His body, a mountain of granite and grief, crumpled. The Oath of Rage, the sacred vow that had turned him into an engine of pure destruction, felt like a joke. A magnificent, terrible, and brutal cosmic joke. He was a man who had dedicated forty years of his life to a truth that did not exist. He was a living ghost mourning a funeral that had never happened. The weight of his grief, a burden he had carried for so long, felt suddenly, violently, and unbearably light. He was nothing. He was a rage without a purpose, a mountain that had been unmade not by a hammer, but by a simple, terrible, and impossible truth. He fell to his knees, his hands a pair of useless, bleeding fists, his body shaking with a profound and terrible rage.

"It's true," he rasped, the words a raw, physical protest against the reality that was unfolding before him. "The ghost road... it has a song."

A sound of boots on stone behind him, and the low, rumbling voices of dwarven guards broke the silent, terrible communion. They had been discovered. The truth, a cold and unforgiving thing, had come to find them. The funeral was over. The war, a war Gundroff had believed was already over, had just begun.

The journey down into the camp was a forced, dazed march through a dream. The dwarven guards, grim faced and clad in mismatched leather and iron, were not hostile. They were... silent. Their hands rested on the pommels of their great war axes, their gazes a mixture of awe and suspicion. They had been told stories of Gundroff, the last son of the Ragingfire clan, a living legend who was a testament to a grief they all carried. Now, they were seeing their legend, and he was a broken, bleeding, and terrified thing.

The camp itself was a brutal, beautiful, and heartbreaking sight. It was not the great city of Hjarta Fell, with its grand, echoing halls and its roaring forges. It was a wound in the mountainside, a sprawling, organic war camp of sod roofed longhouses and hastily built forges. The air was now filled with the low, constant murmur of a people who had learned to live in the silence of war. Gundroff saw a woman with a mane of fiery red hair, her face a road map of old grief, working a forge with a grim, defiant purpose. He saw a man with a face like a slab of grey granite, his hands, clumsy and useless without their hammers, clenched into fists of helpless frustration. He saw his people. They were a people of war, a living testament to a defiance that had not yet been unmade.

They were brought to the heart of the camp, to a large, fire lit longhouse that served as a command tent. The heavy, fur skin door swung open, and they were ushered inside. The air was warm, thick with the scent of pipe smoke and the smell of roasting meat. The man at the center of the room, seated at a long, oaken table, was a ghost. He was clad in a simple suit of worn, battered plate armor, a great black banner with a single, white hammer carved upon it hanging behind him. His face was a grim, stony mask, a road map of a thousand tiny, heartbreaking battles. He was not a prince. He was in a war.

He looked up, his eyes a hard, unforgiving glint of polished obsidian, sweeping over them. They landed on Gundroff, and for the first time in forty years, the mask of the ghost he had become faltered. A single, perfect tear traced a path through the grime and exhaustion on his cheek. "Gundroff," he rasped, the word a low, raw thing, a name that was a promise, a prayer, a ghost of a memory he had thought long dead. "Gundroff. Is it… You?"

The two men, a king without a throne and a hero without a purpose, stared at each other across the distance of a thousand unmade memories. The silent, terrible communion of two men who had believed they were the last.

The man at the table rose slowly. He was taller than most dwarves, his shoulders bowed with the weight of years. He knelt before Gundroff, his armor groaning softly, and placed a hand on his shoulder. "My friend," he said, his voice a low, hard rumble that carried the weight of a thousand secrets. "The war was never over. We went into the dark. We hid. We ran. And we waited."

He looked at Gundroff's poisoned arm, his eyes a glint of brutal, cold fury. "The day Hjarta Fell fell, a splinter of our people, a single clan loyal to the old ways, escaped through the hidden mountain passes. We chose a different path from yours. We chose silence over destruction. We chose to become a ghost army, a weapon that would only be brought to bear when the time was right." He gestured around the room. "These are not the men who fought the demon. These are their sons. Their grandsons. We raised them in the dark, and we taught them to wait." He helped Gundroff to his feet. The weight of his great hammer, the one that had been his only friend for forty years, was gone. But for the first time in forty years, his hands did not feel empty. They were held.

The night deepened, and the cold, unyielding air of the mountains settled around the camp. The king led them from the command tent to the main longhouse, a sprawling structure built into the side of the hill. A great fire pit roared in its center, casting long, dancing shadows on the stone walls and the weathered, grim faces of the dwarves who sat along its length. The air inside was warm and thick with the scent of roasted meat, a comfort Gundroff had forgotten.

He found himself sitting on a bench beside Seraphina and Thaddeus, his gaze fixed on the fire. He felt a hundred pairs of eyes on him, a mixture of awe and suspicion. He was a living legend, a name whispered in their stories, a symbol of a grief they all carried. But he was also a stranger.

A young dwarf with a face like a slab of grey granite and eyes full of old grief knelt before him, offering a bowl of thick stew and a slice of hard, dark bread. Gundroff took it with his uninjured hand, his fingers trembling slightly. He looked at the young dwarf and saw a younger version of his own face, etched with a different sort of war. The dwarf nodded once, a silent gesture of communion, and moved on.

Across the fire, the king sat at the head of a long table, his face a quiet, stony mask. He did not eat. He watched his people, a shepherd overseeing a wounded but defiant flock. He spoke to an old woman with a mane of fiery red hair. Gundroff recognized her as Audhild, his sister's shadow. and she nodded, her eyes full of a grim, familiar defiance.

Gundroff watched his people eat. Their silence was not one of despair, but of a quiet, unyielding patience. They were a people who had learned to live in the dark, to find strength not in glory or victory, but in a shared silence and a common purpose. He was no longer the last. He was a part of a wound, a living testament to a defiance that had not yet been unmade. His Oath of Rage, which had been a lonely, solitary burden, felt different now. He was a weapon that had been found again.

The Prince led them back into the longhouse. He gestured to the maps, crude things of torn parchment and charcoal, spread across the table. His eyes, no longer filled with the sorrow of their reunion, were now brutal and unforgiving.

"The day the demon came," he began, his voice a low, hard rumble that silenced the room. "The day Hjarta Fell fell, the demon's master was a ghost. A whisper on the wind. It unmade us from the inside, a poison in our hearts. It was not a battle of steel and fire, but a battle of our souls. A civil war of the heart." He traced a line on the map with a calloused finger, a line that wound through a mountain pass. "The Grand Council was split. The elders wanted to meet the foe head on, to fight with honor and glory. A fool's errand. They would have all been unmade."

"A few of us, a splinter clan loyal to my father and to the old ways, knew the truth. We knew that we could not win with steel and fire. We chose to become a ghost army. We chose to go into the dark and to wait."

He looked directly at Gundroff, his eyes unyielding. "Your oath, brother, was a sacred vow. We let the world believe it was the final rage of a dying people. We let the world believe we were gone. We let the world believe that you were the last." He swept a hand over the map, over the crude carvings of mountain passes and hidden caves. "This mountain range is our home. We are its veins and its arteries. We have lived in the silence of war for forty years. We have a thousand sons who know nothing but the sound of the forge and the hammer. We are not the end of a story. We are a new beginning. We are the Stonehammer Clan, and we are not a ghost."

A silence fell upon the longhouse, a different kind of silence now. not of grief, but of grim, unyielding purpose. The funeral was over. The war had just begun.

Chapter 22

A Clash of Wars

Prince Fireforge sat at the head of the table, the map of Hjarta-Fell carved into the stone before him. He was no longer the ghost Seraphina had first seen, but a king. His face bore the weight of forty years, every line earned. His massive hands rested flat on the cold stone. not a gesture of control, but of a man holding onto the last solid thing in his world.

The command tent reeked of old grief. Cold mountain stone, yes. But layered over that, pipe smoke thick as fog. Damp wool that never quite dried. The bitter tang of wound salve that couldn't heal what really hurt. The central fire pit hissed and spat. no roar left in it. The flames cast restless orange light across faces carved from granite and loss.

These were not the proud lords from the tapestries. One elder's beard was singed black at the tips. forty years and still it wouldn't grow back white. Another stared into the flames with one good eye and one piece of polished obsidian. Their armor bore patches of scavenged metal. Wrong colors. Wrong clan marks. The respectful silence of a king's council

was absent, replaced by the quiet of men who had run out of words.

"You have heard his name." Fireforge's voice was gravel and iron. "This is Gundroff Ragingfire. The Elf will speak. Give her your silence."

Seraphina stepped forward. Her borrowed leathers creaked too loudly in the quiet. She placed her palms on the stone map, feeling the mountain's pain through cold rock.

"My lords." Her voice was a blade, sharp and clean. "We are fugitives. Hunted by the same shadow that has poisoned your home. But listen. " She raised her hand as she saw Harek shift. "The death of our King and the fall of your kingdom are not separate tragedies. They are wounds in the same body. Symptoms of a sickness that goes deeper than dragons. Deeper than war."

She traced the carved passages with one finger. "The enemy you face. this cult that calls itself the Un Named. they do not simply kill. They unmake. Their alchemy does not merely destroy, it erases. They seek to turn the world's song back to the silence that came before all things. And to do this, they target the Four Pillars of reality itself."

The words hung in the smoky air like incense. Strange. Foreign.

"You have to understand the principles they target. The first is the Moment. the 'now' that keeps the past from bleeding into the future. Then there's the Deep Time, the patient rhythm that builds mountains. The third is the Threshold, the line between what is and what could be. And the fourth..." Her voice dropped. "The Foundation Stone. The simple, bedrock certainty that this world is real." She looked up at their faces. Stone. All stoic.

"This dragon in your mountain. it is not the disease. It is the fever. The real sickness runs in the veins of time itself. I have seen it. Temporal decay that ages a man decades in heartbeats. Spaces that exist in three different centuries at once. The concept of causation beginning to."

"Enough."

The word came from Harek like a boulder falling. The old war master's obsidian eye caught the firelight like a shard of midnight. "Enough of your elven word weaving."

"It is not word weaving," Seraphina said, her composure cracking. "It is a warning. If we do not act."

"If we do not act?" Harek's voice rose like a forge fire catching wind. " Act? Girl, we've done nothing but act for forty years! Forty winters of blood on the stone, forty summers of ash in our beards... and you dare come into the heart of our grief to lecture us on concepts?"

He stood. His chair scraped against stone like a blade on a whetstone.

"You speak of pillars and principles and the weight of reality." He spat. The spittle hissed in the fire. "I speak of my son. My boy, whose shield melted to his arm before the dragon's fire took him. That fire was real, girl. It was hot. It gave no damn for your philosophy."

Another Thane slammed his fist on the table. The stones jumped. "His fire is not natural fire," the man snarled, holding up an arm wrapped in the twisted ruin of what had once been plate armor. "It is profane alchemy, yes. But it burns. It kills. It does not unmake. it obliterates. This was my father's gauntlet. Now it is my prison."

The melted steel gave off a sickly sweet smell. Green veins ran through the metal like poison in a wound. The dragon's fire had not simply melted it. it had perverted it and made it wrong.

Seraphina's hands clenched on the stone map. "You do not understand."

"I understand grief!" Harek's roar filled the tent like an avalanche. "I understand the weight of stone and the heat of flame and the sound my boy made when he died! Do not stand here, in the ruins of our people, and tell us our war is built on ignorance!"

The silence that followed was not quiet. It was the crushing weight of a mountain settling into its foundations.

Prince Fireforge had not moved and had not spoken. His golden brown eyes held the weariness of a man who had buried too many of his people. When he finally said, his voice carried the authority of kingship and the exhaustion of mortality.

"Lady Seraphina," he said, and there was no mockery in the title. "I have heard your words. Your warning. I do not doubt your sincerity. But I am not a philosopher. I am a king. And my duty is not to the cosmos, but to the people who look to me for protection."

He gestured to the map. They could no longer walk in the carved halls.

"For forty years, we have bled for every stone of this mountain. Every passage we have lost, we remember. Every hall that burns, we mourn. You speak of temporal decay and metaphysical threats, and perhaps you are right. Perhaps there is a sickness in the bones of reality." His voice hardened. "But my people die to dragon fire. They starve because our trade routes are ash. They grow old in exile because a monster sits in our home and will not leave."

He stood, his massive frame casting shadows that danced with the firelight.

"So yes, Lady Seraphina. Your war may be older than ours. Deeper than ours. More significant in the grand architecture of existence. But it is not our war. Our war is simple. Our war is this: we want our home back. And if that makes us small and provincial in your eyes, so be it. We are dwarves. We think in stone and iron. And stone and iron are what we understand."

The words settled like burial shrouds. Seraphina stood at the table, her arguments crumbling like houses built on sand. The logic was perfect. The framework was sound. But it meant nothing against the simple, brutal truth of a father's loss.

The council had dispersed like smoke. The Thanes filed out in silence, their faces carved from disappointment and old rage. Fireforge remained at the table, staring at the map as if it might reveal some answer he had missed. Gundroff stood by the fire, his withered arm hidden beneath his cloak.

Seraphina found herself outside, breathing air that tasted of snow and smoke. The exile camp spread below like a wound in the mountainside. Tents and lean tos. Cookfires that burned too low. Children who had never seen the halls their parents mourned.

She wanted to scream. To break something. To help them understand that their mountain, their war, their dead. all of it. was part of something larger. Something that would devour them all if left unchecked.

Instead, she walked.

The camp was laid out with dwarf precision. Even in exile, they maintained their sense of order. The smithies were clustered together, their forges cold but ready. The healers' tents bore the symbol of the mountain's heart. The warriors' quarters faced inward, forming defensive rings around the non combatants.

She found herself drawn to one of the smithies, not by design, but by the sound. Not hammer on anvil. there was no work being done. But the soft, rhythmic scraping of steel on stone. Someone is sharpening a blade in the darkness.

The forge master was ancient even by dwarf standards. His beard was white as mountain snow and reached nearly to his feet. His arms were thick as tree trunks, scarred by decades of sparks and heat. He sat on a low stool, running a whetstone along the edge of a battle axe with the patience of stone itself.

"You are the elf lady," he said without looking up. Not a question.

"I am Seraphina."

"Mmm." The whetstone continued its whispered song. "I heard your speech. From outside the tent."

She sat on an empty crate, uninvited. "Then you know how well it was received."

The old dwarf's eyes flicked up to meet hers. They were pale blue, like a winter sky. "You spoke of rot in the foundations."

"I spoke of temporal decay. Of metaphysical."

"Aye." He returned to his sharpening. "That's what I said. Rot in the foundations."

Seraphina stared at him. "You... understand?"

"Girl, I have been working iron for three hundred years. I know the difference between good steel and bad. I know when a blade has been forged true and when it has been made from poor metal that will snap when you need it most." The whetstone paused. "You speak of time like it was iron. Like someone has been using bad ore."

"That is..." She blinked. "That is remarkably accurate."

"Aye, well." The old dwarf set down his axe and picked up a sword that bore chips and notches from use. "We may not have your learning, but we know our craft. And the first thing you learn about metalwork is this: a flaw in the source makes for weakness in the final product."

He tested the sword's edge with his thumb, frowning at what he found.

"You say this... rot... this bad time iron is spreading?"

"Yes. Corrupting causation itself. Making it so that actions do not lead to predictable consequences. So that the past can be changed retroactively. So that the future becomes..." She searched for words he would understand. "Brittle. Likely to shatter when stressed."

The forge master nodded slowly. "And our dragon?"

"A symptom. A fever caused by the infection, not the infection itself."

"But still killing my people."

"Yes."

He resumed sharpening, but his movements were thoughtful now. Considering.

"In metalwork," he said eventually, "sometimes you get what we call a cascade failure. One flaw in the steel creates stress. That stress causes more cracks. Those cracks weaken the whole piece until..." He made a snapping motion with his hands.

"Yes. Exactly."

"So this cult of yours. they are not just breaking things. They are breaking the way things break."

Seraphina felt something loosen in her chest. Relief, maybe. Or hope. "That is the clearest anyone has understood it."

The old dwarf chuckled, a sound like distant thunder. "Perhaps because I am not trying to be clever. I am just listening to what you are telling me." He held up the sword, examining the edge in the firelight. "But understanding and doing are different things, girl. Even if I believe you. and I do. what would you have us do? We cannot forge a new time like we forge new steel."

"No. But we can find the source of the corruption. Cut out the diseased metal before it spreads further."

"And where might that be?"

"The Deep Core. The oldest, most protected part of your mountain. Where the original Foundation Stone was laid."

The forge master went still. His weathered hands gripped the sword hilt tight enough that his knuckles showed white.

"The Deep Core has not been entered in five hundred years," he said quietly. "It is sealed. Warded. Protected by magics older than our kingdom."

"Which is exactly why the corruption would have chosen it. The most sacred, most protected place. Turn that against itself, and the psychological impact alone would be devastating."

"Aye." The old dwarf set down the sword and stared into the cold forge. "Aye, that has the ring of truth to it." He looked at her with those winter pale eyes. "But girl. even if the council believed you, even if they agreed to help. the Deep Core lies beyond the dragon. Through the heart of fire itself."

"I know."

"It would be a death march."

"Yes."

"For all of you."

"Probably."

The forge master was quiet for a long time. The sounds of the camp drifted through the night. Quiet conversations. A baby is crying. someone singing a lament in the old tongue.

"There is a story," he said finally, "about the first forge fire, how it was lit not with wood or coal, but with the breath of the mountain itself. The fire burned clean and true for a thousand years. But deep in the foundations, where no one looked, another kind of fire began to grow. A cold flame that did not consume fuel but purpose. It fed on the meaning of the work being done above. And slowly, without anyone noticing, the great forge began to produce blades that looked perfect but would shatter at the first blow."

He picked up his whetstone again, turning it over in his hands.

"The smith who discovered the problem had a choice. He could continue working, making beautiful, useless blades. Or he could go down into the foundations, into the darkness where the cold fire burned, and face it alone."

"What did he choose?"

The old dwarf smiled, but there was sadness in it. "That depends on who tells the story, girl. But the version I learned from my master... the smith went into the darkness. Because sometimes, the only way to save your life's work is to risk your life."

The council reconvened at dawn. The same faces. The same silence. But something had shifted in the night. Seraphina could feel it in the air. not hope, exactly, but a kind of grim readiness, as if decisions had been made in the darkness.

Gundroff stood at the foot of the table. His withered arm was no longer hidden beneath his cloak but rested openly on the stone map. The rot was clearly visible. flesh that looked more like ancient parchment than living skin. Veins that showed dark beneath the surface, like cracks in marble.

"I have listened to the lady's words," he began, his voice carrying the authority of kingship and the weight of lived experience. "And I have listened to your grief. Both are true. Both are necessary. But you are thinking too small."

Harek's obsidian eye caught the firelight. "Small? We have fought the largest war in our history."

"No." Gundroff's voice cut across the interruption like a blade. "You have fought the most visible war in your history. But I was there, old man. I was there the day your son fell."

The tent went dead silent.

"I saw the shield melt to his arm. I saw a good dwarf die an honest death, fighting for his home and his people. There was honor in it. Meaning." Gundroff's golden brown eyes held Harek's gaze without flinching. "My own son... he did not get such a clean end."

He raised his withered arm, letting the firelight play across the diseased flesh.

"This is not dragon fire, Harek. This is something else. Something that does not just kill. it lessens. It makes a thing smaller. Weaker. Less than what it was. And it is spreading through every stone of this mountain like poison through a bloodstream."

Prince Fireforge leaned forward. "Gundroff..."

"No, cousin. Let me speak their language." Gundroff turned to address the full council. "The lady spoke to you of pillars and principles. Of cosmic architecture. These are not dwarf words. These are the words of smoke and shadow, and you are right to mistrust them."

Several Thanes nodded. Harek's scowl deepened.

"But I will speak to you in our words. In the language of stone and iron. Of foundation and structure." Gundroff placed both hands on the map. the healthy and the rotted together. "What good is the finest blade if the anvil crumbles when you strike it? What use is the strongest wall if the mortar has turned to dust?"

He traced the passages of the map with one finger. "For forty years, you have fought to reclaim our halls. To drive the dragon from our home. But what if the home itself is dying? What if every victory you achieve is built on a foundation that grows weaker with each passing day?"

The elder with the singed beard spoke up. "The dragon's fire is real enough. It has burned."

"I do not dispute the fire." Gundroff's voice rose slightly, taking on the cadence of a king addressing his people. "I have seen it burn. I have lost friends to it. But tell me this. in forty years of war, have you noticed anything... strange? Passages that lead to different places than they did before? Chambers, where the echoes sound wrong? Stones that weep moisture that should not exist?"

Silence. But Seraphina saw several faces change. recognition flickering like candle flames.

"You have, haven't you?" Gundroff continued. "Small things. Easy to dismiss. Blame it on the dragon. Blame it on the siege. Blame it on forty years of war and grief. But the mountain is sick, relatives. Not just occupied. sick."

He straightened to his full height, and for a moment, he was not just a refugee king but something older. Something carved from the mountain's own stone.

"The dragon is fire in the rafters. A great fire, yes. A consuming fire. It will burn everything we built if we let it. But while you fight the flames above, the foundation stone is turning to ash below. And when it finally crumbles. when the rot reaches its heart. it will not matter if you drive out every dragon in the world. You will have reclaimed a beautiful, hollow tomb."

The words hung in the smoky air like a verdict.

Harek was the first to speak. His voice was quiet now. Thoughtful. "The Weeping Hall."

"What?"

"There is a place. was a place. near the lower merchant quarter. The Weeping Hall. The stones..." He frowned, as if trying to recall something half remembered. "The stones sweat. Not water. Something else. Something that burns the skin if you touch it."

Another Thane nodded slowly. "The Echo Chamber. The acoustics have changed. Voices carry differently. Sometimes you hear whispers when no one is speaking."

"The Shifting Passage," said a third. "Connects the old armory to the grain stores. But sometimes. not always, but sometimes. it leads to chambers that should not exist."

Prince Fireforge was staring at the map with new eyes. "How long have these... anomalies... been occurring?"

"Hard to say," Harek admitted. "We assumed it was dragon work. Structural damage. The mountain is settling after decades of war."

"No." Gundroff's voice was confident. "The dragon burns. It does not change. What you describe is something else entirely. Something that alters the fundamental nature of stone itself."

He looked around the table, meeting each pair of eyes in turn.

"I am not asking you to abandon your war. I am asking you to see it clearly. The dragon is part of a larger sickness. a deeper enemy. Fight the fire, yes. but understand that until you cure the disease, new fires will keep starting. New corruptions will take root."

Fireforge stood slowly. His massive frame cast long shadows across the map.

"And what would you have us do, cousin? Even if we accept your words. even if we believe this rot is real. how do we fight an enemy we cannot see? Cannot touch?"

"The same way you fight any enemy," Gundroff replied. "You find where it lives. And you kill it there."

"Which is?"

"The Deep Core. The oldest part of the mountain. Where the Foundation Stone was first laid. If this corruption has a heart, that is where it beats."

The silence that followed was different from before. Not dismissive. Not angry. Thoughtful.

Finally, Harek spoke. "The Deep Core lies beyond the dragon's lair. The path is guarded by fire and worse things. Even if we could reach it..."

"I am not asking your army to come with me," Gundroff said. "I am asking for a chance. A distraction. Draw the dragon's attention while a small group takes the hidden paths to the Core."

"Hidden paths?"

Gundroff smiled grimly. "Did you think I learned nothing in my years of exile? There are ways through the mountain that even the dragon does not know. Dangerous ways. But they exist."

Prince Fireforge looked at the map for a long time. When he spoke, his voice carried the weight of command and the burden of desperate choice.

"A single war, then. Two fronts, but one enemy. We break ourselves against the gates. Draw the dragon's fire. And you..." He met Gundroff's eyes. "You go into the darkness and try to cut out the heart of this sickness."

"Yes."

"It is a desperate plan."

"It is the only plan we have left."

Fireforge nodded once. A king's decision. Final and irrevocable.

The map looked different in the aftermath of the agreement. The carved stone passages no longer seemed like memories of glory but routes to salvation. Or damnation. The two had become difficult to tell apart.

Prince Fireforge stood at the head of the table, but he was no longer alone. Gundroff had moved to stand beside him. two kings united by necessity and blood. The Thanes remained seated, but their posture had changed. They leaned forward now, warriors planning a campaign rather than mourners remembering the dead.

"The assault will be a diversion," Fireforge said, his voice carrying the cadence of military planning. "But it must be convincing. The dragon cannot suspect our true purpose."

Harek grunted in agreement. "How many will you need for the Deep Core?"

"Small group," Gundroff replied. "Too many and we lose stealth. Too few and we cannot handle what we find there." He gestured to Seraphina and Thaddeus, who had remained silent observers throughout the debate. "The lady's knowledge will be essential. The old man's wisdom likewise. Beyond that..." He shrugged. "Perhaps two or three more. Warriors who know the old ways."

"I will go."

The voice came from the back of the tent. A young dwarf. barely past his majority by the look of him. stepped forward. His armor was patched but well maintained. His axe bore the notches of real combat.

"Thorin Ironfoot," he said, introducing himself with the formal inflection of ancient courtesy. "Son of Dain, grandson of Nain. I know the hidden ways. My grandfather helped carve some of them."

Harek looked skeptical. "Boy."

"I am not a boy," Thorin said quietly. "I have bled for this mountain. I have buried friends in its shadow. And I will not sit above ground while others risk everything to save what we have already lost."

Gundroff studied the young dwarf with appraising eyes. "The Deep Core is not a place for glory seekers."

"Good. I am not seeking glory. I am seeking an end to this. One way or another."

Something in the young dwarf's tone must have satisfied Gundroff, because he nodded. "One more, then. To even the numbers."

"I will provide a guide," Fireforge said. "Someone who knows the current state of the passages. The dragon has changed much in forty years."

"When do we march?" Harek asked.

"Three days," Fireforge decided. "Time enough to prepare. Not enough to lose our nerve."

The council began to disperse, but Fireforge caught Gundroff's arm as he turned to leave.

"Cousin." The word held weight beyond kinship. Beyond rank. "There is something else. Something I have not told the others."

Gundroff waited.

"The Deep Core... it was sealed for a reason and not just protected. sealed. The magic that guards it is older than our kingdom. Older than memory. If this corruption has indeed taken root there..."

"It will not go quietly," Gundroff finished.

"No. It will not." Fireforge's golden brown eyes held depths of worry. "I am sending you into the heart of something that may be beyond fighting. Beyond understanding."

"Then we will face it as dwarves have always faced the unknown," Gundroff replied. "With steel in our hands and stone beneath our feet."

"And if the stone itself has turned against us?"

Gundroff was quiet for a moment. Then: "Then we will teach it to remember what it means to be stone."

Fireforge clasped his cousin's shoulder. the healthy one, not the withered arm. The gesture was formal, but the emotion behind it was real.

"Cleanse our home, Gundroff of the Ragingfire. Cut out this rot. Make the mountain remember its own name." His voice dropped, carrying the weight of command but also the desperate hope of a brother. "And then... then you will return to us. For the final battle."

"The final battle?"

"Win or lose, cousin. after this, there will be no more hiding. No more exile. We retake our home, or we die in its halls. There is no third option."

Gundroff nodded slowly. Understanding. Accepting.

"Then we had better not fail."

Outside the command tent, the exile camp continued its quiet existence. Children played games in the dirt. Women mended clothes by firelight. Men sharpened weapons and spoke in low voices of battles past and battles to come. None of them knew that in three days, their fate would be decided in the depths of a mountain that had become a stranger to them.

But they knew enough. They knew the waiting was almost over.

Seraphina stood at the edge of the camp, looking up at the mountain that loomed above them. Hjarta-Fell. The Everlasting Peak. From here, it looked serene. Majestic. The way mountains were supposed to look in songs and stories.

She knew better now. Beneath that peaceful facade, something hungry was eating the bones of reality. Something that would not stop with one mountain or one kingdom. It would spread. Metastasize. Until the whole world forgot what it meant to be solid.

Three days to prepare. Three days to ready herself for a journey into the infected heart of existence itself.

She touched the hilt of her sword. Steel and leather. Simple. Real. For now.

"Nervous?" Thaddeus appeared beside her, moving with the quiet grace of age and experience.

"Terrified," she replied honestly.

"Good. Fear keeps you sharp. Overconfidence gets you killed."

They stood together in comfortable silence, watching the mountain sleep. Or pretend to sleep.

"Do you think we can do it?" Seraphina asked finally.

Thaddeus was quiet for a long time. When he spoke, his voice carried the weight of years and the wisdom of acceptance.

"I think we have to try. Sometimes that is enough. Sometimes it is not. But it is all we have."

Above them, Hjarta-Fell waited. Patient as stone. Hungry as time.

Three days.

Chapter 23

The gates of Hjarta-Fell

The grim, rhythmic crunch of iron shod boots on frozen stone was the only sound. For hours, the world was a symphony of agony, every note a testament to his own personal hell. Gundroff walked beside the silent, resolute Prince Fireforge, his body a silent protest against the cold, unyielding air that gnawed at his lungs. Every step was an act of profound defiance. This was his home. These were his mountains. And they were dead. He had walked this road a thousand times in his memories, a pilgrimage through the cemetery of his own grief.

He was a ghost walking among the sons of the men he had thought were long dead. The weight of their silent, awestruck gazes was heavier than any armor, heavier, even, than the physical chain he had carried for forty years. He felt the cold, hard weight of it, not as a burden, but as a lifeline, a thing that had kept him from collapsing under the endless sorrow. He saw his own face reflected in their grim, bearded features, his own grief mirrored in the depths of their hard, unyielding eyes. They were a people of stone and silence, and he, who had been the sole keeper of their memory, was now a stranger in his own history. The world, which had once been a living part of him, was now just stone, dead and silent. The wind was a razor's edge of pure, biting cold, whipping through the pass with a mournful, shrieking howl. It tore at his cloak and stung his eyes, a constant physical assault that was a pale echo of the storm that raged within his own soul. The path was a narrow, winding ribbon of ice slicked granite, a treacherous road the Stonehammer dwarves navigated with a slow, grim, and familiar determination. To Gundroff, a master of the stone, every patch of slick ice, every loose rock, was a personal insult. a flaw in a masterpiece that had been left to rot. With every step, he felt the weight of his new reality. He was no longer the last. He was a stranger in his own history.

He saw the first of them then, lining the path at hundred yard intervals: the statues of the forgotten kings. Colossal, thirty foot tall sentinels carved from the living rock of the mountain itself. They were masterpieces of dwarven artistry, their stern, proud faces a testament to a glory that was now a ghost. The biting wind had scoured them, the ice had cracked them, and long, dark streaks of mineral rich water ran from their stone eyes, giving them the appearance of weeping giants, a silent, eternal chorus of grief for a kingdom that was lost. He ran a hand over the weeping stone. VEYRIC THE UNBEARDED.

The name was a spark. Suddenly, the air on the pass didn't smell of ice and wind, but of coal smoke and hot iron.

His father's voice, a low rumble over the clang of a hammer. *Do you know the tale, my son? A fool's oath, born of a boy's pride.*

Gundroff flinched, remembering the shower of orange sparks, the hiss of steam as hot steel met the quenching barrel. an angry sound. The wind whipped at his cloak, a cold shock that pulled him from the memory's warmth. He was still on the pass, his hand on the cold, weeping face of the statue.

An oath is not a boast, Gundroff. It is a chain.

He felt the cold, heavy links of his own chain, the one he had forged in the ashes of his home. It had been his anchor, the only thing holding him together in a world of ghosts. But he looked down at the valley below, at the smoke rising from a hundred living forges.

He was not the last.

The thought wasn't a realization; it was a physical blow. The chain around his soul, once a lifeline, now felt like a hangman's noose. His vengeance was a lie. Forty years of rage for a people who had not been unmade, but had... endured, without him. The chain was still there, but what anchor did it hold now? What was he, if not the last fire?

A small, quiet hand settled on his shoulder. It was Thaddeus. The old man said nothing, but stood beside him, his gaze fixed on the weeping statue, a silent, shared communion of a sorrow that needed no words. He was a paradox of joy and wisdom, a man whose gentle soul held the memory of a thousand unwritten stories, a testament to the idea that a man's history is not a burden to be carried, but a story to be told. Seraphina stood a little apart, her cold, arrogant exterior a shield she used to control the volatile, time bending magic within her. Her analytical gaze swept the statue not as a monument, but as a piece of geological data. "The erosion is profound," she noted, her voice a clinical whisper against the wind. "The constant freezing and thawing of the water has fractured the stone at a structural level. It is a testament to the original craftsmanship that it still stands at all."

Gundroff did not hear her. He heard only the echo of his father's voice, the whisper of a lesson he had failed to learn. He turned from the statue and continued the march, his heart a cold, heavy stone in his chest. They passed other kings, other ghosts, each one a new, silent wound in his soul. King Brodi the Builder, whose stone eyes stared out at a kingdom he could no longer see. King Borass the Dragonslayer, his stone face a mask of grim, final victory, a victory that was now a lie.

The pass was not a road. It was a cemetery of his own history, a final, terrible pilgrimage through the graveyard of his own broken promises. The grief that had been his constant, familiar companion was gone, replaced by a new, and far more terrifying, emotion: shame. And as they finally emerged from the pass and saw the distant, jagged peak of Hjarta-Fell, a black, broken tooth against the cold, grey sky, he felt the last of his old self. the noble, grieving warrior. die.

All that was left was a weapon. a hammer of pure, cold fury, waiting for the anvil of war.

He smelled the rot first. Not the fetid, sweet decay of a living thing gone to seed, but a different, far more insidious stench. It was the sterile, acrid odor of a poison that did not kill, but unmade. It was the temporal decay, a sick, psychic residue from a forgotten wound in reality itself, and it was a smell he knew with an intimate, brutal certainty, a smell that had haunted his dreams for forty years: the scent of his own people, turned to ash and smoke by a profane fire. It was the smell of Mor kin alchemy, a cold, surgical odor that was a profanity in the clean, honest air of the mountains. His head snapped up, and his gaze was drawn to the source. They stood on a final, high promontory, a windswept plateau of jagged, crumbling granite, and below them, nestled in a vast, bowl shaped valley, was his home. It was a wound. The great valley, once a place of verdant life and roaring rivers, was now a dead, silent bowl of cracked, grey stone and ash. The gates, the crown jewel of his people's craftsmanship... were a defilement. The great, iron bound doors of living granite stone were now scarred with a profane, green alchemy. He had expected a tomb. But this was an abomination.

What truly shattered him was the carvings that made the world scream. The elegant, intricate, and beautiful faces of his ancestors had been meticulously, brutally, and artistically defiled. Their stone eyes had been gouged out, a final, unforgivable profanity against the memory of a people who had asked for nothing more than to be remembered. The artistic desecration of a king's face, a final, cold blooded act of unmaking, made his heart. a thing he had thought was a dead, silent stone. leap to his throat and scream. The funeral was over. The war had just begun.

But what truly shattered him was the new, final, and profane work that had been added. A new set of markings, not in the elegant runes of his people, but in the cold, spidery, and geometric scrawl of the Mor kin, had been carved into the crumbling stone of the gate. They were a profane prayer, a litany of cold, nihilistic purpose that spoke of a final, beautiful silence. And over the heart of the great hall, over the silent, echoing space where the great heart of his home had once been, a single, massive, and terrible symbol had been burned into the stone: the cultist spiral of the Dragon Queen. It was not a carving. It was a brand. A silent, physical manifestation of a spiritual abomination that was slowly, systematically, and deliberately unmaking the soul of his home. And in that instant, the grief that had been a cold, heavy stone in his chest exploded. It was a raw, volcanic, and all consuming inferno. It was not grief. It was not a sorrow. It was a hatred so profound, so absolute, it was a work of art in itself. He was a man who had made his peace with a war that was over. He had made his peace with the silence of a people who were ghosts. But this was an insult. A desecration. A final, unforgivable profanity against the memory of a people who had asked for nothing more than to be remembered. The funeral was over. The war had just begun.

He was no longer a mourner, no longer a ghost. He was a weapon. A hammer of pure, cold fury, waiting for the anvil of war. The rage that had shattered Gundroff's grief was no longer a fire, but a cold, hard stone in his gut. The funeral was over. He was a weapon now, and a weapon does not weep. He stood on the wind scoured plateau, his eyes fixed on the defiled gates below, his heart a silent, furious drum. The desecration of his home, the profane markings of the Mor kin carved over the sacred runes of his ancestors, was a physical insult he could feel in his own bones. His past, his shame, his forty year pilgrimage of sorrow. all of it was a lie. The only truth left was the fight.

He looked back at his companions. Seraphina's face was pale, her glacial eyes wide with a horrified comprehension that mirrored his own. The cold, sterile math of her intellect had found a flaw in her own reality, a flaw more terrifying than any demon. She saw the war now, not as an abstract concept, but as a desecration of art, a murder of a symphony she could never hear. Beside her, Thaddeus was a study in grim resolve. The old man's cheerful smile was gone, replaced by a look of sober, unyielding purpose. He was not a warrior, but he was a bulwark, a living testament to the idea that some things, in the face of all the world's fury, will endure.

Gundroff gave a single, sharp nod. It was not a question. It was a command. He turned and began the final descent into the valley, his body. once a silent protest against a world that had abandoned him. now a hard, cold, and terrible promise of a vengeance that had not yet been earned. They moved through the silent, ruined streets of the dead city, the shattered architecture a quiet chorus of their people's glory and fall. The wind, which had been a low, mournful wail, died in the tight, shadowed corridors of the ruined hold, leaving behind an absolute, profound quiet that was more unnerving than any sound. The only noise was the echo of their footsteps against the dead stone, a lonely and defiant tattoo against the silence of a people who had been unmade.

He moved with a hunter's instinct, his massive, scarred frame a blur of motion, a silent, lethal shadow in a city of ghosts. His hands, which had so long known the familiar weight of his own axe, were empty, a fresh and unwelcome wound. But his body, tempered in a thousand battles, was a weapon of its own, a silent, terrible promise. He saw the city not as a home, but as a battlefield, a chessboard of his own making, and he moved with a grim, purposeful grace that was a beautiful and terrifying work of art.

They reached the great gates, the final, terrible monument to their grief. The massive, iron bound doors of living granite stone were open, hanging askew from a single, groaning leather hinge. a gaping, black mouth that promised to devour them whole. Gundroff did not hesitate. He walked to the center of the great, vaulted archway, his body. a mountain of granite and grief. a bulwark against the darkness. He felt the cold, dead stone of the threshold beneath his boots, a stone that had been a living, breathing part of his home just forty years ago.

The smell of the Mor kin's black alchemy was a physical blow, a cold, surgical odor that made his stomach clench. He looked at Seraphina and Thaddeus, and in their eyes, he saw a reflection of his own sorrow, a grief too profound to be expressed in words. They were a shattered trinity, a fellowship forged in the crucible of a cosmic mistake, and they were walking into a war that was not their own. But they were walking it together, a silent, grim, and defiant chorus of a hope that refused to die.

He took a slow, deliberate breath, the stale, cold air a fire in his lungs. He walked a few steps deeper into the city, his body a silent challenge to a darkness he could not see. The vast, echoing silence of the great hall, a space that should have been alive with the sound of hammers and the roar of a thousand forges, was a physical thing, a weight that pressed down on his soul.

And then, without warning, the silence broke. A hail of black fletched arrows, launched from the shadows of the high, vaulted ceiling, sang a low, mournful song of death. The air, which had been so still just a moment ago, was now a maelstrom of screaming steel and whistling wood. Gundroff's body, a coiled spring of lethal intent, moved with the unthinking instinct of a lifetime of war. He threw himself forward, a massive human shield against a torrent of death. The arrows, meant for the soft, unarmored flesh of a human, struck his back with a series of sharp, percussive thuds, their flight arrested by the thick, knotted muscle and scar tissue of his bare hide. The pain was a starburst of white hot agony, but it was a pain he understood, an honest pain he could measure in the simple, physical truth of a wound. This was not the insidious, unmaking poison of a demon. This was war.

Seraphina's hands, a blur of motion, were already weaving a complex pattern in the air. A shimmering, translucent shield of pure, kinetic energy erupted from her fingertips, a wall of light that met a second volley of arrows with the sound of angry bees striking a windowpane. The magical light cast long, dancing shadows that writhed and clawed at them from the darkness. a shadow that seemed to have a life of its own. She screamed a word of power, a word that would have thrown a man fifty feet, and hurled a bolt of pure, concussive force at the ceiling. The force, a bright, coruscating flash of white light, struck the shadows with the force of a hammer, scattering them but leaving the Mor kin, who were the source of the attack, unharmed. They were everywhere. The hall, which had seemed so empty just moments before, was now alive with a new and more terrible kind of life. Figures, clad in dark, grey mail, emerged from the shadows of the high archways. Their scarred skin was the color of cooled ash, their eyes were a cold, alien neon that pulsed in the darkness, and their faces were smooth, utterly devoid of the glorious beards that marked a dwarf's honor. They moved with a silent, graceful, and terrifying precision, their movements a living testament to a cold, nihilistic, and soulless philosophy of war. They were not warriors. They were a machine. A machine designed not to kill, but to unmake.

Thaddeus, for his part, was a silent, unmoving sentinel behind Seraphina. His hands were clasped in quiet prayer, his eyes fixed on the Mor kin, a look of grim, focused resolve on his face. He was not a warrior, but he was a bulwark, a living testament to the idea that some things, in the face of all the world's fury, will endure. He did not move. He did not speak. He existed.

Gundroff, his back a pincushion of pain and steel, let out a roar. a sound of pure, unadulterated fury that had been building for forty years. He drew his war axe from his back, the familiar weight of the polished steel a small, solid comfort in a world that was coming undone. He charged, a blur of leather and rage, into the heart of the chaos, his war axe a flashing, terrible promise of a vengeance that had finally, impossibly, found a name. The first battle for Hjarta-Fell had begun, and it was a battle for the soul of the mountain itself.

Chapter 24

Unbroken Stone

A good crack. Yes. This was a good crack.

It smelled of old, sad stone and the quiet, dusty secrets of spiders. From here, the whole broken world was a pretty, terrible picture. Ankle Shanker settled into her crevice, a happy shadow in a sad place, and watched the noises begin.

Down below, at the ugly, torn gates, the boring things were gathering. The Mor kin. So many of them. They were not a fun noise, like a squealing piglet or a breaking bottle. They were a quiet noise, a shuffling of grey armor and grey faces that was all the same. A un pretty, orderly mess. They made straight lines. They held their pointy things just so. a waste of good chaos.

Ankle Shanker sighed, polishing one of her daggers with a scrap of oily cloth. The hunt was getting boring. The big, sad dwarf and his friends were taking too long. She had followed them through the dark, wet places, and now she was stuck watching the grey things make their boring shapes.

Then, a new thing. A different kind of pretty.

He did not arrive with a noise. He was just… there. Standing on a high, broken archway, I look down at the dull, grey things. He was a masterpiece of a knife cut. Tall and quiet, in clothes the color of a shadow's heart. His skin was a perfect, smooth black, like a river stone from a place with no sun. His hair was a surprise, a splash of snow white against the dark. And his eyes… oh, his eyes were the prettiest thing. Two shiny, purple stones that saw everything and cared for nothing.

284

This was a new kind of quiet. Not her quiet, the sneaky, hiding quiet of the cracks. His quiet was loud. A heavy quiet. When he was there, all the other boring noises stopped. The grey things, with their straight lines and their pointy sticks, all turned their grey faces up to him. They did not cheer. They did not speak. They just... stopped. He made the world hold its breath just by looking at it, a interesting, pretty trick.

The pretty, quiet man raised a hand. A single, elegant hand in a black glove. He did not make a fist. He did not point. He just... held it there.

Ankle Shanker felt a cold feeling, a sudden drop in the air that had nothing to do with the wind. It was the feeling of a door opening into a place that was old and empty.

The sky answered. A shadow fell over the valley, a shadow with wings. It was a big, loud, and *not pretty* thing. A dragon. It was all scales and teeth and a bad, hot smell that ruined the nice, clean smell of the cold stone. It landed with a crash that made the rock crack, sending a shower of dust onto her head.

Ankle Shanker scowled. The big, loud thing was ruining her quiet place. It was making a mess. She looked from the dragon, with its ugly, roaring mouth, back to the pretty, quiet man on the archway. He was still perfectly still, his purple eyes watching the scene with the calm, happy look of a painter who has just finished a good, terrible picture.

This was his noise. He had made the big, loud thing come. A new rule in the game. A interesting, bad knife cut. Down below, the sad, noisy dwarves were still walking, making their little marching sounds, not knowing that the pretty, quiet man had just painted their ending.

The air, once a maelstrom of screaming steel and whistling wood, now hung heavy with a profound and terrible stillness. The scent of ozone and the sterile, acrid stench of Mor kin alchemy clung to the stone, a foul perfume in the heart of a desecrated home. Seraphina stood at the center of it all, the cerulean light of her magic a small, flickering star in a hall of ghosts. They had won. Or, more accurately, they had survived a bloody stalemate. At the foot of their last, terrible stand lay a dozen of the Mor kin, their bodies a grotesque, tangled ruin of dark, grey mail and broken bone.

Her mind. a fortress of causality and arcane law. was cold and clinical. The adrenaline of the fight had faded, leaving a hollow ache in her bones and a clear, razor sharp understanding of what had transpired. This was not a victory. This was an inspection. The Mor kin were a cold, soulless people who fought not with rage, but with a horrifying, pragmatic logic. This ambush was a feint, a probe to test the strength of their enemies. They had tasted the dwarven fury and the chaos of her magic, and they had retreated. They were not defeated. They were... reporting.

"They are not simple beasts," she said, her voice a low, raw whisper that cut through the silence. She knelt beside one of the fallen cultists, her movements slow and deliberate, the scholar in her momentarily eclipsing the warrior. She traced a finger along the cold, soulless steel of their armor, a masterpiece of cold, nihilistic purpose. Their blades were not just steel, but an alchemical alloy that left a faint, acrid scent of bitter almonds and something cold, something that had no name.

"They do not fight with rage," she continued, her voice a cold, clinical instrument of reason. "They fight with logic. This was a feint. A probe." She paused, her gaze sweeping over the carnage. "They knew we would defend the entrance. They knew we would hold this position. They have tasted our strength, and they have retreated. They are not defeated. They are... reporting."

As if on cue, a low, rhythmic drumming, a percussive beat that was not a sound but a vibration that traveled through the stone of the mountain, began in the far distance. It was the sound of a thousand iron shod boots marching in perfect, horrifying unison. The main host was coming.

"We have to move," she said, her voice sharp with an urgency born of pure, tactical necessity. "Now. They will be here within the hour."

Gundroff let out a low growl, a sound of pure, thwarted rage. He looked at the chaos of the battle, at the grim, still forms of their fallen enemies. He was a warrior, and a warrior was meant to hold his ground, to stand and fight until the last foe was slain. But Seraphina was right. This was not a war of glory. It was a war of attrition. A war they could not hope to win in a frontal assault.

"The Deep Core passages," Thaddeus said, his voice a quiet, calm counterpoint to the roaring chaos in Gundroff's soul. The old man, who had spent the entire battle behind a bulwark of Seraphina's magic, was now a picture of serene, unblinking focus. He gestured to a small, unassuming fissure in the great stone wall, a place where the pristine, living rock of the mountain had been fractured and broken, leaving behind a shallow, dark gash. "That is not the main passage. It is not on any map. It is a wound. A place the mountain wants to forget."

Seraphina's mind raced. The logical, cold truth of his words struck her with the force of a physical blow. The Mor kin were a people of order and efficiency. They would not waste their time with a forgotten wound in the stone. They would assume their enemies would take the main passage, the logical path. But they had a different, more ancient, and far more terrifying kind of guide.

"That is our path," she said, her voice a low, hard certainty. "To the heart of the mountain. To the Tomb of the Champions." The words, heavy with a terrible new purpose, hung in the air. This was no longer an abstract quest for a celestial pillar; it was a raid on a sacred, personal grave.

In his eyes, Seraphina saw not a warrior's rage, but the grim, unwavering purpose of a man who had found a new, and far more terrible, kind of war to fight. He was no longer a ghost mourning a funeral, but a brother returned, a warrior with a new battle to fight.

The passage Thaddeus had chosen was a lie. It was not on any of the royal schematics Seraphina had seen, a forgotten wound in the mountain's flesh that had long ago been healed over by time and silence. They moved through a maze of narrow, twisting passages that reeked of damp earth and the profound, dusty quiet of a place that had not seen a living soul in a hundred years. The low, rhythmic drumming of the approaching Mor kin host, a sound that was felt more than it was heard, was a physical weight against their backs, a constant, low grade drumbeat of an impending death that spurred their exhausted bodies into a frantic, desperate march.

Seraphina, her magic a guttering candle after the battle at the gates, focused on the path, a small, silver light from a polished agate illuminating the treacherous, uneven stone. She was the mind, and her mind was a cold, pragmatic instrument of survival. She saw the passages not as a home, but as a chessboard, a series of moves and countermoves that would lead them to their true objective: the Tomb of the Champions.

The tunnels were a testament to the dwarven love of art. The rough, unadorned rock of the outer passages gave way to the smooth, meticulously carved stone of the upper halls. Even here, in the forgotten corridors of the outer perimeter, the artistry of the Anvilheart Compact was on full display. The walls were lined with the faces of their ancestors, their grim, resolute features a silent, eternal chorus of a people who had built their entire civilization on the unyielding strength of a promise kept.

A new sound broke the silence. It was not the cold, rhythmic beat of a thousand marching boots, but a sound of a different, more terrible kind of noise. It was the sound of desecration. It was the rhythmic clang of a hammer, not against an anvil, but against a soul. It was the roar of a forge fire, not a song of creation, but a sound of pure, unapologetic destruction. It was the sound of a beautiful, tragic, and unholy music that was a symphony of their people's final, terrible, and unmade song.

She reached a wide, vaulted archway and, with a silent gesture to Gundroff, peered through the opening. The sight that greeted her made the cold, pragmatic fortress of her mind crumble. They were in a high, echoing hall, a hall that should have been a place of beauty and art, a hall that should have been a testament to a people's heart. It was now a makeshift foundry. A half dozen Mor kin cultists, their dark, grey mail a stark contrast to the brilliant, vibrant artistry of the hall, were tending a large, smoking forge. The flames that erupted from its core were not the clean, roaring, life giving fires of a dwarven forge, but a silent, green alchemy that seemed to consume the air.

And around the forge, in a haphazard, sacrilegious pile, was a mountain of priceless dwarven heirlooms. A great, bronze statue of Grolnir, the Axe Lord, lay shattered on the floor, its face a mask of silent, terrible agony. The elegant, mithril inlaid crest of the Stonehammer Clan, a thing of grace and majesty, was propped up on a heap of coal, a grotesque, silent promise of a pride that was about to be unmade.

One of the Mor kin, a hulking, soulless brute with a face like a slab of dead granite, picked up a shield. It was not a simple piece of iron, but a masterpiece of a young, arrogant artisan. The wood was a dark, rich walnut, and the face of the shield was a riot of elegant, interlocking bronze runes that spoke a prayer to the gods of battle and of a promise to a people who would never be defeated. It was a shield forged by Gundroff's first mentor, a dwarf who had been a father to him, a dwarf whose face was now a ghost in his memories.

Gundroff's breath hitched in his throat. He did not speak. He did not move. He stood there, his hands, which had so long known the familiar weight of that shield, now clenched into white knuckled fists of a profound and terrible shame. The cold, sterile reality of his people's unmaking had found him, and it was a reality that was a thousand times more brutal, a thousand times more personal, than any demon's flame.

The Mor kin tossed the shield onto the coals with a contemptuous thud. The runes, once a living, breathing testament to a people's heart, began to shimmer, to writhe, to dissolve into a fine, black, acrid powder. The shield was not just melting. It was being unmade.

A low, guttural growl, a sound of pure, volcanic fury that was a thousand years old, tore itself from Gundroff's throat. He was a son, and he was watching his father die a second time. He was a smith, and he was watching his people's greatest art be turned to ash. He was a weapon, and he was being asked to stand down while the last, beautiful piece of his home was being erased from the world.

"No," Seraphina whispered, her hand on his massive shoulder, a small, fragile anchor against a storm that was threatening to tear her own soul from its moorings. "Not yet. We need to find the passage. We need to find the Tomb of the Champions."

Her words, the cold, pragmatic truth of their mission, cut through the red haze of Gundroff's rage. He looked at the smoking ruin of the shield, at the blank space where a memory had once been, and his rage, which had been a fire, turned to ice. He was not a warrior. He was a weapon, and a weapon, in the end, must be aimed.

He nodded once, a single, sharp gesture of a grim, terrible resolve, and together, they plunged back into the dark, leaving the desecrated foundry behind them.

The halls of Hjarta-Fell were a labyrinth of stone and shadow, a ghost of a home that was now a battlefield. Seraphina moved through the chaos with a desperate, frantic grace, her mind a fortress under siege. The Mor kin were not a disorganized rabble of monsters; they were a legion of silent, soulless soldiers, a machine of war that was designed not to kill, but to unmake. They moved with a terrifying, soulless precision, their movements a living testament to a cold, nihilistic purpose. They did not pursue the fellowship with a battle cry, but with the grim, unyielding efficiency of a predator herding its prey into a trap.

The War of Attrition was a constant, grinding agony of steel and will. Seraphina's magic was a flicker of light against a sea of darkness, a last, desperate shield against a storm of a thousand screaming blades. She wove a shimmering, translucent shield of pure, kinetic energy around them, a wall of light that met a torrent of black fletched arrows with a sound of angry bees striking a windowpane. The magical light cast long, dancing shadows that writhed and clawed at them from the darkness, a shadow that seemed to have a life of its own. Gundroff, a blur of leather and rage, fought beside her, his war axe a flashing, terrible promise of a vengeance that had finally, impossibly, found a name.

But the Mor kin were relentless. They did not attack with force, but with a cold, elegant, and terrible logic. They were not trying to defeat them with a glorious, final blow. They were trying to exhaust them. To break them piece by piece. They would lay a trap, a simple and obvious thing, and then retreat, leaving them to choose between a glorious, suicidal charge and a grim, endless war of attrition.

A new sound cut through the chaos of their desperate flight. It was not the cold, rhythmic beat of a thousand marching boots, but a single, heart stopping sound of a final, terrible defeat. It was the sound of a scream. A deep, guttural, and profound cry of agony that was the sound of a world that had been unmade.

Seraphina's mind, which had been focused on the immediate, grinding tactical needs of their escape, reeled. The sound was not in the hall with them. It came from the main assault. It was the voice of a man she had only just met, a man whose sorrow was a mirror of her own. It was the voice of Prince Fireforge.

Her mind, which had been a fortress, felt a sudden, profound, and devastating emptiness. She saw a vision of a great, booming forge, a fire that had been tended for a thousand years, a song of a people who had built their entire civilization on a promise of a future that would never be unmade. And then, without warning, she saw the forge crumble. The fire went out. The song died.

The Mor kin had not defeated the dwarven army in a glorious, final battle. They had defeated them with a single, brutal, and elegant act of psychological warfare. A trap. A cold, terrible, and brilliant trap. They had not killed a king. They had broken the heart of a people.

The retreat was a rout. The dwarf army, their courage and their pride shattered by the fall of their king, were a disordered, chaotic mass of fear and regret. They scrambled back from the heart of their home, their only thought to escape a war they had just, impossibly, lost.

Gundroff, a few feet ahead of Seraphina, let out a roar, a sound of pure, unadulterated fury that had been building for forty years. He turned, his war axe a blur of motion, and charged back into the fight. He was a son, and he was watching his father die a second time. He was a smith, and he was watching his people's greatest art be turned to ash. He was a weapon, and he was being asked to stand down while the last, beautiful piece of his home was being erased from the world.

The rage that had been a cold, heavy stone in his chest, a companion he had thought was a part of him, exploded. It was a raw, volcanic, and all consuming inferno, a fire that was a hundred times hotter than the dragon's, a thousand times purer than the divine fire he had once commanded. It was not grief. It was not a sorrow. It was a hatred so profound, so absolute, it was a work of art in itself.

He was a man who had made his peace with a war that was over. He had made his peace with the silence of a people who were ghosts. But this... this was an insult. A desecration. A final, unforgivable profanity against the memory of a people who had asked for nothing more than to be remembered.

The battle for the Upper Halls was a desperate, losing affair. The fellowship, along with a handful of grim faced dwarven warriors, was a small, defiant island in a sea of Mor kin fury. They were cornered, trapped in a grand, vaulted hall that had once been the royal armory.

The Mor kin, their movements a living testament to a cold, nihilistic purpose, advanced slowly and methodically, a phalanx of silent, soulless soldiers. They did not attack with a battle cry, but with a chilling, disciplined precision. They did not need to. The knowledge of their king's crippling, the sound of his final, guttural scream, had done more to break the dwarves' spirit than any arrow could.

Gundroff, a blur of leather and rage, fought with a primal, animalistic fury. His war axe, a blur of polished steel and righteous anger, was a flashing, terrible promise of a vengeance he would not be able to deliver. He fought not to win, but to die a good death. He was a mountain of defiant, glorious rage, a living monument to a people who would not be forgotten.

But the Mor kin were relentless. They were a force of nature, a living, breathing testament to a cold, surgical, and utterly soulless philosophy of war. They did not fight with rage; they fought with logic. They were a machine, and a machine does not tire.

The fellowship was trapped. The Mor kin, a wall of dark, grey mail and polished steel, had them surrounded. The grim faced dwarven warriors, their axes held high, were a small, defiant shield against a tide of overwhelming, soulless rage. The funeral was over. The war had just begun. The only question now was how to end it.

The old war master, Harek, who had been a silent, grim faced observer of their desperate stand, moved. He did not speak. He stood there, his hands, massive and calloused, resting on his axe haft. His face was a mask of granite, a roadmap of a thousand tiny, heartbreaking battles. He was a warrior of a forgotten age, a man who believed that a good death was not an end, but a final, glorious battle for a cause that was simple, noble, and brutally tangible.

He looked at Gundroff, his gaze a final, silent communion of a shared sorrow. He looked at Seraphina and Thaddeus, his eyes a grim, silent acknowledgment of a truth he had only just begun to understand. He was not a fool. He was a pragmatist. And he knew that a single, glorious death was a better investment than three.

"The Deep Core passages," he said, his voice a low, gravelly rasp that was the sound of a rock grinding against a stone. "There, on the north wall. The old well shaft. It is hidden. They will not be watching it." He looked directly at Gundroff, a king's command in his eyes, but a brother's plea in his heart. "You will go to the Deep Core, brother. You will cleanse our home of this rot."

He then looked at Seraphina and Thaddeus, and his gaze softened. "And you… You will help him. He is a hammer without an anvil. He is a forge without a fire. He is a king without a kingdom. You will be his home."

He looked back at Gundroff, his eyes a glint of hard, cold fury. He was a king who had lost his kingdom. He was a father who had lost his son. He was a man who had lost his world. He was a warrior, and he was being asked to stand down while the last, beautiful piece of his home was being erased from the world.

"You will return to us, brother," he said, his voice a low, hard, and final promise. "For the final battle. And you will not be alone. We are a people who have lived in the dark. But we have not forgotten our song."

He turned from them and, with a final, glorious roar that was the sound of a thousand hammers and a thousand forges, he charged into the heart of the Mor kin phalanx, his war axe a flashing, terrible promise of a vengeance he would not be able to deliver.

The Mor kin met his charge with the grim, unyielding efficiency of a machine. They did not attack with a battle cry, but with a cold, elegant, and terrible logic. They were a force of nature, a living, breathing testament to a cold, surgical, and utterly soulless philosophy of war.

Gundroff did not move. He stood there, his back to the battle, his eyes fixed on the small, unassuming fissure in the great stone wall. The scream of Harek was a raw, visceral sound that was the sound of a world that was being unmade. He did not move. He did not speak. He stood there, his hands, which had so long known the familiar weight of his own axe, now clenched into white knuckled fists of a profound and terrible shame.

He was a son, and he was watching his father die a second time. He was a smith, and he was watching his people's greatest art be turned to ash. He was a weapon, and he was being asked to stand down while the last, beautiful piece of his home was being erased from the world.

The rage that had been a cold, heavy stone in his chest, a companion he had thought was a part of him, exploded. It was a raw, volcanic, and all consuming inferno, a fire that was a hundred times hotter than the dragon's, a thousand times purer than the divine fire he had once commanded. It was not grief. It was not a sorrow. It was a hatred so profound, so absolute, it was a work of art in itself. He was a man who had made his peace with a war that was over. He had made his peace with the silence of a people who were ghosts. But this... this was an insult. A desecration. A final, unforgivable profanity against the memory of a people who had asked for nothing more than to be remembered.

Chapter 25

The Deep Core

The halls of Hjarta-Fell, once a labyrinth of strategic chaos and a testament to the brutal, elegant laws of dwarven warcraft, became a narrow, purposeful descent. The frenzied grace of their flight, born of the primal need to survive, gave way to a measured, deliberate trudge. Each footfall on the worn stone stairs was a slow, agonizing beat in the silent funeral march of their hope. The echoing clamor of the main assault, a storm of iron and rage that had consumed the upper levels of the fortress, faded into a low, distant tremor. It was not a sound that could be heard so much as it was a vibration that travelled through the marrow of their bones, a constant, low grade drumbeat of an impending death that spurred their exhausted bodies into a frantic, desperate march.

They descended into the forgotten underbelly of the mountain, a place so old it felt as though the rock remembered a different, softer world. The air grew colder, heavier, smelling not of the iron and gore of the battle above, but of a profound, dusty quiet. It was the scent of a place where a thousand years of forgotten grief had settled into the stone, where every mote of dust was a memory and every whisper of the wind was a sigh. The passages spoke of an ancient, pre war age. a time when the mountain was not a fortress, but a home. The carvings on the walls were not of glorious battles and conquering kings, but of families laughing around a hearth, of children playing at the knees of their fathers, of the sacred, quiet beauty of a people who had built their entire world on a song of stone and of songs.

After what felt like an eternity, they reached an immense, vaulted cavern. A deep, abyssal chasm split the floor, a wound in the world that seemed to drink all light and sound. The air at the edge of the abyss was still, utterly silent. It was a silence that was not a rest, but a profound and terrible emptiness, a void that seemed to reach out with a physical weight to crush their souls. Spanning this impossible divide was a bridge. It was not a grand arch of polished stone or crafted metal, but a thing of pure, unadulterated thought. a shimmering, translucent expanse of solidified mist that pulsed with a faint, sorrowful light. Its surface was the color of a winter sky, and it seemed to hum with a thousand whispered regrets. This was not a ward of brute force, but of soul. This was the Bridge of Sorrows.

Seraphina was the first to approach, her mind a fortress of logic and arcane law, yet a chill of disquiet settled in her bones. The bridge was a lie, a psychic construct meant to test their will. A low, sorrowful moan seemed to echo from its depths, a sound that was not heard with the ears but felt in the hollow places of the soul. The bridge would only solidify if they confessed a profound, heart wrenching failure. It was an impossible price. They were warriors, not penitents.

"This is a ward of pure will," she said, her voice strained. "It is not seeking strength, but honesty. This is a place where we must bare our souls."

Gundroff, his fury from the battle still a low, simmering ember in his chest, stepped forward. He looked at the bridge, and his grim face, a roadmap of a thousand battles, seemed to soften. He knew this kind of pain. This was a war he had been fighting for forty years. He looked at the translucent path and saw not a road to salvation, but a mirror. He was the last of the Ragingfires. The previous, defiant light of a fire that had been extinguished a hundred years ago. And his greatest shame, his most profound failure, was not that he had lost his home, but that he had walked away from it. He had let the silence become a grave. He had let his people become a ghost in the annals of a forgotten age.

He took a slow, deep breath, the air filling his lungs with a scent of cold, forgotten dust. He spoke not to the others, but to the bridge, a confession to a wound in the world that was a mirror of his own. His words were a low, gravelly rasp that felt like a confession of a man who had lost his home, and now, his king. "My greatest failure," he said, his voice raw with an ancient pain, "was not that I lost my home, but that I walked away from it. I let the silence become a grave. I was so caught up in mourning a funeral that I forgot to fight a war." As the words left his lips, a small, fragile tremor ran through the bridge. A small section of the surface, a circle of about a man's span, solidified into a solid, unyielding stone.

Seraphina watched as the stone solidified under Gundroff's words. Her mind, an engine of causality, tried to process the event. It was not a magical reaction; the bridge was not a lock to be picked by an arcane key. It was a wound responding to the salt of a shared grief. The low, sorrowful moan that echoed from its misty depths shifted, taking on a new texture. the faint, heartbreaking sound of a child's cry in a distant room.

Her breath caught. The cold, dusty air of the cavern vanished.

A high balcony of white marble. A sky of the softest summer blue. The scent of salt and sun-warmed stone. Alexander stood beside her, his kingly gaze not on the glittering city below, but on the small, sleeping bundle in her arms. His hand, so accustomed to the pommel of a sword, trembled as he traced the crescent-shaped birthmark behind their daughter's ear.

"We cannot," he had whispered, his voice thick with a sorrow that was a premonition. "The Council would tear the kingdom apart. My father's line... the succession..."

She had looked from his face, a landscape of love and trapped duty, to the face of her child, Juniper. Her child. She saw the impossible equation. A kingdom's stability on one side of the scale; this small, perfect, breathing life on the other. Her mind, her greatest strength and her most terrible curse, presented the solution with the cold, clean precision of a surgeon's blade.

"It is the only logical choice," she had said, the words tasting like glass in her mouth. She had kissed her daughter's brow one last time, a ghost of a touch, and placed her in the arms of the quiet, sorrowful man who would take her far away, to a place of sunlight and lavender.

She had called it logic. She had called it duty. She had called it sacrifice.

The bridge wailed, a sound of profound and terrible empathy, and she knew the truth. It had been fear.

The entire span before her solidified in a rush, the mist hardening into a solid, unyielding road of pale, tear-stained stone. It was a monument to a grief that had, at last, found its name. Gundroff and Thaddeus were staring at her, their faces etched with concern in the sorrowful light. A single, hot tear traced a path through the grime on her own cheek.

"I am a mage of pure causality," she said, her voice a low, raw whisper that felt like a sound from a different, far more broken world. "I see a problem, and I see a solution. I can calculate the trajectory of a falling star and chart the course of empires."

She looked at Gundroff, at the raw, honest pain in his eyes.

"But I stood on a balcony with a king who would have given up his throne for me, and I held our daughter in my arms. I saw the chaos our love would bring. civil war, a fractured kingdom, a throne built on a lie. I weighed the fate of a nation against the life of my own child." Her voice cracked, a brittle, shattering sound. "I chose the kingdom. I chose the law over the heart. And I left her with Master Nightshade. I dont know what he did with her but i hope she is safe."

They crossed the bridge in silence, a man and a woman who had, for a moment, been stripped of their armor, their titles, and their pride. They were simply two souls who had confessed a terrible, brutal truth. They had not defeated the bridge. They had become a part of it.

They stepped from the solid, unyielding stone of their confessions and into a hall of mirrors. It was an immense, perfectly circular chamber, its walls a polished, obsidian smooth surface that reflected their forms in a distorted, haunting chorus. The air was heavy, thick with the scent of ozone and the profound silence of a mind without a heart. At the center of the chamber, a great, black sphere hung in the air, a thing of profound and terrible stillness that hummed with a low, resonating beat.

The moment they crossed the threshold, a wave of psychic pain, a profound and devastating echo of a mind that had been shattered and remade, crashed into them. It was a sound that was not heard with the ears, but felt in the bones. It was the sound of a beautiful, tragic, and unholy music that was a symphony of a god's final, terrible, and unmade song.

For Gundroff, the sound was a hammer blow to his soul. It was the rhythmic, sacred clang of a thousand forges, but each strike was a cold, alien thing that did not shape metal, but broke it. His mind, so used to the honest, tangible truth of a hammer against an anvil, was now faced with an assault that defied all reason. The fire in his soul, the glorious, volcanic rage that had sustained him for forty years, flickered. In its place came a profound and terrible sense of futility, a cold, grinding knowledge that his purpose was a lie, his vengeance a meaningless echo. His body, a mountain of granite and grief, shuddered, and he fell to his knees, his hands a pair of useless, bleeding fists. He heard the voices of his ancestors, but they were no longer a battle cry; they were a mournful chorus, lamenting a purpose that could never be fulfilled.

For Seraphina, the pain was a violation of a different kind. Her mind, a fortress built upon causality and arcane law, was under siege. The psychic assault was a relentless, chaotic static that made her precise, linear thoughts feel like a fool's game. She saw a world of beautiful, intricate equations, a universe of perfect, elegant laws, and then she saw it all unmade, all the numbers turning to screaming, nonsense. Her magic, her cold, pragmatic truth, had no answer for this madness. The sound was a discordant chord in the heart of her own sanity. She pressed her hands against her temples, a thin line of blood running from her nose as she fought a battle she was never meant to wage, a battle against a mind that was not sane, but perfectly, terribly, mad.

It was Thaddeus, the old man who had seemed so frail and so lost, who was now a picture of serene, unblinking focus. He saw not chaos, but a story. He saw a mind that had shattered itself to become a god. He saw a man who had loved his world so fiercely that he had unmade it. He gestured to a series of glyphs that were etched into the floor, a complex, paradoxical runic puzzle that was a thing of impossible, elegant chaos. It was a puzzle that could not be solved with a hammer or a sword. It was a puzzle that could only be solved with a soul.

"It is a riddle of paradox," he said, his voice a low, calm counterpoint to the howling chaos in their minds. "The sphere reflects a mind that is at war with itself. You must solve the puzzle with the opposite of what you are."

Gundroff, a man who had only ever known the simple, tangible truth of a hammer against an anvil, saw a different kind of truth in the intricate, swirling chaos of the runes. He saw a series of impossible, beautiful, and unmade promises. He saw a hammer without an anvil. He saw a forge without a fire. He saw a king without a kingdom. He saw himself. "It's not about what the runes say," he said, his voice raw with a sudden, profound understanding. "It's about what they don't say. They are an unmade promise. They are a song that was never sung. They are a riddle that has no answer because the answer is not on the board. The answer is in the unmaking."

Seraphina, her mind reeling from the psychic shockwave of his fall, looked at the runes. She saw a series of impossible equations. She encountered a series of contradictory laws with no clear solution. She saw a series of unmade promises. She saw a man who had lost his home. She saw a man who had lost his kingdom. She saw a man who had lost his world. And she saw herself.

She reached out a hand, and with a small, fragile gesture of a sudden, profound understanding, she touched the first rune. The rune, once a symbol of a brutal, cold logic, began to shimmer, to writhe, to dissolve into a fine, black, acrid powder. She was not a warrior. She was a scholar. And a scholar, in the end, must be aimed.

She and Gundroff worked in unison, he providing the raw, emotional truth, and she providing the knowledge to complete the circuit. With each unmade rune, the psychic wail from the sphere lessened. When the last rune was gone, the sphere was silent. The psychic pain was gone. The puzzle was solved. They had not defeated the pain. They had absorbed it.

The psychic storm had passed. In the profound and ringing silence, the obsidian walls of the Hall of Echoes returned to a simple, unmagical reflection. The black sphere at its center, now cold and utterly inert, hung as a testament to a pain they had both absorbed and overcome. But their brief victory was shattered by the simple, brutal truth of their exhaustion. Seraphina was on her knees, her body trembling with the aftershocks of a mind shattering psychic assault. Gundroff, his own face a mask of raw exhaustion, stood over her, his hands, once again, a pair of useless, bleeding fists.

Thaddeus, ever the quiet anchor in their chaos, knelt beside them. He did not offer a story or a prayer. He placed a steadying hand on each of their shoulders, a silent, unequivocal statement of a presence that was more powerful than any spell or sword.

They stepped from the echoing chamber and into a new kind of silence. The air was heavy, thick with a cold, damp grief that clung to their skin like a shroud. The final ward, the Weeping Gate, stood at the far end of the hall. It was a massive, circular seal of polished obsidian that was not a door, but a monument to a grief that had been frozen in time. The surface of the stone was a mirror, a thing of such perfect, unyielding blackness that it reflected nothing but their own weary, broken faces. But from the center of the door, from a pair of perfectly carved, closed stone eyes, a constant, viscous stream of silver tears wept down the surface of the obsidian, pooling at the base in a small, still, and heartbreaking sea of a people's profound and terrible sorrow. The sound was a low, sibilant hiss, a quiet sobbing that spoke of an ancient, inconsolable pain.

In the center of the door, a perfectly smooth, heart shaped indentation sat empty, a void waiting to be filled.

Seraphina was the first to approach. Her hands, still trembling from the psychic assault, hovered over the space. Her mind, an engine of arcane law, raced for a solution. She poured her will into the stone, attempting to find a temporal loop, a causal flaw, anything that would give her a foothold. Her magic, the precise, mathematical truth she had always relied on, dissolved against the obsidian with a quiet, useless hum. It was a lock of a different nature entirely, and her logic was a child's toy against its impenetrable sadness.

Gundroff, his hands a pair of useless, bleeding fists, stepped forward. His blood, a crimson contrast to the pristine obsidian, dripped onto the stone, and the tear pool at the base of the gate hissed as it sizzled into steam. With a low growl of pure frustration, he raised his greataxe and brought it down with a thunderous crash. The weapon, forged for battle against tangible foes, sank into the surface with the muffled thud of a blade hitting a sandbag. It left no mark. The stone did not even tremble. He felt a profound sense of futility, as if he were trying to strike a memory. He was a creature of the physical world, and this door was a thing of the spirit.

Thaddeus watched, his face a landscape of ancient grief. He understood this place. "Grief may be the lock," he said, his voice a low, hard rasp that was a sound of gentle storytellers and old kings. "But love has always been the key."

Gundroff looked at the obsidian, and in the reflection of his broken face, he saw not just his own image, but the reflection of a thousand ghosts. He saw the laughing, bearded face of his father, the tear streaked face of his mother, and the defiant smile of his sister, Audhild. He looked from his reflection to the face of the king on the gate, and he saw the grief of a people, and a promise that had been unmade. He reached into his pouch, his fingers tracing the shape of the Sun Petal, a simple, beautiful thing that he had found in a tomb of a forgotten clan lord. He remembered the feeling of that moment. a quiet, somber peace in a place of great sadness. The Sun Petal was not a weapon. It was a memory.

"The key is not a grand artifact," he said, his voice a low, hard certainty. "It is a simple, beautiful thing."

He held it to the heart shaped indentation. The moment the crystal touched the stone, the weeping stopped. The air, which had been heavy with grief, was now still. The sorrowful light in the stone gave way to a brilliant, life giving golden light, a light that seemed to be a perfect echo of the sun. The tears, which had been a thing of sorrow, now ran down the face of the door with a profound and terrible joy. The obsidian, which had been a thing of frozen, unyielding grief, began to shimmer, to writhe, to dissolve into a fine, black, acrid powder. The door was not just melting. It was being unmade.

The great stone eyes of the king on the door ground open with a sound of ancient, grinding joy, revealing the tomb. It was not a grand, vaulted chamber of polished stone and gilded monuments. It was a perfect, circular hall carved from a single, seamless piece of living stone that seemed to drink the light, giving forth a soft, shadowless luminescence. The air within was cold, still, and smelled of dust and heroes. It was a sanctuary, a place of profound, hallowed peace, a final, unmade promise of a people who had built their entire civilization on a song.

And in the profound silence, a new sound reached them. It was a sound that was not heard with the ears but felt in the bones. It was a deep, resonant BOOM of a battering ram, a vibration that traveled through the stone of the mountain, a sound of a war that had been fought and lost long ago. It was the sound of Fireforge's last, desperate assault.

Gundroff, a man who had thought his heart was a dead, silent stone, felt a sudden, profound beat of a drum against his soul. It was the sound of a war he had believed was already over. He thought it not just in his ears, but in the marrow of his bones, a slow, insistent thud that was a call to arms and a brutal desecration. The peace of the tomb was a fragile, beautiful thing, but it was being shattered by a new and more terrible kind of silence. The war had just come to their doorstep. The air, which had been a still, sterile thing, was now alive with a thousand different, magnificent sounds. The rhythmic clang of a thousand hammers, a sound that was a prayer and a promise. The low, rumbling roar of a thousand forges, a fire that burned with the unyielding strength of stone. The shouts of dwarven guards, their voices a deep, rumbling command that was a testament to a strength that had not yet been unmade. The air was thick with the scent of hot iron, of coal smoke, and of a life that was still, impossibly, being lived.

For Seraphina, the sound was not a melody of war, but a cacophony of shattered data. Her mind, so used to the elegant rhythm of causality, was now under assault by a brutal, chaotic frequency. She pressed her hands to her temples, a thin line of blood already dry beneath her fingers, as her senses threatened to overload. The sound of the drums was a relentless, asymmetrical beat that made her feel sick to her stomach, a physical manifestation of a paradox she could not solve. She could see the equations of physics, the perfect, elegant laws of the universe, begin to shudder and fray at the edges, a testament to the unholy chaos of the cult's purpose.

Thaddeus closed his eyes. For a man who had lived his life as a quiet, cheerful shepherd, the sound of war should have been terrifying. But it was not. He felt a profound, aching sorrow. He had found his purpose in the peace of his faith, in the solace of quiet parables and the gentle wisdom of his god. He had made his peace with a world of silent tombs.

But now, in the heart of this ancient, quiet sanctuary, a new war had come, and it was fighting for the soul of the living. He stood, a small, still point of quiet desperation, the low, steady thrum of the drums echoing in his soul where the voice of his god should have been.

They stood before the massive, obsidian doors of the tomb, a thing of pure, unadulterated sorrow that wept silver tears. They had been told of the tomb by a man of stone, a man of hammers and of songs, a man who had been a ghost walking a ghost road. And in the profound, terrible, and glorious truth of a new and horrific battle, the two worlds, a world of beautiful, tragic lies, and a world of cold, honest truths, had just met. The struggle for the soul of the mountain had just begun.

A single, iron word was branded into the core of Gundroff's being, a command and a curse in one: endure. He was a man who had made his peace with a war that was over. He had made his peace with the silence of a people who were ghosts. But this… this was an insult. A desecration. A final, unforgivable profanity against the memory of a people who had asked for nothing more than to be remembered. His body, which had been a symphony of exhaustion and pain just a moment before, was now alive with a new, terrible fire. He felt the ancient, sacred tattoos on his body begin to hum with a low, vibrant power, a power he had not felt since the fall of his home. His greataxe, which had felt like a useless weight just moments before, now felt like a part of his soul, a living weapon of vengeance. He was no longer a ghost; he was a warrior reborn.

The air of the tomb, which had been a silent, sterile thing just moments before, was now alive with a thousand different, magnificent sounds. The rhythmic clang of a thousand hammers, a sound that was a prayer and a promise. The low, rumbling roar of a thousand forges, a fire that burned with the unyielding strength of stone. The shouts of dwarven guards, their voices a deep, rumbling command that was a testament to a strength that had not yet been unmade. The air was thick with the scent of hot iron, of coal smoke, and of a life that was still, impossibly, being lived. He could see it now, flashes of steel and magic, the frantic, defiant movement of his kin against an enemy he had thought long dead. He saw a single, bloodied dwarf fall, his defiance silenced. He saw the proud, defiant look of Prince Fireforge as he rallied his troops.

Gundroff's heart, which he had thought was a dead, silent thing, stuttered and then began to pound with a slow, heavy, and profound beat. He looked at the great banner that snapped in the cold wind, a great black banner with a single, white hammer carved upon it. It was the banner of the Stonehammer Clan, the royal line of Hjarta Fell. His eyes, which had been a glint of hard, cold fury just a moment before, were now wide with a profound, unadulterated horror. They were no longer the last. They were a people of war, a living testament to a defiance that had not yet been unmade. The two worlds, a world of beautiful, tragic lies, and a world of cold, honest truths, had just met. The battle for the soul of the mountain had just begun.

The three of them, a shattered dwarf, a broken mage, and a sorrowful shepherd, did not speak. They did not need to. Unconsciously, drawn by a gravity more powerful than fear, they moved closer together until their shoulders were nearly touching. Gundroff stood in the center, his body a shield against the coming storm. Seraphina stood to his right, her hands clenched into a fist, a silent promise of magic yet to be wielded. Thaddeus stood to his left, his hand resting on Gundroff's shoulder, a gesture of profound and quiet strength. They were a small, defiant point of life in a world of impending chaos, their shared past a silent bond that was stronger than any stone. They had not come to a tomb.

Chapter 26

The Hydra's Lament

The silence that followed the war drum's cry was not a peace, but the terrifying quiet before a hammer falls. The three of them stood in the tomb's antechamber, the new and glorious silence of living dwarves now a raw, painful absence in the ringing of their souls. The air, which had been thick with the scent of hot iron and life, was now once again still, cold, and heavy with a premonition of death. They were no longer in the heart of a sanctuary, but on the precipice of a vast, natural cavern, its ceiling lost in a darkness that the silver mineral light of the walls could not pierce. Before them lay a perfectly still, black subterranean lake, its waters as smooth and depthless as polished obsidian. In the center of the cavern, a single, massive, marble white island rose from the black water, connected to their ledge by a single, elegant stone causeway. Carved into the island was another, even grander set of obsidian doors. the true tomb. Faintly etched above the doors, so worn by time as to be almost invisible, was a single line of script in a forgotten tongue. Thaddeus squinted, his brow furrowing as his lips silently formed a syllable he couldn't quite grasp, before he shook his head in frustration.

Gundroff felt it first. A deep, earth shaking, and utterly primal ROAR of a great beast, a sound that came from the world below them. It was the sound of a living thing, a sound of such profound and ancient malice that it made the hairs on the back of his neck stand up. He looked at Seraphina, whose jaw was tight, her eyes wide with a cold, intellectual terror. He looked at Thaddeus, whose cheerful mask was gone, replaced by a grim landscape of quiet fury. "Ash Heart," Gundroff breathed, his voice barely a whisper. "The dragon has joined the fight."

As if in answer to that distant rage, the black lake before them began to stir. Rather than ripples, it was a slow, oily disturbance. The surface broke, and the guardian of the tomb rose from the silent depths. It was a Gilded Hydra. Five serpentine heads, each the size of a warhorse, rose on long, pale necks, their skin the color of old bone. It was blind, its ancient eyes sealed shut under folds of translucent skin. Its necks were a pale, horrifying canvas, etched with faint, shimmering bands of silver light. They tightened for a moment, like ghostly shackles, before fading again, only to reappear on another neck. From beneath the sealed lids, a constant, viscous stream of shimmering, silver tears wept down its cheeks, sizzling and steaming as they struck the water. Where the tears touched the stone of the causeway, the rock hissed and dissolved into a fine, grey slush. It did not roar. It simply raised its five heads and let out a low, mournful, multi toned moan.

For a dizzying second, the black lake before Gundroff was the blood soaked floor of his home, and the Hydra's moan was the scream of his sister, Audhild. He saw his home in the hydra's weeping, his grief in its tears. The cold ache in his chest became a white hot forge of forty year old fury. The battle for the tomb had begun. He charged onto the causeway, his greataxe a flaming sun, a weapon of pure, unadulterated vengeance. The sound of his own heavy, iron shod boots on the causeway, a thunderous echo in the stillness, was a declaration of defiance. He bellowed, a sound of pure, animal rage, a sound that he had not made in forty years. "Grolnir, Father of the Forge," he whispered, his voice a raw prayer. "Grant my steel one final fire. One true strike."

Seraphina whispered the first syllables of a powerful binding spell, but the sound of the incantation, a soft hiss in the vast cavern, drew an immediate, lashing strike from one of the heads that nearly took her own. Gundroff was driven back. Pinned down, the corrosive tears eating away at their path, he clutched his axe, its divine fire flickering. It was then that Thaddeus, his back pressed against a cavern wall, saw the pattern. "It weeps for the noise!" he yelled. "The sound of battle is a torment to it! It strikes at the sound!" Seraphina understood. She slammed the butt of her staff on the far side of the cavern, and with a powerful spell, amplified the sound a hundredfold, creating a deafening CRACK that echoed through the grotto. Four of the Hydra's heads whipped toward the sound, lashing out blindly at the empty wall, leaving the single, central head focused on the causeway.

It was the opening he needed. He didn't just charge; he bellowed, a sound of pure, animal rage. His axe was no longer a blur of divine fire; it was a hammer of vengeance. The first blow he struck against its pale hide rang with the name of his father. The second, for his mother. The third, for his clan. He was no longer fighting a monster; he was fighting a memory, and he would not be a coward again. Steel bit deep. The Hydra shrieked, a sound of pure, physical agony, but beneath it was a deeper, resonant note. a final, sorrowful exhalation as its millennia long torment came to an end. In its death throes, it unleashed its final, devastating attack.

All five heads reared back, not to strike, but to unleash a torrent of corrosive sorrow. A tidal wave of shimmering, hissing tears surged from its mouths, a wall of liquid death that would not just kill them, but unmake the stone they stood upon. There was no time to run. Gundroff looked at the wave, at the island, at his two companions. Forty years he had lived as a weapon of vengeance. He had run from the fire that took his first clan. He would not run from the water that threatened his new one. In this moment, he was not a ghost. He was a shield. He slammed his body into Seraphina and Thaddeus, shoving them towards the island at the end of the causeway. "Live!" he roared. He turned back, his warrior's gaze replaced by the discerning eyes of a smith. He saw the architecture not as a path, but as a creation. And in its heart, he saw the single, load bearing keystone. the flaw Grolnir himself would have left to unmake it. A prayer of understanding left his lips as he raised his great axe. "The stone endures!"

He brought the axe down. The ancient stone groaned, spiderweb cracks erupting from the point of impact. The wave of tears hit him as the causeway collapsed. A cascade of stone, a falling dwarf, and the wall of corrosive tears all plunged into the black lake in a chaotic, churning vortex. Gundroff's roar of defiance was cut short by a sharp cry of agony as the acidic tears washed over his back and legs. The violent collapse of the bridge dissipated the main force of the attack, which splashed harmlessly against the shores of the tomb's island. The Hydra, its final lament spent, collapsed back into the black water and was gone. The cavern was suddenly, terribly silent. For a heart stopping moment that stretched into an eternity, there was only the black, still water. Then, a single, scarred hand broke the surface.

Seraphina reached into the water, her magic a shimmering tendril that wrapped around his arm and hauled him ashore. Her jaw was set, her knuckles white where she gripped her staff. Her eyes, wide and fixed on Gundroff's ruined form, were not wet with tears but burned with a cold, protective fire. The sacred chronicle of his people tattooed on his back was a ruin of melted, fused flesh, the ink of his ancestors' glory burned away by the acidic sorrow. His legs were covered in horrific burns that had eaten deep into the muscle. He was a bastion. The silent shepherd and the furious mage knelt beside the crippled dwarf, beginning the grim work of tending to the broken shield. Without a word, they turned their faces toward the massive obsidian doors.

The Gilded Hydra did not strike again. It simply waited. Its five heads swayed in a silent, grotesque ballet above the black lake, a horrifying sculpture of bone and sorrow. From its throats, a low, mournful, multi toned moan, a sound that was a symphony of a thousand heartbreaks, echoed through the cavern. For Gundroff, the sound was a physical weight against his chest, a low, constant pressure that made his lungs feel small, as if they were trying to breathe in water. He could feel it in the soles of his boots, a vibration that crawled up his spine and settled in his skull with a chilling dread. He was a creature of a forge, a place of noise and purpose, and this... this was the sound of a universe that had lost its meaning.

He looked from the beast to his companions. Seraphina stood a few feet from him, her body a rigid, trembling line of defiance. Her eyes, wide and fixed on the creature, were not wet with tears but burned with a cold, intellectual terror. He could see her mind racing, a fortress of pure logic under siege by an enemy that defied all her understanding. The sight of the Hydra's necks, their skin a pale, horrifying canvas etched with faint, shimmering bands of silver light, made her arcane instincts recoil. This creature wasn't just a monster; it was a paradox made flesh.

And Thaddeus... Thaddeus was a study in profound, quiet sorrow. His face, so often a landscape of benign cheer, was now a grim, weary mask. He watched the creature, his eyes filled with a heartbreaking empathy. A man who had lived his life in the gentle faith of his god, he was now faced with a beast that was a living blasphemy, a creature that wept tears of pure, unadulterated grief.

The Hydra moved. One of its five heads, with a fluid, horrifying grace, dipped low to the surface of the lake. It did not roar. It simply released a torrent of its silver, hissing tears, a stream of corrosive sorrow that struck the first five feet of the causeway. The stone hissed and steamed, dissolving into a fine, grey slush in a matter of seconds. The causeway, once a path to the tomb, was now a rotting corpse of crumbling stone and foul, smoking sludge. "It knows we are here," Seraphina said, her voice a low, raw whisper that felt like a sound from a different, far more terrible kind of world. "It is not seeking strength. It is not trying to kill us with brute force. It's trying to cut us off. It's trying to make us a part of its grief."

Gundroff looked from the ruined causeway to the Hydra's five heads, a horrifying, multi faceted terror, and he felt a cold, grinding knowledge settle in his bones. This was a battle he could not win with a hammer or a sword. This was a battle he could only win with a shield. He looked at the creature's five serpentine heads and saw a hundred different ways he could die. The cold, logical part of his mind, the part that had been forged in the crucible of his ancestors, began to analyze the Hydra's movement, its weaknesses, its strengths. But his instincts, the part of him that was pure, elemental fury, screamed for him to charge. He felt the cold fury of his Ragingfire ancestors boil in his blood, and he raised his axe, its divine fire a single, defiant point of light in the profound darkness.

Seraphina moved to his side, her staff in hand. She began to chant, her voice a low, humming incantation, a symphony of arcane law. A small, shimmering dome of silver light erupted around the three of them, but the moment the sound of her magic, a soft hiss in the vast cavern, reached the creature, one of the Hydra's heads whipped toward the sound, lashing out blindly at their position. Its breath, a cold, mournful wind, nearly extinguished the divine flame on his axe, and the foul, rancid scent of its breath, a smell of grave dust and primordial rot, made his stomach turn. The Hydra's head lashed out again, a fluid, elegant strike that nearly took her own, and Gundroff was driven back.

Pinned down, the corrosive tears eating away at their path, he clutched his axe, its divine fire flickering. It was then that Thaddeus, his back pressed against a cavern wall, saw the pattern. "It weeps for the noise!" he yelled. "The sound of battle is a torment to it! It strikes at the sound!" Seraphina's mind, a fortress of logic, recoiled at the simple truth. It wasn't a tactical genius; it was a creature of immense and terrible grief, tormented by the noise of the living world. The screams of the dwarves, the clang of hammers, the sound of war. this was a torment to its unmade soul. Seraphina understood. She slammed the butt of her staff on the far side of the cavern, and with a powerful spell, amplified the sound a hundredfold, creating a deafening CRACK that echoed through the grotto. Four of the Hydra's heads whipped toward the sound, lashing out blindly at the empty wall, leaving the single, central head focused on the causeway. It was the opening he needed.

It was the opening he needed. The Hydra's attention, a vast and terrible thing of sorrow, was now focused on the amplified sound of Seraphina's staff. Gundroff didn't just charge; he bellowed, a sound of pure, animal rage, a sound that ripped from his chest with the force of a battering ram. He was no longer a man on a mission. He was a creature of a forge, a vessel of vengeance, and his axe was its hammer. The stone of the causeway was a blur beneath his heavy, iron shod boots. He felt the cold fury of his Ragingfire ancestors boil in his blood, and in that moment, he was not a ghost; he was a god of war, a living testament to a defiance that had not yet been unmade.

He moved with the terrible grace of a predator, his body a solid bastion of unyielding stubbornness. His axe was no longer a blur of divine fire; it was a hammer of vengeance. The first blow he struck against the Hydra's pale hide rang with the name of his mother. The second, for his father. The third, for his clan. The steel bit deep, and the creature shrieked, a sound of pure, physical agony, but beneath it was a deeper, resonant note. a final, sorrowful exhalation as its millennia long torment came to an end.

He was no longer fighting a monster; he was fighting a memory. He saw the face of his mother as he charged, her kind, strong face twisted in a silent scream. The face of his father, a master smith, as he fell to the dragon's fire. The faces of his kin, the joyous, vibrant halls of Hjarta Fell in ruins. He was fighting for all of them. He would not be a coward again. He would not run from the fire that took his first clan. He would not run from the water that threatened his new one. In this moment, he was not a ghost. He was a shield.

He brought the axe down again, this time with the full, unyielding weight of forty years of vengeance. The Hydra shrieked, a sound of pure, physical agony. Its head, a horrifying sculpture of bone and sorrow, writhed in pain. But it did not die. It simply raised its five heads, not to strike, but to unleash a torrent of corrosive sorrow. A tidal wave of shimmering, hissing tears surged from its mouths, a wall of liquid death that would not just kill them, but unmake the stone they stood upon.

There was no time to run. Gundroff looked at the wave, at the island, at his two companions. Forty years he had lived as a weapon of vengeance. He had run from the fire that took his first clan. He would not run from the water that threatened his new one. In this moment, he was not a ghost. He was a shield. He slammed his body into Seraphina and Thaddeus, shoving them towards the island at the end of the causeway. "Live!" he roared. He turned back, his warrior's gaze replaced by the discerning eyes of a smith. He saw the architecture not as a path, but as a creation. And in its heart, he saw the single, load bearing keystone. the flaw Grolnir himself would have left to unmake it. A prayer of understanding left his lips as he raised his great axe. "The stone endures!"

He brought the axe down. The ancient stone groaned, spiderweb cracks erupting from the point of impact. The wave of tears hit him as the causeway collapsed. A cascade of stone, a falling dwarf, and the wall of corrosive tears all plunged into the black lake in a chaotic, churning vortex. Gundroff's roar of defiance was cut short by a sharp cry of agony as the acidic tears washed over his back and legs. The violent collapse of the bridge dissipated the main force of the attack, which splashed harmlessly against the shores of the tomb's island.

The Hydra, its final lament spent, collapsed back into the black water and was gone. The cavern was suddenly, terribly silent. For a heart stopping moment that stretched into an eternity, there was only the black, still water. Then, a single, scarred hand broke the surface. Seraphina reached into the water, her magic a shimmering tendril that wrapped around his arm and hauled him ashore. Her jaw was set, her knuckles white where she gripped her staff. Her eyes, wide and fixed on Gundroff's ruined form, were not wet with tears but burned with a cold, protective fire. The sacred chronicle of his people tattooed on his back was a ruin of melted, fused flesh, the ink of his ancestors' glory burned away by the acidic sorrow. His legs were covered in horrific burns that had eaten deep into the muscle. He was a bastion. The silent shepherd and the furious mage knelt beside the crippled dwarf, beginning the grim work of tending to the broken shield. Without a word, they turned their faces toward the massive obsidian doors. The Hydra, its attention now fractured by Seraphina's spell, was a dying star. Its five heads thrashed in a final, horrifying symphony of pain, a terrible, guttural wail of agony that was the sound of a millennia long torment coming to an end. It was the last, desperate lament of a creature born of sorrow. Gundroff watched its thrashing body, a mountain of bone and hate, and he felt a cold, grinding knowledge settle in his bones. The Hydra had been a monster, yes, but it had also been a mirror. And in its final moments, he saw his own pain, his own terrible sorrow, reflected in its unmade soul.

In its death throes, it unleashed its final, devastating attack. All five heads reared back, not to strike, but to unleash a torrent of corrosive sorrow. A tidal wave of shimmering, hissing tears surged from its mouths, a wall of liquid death that would not just kill them, but unmake the stone they stood upon. It was a final, horrifying act of pure, unadulterated grief.

There was no time to run. Gundroff looked at the wave, at the island, at his two companions. Forty years he had lived as a weapon of vengeance. He had run from the fire that took his first clan. He would not run from the water that threatened his new one. In this moment, he was not a ghost. He was a shield. He slammed his body into Seraphina and Thaddeus, shoving them towards the island at the end of the causeway. "Live!" he roared, a sound of a hundred different emotions. of a warrior's fury, a father's love, a captain's command, and a friend's final farewell. He turned back, his warrior's gaze replaced by the discerning eyes of a smith. He saw the architecture not as a path, but as a creation. And in its heart, he saw the single, load bearing keystone. the flaw Grolnir himself would have left to unmake it. A prayer of understanding left his lips as he raised his great axe. "The stone endures!"

He brought the axe down. The ancient stone groaned, spiderweb cracks erupting from the point of impact. The wave of tears hit him as the causeway collapsed. A cascade of stone, a falling dwarf, and the wall of corrosive tears all plunged into the black lake in a chaotic, churning vortex. Gundroff's roar of defiance was cut short by a sharp cry of agony as the acidic tears washed over his back and legs. The violent collapse of the bridge dissipated the main force of the attack, which splashed harmlessly against the shores of the tomb's island. The Hydra, its final lament spent, collapsed back into the black water and was gone. The cavern was suddenly, terribly silent. For a heart stopping moment that stretched into an eternity, there was only the black, still water. Then, a single, scarred hand broke the surface.

Seraphina reached into the water, her magic a shimmering tendril that wrapped around his arm and hauled him ashore. Her jaw was set, her knuckles white where she gripped her staff. Her eyes, wide and fixed on Gundroff's ruined form, were not wet with tears but burned with a cold, protective fire. The sacred chronicle of his people tattooed on his back was a ruin of melted, fused flesh, the ink of his ancestors' glory burned away by the acidic sorrow. His legs were covered in horrific burns that had eaten deep into the muscle. He was a bastion. The silent shepherd and the furious mage knelt beside the crippled dwarf, beginning the grim work of tending to the broken shield. Without a word, they turned their faces toward the massive obsidian doors.

Chapter 27

Heart of the Mountain

The silence that followed Gundroff's ordeal was a hallowed thing, a quiet purchased with flesh and fire. The thunderous echo of the collapsing causeway had died into a profound stillness that seemed to swallow even the muffled thrum of the war above. They crossed the final, treacherous stretch to the doors in a grim, somber procession. The only sounds were the soft, rhythmic shuffle of their boots on the marble white stone, the ragged, pain filled breaths of the crippled dwarf, and the soft drip of water from the cavern's roof, each drop a tiny, lonely tolling in the stillness.

As they approached, the air grew colder, heavier, charged with a strange, spiritual energy that made the hair on Seraphina's arms stand on end. The great obsidian doors of the true tomb stood before them, a silent, final sentinel against a world of violence as they drew near, five worn sigils etched above the door began to glow with a soft, internal light, each one a different color: a fiery gold, a deep sapphire, a stony grey, a pure, divine silver, and a shadowy amethyst. There was no grinding of stone; the doors parted with the sigh of air that had been held captive for millennia, separating like a curtain to welcome the inheritors of their long held sorrow.

The chamber within was a sanctuary. It was a perfect, circular dome, its walls carved from a single, seamless piece of living stone that seemed to drink the light, giving forth a soft, shadowless luminescence. The air within was cold, still, and smelled of dust and heroes. It was a place of profound, hallowed peace, a final, unmade promise of a people who had built their entire civilization on a song. The walls seemed to hum with a silent, ancient music, a sound that was felt in the heart, not heard with the ears. In the center of the room, facing inward in a silent, eternal council, stood four life sized statues of the First Fellowship, with a single, empty plinth of black obsidian at the center of their circle. a wound in the heart of their fellowship.

Each statue was a masterpiece of a forgotten age, a perfect, heartbreaking effigy of a fallen hero, their faces so full of life and sorrow that it felt as though their souls had been sealed within the stone. There was Kaela the Beacon, a serene cleric carved from white marble, her face a mask of fierce, unwavering compassion. And Jostein the Unbreakable, a stoic half stone giant carved from grey granite, his powerful form a testament to loyalty. There was Corvin the Scholar, a focused mage carved from pale, veined marble, his features a study in fierce, intellectual concentration. And finally, Aela the Shadow, a lithe dark elf carved from a deep, amethyst veined stone, her hands poised as if to draw two daggers that were not there, a silent testament to a desecration of this holy place.

Seraphina moved toward the statue of Corvin, her feet silent on the floor. For a fleeting, painful moment, she saw him not as a figure of legend, but as a man, seeing the familiar lines of his face and the grief in his posture. This place was not a monument to their glory, but a testament to their love, a thing that was a thousand times more painful and beautiful. She took up the heavy, leather bound spellbook from its stone hands. It was not the dark grimoire she knew, but a personal tome, and as she touched the cool leather, she felt a faint echo of her master's profound, soul deep exhaustion. The book was his legacy, and it felt heavier in her hands than any stone, a burden she did not feel she deserved.

Gundroff, leaning heavily on Thaddeus, limped toward the statue of Jostein the Unbreakable. He looked upon the face of the stone giant, a creature of unbreakable loyalty, and saw a kindred spirit. He, too, had made a promise to his people that he could not keep. He reached out and took the Battle Axe of the Titan from the statue's stone grasp. The weapon was colossal, its weight almost more than his wounded body could bear. It felt alien in his grip, a physical burden of a legacy he was not sure he could fulfill, a tool not of vengeance but of duty.

Thaddeus approached the statue of Aela the Shadow. He looked at her empty hands, at the spaces where her daggers should have been, and a profound, inexplicable sorrow washed over him. It was a grief that felt ancient and vast, as if he were mourning not just for the statue, but for a loss he could not name. He bowed his head, a single, silent tear tracing a path down his cheek, though he did not know for whom it fell. He took no weapon.

For a long moment, the three of them stood in the shadowless light, armed with the legends of a fallen age. The legacies they now carried felt heavier than any stone, a burden of a past they had not lived but were now, impossibly, a part of.

Their somber inheritance was shattered. A low, guttural roar echoed from the passage behind them, the sound of a Mor kin commander rallying its troops for a final, killing blow. The war had found them again. They turned, a trio of living ghosts in a tomb of dead heroes, to see the antechamber fill with the dark, grey shapes of the Mor kin. They poured through the main entrance, their movements a silent, horrifyingly efficient tide of steel and malice. There were dozens of them, a wall of interlocking shields and razor sharp spears blocking their only exit.

"So," Gundroff growled, his voice a low rumble of pure, defiant hatred as he hefted the Titan's Axe. "It ends here."

Seraphina's hands, already weaving the complex patterns of a defensive ward, crackled with the last of her dwindling power. But she knew it was not enough. They were surrounded, exhausted, and hopelessly outnumbered. As the Mor kin phalanx began its slow, inexorable advance, Thaddeus did not prepare for a fight. His gaze was not on the wall of shields, but on the high, vaulted darkness above. He had seen a flicker of movement, a thing that did not belong. a flicker of chaos in the crushing, perfect order of their doom.

A black fletched crossbow bolt, silent as a thought, sprouted from the throat of the advancing Mor kin captain. The creature's eyes went wide with surprise as it crumpled to the stone. Before the others could react, a second bolt from the opposite side of the cavern took another

Mor kin in the eye. A third, from a shadow near the ceiling, punched through the shield of another, causing the disciplined line to falter in confusion.

Thaddeus's eyes followed the impossible trajectories. This was not the work of a single archer. It was the work of a shadow that seemed to be in a dozen places at once. And in the split second before the shadow in the high rafters vanished, he saw it: the glint of two luminous purple eyes and the unmistakable silhouette of an overly long and twitching goblin ear.

He saw the pattern in the goblin's chaos. The bolts were not aimed at the main host, but at the specific warriors who broke from the line, the ones whose path would lead them directly to him. A cold, strange thought, a story he had never heard before, surfaced in his mind: a predator so fond of a particular songbird that it would kill the hawks that hunted it, just to listen to it sing a little longer. The Mor kin line, their perfect, logical advance shattered by an impossible, chaotic variable, devolved into a confused rage.

"Now!" Seraphina screamed, seizing the moment of confusion.

Gundroff let out a final, glorious roar, a sound not of despair, but of a sudden, impossible hope, and charged. His charge was a geological event. The Battle Axe of the Titan was a weapon forged for a being of living stone, and in his hands, it was a clumsy, brutal, and almost uncontrollable thing. It was too heavy, its balance all wrong, a parody of the elegant fury of his own lost axe. He did not swing it with skill; he aimed its crushing weight and let it fall. The first Mor kin met his charge with a raised shield. The Titan's Axe shattered it, along with the arm and shoulder behind it, with a sickening crunch of pulverized bone and iron. The blow was so powerful it buried the axe head a foot into the stone floor, and for a terrifying second, Gundroff was a defenseless bastion, his weapon hopelessly stuck.

A half dozen spears lanced toward him. He roared, a sound of pure, animal frustration, and heaved. The stone floor cracked and split as he ripped the axe free, the sheer, unyielding force of his will more powerful than the mountain's own grip. He became a whirlwind of clumsy, devastating force, a living battering ram that cared nothing for parries or feints, only for the brutal, honest work of unmaking.

While Gundroff was the anvil, Seraphina became the hammer's eye. Her own magic was a guttering candle, too weak for grand wards or destructive bolts. She fell back, shielded by Thaddeus's quiet, unmoving form, and desperately scanned the pages of Corvin's tome. It was not a book of simple spells, but of complex, arcane theory. Her mind, a fortress of logic even in the chaos, raced, searching for a flaw, a variable, an equation she could use. Her eyes landed on a passage, a footnote on the metallurgical properties of Mor kin alloys. "...a profound weakness to sonic resonance... the metal, forged in absolute silence, cannot abide a pure, sustained chord..."

She looked up from the book, her gaze sweeping over the Mor kin phalanx as they struggled to reform against Gundroff's onslaught. They were a wall of silent, logical death. And she had just found the word that would make their armor betray them. Ignoring the spears and the chaos, she began to chant. It was not a spell of power, but a single, perfect, and impossibly pure note of music that emanated from her throat. The note hung in the air of the tomb, a perfect, crystalline vibration that was anathema to the dead silence of the Mor kin's world.

The effect was instantaneous and horrific. The Mor kin's dark, grey mail began to vibrate violently, the metal screaming with a high pitched, harmonic shriek. The warriors cried out, dropping their weapons, their hands flying to their armor as it began to glow with a dull, red heat. It was not a fire; it was a fever in the soul of the steel.

Thaddeus, watching the chaos, saw another crossbow bolt fly from the darkness, not at a warrior, but at a Mor kin shaman who had been attempting to cast a counter spell of silence. The bolt took the shaman in the throat, his spell dissolving into a choked gasp. The goblin in the rafters, Thaddeus realized with a chill, was not just a chaotic force. She was a brutally efficient protector, and her sole focus was keeping him alive.

The Mor kin, their discipline shattered by an enemy they could not see and a sound that was physically annihilating their armor, finally broke. They did not retreat in a rout, but with a cold, logical pragmatism. They fell back, abandoning their dead, their movements a silent, efficient withdrawal that was more terrifying than any battle cry. They were not defeated. They were recalculating.

The silence that descended upon the tomb was a profound and terrible thing, broken only by the echo of Seraphina's perfect, dying note and the ragged, heaving breaths of the survivors. Gundroff stood in a circle of his own making, the bodies of a dozen Mor kin a testament to his clumsy fury. The adrenaline of the fight drained away, leaving a cold, hard reality in its place.

"They will return," Thaddeus stated, his voice a quiet anchor in the echoing silence. "That was not a rout. That was a tactical withdrawal."

"He's right," Seraphina said, her voice a strained whisper. The sonic spell had left her throat raw. She slumped against the base of Corvin's statue. "They are a tide. They will recede, gather their strength, and crash upon us again. We cannot win a war of attrition."

Gundroff knew she was right. His gaze swept the tomb, landing on the empty plinth at the center of the circle of heroes. They had found their legacies, but they had also discovered their tombstone. "Harek's path," he grunted, the words a painful rasp. "The old war master spoke of a well shaft. A hidden way to the Deep Core."

Seraphina's eyes, clouded with exhaustion, sharpened. The tome. It was not just a weapon; it was a key. She forced her aching fingers to trace the spidery script of Corvin's personal notes, not for a spell, but for a memory. Her finger stopped on a small annotation next to a schematic of the tomb. It was a single, elegant dwarven rune: Hydra's Lament.

"The hydra's spring," she breathed. "It wasn't just a lair. It was a cistern. Harek wasn't speaking of a simple well. He was speaking of the source." She looked toward the back of the tomb, at a seamless section of the wall. "There."

Gundroff followed her gaze. It was a solid wall, a dead end. "There is no door."

"Because it is not a door for the living," she countered, pushing herself to her feet. "It is sealed not by a lock, but by a rite. The only way through is to perform the dwarven last rites, to declare this place a true and final tomb."

The weight of her words settled upon them. To open the path, they would have to consecrate this sanctuary as a grave. Gundroff took a slow, heavy breath. He was the only one who knew the old words. The duty fell to him. He limped to the center of the room and faced the statues, the silent, stone witnesses.

"The stone remembers," he began, his voice a low, gravelly chant, the ancient words of the Hydra's Lament a rough music in the hallowed silence. He moved first to Jostein. "Your shield is broken, but your loyalty endures. Rest in the quiet heart of the stone." He moved to Corvin, giving a stiff, formal bow. "Your knowledge was a heavy price. May your mind find peace in the final silence." He paused before Aela, glancing at Thaddeus, who bowed his head. "Your daggers are lost, but your courage is not. May you find the light you fought so hard to protect." He looked upon Kaela's serene face. "Your light has faded, but your faith... your faith remains."

Finally, his gaze was drawn to the empty plinth, the black, obsidian wound. He had to give a name to the ghost. "And for the nameless hero. The hero who fell. We do not mourn your glory. We mourn the man you were. We commit your memory to the stone as a brother."

As the final word died, a low, grinding groan echoed through the chamber. A single, vertical crack of absolute darkness appeared in the back wall, widening slowly, revealing not a passage, but a void. The air that issued from it was ancient, cold, and utterly devoid of life. The way was open.

Gundroff took the first step into the absolute blackness. The air that greeted him was ancient, cold, and hummed with the low, resonant energy of the mountain's living heart. It was a song of home he had not felt in forty years, but it brought him no comfort. He was a discordant note in its ancient melody, a ghost haunting his own history.

Seraphina followed, a small sphere of pearlescent light blooming in her palm, casting long, dancing shadows down the natural, fissure like passage. Thaddeus brought up the rear, his hand a steady, silent presence on Gundroff's shoulder.

They walked in a procession of the damned, each step a testament to the price of their survival. The victory in the tomb had not been a triumph; it had been a brutal act of culling that had left them hollowed out. Gundroff's body was a map of new and terrible pains. The acid burns on his back and legs were a searing fire, a constant reminder of his failure as a shield. The temporal wound on his arm was a deep, soul chilling cold, a piece of his own death he was forced to carry while still living. He was a walking paradox of fire and ice, and the conflict was tearing him apart from the inside.

He leaned heavily on the Titan's Axe, its unfamiliar weight a clumsy substitute for the limb he could no longer trust. Beside him, Seraphina's own exhaustion was a palpable thing. Her face was pale, her breath a shallow whisper in the cold air, and the light she carried flickered with the unsteadiness of a will that had been scraped clean.

They had not been walking for more than an hour when the first, muffled *BOOM* reached them. It was a sound that was felt more than it was heard, a deep, percussive tremor that vibrated through the soles of their boots and up into their bones.

To Gundroff, it was the sound of a battering ram. the sound of war.

But the sound struck Thaddeus not as a simple echo, but as a memory. He felt a ghost of an impossible weight settle on his brow, the cold kiss of a crown he had never worn. His hand, resting on his simple wooden staff, suddenly felt the phantom heft of a colossal Axe, a tool of creation and of terrible, righteous fury. And with it came a surge of emotion so powerful it buckled his knees. a fierce, paternal, and heartbreaking love for the mountain and the unseen dwarves fighting within it, a love that was not his own.

He stumbled, catching himself against the cold stone, his heart hammering with the echo of a stranger's sorrow. *A trick of the echo,* he thought, his mind scrambling for a logical anchor. *A sorrow of the stone itself.* But the feeling lingered, a profound and terrible ache for a loss he could not name.

Gundroff stopped dead, his head snapping up. The sound was a spark in the tinder of his soul. It was a sound of defiance. a sound of life.

"Fireforge," he breathed, the name a raw, desperate prayer. For the first time since he had seen the desecrated gates, a flicker of something other than grief or rage ignited in his eyes: a wild, impossible hope. His king was still fighting. His people still lived.

Thaddeus, his face a mask of ancient grief, whispered to the stone, "A king should never have to watch his home die twice."

Seraphina's head whipped around, her brow furrowed. The words were a strange and terrible poetry, a wisdom that seemed to come not from the cheerful cleric, but from a sad and ancient king. Before she could question him, Gundroff's own soul, deaf to all but the song of battle, screamed for him to turn back, to join the fight, to lend the clumsy, terrible power of the Titan's Axe to their cause.

"No, Gundroff," Seraphina's voice was sharp, a cold, hard anchor against the tide of his rising hope. Her logic was a cruel and undeniable blade. "Harek's sacrifice, Fireforge's charge. it was all to buy us this path. Their fight is for the gate. Ours is for the heart. To turn back now is to make their deaths meaningless."

He knew she was right. The knowledge was a physical agony, a chain that bound him to this dark, lonely path while his heart yearned for the fire of the battle above. He was a warrior, but he was told that the only way to win the war was to abandon it.

Before he could voice the protest that was a fire in his throat, a new sound cut through the gloom. A high, keening shriek of a dwarven war horn, a sound of glorious, suicidal defiance.

Gundroff's head snapped up, the agony on his face momentarily erased by a surge of pure warrior's joy. He turned, taking a half step back towards the battle, his grip on the Titan's Axe so tight his knuckles were white. A low growl of anticipation rumbled in his chest.

"That is the sound of the Unbroken Stone!" he roared, his voice a clarion call of belief in the echoing dark. "They are turning them! They are turning them back!"

"Gundroff, wait…" Seraphina said, her own voice a thin whisper of dread. Her arcane senses did not feel the clean, triumphant energy of a victory. She felt a chaotic, frantic surge. the energetic signature of a final, desperate, and failing charge.

Her warning was swallowed by the guttural, alien braying of a Mor kin horn that answered the dwarves' cry. The two sounds clashed for a single, terrible moment. a discordant symphony of a world breaking. It was followed by a sickening crunch of breaking steel and splintering stone.

And then, silence.

A profound, terrible, and absolute silence. The drumming was gone. The battle cries were gone. The hope was gone. The war was over.

Gundroff staggered as if he'd been struck. The Titan's Axe fell from his numb fingers, its colossal weight crashing to the stone with a final, echoing clang. The wild, beautiful hope that had lit his eyes just a moment before was violently extinguished, leaving only a cold, dead ash. He didn't just hear that the battle was lost; he felt the future he had just started to believe in be murdered in that silence.

He collapsed to his knees, his body, a mountain of defiance, finally crumbling. His heart, which had just begun to remember the song of his people, now felt a final, terrible stillness. He was too late. He was always too late.

He was a ghost again, in a new and more terrible tomb, mourning a funeral he had been forced to abandon. The path ahead was no longer a mission. It was a penance.

The hush after Gundroff's sacrifice was sacred, bought at the price of pain and fire. The echo of the fallen causeway faded, leaving only a thick silence that pressed in on the survivors as they crossed the last stretch to the doors. a procession of exhaustion and resolve. Every footfall, every ragged breath, marked their passage from chaos into the charged stillness before the true tomb.

As they neared, the air grew heavier, electric with memory and loss. Five sigils above the obsidian doors glowed softly. gold, sapphire, grey, silver, and amethyst. as the doors sighed open, revealing a sanctuary carved from seamless stone. In this circular chamber, light shimmered without shadow. Four statues. Kaela the Beacon, Jostein the Unbreakable, Corvin the Scholar, Aela the Shadow. stood in eternal vigil, the plinth between them empty, a wound left for the absent fifth. Their faces, carved with impossible life and sorrow, watched over the chamber, making the air hum with the silent music of an ancient age.

Seraphina stepped softly to Corvin's statue, drawn as if by gravity. Seeing his features not as legend but as memory, she felt a tide of unworthiness crash through her when she lifted his spellbook from stone hands. The weight of legacy pressed on her. heavier than any blade or burden.

Gundroff, leaning on Thaddeus, limped to Jostein. The giant's stone gaze met his, and Gundroff took the Battle Axe of the Titan.

Its unwieldy bulk was a test of will, not skill. a warrior's duty, not vengeance.

Thaddeus lingered by Aela's statue, her hands empty. He bowed his head, emotion welling up for a loss too old to name. He took no weapon, but bore the weight of her absence.

A guttural roar from behind shattered their moment. Mor kin, pouring in, a disciplined wall of shields and spears. Gundroff braced the Titan's Axe, Seraphina's hands began a ward, and Thaddeus searched the shadowed heights. Suddenly, a black fletched bolt pierced the Mor kin leader's throat. Another fell a second, chaos rippling through the phalanx as more bolts struck unseen. Thaddeus caught a glimpse: a shadow with luminous purple eyes and a twitching goblin ear, moving impossibly fast through the rafters.

The bolts didn't target the mass, but the outliers. those who might reach Thaddeus. The Mor kin's formation fractured.

"Now!" Seraphina called, seizing the opening.

Gundroff charged, the Titan's Axe smashing through shields, bone, and stone. The weapon was unwieldy, but his intent was clear; each swing was a blow against extinction. Spears jabbed toward him. he ripped the axe free, scattering his attackers with brute force.

Seraphina, nearly spent, scanned Corvin's tome. Her eyes caught a note. Mor kin alloys shatter at pure resonance. Without hesitation, she sang a single, piercing note that made their armor scream and glow with heat.

The effect was instant. Mor kin guards staggered, clutching burning mail, discipline crumbling. Another bolt from the shadows struck a shaman mid spell, silencing a counterattack. Their line broke. not in panic, but in cold calculation, falling back to regroup. The tomb rang with Seraphina's fading note, the survivors' breaths ragged in the aftermath.

"They'll return," Thaddeus said, steady as bedrock. "That was not a rout, but a retreat."

Seraphina nodded, throat raw. "They're a tide. This was only the first wave."

Gundroff's gaze fell to the black plinth. "Harek's path," he rasped. "A well shaft. the Deep Core."

Seraphina's mind, sharpened by exhaustion, found the rune in Corvin's notes: Hydra's Lament. "The hydra's spring. it's the entrance. We must consecrate this sanctuary as a tomb to open the way."

Gundroff stepped to the center, bearing the ritual alone. Each invocation honored the fellowship, each word a stone laid on the path of memory. When he named the fallen king, the chamber opened. a crack of darkness blooming in the wall, ancient air spilling forth.

They entered, Gundroff forward, wounded but resolute, Seraphina's light flickering behind, Thaddeus the anchor at their rear. The passage pressed in, cold and humming with mountain song. a song of home.

Not far along, a thundering boom tremored through the stone. a call to battle. Gundroff's heart leapt; Thaddeus staggered, a surge of grief and borrowed love overwhelming him. The echoes of war, of loss and hope, beat through them all.

The urge to return, to join the fight, was nearly overwhelming. But Seraphina's logic cut through. this path was bought by sacrifice. Their duty was here. The battle above was not theirs to win.

Then. a dwarven war horn, defiant and wild. Gundroff's hope surged, but Seraphina sensed only desperation, not victory. A Mor kin horn answered, followed by a terrible silence. Gundroff dropped the Titan's Axe, hope extinguished, the weight of failure final.

He sank to his knees, lost once more in grief, burdened by a penance that was his alone to bear. The path ahead was not triumph, but atonement.

A hush thick as velvet enveloped Gundroff and his companions, a quiet earned by pain and sacrifice. The crash of the causeway's ruin faded, and what remained was a stillness so complete it pressed against their ribs. a dense, living presence that seemed both comfort and warning as they approached the obsidian doors. Each step was a negotiation with exhaustion and fear, marking their passage from chaos into the charged anticipation of what lay beyond.

The air grew colder, tinged with a subtle current of ancient magic. dust motes glimmered like embers, swirling in patterns that hinted at old, protective wards. Five sigils glowed above the doors: gold, sapphire, granite, silver, and amethyst, each color pulsing with the breath of history. They parted with a gentle sigh, admitting the travelers into a sanctuary that felt more secret than sacred.

Inside, the tomb's dome crowned them with a soft, unshadowed luminescence. Four statues stood sentinel, carved with unsettling realism. Kaela the Beacon, Jostein the Unbreakable, Corvin the Scholar, and Aela the Shadow. each face etched with longing and sorrow. Their arrangement was a council of memory, every gesture and detail a piece of lost lore. The black, obsidian plinth at the center was a wound in their fellowship, a testament to what was missing.

Seraphina drifted toward Corvin's statue, her steps faltering. Despite her fatigue, a memory flared. her mentor's voice, sharp and encouraging, urging her to endure when she wanted to falter. The spellbook she retrieved from stone hands was not just a legacy; it was a promise she had made before their departure: to return with knowledge, to be worthy of the trust Corvin had placed in her. The weight of that oath pressed against her, more demanding than any physical burden. As she thumbed through the tome, she felt not just responsibility, but kinship. a reason to persevere that transcended mere survival.

Gundroff, leaning heavily on Thaddeus, limped to Jostein's statue. The giant's granite countenance was a mirror to Gundroff's own stubborn loyalty. He gripped the Titan's Axe, its heft an inheritance that thudded against his old wounds and pride. For a moment, he wavered. caught between the urge to rush back to the fight and the knowledge that their quest now depended on him. He thought of his clan's destruction, the fire and water he had run from, and the weight of being the last shield. Conflict seethed beneath his battered exterior; duty demanded endurance, but grief yearned for action. His knuckles whitened on the axe, and the ache of those memories finally nudged him forward. not out of surrender, but acceptance that every step was for those he had lost.

Thaddeus hesitated by Aela's statue, the empty hands drawing him into their silent mystery. He bowed his head, and the absence called forth old wounds. Years ago, he had watched his village succumb to infection, powerless to halt the spread. That memory, buried deep, throbbed now as the echoes of war reached them. reminding him of every promise unkept, every life lost to forces beyond his reckoning.

The mountain's toll was not only blood, but memory. The war above felt personal: he recognized in the dwarven struggle the same desperate hope that had driven him to become a healer, to try and mend what could not be saved. The connection was more than empathy. it was kinship with loss, a silent prayer for redemption. He let the sorrow fill him and resolved to carry it, not as a wound but as a reason to press on.

As the trio stood poised for their inheritance, a guttural roar echoed from behind. the Mor kin's disciplined ranks flooding in. Gundroff braced the Titan's Axe, his mind a battlefield of regret and resolve. Seraphina's hands, trembling, began a protective ward, her mind racing with the equations Corvin taught her. Thaddeus looked not at the enemy, but along the archways, seeking any sign of hope.

Suddenly, black fletched bolts struck from the darkness; a shadow with purple eyes and a twitching goblin ear moved impossibly fast among the rafters, picking off key Mor kin warriors. Thaddeus felt a surge of gratitude, recalling stories of unlikely saviors from his youth. beings who intervened in moments of desperate need. The Mor kin formation broke, the chaos giving Seraphina a chance. She remembered a note in Corvin's tome. Mor kin alloys fractured by pure resonance. Her voice, hoarse but unwavering, sang out a crystalline note that reverberated through the tomb, causing the enemy's armor to shriek and sear.

The Mor kin faltered, their discipline unraveling. Another bolt felled a shaman mid spell. The enemy retreated, not in panic but with cold calculation, their absence leaving the survivors surrounded by the lingering residue of battle. a stench not just of blood, but of scorched hope.

"They'll regroup," Thaddeus said, voice steady, shaped by the habit of tending wounds in the aftermath of disaster.

Seraphina nodded, swallowing back exhaustion. "We can't wait for them to return. We have to find Harek's path." She traced the rune of Hydra's Lament, recalling not only the hydra's spring but a passage her mentor once described as "a door for the dead". a ritual to open the way.

Gundroff stepped forward, the conflict in his soul finally settled. He performed the dwarven last rites, each invocation a stone laid for those he had sworn to protect. As the final word echoed, a fissure yawned open in the wall, cold air spilling forth. The way to the mountain's heart revealed itself.

They entered, Gundroff first. his stride heavy, his thoughts a tangle of regret and resolve. Seraphina's orb of light flickered in her palm, fueled by the memory of her promise. Thaddeus anchored the rear, his sorrow for the lost guiding him as much as hope for those yet to be saved.

Their passage was marked by sensory details: the stone cool and damp underfoot, runes glowing faintly in the walls, the echo of distant water suggesting the mountain's veins. Not far along, a deep boom vibrated through the ground. war's drum, striking each of them differently.

For Gundroff, it was a summons. a plea to return and fight. His heart pounded, the temptation to abandon the mission nearly overwhelming. But the faces of his kin, the weight of his promise, held him back. He grappled with the urge, finally surrendering to the necessity of going forward; the fire of hope turned to bitter resolve.

For Thaddeus, the echo called forth the old ache of loss. He remembered the day his family was lost, the weight of helplessness pressing on him then as it did now. The mountain's grief became his own, a thread connecting past failure to present duty.

Seraphina, sensing the battle's energy, drew strength from the memory of Corvin's encouragement. "We haven't failed yet," she murmured, recalling a promise made over a small table years ago.

When the dwarven war horn sounded, Gundroff surged with hope, nearly turning back. But Seraphina's logic held him. reminding him that their path was bought with sacrifice, that the most incredible honor was to finish what the fallen had started. He trembled, torn between longing and obligation, before yielding to the burden of leadership.

A Mor kin horn answered, then a final, crushing silence. Hope snuffed out, Gundroff crumbled, the inheritance of pain settling into his bones. The path ahead became not triumph, but atonement. a journey marked by memory, regret, and the enduring promise that even in defeat, their story would linger in the stone.

The chamber behind them lay in silence, but it was the silence of history, thick with the pulse of ancient magic and memory. a world alive with the weight of lore, and the echo of every step they now took into shadow.

Chapter 28

A King's Ransom

Silence fell upon them. It was a hallowed thing, a quiet purchased with flesh and fire. As they burst through the door, the Upper Halls greeted them with a cacophony of absolute, unmitigated carnage. The dwarven assault had shattered. The Great Hall was a charnel house, the air thick with the iron tang of blood, the sharp ozone of spent magic, and the acrid, unfamiliar stench of Mor kin ichor that clung to the back of the throat. The silence they had just left was now a brutal, horrifying absence, a peace that had been brutally murdered.

Gundroff's stomach, a solid bastion of unyielding stubbornness, lurched with a profound, bone deep disgust. He had expected to see a battle, a glorious, final war, but this was a slaughter. He saw the bodies of his kin, of the last of the Ragingfire Clan, lying in grotesque, unyielding stillness. He saw the proud banners of their clans, torn and trampled into the blood slick stone. He saw the walls of the Great Hall, once a testament to their unwavering strength, now marred with the blood and fear of his people.

His gaze fell upon a single dwarf, his face frozen in a mask of pure terror, a Mor kin arrow protruding from his eye. He was a boy, no more than twenty years old, and Gundroff had known his father. He felt a wave of cold, desolate sorrow wash over him, a feeling that had nothing to do with rage and everything to do with a profound and terrible pity. They were ghosts, a people who had asked for nothing more than to be remembered, and he had returned to find their memory being unmade.

Seraphina, her face a pale mask of exhaustion, stumbled backward, her hand flying to her mouth to stifle a cry. Her mind, an engine of arcane law, had no equation for this chaos. This was not a problem to be solved, but a truth to be endured. The sight of the carnage was a visceral violation of her senses. She saw the bodies not as fallen warriors, but as a series of complex, broken systems, their lives an equation that had been unmade. She felt the chill of the death that had filled the hall, a cold, unnatural stillness that was a testament to a life that had been extinguished.

Thaddeus, ever the quiet anchor, bowed his head, his face a landscape of ancient grief. He had seen this before. The blight. The sickness. The way that life, a profound and terrible truth, could be unmade. He looked upon the scene and saw not a battlefield, but a garden that had been razed by fire, its promise of life a quiet, brutal, and unmade thing. He felt a profound and terrible sadness, a sorrow that was a testament to a love that had been lost.

The air was a heavy soup, thick with the iron tang of blood, the sharp ozone of spent magic, and an acrid, unfamiliar stench that clung to the back of the throat. the ichor of a creature ancient beyond reckoning. The few dwarves left standing moved through the carnage of their kin like specters, their faces grim masks of soot and sorrow. Their eyes, vast and vacant, held the terrible stillness of men who had stared into the abyss and found no bottom.

Gundroff, a man who had thought his heart was a dead, silent thing, felt a sudden, profound beat of a drum against his soul. It was the sound of a war he had believed was already over. He had made his peace with a war that was lost, and now, he had returned to find a new war being waged. The peace of the tomb was a fragile, beautiful thing, but it was being shattered by a new and more terrible kind of silence. The war had just come to their doorstep. He had returned, not to a glorious end, but to a bitter, awful, and most of all, painful beginning.

They were no longer the last. They were a people of war, a living testament to a defiance that had not yet been unmade. The two worlds, a world of beautiful, tragic lies, and a world of cold, honest truths, had just met. The battle for the soul of the mountain had just begun.

The stench hit Gundroff first, a physical blow that staggered him. It was a vile alchemy of blood, burned hair, and something far worse. the metallic, acidic tang of Mor kin ichor, a smell he had not encountered since the last, desperate days of the war. His stomach, a solid bastion of unyielding stubbornness, lurched with a profound, bone deep disgust. He had expected to see a battle, a glorious, final war, but this was a slaughter.

The hall, once a monument to a people's unwavering strength, was now a charnel house. The great, iron bound doors of the upper forge lay splintered and broken, their proud seals of the Stonehammer Clan torn away. The high arches, carved with a thousand years of dwarven history, were marred with streaks of gore and soot. The floor was a slick, treacherous expanse of blood and splintered bone, a grotesque tapestry of his people's final stand. The silence that had filled the tomb was now a brutal, horrifying absence, a peace that had been brutally murdered.

Gundroff's gaze fell upon a single dwarf, his face frozen in a mask of pure terror, a Mor kin arrow protruding from his eye. He was a boy, no more than twenty years old, and Gundroff had known his father. He felt a wave of cold, desolate sorrow wash over him, a feeling that had nothing to do with rage and everything to do with a profound and terrible pity. They were ghosts, a people who had asked for nothing more than to be remembered, and he had returned to find their memory being unmade.

Seraphina, her face a pale mask of exhaustion, stumbled backward, her hand flying to her mouth to stifle a cry. Her mind, an engine of arcane law, had no equation for this chaos. This was not a problem to be solved, but a truth to be endured. The sight of the carnage was a visceral violation of her senses. She saw the bodies not as fallen warriors, but as a series of complex, broken systems, their lives an equation that had been unmade. She felt the chill of the death that had filled the hall, a cold, unnatural stillness that was a testament to a life that had been extinguished.

Thaddeus, ever the quiet anchor, bowed his head, his face a landscape of ancient grief. He had seen this before. The blight. The sickness. The way that life, a profound and terrible truth, could be unmade. He looked upon the scene and saw not a battlefield, but a garden that had been razed by fire, its promise of life a quiet, brutal, and unmade thing. He felt a profound and terrible sadness, a sorrow that was a testament to a love that had been lost.

The air was a heavy soup, thick with the iron tang of blood, the sharp ozone of spent magic, and an acrid, unfamiliar stench that clung to the back of the throat. the ichor of a creature ancient beyond reckoning. The few dwarves left standing moved through the carnage of their kin like specters, their faces grim masks of soot and sorrow. Their eyes, vast and vacant, held the terrible stillness of men who had stared into the abyss and found no bottom.

Gundroff, a man who had thought his heart was a dead, silent thing, felt a sudden, profound beat of a drum against his soul. It was the sound of a war he had believed was already over. He had made his peace with a war that was lost, and now, he had returned to find a new war being waged. The peace of the tomb was a fragile, beautiful thing, but it was being shattered by a new and more terrible kind of silence. The war had just come to their doorstep. He had returned, not to a glorious end, but to a bitter, awful, and most of all, painful beginning.

They were no longer the last. They were a people of war, a living testament to a defiance that had not yet been unmade. The two worlds, a world of beautiful, tragic lies, and a world of cold, honest truths, had just met. The battle for the soul of the mountain had just begun.

The stench of the massacre was a physical blow that staggered them. It was a vile alchemy of blood, burned hair, and something far worse. the metallic, acidic tang of Mor kin ichor, a smell Gundroff had not encountered since the last, desperate days of the war. His stomach, a solid bastion of unyielding stubbornness, lurched with a profound, bone deep disgust. He had expected to see a battle, a glorious, final war, but this was a slaughter.

He saw the great, iron bound doors of the upper forge, the last line of defense, lying splintered and broken. Their proud seals of the Stonehammer Clan were torn away, their purpose unmade. The high arches, carved with a thousand years of dwarven history, were marred with streaks of gore and soot. The floor was a slick, treacherous expanse of blood and splintered bone, a grotesque tapestry of his people's final stand. The silence they had just left was now a brutal, horrifying absence, a peace that had been brutally murdered.

Gundroff's gaze fell upon a single dwarf, his face frozen in a mask of pure terror, a Mor kin arrow protruding from his eye. He was a boy, no more than twenty years old, and Gundroff had known his father. He felt a wave of cold, desolate sorrow wash over him, a feeling that had nothing to do with rage and everything to do with a profound and terrible pity. They were ghosts, a people who had asked for nothing more than to be remembered, and he had returned to find their memory being unmade.

Seraphina, her face a pale mask of exhaustion, stumbled backward, her hand flying to her mouth to stifle a cry. Her mind, an engine of arcane law, had no equation for this chaos. This was not a problem to be solved, but a truth to be endured. The sight of the carnage was a visceral violation of her senses. She saw the bodies not as fallen warriors, but as a series of complex, broken systems, their lives an equation that had been unmade. She felt the chill of the death that had filled the hall, a cold, unnatural stillness that was a testament to a life that had been extinguished.

Thaddeus, ever the quiet anchor, bowed his head, his face a landscape of ancient grief. He had seen this before. The blight. The sickness. The way that life, a profound and terrible truth, could be unmade. He looked upon the scene and saw not a battlefield, but a garden that had been razed by fire, its promise of life a quiet, brutal, and unmade thing. He felt a profound and terrible sadness, a sorrow that was a testament to a love that had been lost.

The air was a heavy soup, thick with the iron tang of blood, the sharp ozone of spent magic, and an acrid, unfamiliar stench that clung to the back of the throat. the ichor of a creature ancient beyond reckoning. The few dwarves left standing moved through the carnage of their kin like specters, their faces grim masks of soot and sorrow. Their eyes, vast and vacant, held the terrible stillness of men who had stared into the abyss and found no bottom.

Gundroff, a man who had thought his heart was a dead, silent thing, felt a sudden, profound beat of a drum against his soul. It was the sound of a war he had believed was already over. He had made his peace with a war that was lost, and now, he had returned to find a new war being waged. The peace of the tomb was a fragile, beautiful thing, but it was being shattered by a new and more terrible kind of silence. The war had just come to their doorstep. He had returned, not to a glorious end, but to a bitter, awful, and most of all, painful beginning.

They were no longer the last. They were a people of war, a living testament to a defiance that had not yet been unmade. The two worlds, a world of beautiful, tragic lies, and a world of cold, honest truths, had just met. The battle for the soul of the mountain had just begun.

The stench hit Gundroff first, a physical blow that staggered him. It was a vile alchemy of blood, burned hair, and something far worse. the metallic, acidic tang of Mor kin ichor, a smell he had not encountered since the last, desperate days of the war. His stomach, a solid bastion of unyielding stubbornness, lurched with a profound, bone deep disgust. He had expected to see a battle, a glorious, final war, but this was a slaughter.

He saw the great, iron bound doors of the upper forge, the last line of defense, lying splintered and broken. Their proud seals of the Stonehammer Clan were torn away, their purpose unmade. The high arches, carved with a thousand years of dwarven history, were marred with streaks of gore and soot. The floor was a slick, treacherous expanse of blood and splintered bone, a grotesque tapestry of his people's final stand. The silence they had just left was now a brutal, horrifying absence, a peace that had been brutally murdered.

Gundroff's gaze fell upon a single dwarf, his face frozen in a mask of pure terror, a Mor kin arrow protruding from his eye. He was a boy, no more than twenty years old, and Gundroff had known his father. He felt a wave of cold, desolate sorrow wash over him, a feeling that had nothing to do with rage and everything to do with a profound and terrible pity. They were ghosts, a people who had asked for nothing more than to be remembered, and he had returned to find their memory being unmade.

Seraphina, her face a pale mask of exhaustion, stumbled backward, her hand flying to her mouth to stifle a cry. Her mind, an engine of arcane law, had no equation for this chaos. This was not a problem to be solved, but a truth to be endured. The sight of the carnage was a visceral violation of her senses. She saw the bodies not as fallen warriors, but as a series of complex, broken systems, their lives an equation that had been unmade. She felt the chill of the death that had filled the hall, a cold, unnatural stillness that was a testament to a life that had been extinguished.

Thaddeus, ever the quiet anchor, bowed his head, his face a landscape of ancient grief. He had seen this before. The blight. The sickness. The way that life, a profound and terrible truth, could be unmade. He looked upon the scene and saw not a battlefield, but a garden that had been razed by fire, its promise of life a quiet, brutal, and unmade thing. He felt a profound and terrible sadness, a sorrow that was a testament to a love that had been lost.

The air was a heavy soup, thick with the iron tang of blood, the sharp ozone of spent magic, and an acrid, unfamiliar stench that clung to the back of the throat. the ichor of a creature ancient beyond reckoning. The few dwarves left standing moved through the carnage of their kin like specters, their faces grim masks of soot and sorrow. Their eyes, vast and vacant, held the terrible stillness of men who had stared into the abyss and found no bottom.

Gundroff, a man who had thought his heart was a dead, silent thing, felt a sudden, profound beat of a drum against his soul. It was the sound of a war he had believed was already over. He had made his peace with a war that was lost, and now, he had returned to find a new war being waged. The peace of the tomb was a fragile, beautiful thing, but it was being shattered by a new and more terrible kind of silence. The war had just come to their doorstep. He had returned, not to a glorious end, but to a bitter, awful, and most of all, painful beginning.

They were no longer the last. They were a people of war, a living testament to a defiance that had not yet been unmade. The two worlds, a world of beautiful, tragic lies, and a world of cold, honest truths, had just met. The battle for the soul of the mountain had just begun.

Chapter 29

The Unseen Wound

The dragon's descent was not a flight but a physical manifestation of malice. It did not so much land as it simply arrived, a final and brutal judgment upon the last, desperate stand of a dying people. Its immense, clawed foot, the size of a dwarf gate, slammed into the dwarven line. The earth shaking impact was a sound of absolute finality, a sound that said, with a quiet and brutal truth, that a long and glorious war had just come to an end. It was the sound of a world breaking. Prince Fireforge, seeing his men about to be annihilated, seeing the terrible truth of their defeat in the dragon's molten gaze, moved. He did not move with the wild, unthinking fury of a man about to die, but with the grim, quiet purpose of a king. He planted his feet and, with a final, desperate roar, took the full, crushing force of the blow. The sickening crunch of his shield, his armor, and the bones beneath was a sound of absolute finality. He was broken utterly and cast across the hall like a child's toy.

Gundroff witnessed it. He saw the last king of his people shattered, his oldest friend. Grief, vast and terrible, erupted in his soul, as if a star had fallen and been quenched within him. His gaze met Seraphina's across the chaos. She was a pale mask of exhaustion, her hands trembling as she held the temporal spell, but her eyes were filled with a cold, tactical fire. She gave him a single, sharp, almost imperceptible nod. No words were needed. Hold the line. At the same time, Thaddeus, his cheerful mask finally dissolved, moved with surprising speed, using his own body as a shield to drag the wounded Harek to safety, creating a clear path. It was not a plan discussed; it was a symphony of desperation, executed in a single, shared heartbeat. They were three parts of a single, functioning weapon. He let out a roar, a sound of pure, cosmic rage, and charged.

The dragon's laughter ceased, replaced by a low, guttural growl that vibrated in Gundroff's bones. He charged without waiting. The Titan's Axe was a torrent of motion, a force he could barely guide, and he brought it crashing down upon the creature's extended claw. The impact rang with a world splitting peal of thunder. Stone chips flew from the axe's edge, though the dragon's obsidian hide was not even scratched. Ash Heart tilted its head, its molten eyes filled with a scornful amusement, and swatted him aside with a flick of its tail.

Gundroff's charge, however futile, was the signal. A wave of dwarven fury, the last of their number, broke against the beast. They were a tide of iron and desperation, their axes and hammers raised in a final, suicidal chorus. Their weapons, forged with the pride of a kingdom, glanced from the dragon's scales with pathetic, ringing chimes. Ash Heart roared, a blast of furnace heat and fury, and began to dismantle them. A claw swept through the line, sending dwarves flying like scattered stones. A snap of its jaws ended the life of a warrior mid cry. It was a culling.

From the edge of the carnage, Seraphina fell to her knees, her legs. once elegant pillars of grace. buckling and sending her sprawling onto the cold, blood slick stone. The heavy tome, a thing of immense and unyielding power, felt like a lead weight in her trembling hands. The pages, brittle and yellowed with time, smelled of dust and forgotten knowledge. She could hear the rhythmic clang thud shriek of the battle, a symphony of a world breaking. But her mind, a fortress of arcane law, had no equation for this chaos. This was not a problem to be solved, but a truth to be endured. She frantically flipped through the pages, her hands trembling so violently the parchment threatened to tear. She was a scholar, a creature of cold, pragmatic truth, and she had no equation for this. This was not a problem to be solved, but a truth to be endured. The elegant, spidery script blurred before her exhausted eyes. She could feel the life force of the dwarves being extinguished around her, each death a pinprick against her soul, a silent, terrible scream of a promise unmade. She chanted, whispered, and pleaded with the ancient ink, pouring her fading will into phrases she barely understood. A shield of light shattered before it was fully formed. A bolt of pure magic dissolved harmlessly against the creature's hide. Nothing worked.

Tears of desperation streamed down her face, sizzling on the leather cover of the book. She had nothing left. Her mind, a fortress built upon causality and arcane law, was under siege. The psychic assault was a relentless, chaotic static that made her precise, linear thoughts feel like a fool's game. She saw a world of beautiful, intricate equations, a universe of perfect, elegant laws, and then she saw it all unmade, all the numbers turning to screaming, nonsense. The sound was a discordant chord in the heart of her own sanity. She pressed her hands against her temples, a thin line of blood running from her nose as she fought a battle she was never meant to wage, a battle against a mind that was not sane, but perfectly, terribly, mad.

There was one last section, a chapter of esoteric lore on the nature of being, of time and substance. It contained theory, though she needed practical magic. She had nothing left. Her fingers, stained with grime and ink, traced a complex diagram. a rune of seeing, one meant for viewing the past that lingers in all things. It was a spell that demanded a price. Ignoring the warning in the text, she screamed the final incantation.

Light, pure and silver, erupted from her eyes. The world of stone and fire dissolved into a grey, shimmering sea of echoes. She saw the dragon as it had been across millennia. a coiled serpent in the heart of the world, a shadow against a forgotten sun. On one scale, near its heart, she saw a faint, silvery hairline crack. It was a wound in time itself, a scar from a battle fought before dwarves had ever carved their first hall.

"GUNDROFF!" Her voice was a raw shriek, tearing from her throat. Blood trickled from her nose and the corners of her blazing eyes. "IT'S LEFT SIDE! BENEATH THE FORELIMB! THERE IS A WOUND YOU CANNOT SEE! STRIKE THERE!"

Gundroff, staggering to his feet, heard her cry over the din. He saw her, a collapsed figure wreathed in a terrible light, and understood the price of her knowledge. He had one strike left. He bellowed the dragon's name, a challenge and a curse, drawing the great head toward him. As the beast lunged, its jaws gaping like the entrance to a fiery hell,

Gundroff dodged beneath it. The heat of the dragon's breath scorched his beard. He swung the Battle Axe of the Titan with every ounce of grief, fury, and loyalty left in his soul. His target was the invisible space she had revealed.

The axe struck with a sickening, crystalline crack, like a glacier calving into the sea. The sound was followed by a shriek that was nothing of malice or rage, but of pure, undiluted agony. The ancient temporal wound, struck in the present, tore open. A fissure of blinding white light erupted in the dragon's side. Ash Heart convulsed, its massive body thrashing in a cataclysm of pain, bringing down stalactites and arches from the ceiling. It released its grip, no longer a predator, but a wounded animal. It scrambled back into the darkness of the mountain's depths, its terrible screams echoing behind it until they faded into a hateful silence.

The dust began to settle. The battle was over. The silence that followed was the silence of a tomb.

The Great Hall was still, save for the crackle of a few dying torches and the whimpering of the wounded. Gundroff collapsed to his knees, his body a symphony of pain and exhaustion. He looked at the wreckage of the battle, at the fallen dwarves, at the still, broken form of Fireforge being attended to by Harek. He looked at the Battle Axe of the Titan, its immense weight feeling heavier than any mountain.

He struggled to his feet and limped toward the great, carved stone throne at the head of the hall. He did not make it. His legs, pillars of crumbling stone, gave out, and he collapsed to the floor a few feet before it, the cold, unyielding stone a small comfort against his trembling, broken body.

He closed his eyes, overcome by a profound, bone deep weariness he hadn't felt in forty years.

The pain became a distant echo, the cold of the stone a fading memory. The low crackle of the torches in the hall deepened, becoming the steady, burning coals in a god's eyes. The world of the living dissolved.

He stood in a vast, smoky hall, the sound of a thousand dwarven warriors singing a battle hymn shaking the foundations of his soul. The air smelled of roasting boar, spilled ale, and forge fire. On a throne of blackened iron and dragon skulls sat Grolnir, the Axe Lord, a tankard the size of a barrel in his fist. Fiery tears cut paths through the soot on his cheeks.

"YOU HAVE ENDURED!" the god boomed, his voice the sound of a thousand war hammers. "THE OATH IS FULFILLED! A GRIM TASK IT WAS, AND WITHOUT A DROP OF ALE TO WARM THEE, BUT DONE NONETHELESS! YOU HAVE EARNED YOUR PLACE AT MY TABLE, SON OF THE RAGINGFIRE! THE DRAGON IS WOUNDED! YOUR KING IS BROKEN! YOUR WORK IS DONE! ASK FOR YOUR END, AND I WILL GIVE YOU A FINAL BATTLE WORTHY OF SONG!"

Gundroff looked at the hall of glorious ghosts, at the endless ale, at the laughing, grieving god. He felt a duty to the quiet, whimpering sounds of the living he had left behind that overshadowed any longing for rest.

"I seek no end while my king still draws breath," he said, his voice a low, fierce plea. "My debt to you is paid. My debt to my living kin is not. Give me the strength to be their shield."

A great, booming laugh that was half sorrow and half pride shook the hall. "A FOOL'S CHOICE!" Grolnir roared. "TO CHOOSE THE WOUNDED OVER THE WHOLE! TO CHOOSE A SHIELD OVER A SWORD! IT IS A CHOICE WORTHY OF MY FINEST SON! IT IS DONE! NOW GO! YOUR KINGDOM AWAITS!"

Gundroff's world dissolved in a blast of heat, a searing, white hot fire from a divine forge. He awoke with a gasp to the grey, cold stone of the Great Hall. The pain was gone. The exhaustion was a fading memory. He pushed himself to his feet, feeling the quiet song of a body made whole. He looked at Seraphina, at Thaddeus, and then at the still form of his king.

Chapter 30

The Unquiet Throne

The Great Hall breathed a silence born of exhaustion and choked with the ghosts of the past. Victory was a word for songs and histories; what lingered here was the butcher's quiet. The hiss and crackle of failing torches was a lonely sound in the vastness, punctuated by the soft, animal whimpering of the wounded. The air was a heavy soup, thick with the iron tang of blood, the sharp ozone of spent magic, and the acrid stench of dragon ichor that clung to the back of the throat. The few dwarves left standing moved through the carnage of their kin like specters, their faces grim masks of soot and sorrow. Their eyes, wide and vacant, held the terrible stillness of men who had stared into the abyss and found no bottom. They had won the mountain. It had cost them the world.

Thaddeus moved through the ruin, a quiet island of purpose in a sea of despair. The cheerful cleric was gone, replaced by a shepherd tending to a shattered flock. He knelt beside a young dwarf, a boy no older than Thorin, whose leg was pinned beneath a fallen piece of the ceiling. The boy was not crying; his face was a pale, stoic mask, his knuckles white where he gripped the stone. Thaddeus's hands were gentle as he assessed the wound, his voice a low, calming murmur that cut through the boy's silent pain. He worked with a healer's quiet efficiency, binding the wound, his touch a small, defiant act of mending in a world that had been so brutally unmade.

Near the shattered throne, Seraphina knelt in a pool of dragon blood that was not red, but a deep, iridescent black, like oil on water.

The terrible, silver light of her final spell had receded from her eyes, but it had left behind a profound, hollow ache, a weariness that felt older than the mountain itself. Before her, the old war master Harek was a mountain of grief, his massive shoulders slumped as he cradled the head of his broken king in his lap. Fireforge was alive, but only just, his breath a shallow, ragged whisper against the silence. Harek did not weep. He stared at his king's pale, still face, his own a mask of such utter desolation that it was a wound in itself. Seraphina reached out, not with magic, but with a simple, human touch, her hand resting on the old dwarf's trembling shoulder. He did not flinch. He did not look at her. He endured, and she, the scholar who had once seen the world as a complex equation, now understood that some griefs had no solution. They could only be shared.

And through it all, Gundroff walked.

He had awoken from his divine communion to a body made whole, the pain and exhaustion scoured from him by a god's fire. But the strength that now flowed through his limbs was not a triumphant thing; it was a burden. He moved through the hall, a living bastion of vitality in a charnel house, and the contrast was a fresh and terrible kind of agony. He saw the faces of the dead, dwarves he had fought beside just hours ago, their faces frozen in final, desperate snarls. He saw the great, iron bound doors of the hall, the last line of their defense, now splintered and torn from their hinges. He saw the Battle Axe of the Titan, lying where he had dropped it, its immense weight a testament to a victory that felt like a lie.

He was no longer a ghost, but he was a stranger in his own home, a memory of a strength his people no longer possessed. He reached the foot of the throne and saw his king, broken and bleeding, and Harek, a father who had lost a son, now on the verge of losing his king. He saw Seraphina, the proud elf mage, her face streaked with soot and blood, her hand a small, fragile anchor in Harek's storm of grief. He saw the cost. And he knew, with a certainty that was colder and harder than any stone, that his own war, the one he had waged for forty years in the wilderness of his own soul, was a child's game compared to this. The true battle had just begun.

The council convened amongst the ghosts of their past. They did not gather in a formal chamber, but in the center of the Great Hall, a small circle of chairs and crates arranged around a low, sputtering fire. The great stone throne at the head of the hall sat empty, a monument to a king who now slept a fitful, shallow sleep in the healers' care. Torn banners of their fallen clans hung like burial shrouds from the high, vaulted ceiling, their proud sigils obscured by soot and blood. The air still reeked of the battle's aftermath, a smell the living would carry in their memories forever.

Prince Fireforge presided, though not from the throne. He sat in a simple, high backed wooden chair, his body bound in splints and bandages, his left arm in a sling of oiled leather. Every movement was a slow, deliberate act of will against a pain that was etched in the deep lines of his face. He was a king in all but name, a broken shield for a broken people.

Harek, his face a mask of grim practicality, stood before him. The raw, volcanic grief had cooled into a hard, cold stone. He was a war master again, and his words were the grim mathematics of their survival.

"The count is done," he said, his voice a low, gravelly rasp. "We have lost one hundred and seventeen. Forty three are grievously wounded. We have fewer than two hundred warriors fit to stand a watch." He paused, his obsidian eye fixed on the fire. "The dragon... it is wounded. Badly. We have seen no sign of it, but the tremors from the deep places have ceased. It has retreated to its lair to heal. Or to die."

No one cheered. The knowledge that the beast was still alive, still breathing in the heart of their home, was a poison that leached the warmth from the fire.

Seraphina stepped forward, her borrowed leathers now seeming to belong to her. She looked at the faces around the fire. at Gundroff, a silent, reforged bastion; at Thaddeus, his quiet sorrow a palpable presence; at Harek, his grief now a tool of war.

"The dragon will heal," she said, her voice a quiet, sobering reality that no one could now deny. "And the cult that commands it will not be idle. The Un Named have lost a battle, but their war is against time itself. They will be back. They are a tide, and this was only the first wave."

Fireforge looked up from the fire, his eyes holding the weary weight of his new crown. He looked from face to face, at the small, shattered remnant of his people. He saw not despair, but a quiet, stubborn, and unyielding resolve. The fire of their grief had not consumed them. It had forged them into something harder.

He gripped the arms of his simple chair, his knuckles white. "The war for this mountain is over," he said, his voice a quiet, grim promise that echoed in the silence of the hall. "Now begins the war for our people." He straightened, the movement costing him a sharp intake of breath. "Let the word go forth. We are not a broken clan. We are not a defeated army. We are the Stonehammer Clan. And we will not be broken again."

Later, when the moon was a silver chip in the black sky, Gundroff stood on a high balcony overlooking the valley. The biting wind had softened to a cold, clean whisper. Below, the camp was a patchwork of quiet, defiant lights. A single forge still glowed, its embers a warm, orange heart in the darkness, and the distant, rhythmic *clang... clang...* of a lone hammer shaping steel was not a sound of war, but a song of mending. He was no longer a ghost in a dead city; he was a watchman over a wounded, but living, home.

He did not hear her approach, but he felt the shift in the air. Seraphina came to stand beside him, not as a rival or a commander, but as a quiet presence at his shoulder. She held a greataxe in her hands.

It was not the colossal, unwieldy weapon of the Titan. This was a dwarf's axe, forged in the last day with a grim and beautiful purpose. The haft was dark, unadorned ironwood, wrapped in fresh leather. The head was a single, massive piece of blued dwarven steel, its edge honed to a razor's sharpness. It was a brutal, practical weapon, made for a single purpose. But inlaid along the blade's spine was a single, impossibly fine line of shimmering, starlit silver. a seamless fusion of her magic and their steel.

She held it out to him. "A shield needs a blade to guard its back," she said, her voice quiet in the vast stillness.

Gundroff took the axe. The weight felt right. It was not the familiar comfort of his old companion, but something new. a shared strength. His hands, whole and hale, closed around the haft, the healthy flesh of his left arm a stark and beautiful contrast to the memory of its withered ruin.

He looked from the silver inlay on the blade to her face. He saw no pride in her eyes, only a deep, weary, and hard won understanding.

"The world is a vast and complex equation," Seraphina said, her gaze on the valley below, at the small, flickering lights of life. "And I believe I am only just beginning to understand the variables."

A quiet footstep announced Thaddeus's arrival. He came to stand on Gundroff's other side, placing a steadying hand on his shoulder. The old man looked at Gundroff, at the new axe in his hands, at the sleeping kingdom at their feet, and a gentle, sad smile touched his lips.

"A king is a shield for his people," Thaddeus said, his voice a murmur on the wind. "And a shield, my friend, is not meant to stand alone."

Gundroff gripped the axe, its weight a promise. He looked out at the valley, at the jagged peaks of the mountains silhouetted against a sky that was beginning to soften from black to the deepest purple. He was no longer a ghost haunted by a funeral. He was a protector, a part of a fellowship, a shield awaiting the inevitable dawn.

EPILOGUE

The wind, a thief that stole sound and warmth, was a familiar companion. For two weeks, Ankle Shanker had made her home in the high, razor sharp ridges overlooking the dwarven camp. The air, thin and cold, smelled of iron and ozone and the sharp, clean scent of a battle that had just ended. Below, in the vast, bowl shaped valley, lay the war camp of the dwarves, no longer a funeral, but a quiet, powerful celebration.

Her home was not in a place of stone and warmth, a place of boring, sturdy things that stayed where you put them. Her home was the silence between heartbeats. The dust under a king's bed. The dark, wet place behind the walls where the rats went to die. She was a creature of the cracks, a thing of whispers and of rust. Her world was a place of quiet, fascinating, pretty things that she, and she alone, was clever enough to get. It was a perfect world.

This was a *bad knife cut*. The dwarves down there are supposed to be broken, but they are not. They were supposed to be soft things, hollowed out by their grief and ripe for the plucking, but their sorrow is a thing of stone, and they are using it to build. The loud one, the one with the sad memories, is supposed to be a quiet ruin. He is supposed to be a hollowed out thing that she, a professional, could have just ended. But his heart... it beats with a new, slow, and stupidly strong beat. She did not like this. It made the world a terrible place. The fires below were too bright, their flames a boast. The hammers were too loud, a song that hurt her ears. The pretty thing had a nasty knife cut.

She had been tasked with hunting them, with finding their flaw, with reporting their story back to Malakai so that he could end it. She had, in a fit of artistic pique, decided to sculpt a masterpiece of her own.

347

A creature of pure, unmade sorrow, a monster that fed on grief and amplified despair. She had found a wisp of a whisper from a long dead god, and with it, she had woven a thing of pure unmaking. She had set the stage, sent the monster, and waited for the cute, predictable chaos. She had expected to see them consumed by despair, to watch their society fall into a silent ruin. But the chaos had not been predictable at all. They had, in a single, cute, and terrible moment, unmade her monster. It had not been with a great battle, or a clever trap, but with a simple act of shared grief, a song of sorrow that had been so honest, so pure, that her monster, a thing of echoes and lies, had ceased to be. Her masterpiece, a cute and artistic hunt, was a failure. And it was a failure that she, a professional, could not abide.

A failure is a broken thing. A professional does not leave broken things. She must fail at this, understand the reason for it, find the answer, and give it to her master. This is the new hunt. A hunt for a truth that is not a pretty thing at all. It is a terrible thing, a truth that screams with noise and is warm with light. It is a new kind of cute. A, bad knife cut that she must understand before she can fix it.

She had to see the end of the story. She had to understand how a small, limping herd of broken things could have defeated a masterpiece of unmaking. She scuttled down the ridge, her feet making no sound on the loose scree, and found a small, sheltered crevice near the edge of the camp. She did not need to see. She needed to listen.

The sound that reached her was no longer the mournful chant of a funeral. It was the rhythmic clang of a thousand hammers, a song of creation. It was the low, rumbling roar of a hundred forges, a fire that burned with the unyielding strength of stone. It was people who, at last, were rebuilding their homes. The scent of burnt metal and molten ore reached her, a bitter sweet perfume on the wind. She watched as one dwarf, his face streaked with soot, laughed with another, a laugh that was a sound of absolute, unadulterated joy. She watched as an old dwarf, his hands trembling with age, hammered a new shield, his face a landscape of quiet, stubborn resolve. She saw a young dwarf woman, her braids adorned with tiny pieces of obsidian, teaching a small child to polish a sword. She saw life, and she saw it in a way that defied all logic, all of her own quiet, cynical philosophy.

Burials. So many orders. So much waste. So many good bites, just left in the ground. Why? The pretty thing has no answer. It is a cute, terrible flaw. Their sorrow is a thing of stone and not of water. It is not something she can drink. It is a noise she cannot use. It is a waste. This laughter, this new song of hammers, it is all so wrong. It is a noise that has no place in a world of silence. It is a noise that makes her feel small, and she dislikes feeling small. This is not how it is supposed to go. This is a terrible story. She must find the flaw. She must find the knife cut.

She saw him then. **Thaddeus**. He was standing near a great, roaring forge, his hands clasped in silent prayer, his face a mask of profound, unreadable sadness. She watched him, a quiet, unseen sentinel in a world of grief she could not comprehend. His sadness was not the kind that created a hollow space inside, a dark, quiet place for her to hide. It was a solid, palpable thing, a sadness that was a part of him, a truth that made him stronger. She, a creature of the cracks, a master of silence, a sculptor of the shadows, was completely and utterly captivated. This was a pretty thing she had never seen before. a truth she had never encountered. This was a man who, in the act of living, had defeated the same concept of unmaking.

She stayed until the sky, a vast, aching, and impossible expanse of black, was filled with the hard, cold light of a thousand, indifferent stars. The fire was a ghost now, a red, dying ember in a bed of white, silent ash. The dwarves, their songs of mourning finished, had retreated into their longhouses, their grief a heavy, palpable presence in the night. The camp was silent. She, a quiet shadow in a silent world, was alone.

The night held a different kind of quiet. Not the quiet of despair, but the quiet of a simple, cute, and utterly predictable chaos. She saw a small, fat, pink piglet, a thing of utter innocence and a delicious, messy, and intriguing kind of noise, wander away from its pen. Its tiny, cloven hoofs made a soft, rhythmic pat pat pat against the cold ground, a sound that was a prayer and a promise. It was a cute, terrible, and utterly predictable noise. A pretty thing that she, and she alone, was clever enough to get. She watched it as it snuffled at the ground, its little pink nose twitching with delight at the new scent. She watched as it bumped into a rock, squealed in surprise, and then trotted on, completely unbothered.

The piglet. It is perfect. A thing of tiny, chaotic joy. So many good bites. The soft skin. The pink nose. The funny, squeaky

noise. A toy. A gorgeous toy. She would keep it until the noise was boring. It would be a pretty noise. She wants to see what it will do when she squeezes it. What new noise will it make? A different kind of pretty noise. A new experiment. A new project. A new friend. A new life to unmake, and she is the master of it.

She scuttled forward, a blur of motion in the dark. She did not want to hurt it. She did not want to kill it. She wanted to… keep it. A creature of order and silence, she was captivated by a thing of chaos and noise. A whim, she thought. A temporary detour. She would keep it until it was no longer interesting. A new project. A new, pretty thing. A new friend.

She was so focused on the piglet's soft, rhythmic pattering that she did not hear the sound of boots on stone. She did not see the figure that, in a simple, quiet, and utterly predictable manner, had stepped out from the main longhouse to watch the stars. He was a creature of routine, of habit, of a quiet and gentle kind of chaos. A predictable thing she had not seen before. She did not hear him until it was too late.

Her shoulder slammed into a warm, soft, and utterly solid mountain of a man. The impact was not violent, but it was absolute. It was the feeling of hitting a wall that was a part of the world, a wall that was warm and soft. She stumbled back, her grip on the piglet's fat, squealing body faltering. She looked up, her purple eyes wide with a frantic, disorganized, and cute chaos. This is not part of the plan. This is not how it is supposed to go. This is a new noise. A new, big noise. This is the truth. The truth she has been hunting for.

Who was this man? She had seen him as a fool, a simple vessel for a cute, terrible magic. But here, in the cold, honest silence of the night, he was a different kind of pretty thing. He saw her not as a monster, but as a pretty thing, not as a shadow, but as a child. He saw her. A single, perfect, and impossible truth in a world of lies. He saw her. The whisper, the thief, the silent shadow. And in his eyes, she saw a home. She saw a home that was not made of stone or warmth, but of kindness. A home that was a man who had seen too much sorrow to ever lose his own. She looked at him, and her cute, terrible, and impossible pretty thing . a pretty thing that had no answer, and no end . had just found a key. A key to a door she did not know was closed. A key to a new kind of pretty thing, a warm, soft kind of pretty thing that made her stomach feel strange.

He looked down at her, his face a landscape of gentle, sleepy amusement. His beard, which was as white as a mountain peak and smelled of pipe smoke and a quiet, patient wisdom, was a thing of soft, comforting, and utterly predictable goodness. His eyes, a deep and gentle blue, seemed to hold the weight of the night sky, encompassing all the stars and the vast empty space between them. This was not a warrior. This was not a god. This was a man who had seen too much sorrow to ever lose his own.

He reached out a hand, not to console, but to steady her, and in his eyes, a deep and gentle blue, she saw a truth that made her heart, a thing of silence and dust, feel a sudden, jarring beat. His hands are warm. Like a fire. Like a home. This is a pretty thing that is not quiet at all. It is so loud. It is a different kind of loud. Not the loud of the hammers, but the loud of a heart. This noise is not a waste. He saw her not as a monster, but as a pretty thing, not as a shadow, but as a child. He saw her.

The piglet, a single, perfect note of utter, cute, and predictable chaos, finally escaped her grasp. It let out a triumphant squeal, a sound of absolute, unadulterated joy, and scurried back to its pen. She, the silent shadow, a master of a thousand different, cute, and terrible kinds of chaos, was left alone in a silence that was a thing of profound, terrifying, and utter truth. She looked at him, and her cute, terrible, and impossible pretty thing . a pretty thing that had no answer, and no end . had just found a key.

"Dad?" she whispered, the word a raw, broken thing, a sound of a girl who had just found her home.

He looked down at her, a low, gentle chuckle shaking his great, rumbling chest. He reached out a hand, not to steady her, not to console, but to touch the fine, elegant line of her face, a gesture that was a prayer and a promise. His thumb, calloused and rough from years of hammering, gently brushed away a stray tear she had not even known was there.

"Well," he said, his voice a low, gentle rumble, a sound of a man who had found a new and more terrible kind of truth. He bent down on one knee, bringing his kind, weary eyes closer to her level. "A man spends his life building things, and sometimes, he finds something so broken that he can't fix it. Something so quiet, it makes a kind of silence he's never heard before. He doesn't know what to do with it. He doesn't have the tools. He doesn't have the words." He paused, his thumb still on her cheek. "I was never promoted to a father. But I suppose we can go with that. A man should never turn away a child who needs a home. A child is a new kind of pretty thing, a new kind of loud noise, and a new kind of purpose. A man should never turn away a child who needs a home."

He helped her to her feet, his hands rough yet reassuring, their steady grip grounding her. He guided her back to the fire, where warmth and flickering light promised safety, opening her eyes to a world she had never known before.

Ankle Shanker, a master of a thousand different, cute, and terrible kinds of chaos, a hunter of the silent shadows, and a scholar of a world of dust and silence, was, at last, going home.